GRIP TAYLOR

C.J. PETIT

GRIP TAYLOR

TABLE OF CONTENTS

Printed in the United States of America

ISBN: 9798695624892

PROLOGUE

May 19, 1878
Ann Arbor, Michigan

It was early afternoon and Grip was at his desk reading *The Ballistics of Projectiles* when the door burst open behind him and he didn't bother taking his eyes away from the chart knowing who had just exploded into the room.

"Hey, Grip! The dean of students wants to see you right away," Henry Leopold exclaimed before throwing himself onto his bed.

Grip turned to look at his roommate and asked, "Do you know what he wants?"

"Nope. I was signing up for the mechanical drawing class and he spotted me. He seemed kind of serious. Did you do something that I don't know about?"

"Oh, my goodness! You don't think he found out about my indiscretion with Miss Horner; do you?"

Henry snickered then replied, "That would be funny. I swear, Grip, if I knew you were fooling around with his secretary, I'd be the first one to question your sanity."

Grip stood, closed his book and said, "So, would I. She's a bit too old for us, but I wouldn't be surprised if Dean Wormwood wasn't spending some extra office time with her."

His roommate chuckled before he said, "I think you may have something there, Mister Taylor. You'd better get over there before they share some of that private time in his office while you wait outside."

Grip pulled on his light jacket then his hat before exiting their room and walking down the hallway wondering why the dean wanted to see him. He suspected that it had something to do with his father as he had no personal problems on campus. At least none that he knew about.

He quickly crossed the expansive grounds and entered the administrative building. He took the stairs two at a time and after reaching the second floor, he headed for the dean of students' office near the end of the hallway. It was a large corner office that had a separate outer office for the dean's secretary, the aforementioned Miss Lorraine Horner.

He entered the outer office and smiled at Miss Horner as he said, "I was told that Dean Wormwood needed to see me."

She smiled back and replied, "Yes, he does. Have a seat Mister Taylor and I'll tell him that you've arrived."

"Thank you."

Grip's butt had barely touched the chair's cushion when Miss Horner waved him into the dean's office.

He entered the dean's inner office and Miss Horner closed the door behind him.

Dean James Wormwood smiled at him and said, "Please have a seat, Mister Taylor."

"Thank you, sir," Grip said as he sat down across the desk from the dean.

"Mister Taylor, I'm afraid I have some terrible news for you and I'm not one to try to mitigate the shock by any long preparatory speechmaking. I know how difficult this will be for you and as much as I'd like to soften the blow, I think that it's better if I simply give you the sad tidings without trying to prattle on with superfluous oratory."

Grip managed to refrain from rolling his eyes as he waited for the long-winded dean to just give him whatever terrible news he was about to deliver.

"Mister Taylor, we just received a telegram a little while ago, and I'm sorry to have to tell you that your father has died unexpectedly."

Grip was surprised and far from despondent, yet he was curious.

"Why did you receive the telegram and why wasn't it sent directly to me?"

"Apparently, the sender only knew that you were enrolled here, but not your address."

"Oh. May I see the telegram, please?"

"Of course," Dean Wormwood said as he slid a sheet of paper across his desk.

Grip picked it up and read:

AGRIPPA TAYLOR UNIV OF MICH ANN ARBOR MICH

FATHER KILLED MAY 10
NEED YOU TO RETURN AS SOON AS POSSIBLE

JAMES ELLIS ESQ 243 WILLOW ST LOUIS MISSOURI

After he read the short message, he folded the sheet and said, "I'll be packing my things and returning to St. Louis, Dean. I won't be returning, so please disenroll me from my classes."

"Of course. I'm sorry for your loss and still hope that you'll return to our school and complete the work on your doctorate."

Grip stood, smiled at the dean and shook his hand before saying, "I'll think about it," then turned and left the office.

As he walked down the hallway, he wondered how his father had died. His father's lawyer had written that he had been killed, not that he had died. Grip wasn't surprised if his father had met his end in a violent manner but was curious about who had ended his life.

He returned to this room and told Henry about the telegram and his meeting with the dean. Unlike the dean, his roommate understood Grip's disdain for his father, so after Grip told him about his father's death, Henry knew that he'd never see his friend again.

———

Grip didn't hastily pack and race to the train station because he knew his father would be buried long before he returned to St. Louis anyway. It was another week before he departed from the university.

CHAPTER 1

May 28, 1878
St. Louis, Missouri

Grip stepped down from his black gelding before his father's mansion and after tying him off at the closest iron hitching post cast to look like a small cannon, he marched to the front of the extravagant house and climbed the eight steps to the polished maple floor of the wide porch.

He didn't even touch the large brass door knocker shaped like Roman fasces, but just pulled open the heavy right-side door and entered the large foyer.

The door had barely closed when Grip heard hurried footsteps crossing the uncarpeted section of the parlor's floor.

As he hung his hat on the first brass hook on the foyer's wall, Richard Bennett, the household steward, stopped at the room's entrance and said, "Welcome home, Master Taylor. I'm sorry that you had to return under these tragic circumstances."

Grip looked at him in silence for a few seconds before saying, "Tragic, Richard? I hardly think one would call it tragic. If anything, it was justice well served."

Mister Bennett didn't reply as Grip unbuttoned his light jacket and hung it on the adjoining brass hook.

Grip could see that he was putting the steward in an awkward position, so he smiled and placed his hand on Richard's left shoulder.

"I'm sorry, Richard. I was just being flippant when I know you meant well. Please forgive me."

Mister Bennett relaxed and asked, "May I ask what you plan to do now, sir?"

"Can you gather the staff together and we'll meet in the kitchen? I'll explain what I want to do, and I will need all of your support."

"Most certainly, sir," Richard said before he turned and quickly walked away.

Grip sighed and entered the big parlor but didn't take a seat on any of the opulent chairs, settees, or the excessively large couch. He hated the room more than most, which was why he had asked to meet everyone in the kitchen.

He hadn't expected to return to St. Louis so soon, if ever, but his father's unexpected death had brought him back to the city where he'd been born. He knew he wouldn't be staying St. Louis and had already picked his new home before he had even boarded the train in Ann Arbor. He'd done a lot of research and it seemed to be the ideal location.

He figured that it would take about ten minutes for Richard to gather the household staff together, so while he was hunting for everyone, Grip headed to his father's office.

After opening the door, he strode to his father's enormous mahogany desk and sat in the thickly padded leather chair. He had never been granted access to whatever his father kept in its drawers, and Grip knew that his father hadn't had the opportunity to empty them before he was killed. The hidden safe was probably untouched as well. If anyone had found it, he would have been shocked. His father didn't even know that he had found its hiding place.

While Richard gathered the staff, Grip began opening drawers and scanning each one's contents. There was one locked drawer that he didn't have time to open, but he'd look later when he came back to open the safe.

Nothing that he found really surprised him and he didn't expect to find any shocking revelations in the locked drawer or the safe, but what he did discover confirmed what he already suspected about his father and how he had accumulated much of his vast wealth.

Lawrence Preston Taylor wasn't much different than other men who sought power and wealth, and Grip knew that most were no less corrupt than his father. But the manner of his death and what he had done that precipitated it had marked him as a man who simply didn't understand the people whom he employed to give him that power and wealth.

Grip stood and then left the office leaving the door open behind him. He wasn't concerned that one of the staff would do any snooping. He was sure that each of them knew his father even better than he did.

He turned down the long hallway and stepped quickly toward the kitchen.

When he entered the large space, he found the staff standing almost as if they were in a police lineup awaiting his arrival.

He held back his smile before saying, "Please, would you all have a seat at the table?"

"Thank you, sir," escaped quietly from several of their lips as they slowly made their way to the chairs surrounding the large oak table.

Once they were all seated and staring at him, Grip said, "What I do want each of you to understand is that I am not my father. I am as far removed from him in personality and character as possible and that is why I asked to go with you. I am not going to live in this mausoleum or in St. Louis for very long. Tomorrow, I'll meet with Mister Ellis to settle the estate and then I'll go to the bank and make arrangements to sell this place and most of my father's other assets."

He saw the expected concern in their eyes but hoped to alleviate their worries with what he told them next.

"I can tell that you are all worried about my decision. You were probably already concerned after my father's death, but please set those apprehensions aside. While I may not be staying, I will obviously be needing to find another place to live. I will definitely not be buying a mansion like this, but I will still need help in managing the household. If any of you don't wish to follow me halfway across the country, then I'll give you a year's severance pay and a good recommendation."

Mister Bennett then said, "Excuse me, sir, but you said that you'd be moving halfway across the country. Which direction would that be?"

Grip smiled before he replied, "West. I expect to be leaving the city within a month or so. I'm going to return to my father's office for a little while before I come back to talk to you again. My trunk should be delivered by then. I don't need your answers about whether you'll stay with me for at least a week, but I'll let you know that I've decided to live in Ogden, Utah."

"Utah?" asked Tom Truax, the horse keeper and his father's driver.

"Yes, Tom. It only took a day of research to determine that Ogden is the ideal location for what I want to do. I'll explain that after I meet with Mister Ellis tomorrow. I'll be back in another hour or so, and if you already know that you don't want to board a train to Utah, let me know."

Grip stood, smiled at their still disbelieving faces then returned to the office and searched for the key to the locked drawer. It wasn't anywhere in the room, so he suspected it was on his father's heavy keyring that was on the other end of his pocket watch. He assumed that he'd be given his father's personal possessions when he met with Mister James Ellis, Esquire, in the morning.

He expected that would be an interesting meeting as he barely knew the man and he suspected that the attorney would harbor hopes that Grip would simply take over his father's business and retain him. But what he did know about the lawyer was enough to remove any possibility of giving him any opportunity to do anything more than administer his father's will. He simply didn't trust the man, and he would need someone he could trust in Ogden. One of the few men he could trust in St. Louis was sitting in the kitchen talking to his wife about whether or not to join him in Utah. Another was in his bank and he'd depend on him for totally different reasons.

After his brief and futile search for the key to the drawer, he walked to the opposite side of the office and opened a narrower door. This was his father's favorite room in the house and Grip had to admit that it was his as well. It wasn't even as large as the downstairs bathroom and just had a single chair and a narrow, heavy table for furnishings.

The far wall had two tall, ladder-like racks and each set of heavy wooden supports held a rifle, musket or shotgun. The wall on the left had a series of vertical racks with more long-barreled guns. On the right side of the room, there were four long shelves with handguns of all sorts, from matchlocks to the latest double-action revolvers. Below the shelves was a row of heavy drawers filled with well-sealed ammunition of all calibers and types. He knew that there were two small kegs of gunpowder near the door as well. The room would turn any fire into a fireworks display.

The only non-firing weapons in the room were displayed in a line across behind the workbench. It was a row of sharp blades from bayonets and sabers to gleaming bowie knives and daggers.

The table and chair were for working on the guns and reloading cartridges, which was obvious to anyone who knew what the heavy piece of equipment was that was bolted to the heavy table. The tools were hung on a small backboard and in a large flat drawer under the tabletop. The oils and cleaning fluids where kept in airtight heavy boxes on either side of the table. The smell was still there, but Grip knew they would dominate the entire south side of the house if they weren't stored in the boxes.

But he wasn't there to work on a gun or even admire their condition. He wanted to open his father's safe.

The gun room was almost a façade in itself as it would usually stop any examination just because the inspector would want to admire the extensive collection of weaponry. It was only Grip's love of those weapons that had led him to the discovery of his father's secret room with the safe and also to quickly think of its combination.

He closed the door, walked to the back of the room and when he stood before the left ladder of rifles, he put his hand between a Kentucky rifle and an unmarked flintlock and pushed on the wall behind the rack.

There was a loud click as the board depressed just a quarter of an inch, then Grip pushed the entire ladder of rifles back. It moved just three inches, but when it was out of the way, it revealed a latch on the left wall that had been hidden by the wall.

He popped open the latch and pushed open the narrow door. It was dark inside, but he knew that there was a wall lamp on the left just beside the door jamb.

Grip stuck a match, lit the lamp, then after blowing out the match, he stepped into the narrow room until he reached his father's safe. It wasn't a typical safe, but more like a steel door. It was only eighteen inches wide, but almost five feet tall. The door wasn't very thick because it didn't need to be. He'd only opened it once and that was before he went off to college. When he'd discovered the secret, he hadn't spent much time to examine its contents in fear that his father might return unannounced. But that fear was long gone even before his father died, so Grip could take his time.

He took a breath and began to spin the dial. Most men who used combination safes used their wife's or children's birthdays or maybe even their own if they were careless. But Lawrence Preston Taylor probably didn't even know the birthdays of his two wives and Grip wasn't sure if he knew his only son's. Grip's birthdays were usually spent elsewhere. His father wasn't careless either, so he wouldn't use his own birthday.

But as soon as he had discovered the safe, it only took Grip a few seconds of thought to determine the combination. He had guessed 45-32-44. They weren't a large woman's measurements, but calibers for his favorite three pistols. The order had been the only question, but it hadn't taken him long to open the safe's door.

Now he spun the dial with certainty. His father may have changed the combination in the past few years, but Grip doubted it. He suspected that no one, not even Mister Ellis knew about the safe, much less the combination. It was why he felt it was so important to finally reveal its contents.

After setting the dial on 44, he turned the handle and was gratified when it moved. He'd had a small suspicion that his father had somehow discovered that his secret had been compromised, but if he did, he still hadn't changed the combination.

He swung the door open and began extracting the papers that were inside. There was a reasonably sized stack of cash, but that wasn't important. Grip wanted to know what was so critical to his father that he had to hide it in the safe.

There wasn't a table in the room, so he returned to the gun room and set the papers near the reloader.

He began reading and was disappointed that the first few pages were just deeds to buildings and businesses that he wasn't sure still existed. Most of them were on the shady side of the law, including two brothels and one farm that his father probably used as a secret distillery for making illegal whiskey just to avoid the tax. To most people, a man as wealthy as his father doing something this risky made no sense, but they didn't know Lawrence Preston Taylor. He felt free to do anything he wanted, and the law would just smile with their hands out.

It was only when he reached the fourth page that things began to get interesting. His father had been paying bribes to all sorts of city, state and Federal officials and had documented dates and times as a way of keeping him safe from reprisals or blackmail. It hadn't protected him in the end as none of those he'd paid off were among the people who had killed him.

When he reached the next page, he felt his stomach twist in a knot. *How could he not have known this?* Granted, he'd spent almost all of his boyhood at military schools, so he really didn't understand what was happening in this big house, but he still believed that he might have had some inkling of what he held in his hand.

It was an old birth certificate. He had a sister.

She might only be a half-sister, but the shock of finding that he had even a half-sibling was disturbing.

He remembered her mother, Charlotte Marley, even though he was just six years old when she'd been fired by his father. What surprised him was why his father had even kept her birth certificate when his name wasn't listed as the father. That space was left blank by the doctor and the only reason he had assumed that the baby was his father's offspring was that he had kept the birth certificate. He probably kept it as some form of insurance but that made no sense to him either. He had only recalled the mother's name, Charlotte Marley because as a six-year-old, he had called her Charlie Marley, but only when he knew his father was beyond hearing.

He supposed that there could be another reason for the birth certificate being in the safe, but nothing else made sense.

He quickly read the remaining pages that were no different than most of the others, then stood and returned to the safe room. After leaving all of the papers inside except for the birth certificate, he closed the heavy steel door and spun the dial.

After blowing out the lamp, he exited the small room and returned it to its invisible state. That one scrap of paper had inserted an unexpected twist into his plans, but he simply had no idea of what he would do with it. He needed to talk to Richard Bennett and his wife. They were the longest serving members of the staff, but Charlotte Marley had been fired years before they began working for his father. He hoped that they might have heard some stories and not be afraid to repeat them, regardless of the sordid details about his father that they would have to reveal. He also hoped that they would accompany him to Ogden. He liked Richard and Wilma Bennett and he was friendly with Tom Truax because they both liked horses. He was less familiar with Tom's wife, Jenny, and didn't know the two maids much at all, but he hadn't seen them in the kitchen. He wondered if they had already gone to seek new employment.

When he returned to the kitchen, he found Wilma Bennett and Jenny Truax preparing to cook dinner.

Tom Truax and Richard Bennett were talking near the pantry door, but when Grip entered, Richard broke off the conversation and approached him.

"Master Taylor, your trunk and bag arrived. I put them in your bedroom."

"Thank you, Richard."

"We've all discussed your offer, and my wife and I have decided to continue our service to you in Utah, as have Mr. and Mrs. Truax. Miss Elizabeth and Miss Anne have already departed the household after your father's death and are employed elsewhere."

"I'm glad to have you and your wife join me and Tom and Jenny as well. I'd like to talk to you and Tom in my father's office where I will explain what I want to do when we get to Ogden."

"Of course, sir," Richard replied.

He didn't have to ask Tom Truax to come along as he was just three feet away, so as soon as Grip turned to the long hallway, the two men quietly followed.

After they reached the office, Tom closed the door but neither man took a seat until Grip said, "Please, sit down, gentlemen."

They both nodded, chose their chairs and sat in two of the three heavy chairs against the wall opposite the desk.

Grip just leaned his butt against the desk and braced himself with his hands on the edge.

"There will be many changes ahead for us and those changes will begin right now. From this moment, I am not Mister Taylor nor sir or master. I am Grip and you will address me as such. I need your help in what I will be doing, and I don't want you to hesitate to tell me when I'm about to screw up. I may have spent a lot of time learning, but aside from all of my martial and athletic training, it's all been academic. I need to keep learning about people and how they live their lives.

"I only know the basic facts of my father's death from the official reports I received before I left, but I'm sure that there is much more to it than what was written in those pages."

His gray eyes bore into them as he said, "I'm going to ask you both some questions that may make you uncomfortable, but I want direct answers."

Then he focused his intense gaze onto Tom Truax and said, "Tom, you were driving the carriage that night, so you can tell me the exact details. I want to understand not only the event itself, but what drove the men to do it."

Tom nodded, then after he glanced at Richard, he said, "Well, sir…"

"Grip."

"Yes, sir…I mean, Grip. We were going to one of your father's places of business that night…"

"You mean one of his whore houses," Grip interrupted.

Tom blinked, swallowed, then after a short pause, he nodded and continued.

"Yes, to the Mason Street Hall and Billiard Parlor. We had just turned onto Lafayette Street when I had to pull the carriage to a sudden stop because a wagon unexpectedly appeared from an alley. The moment we stopped moving and before I could react, I was set upon by two men armed with heavy clubs. One knocked me to the cobblestones and the other bound me quickly with a cord.

“I watched helplessly as other men quickly used cords to secure the doors while two others splashed kerosene across the carriage. I could hear your father shouting at the men, but I was being held and was dizzy as well.”

“I don’t place any blame on you, Tom,” Grip said quietly.

“Thank you…Grip. I’m ashamed to admit that my first concern was for the horses, but that concern vanished when two men set their torches ablaze, and another man unhitched the yoke and moved the team away from the carriage. Then all I could do was watch as the carriage burst into flames. The men didn’t even stay to watch the results of their handiwork. I assume that they expected the imminent arrival of the fire brigade who would bring police with them.

“I was left on my knees with my wrists bound and couldn’t approach the intense blaze. All I could do was listen to your father’s screams that were even louder than the roaring fire. The fire brigade and police didn’t arrive for another ten minutes and by then, there was nothing left to save. The team was left a block away and there was almost nothing left of your father to bury.”

"I'm guessing that his manner of death had something to do with the foundry fire?"

Richard replied, "Yes, sir. That was my first thought after Tom gave me the news. It was the only reason that made much sense to any of us."

Grip nodded then said, "Thank you both. My father wasn't a very scrupulous man, and I don't really blame those men for acting as they did. When I learned of the loss of the foundry, I didn't doubt for a minute that my father had arranged the arson to collect the insurance money. The foundry hadn't been very profitable since the war and needed expensive upgrades that he wasn't about to buy. When it burned, almost two hundred men were suddenly jobless, and my father probably didn't even know any of their names."

Richard said, "Three days before the fire, a delegation of workers had approached him in his offices at the furniture factory and complained about the poor state of some of the forges. Your father joked about it that evening at dinner. He had told them that if they didn't want to keep working, they could go for a bath in the molten iron."

"It may not have been poetic justice, but it was close," Grip replied before saying, "Richard, I don't need you to be the household steward any longer. I need you to be more of a personal secretary and confidant. I need your advice and yours as well, Tom. I need men and women I can trust. That's why I want you to address me using my Christian name. I want to learn more about regular people. For years, I've been surrounded by the well-to-do, even in college. So, I need you both to be more like wise uncles than hired servants. I know that it will be difficult for you both after years of being treated as nothing more than furniture, but it's what I expect from each of you and your wives."

Richard said, "It will be difficult to change quickly…Grip."

Grip grinned and replied, "You're learning, Richard, and we'll have at least a month here before the adventure begins."

He looked at his father's horse keeper and asked, "Tom, how are the horses?"

Tom Truax quickly replied, "All of them are in great condition. One of the mares is in foal and should drop in another couple of months."

"There is the one stallion, four geldings and six mares now. Is that right?"

"Yes, sir, but we have three fillies from last year, too."

"They'll all be coming with us and I have one more question for you, Tom. How are you with dogs?"

Tom broke into a grin before he replied, "I love dogs, but your father hated them and called them curs regardless of their sex."

"I know. It was one of the many boyhood pleasures that he denied me. When we get to Ogden, you and I will finally get to have our dogs."

Richard then asked, "Why did you choose Ogden and what are your plans when we get there?"

"Ogden, Utah is almost like the center of a web of railroads that spread out across the West. Within a day or so, I would be able to reach anywhere from Kansas to Nevada and the Dakotas to Idaho. What I plan to do is try to make amends for the life my father led. It won't undo the harm he caused, and I won't be able to help as many people as he hurt, but I want it to be personal. I want to use his accumulated wealth to help innocents who need help."

"You could just donate it to charity right here and not risk personal injury."

"I intend to leave a substantial amount of his fortune to charities, but if I don't risk anything, then it has no value to me."

"So, it is your intention to become almost like a Robin Hood but in the setting of the vast expanse of the American West and not Sherwood Forest."

"I won't be robbing from the rich as my father has already committed enough thievery in the Taylor name. I will probably run afoul of a sheriff or two, but if they're honest men, then it won't be a problem. But there are as many dishonest lawmen as there are those who follow the laws. There are also greedy men like my father who take what isn't theirs or crush those who oppose them. I intend to do whatever I can to stop them."

Tom glanced at Richard, smiled then looked back at Grip and said, "That sounds interesting, Grip."

Grip grinned in return then replied, "It's going to be very different from what you've been doing with your lives, but I'll grant you that it will be interesting. It's going to be a very busy few weeks before we make the move. I'll be taking the books and the contents of the weapons room, but nothing else. I'll leave it to you and your wives to decide what they'll need to set up our new homes in Ogden. I'll be having houses built for each of you, so you'll finally be able to enjoy some measure of privacy."

"Thank you, Grip," Richard replied, "I'm sure that Wilma will be thrilled."

"If you really want to make her happy, tell her that neither she nor Mrs. Truax will ever do laundry again. I'm going to contract with a laundry service in Ogden to handle that chore because I'll be living alone and don't intend to do my own laundry either."

Tom grinned and said, "Thank you, Grip. My Jenny will be delighted."

Now that he believed he could get an honest answer, Grip pulled the birth certificate from his pocket and after unfolding it, he looked at Richard and said, "I found this birth certificate in my father's hidden safe. It's for the birth of a baby girl named Julia to Charlotte Marley. Do you remember hearing anything about her, Richard? I know that she was one of my father's maids or housekeepers when I was just a young boy."

Richard nodded then replied, "I don't recall her name at all. She must have been gone before we were hired."

Grip sighed then looked at the birth certificate again before saying, "That's what I thought, but I had hoped that you might have heard whispers. I know he used many of his maids as his private whores, but those who became pregnant were just sent away, or worse. I have no idea why he would keep this one. He's not listed as the father, so it doesn't make any sense at all. I would think that if he was concerned about being blackmailed by the woman, he would have taken more drastic action."

"I would imagine so," Richard replied.

"I think I'll have a detective see if either the mother or daughter can be found before we leave. If nothing else, the mystery of my father's need to keep it in his safe won't keep nagging me."

"If she's your half-sister, then what will you do?" asked Richard.

“If she is, then she and her mother can join us in Ogden if they wish. If not, I’ll give them this house and a large settlement so they can live in peace.”

Richard nodded as Grip folded the birth certificate and slipped it back into his pocket.

“Let’s go and have dinner and you can tell your wives what to expect. Tomorrow will be the first big day of change when I meet with Mister James Ellis, Esquire.”

Richard quickly said, “I wouldn’t trust that man, Grip.”

Grip stood straight and replied, “I never have, Richard.”

He may not have trusted his father’s attorney, but there was the one other man he had trusted before and would need to trust him much more now. He’d talk to Warren Stone tomorrow after he had his chat with James Ellis, Esquire. The one with the banker should be a much more pleasant and interesting conversation.

———

That night he slept in the same bed he’d used whenever he had stayed in his father’s house. He never had thought of it as his house, room or even his bed. It was almost as if it was a hotel room in one of the fanciest hotels in the city.

He tried to think of the longest length of time that he’d stayed in the room since he had been sent away to St.

Michael's Military Academy when he was seven. Most of his summers were spent at the school, but he did spend a few holidays and a rare summer here. The last full summer he'd lived in the house was when he was sixteen. It had been a memorable summer because of one momentous and revealing night.

It was a very clear memory for him because it was in this room where he had his introduction into the world that his father cultivated and enjoyed. It was the twenty-first of June in 1869, his sixteenth birthday. The war was over, and his father had reaped enormous profits from the conflict that had taken so many lives and destroyed so many families.

But it wasn't the war or anything dealing with those profits that had that immense impact on sixteen-year-old Agrippa Samuel Taylor.

His father hadn't sent him off to St. Michael's Military Academy to prepare him for a career in the army, but to harden him and teach him discipline. When Grip was six years old, his father had seen him playing with the eight-year-old daughter of the cook. He had yanked him into his office and told him that no son of his would grow up to be a sissy.

When he'd been sent away to St. Michael's Military Academy, he had written a letter to the headmaster with instructions to be hard on his son and to ensure that he learned every way possible to kill a man. For a boy of seven, it was a stunning entry into a world of harsh discipline and an almost tortured daily life.

Grip could have turned into an angry, resentful and hate-filled youth, but even though the study, training and discipline were almost enough to break him, he saw each of them as a challenge. He vowed to be the best he could be at everything, but not to impress his father. He wanted to prove to himself that he could do it and to defy his father in the process.

He excelled in whatever was required of him as he progressed in his education. He never received a word of praise from his father when he did return to St. Louis, but he hadn't expected any.

It was his father's treatment of the women who worked for him that really angered Grip, but that was before he understood the full measure of his father's other pursuits.

Lawrence Preston Taylor had married his mother, Alicia, when he was young, and Grip was born in 1853. His father had never explained why he had given him the name of the Roman general, but it never really mattered, and the unusual name had come in handy in the classes on the history of warfare at St. Michael's.

He never met his mother as she died in childbirth when he was three. His father had remarried the following year, but his second wife had died giving birth to a baby girl, who had followed her mother into the afterlife after just three tiny breaths.

After losing his second wife, Grip's father simply began using a string of mistresses, most of whom were hired as either maids or housekeepers. The first one he recalled was Charlotte Marley.

It was on the evening of his sixteenth birthday when he was more formally introduced to Mary Duffy, his father's newest maid and mistress. She was a handsome young woman with bright red hair and blue eyes. He had met her just a few days earlier when he'd returned from St. Michael's and had liked her.

He was in his room and preparing for sleep when the door opened, and Mary entered. Grip had been startled and asked what she was doing in his room.

She was upset and he could tell that she didn't want to be there, but eventually she told him that his father had told her to come to his room to 'make him a man'. Grip had been sorely tempted because she was a pretty young woman, but he wasn't about to take advantage of her just to prove that he wasn't the sissy that his father obviously still believed him to be.

He had sat with her on the edge of the bed for a few minutes, then after a short discussion, the pair had laid on the same bed he was now using and began to bounce up and down rhythmically. It was such a silly thing, so it wasn't long before each of them was laughing, but Mary was quick enough to mix in some loud moaning as proof of their passionate exercise.

They kept the façade alive for the length of time that Mary thought was appropriate before they slowed and then stopped. Even though it had been a comedy, Grip had found it difficult to avoid turning the faux sex into a serious drama. He wasn't close to being the sissy that his father perceived him to be and Mary Duffy was inspirational. Yet he had managed to restrain his teenage boy's raging hormones. The deciding inhibitor had been his refusal to give his father the satisfaction. They had spent another hour just talking and that was when Grip also began to learn much more about his father. It was an educational experience much different than the one his father had anticipated.

When she stood to leave, he told her that would never take advantage of a woman and vowed to wait until he found the right woman, and once he did, he'd never be unfaithful to her.

Mary thanked him and gently kissed him on the lips before leaving the room. Grip was sure that if he had asked her politely, she wouldn't have hesitated to join him, but he wasn't about to give his father his victory.

The next day, his father treated him much differently. Obviously, Mary had given the master of the house high praise for his son's performance.

It was then that his father had shown him the weapons room for the first time. Grip had impressed his father with his detailed knowledge of each of the guns. He almost shocked his father when he demonstrated his prowess in the use of a knife when he lifted one of the sharp daggers from the wall and without a moment's hesitation, threw it the length of the room. The point rammed exactly on his announced target when it stuck into the small space between a Sharps breech loader and a Henry carbine.

That day marked a serious shift in their relationship, but only for his father. His father had actually asked him to stay in St. Louis, but Grip said that he needed to finish his studies at St. Michael's. He wasn't being dishonest, but he knew it would be difficult for him to stay in the house because he suspected that his father would expect him to take over his widely varied businesses in a few years. He wanted no part of any of them, so after he graduated first in in his class at St. Michael's, he left for the University of Michigan after explaining to his father that it had the best engineering school in the country.

His father had seemed to lose all interest in Grip's future before he received his undergraduate degrees in engineering and a second in history, so Grip stayed in Michigan and was working on his doctorate in engineering until that fateful and surprising summons to Dean Wormwood's office.

Now he was back and would dismantle his father's empire starting tomorrow after meeting with Mister Ellis. He'd visit the bank and begin the process of removing the name of

Lawrence Preston Taylor from St. Louis. The only place that name would exist by the time he left for Ogden would be the one carved into the marble of his father's gravestone.

CHAPTER 2

The next morning after having a pleasant breakfast with the more relaxed staff, Grip mounted his black gelding, Pitch, and rode down the long, graveled drive to the road where he turned left. He had committed a gentleman's faux pas when he had made his own bed that morning but explained that after all those years in military schools, it was difficult to break the habit.

He was actually looking forward to the meeting with his father's lawyer. He wanted to see how much groveling the man's dignity would permit in the belief that Grip would be keeping the status quo. He wasn't about to let the attorney know his real plans. Not that he believed any of the staff would pass that information along, he had still asked them to keep his plans within the walls of the house.

After he'd had his breakfast, he'd paid another visit to the safe to collect the deeds. He still had the birth certificate in his pocket and would talk to Warren Stone about it as well and ask for a recommendation for a private investigator. It was part of his plans for the house anyway.

As he trotted Pitch through the busy St. Louis streets, he wondered what his half-sister looked like. According to her birth certificate, she was born on the 11th of October in '59. So, she would be an almost nineteen-year-old young woman by now and he was curious if he'd be able to see any of his father's features in her face.

He shared his father's black hair but that was all. His father had dark brown eyes while his were gray. His father's oval face and thick nose died with him as Grip must have mimicked his mother's slimmer face and more subtle nose. He was by all measures a handsome young man, standing within a fraction of an inch of six feet and weighing a very muscular one hundred and ninety pounds. The physical effect of his years of punishing training at St. Michael's hadn't been neglected in his years at Ann Arbor. He'd continued to push himself in his athletic endeavors, so his physical conditioning was at its peak and he intended to keep it there for as long as he could.

One of his great joys was simply running. He'd been running for as long as he could recall, and it was one of the reasons that his father had sent him to St. Michael's as he viewed running itself as a cowardly pastime. But they had encouraged him to run as a form of exercise, so he had enhanced his stamina by making longer and longer runs through the hills around the military school.

He had lived in a world of boys and men for most of his life and was still embarrassingly shy around women, which was difficult for a twenty-five-year-old man who by all criteria, would be considered a stud male of the species. He was a handsome, virile and incredibly wealthy young man who would still sometimes blush if a pretty female made a mildly suggestive comment. It was another reason for his desire to leave St. Louis. It wouldn't be long before the word of his return would leak out and he didn't doubt that he'd be inundated with the cream of St. Louis society's available ladies. The expected tidal wave of men trying to ingratiate themselves with Emperor Taylor's heir hadn't begun yet either and he hoped that when it did, it would crash against the walls of an empty Taylor estate.

But today wasn't about meeting women or begging supplicants. He had to start his plan to put his father's empire into the trash bin. He knew it wasn't going to be a simple operation as his father's enterprises were vast and some were quite shady, as evidenced by the deeds he had in his inner jacket pocket. But once it was gone, he could live his life as he wished. He still didn't know exactly what he would do, but he had the education and skills to do almost anything. It was simply a question of what would interest him.

He turned onto Willow Street and soon pulled up before the large brick building that housed the offices of James M. Ellis, Esquire. Grip never did hear what the lawyer's middle name was and began to come up with some seriously funny options. Of course, a man with the first name of Agrippa can't really point fingers.

He dismounted, tied the gelding to one of the hitching posts then stepped onto the sidewalk and climbed the four stone steps to the front door and entered the building.

Mister Ellis' office was on the second floor, so he headed for the stairs and took them two at a time.

He strode down the hallway and soon reached the glass door to the lawyer's outer office door. He had only been to the office once before and that was before he left for college and his father had brought him along to show him his new will. It was at that meeting that he had formed his opinion of the attorney.

He took a breath and swung the frosted glass door open and smiled at his clerk.

"Good morning, I'm Grip Taylor and I need to speak to Mister Ellis about my father's estate."

The clerk popped out of his chair as if Grip was royalty, then smiled back and replied, "Yes, sir. Of course, sir. Won't you please have a seat? Mister Ellis is with a client right now, but he should be finished shortly."

"Thank you," Grip replied as he removed his hat and took a seat in one of the four plush chairs.

The clerk tapped on the inner office door, stuck his head inside and in a low voice said, "Mister Ellis, Mister Taylor is here."

The attorney must have just used a sign to tell his clerk that he would be done in a minute because Grip didn't hear a reply before the clerk closed the door and returned to his chair behind his desk.

As the clerk resumed his work, Grip stared at the hat in his hands. It was an acceptable piece of headgear for St. Louis or even the halls of the University of Michigan, but he suspected that it would look out of place in Utah or anywhere else he might go in his travels throughout the West. He'd have to change his wardrobe before he got on the train.

Mister Ellis must have cut short his meeting with his less important client because just two minutes after the clerk told him of Grip's arrival, the door opened again, and an incredibly obese man barely squeezed through the door. He smiled at the clerk and as Grip was rising from his chair, the man stepped before him and offered him his hand.

Grip grasped his pudgy palm and the man said, "I'm sorry for your loss, Mister Taylor. We all had the greatest respect for your father."

Grip nodded and replied, "Thank you."

The chubby man smiled at him again then waddled away and exited the outer office.

Before Grip could ask the clerk who he was, James Ellis strode from his inner office and said, "Please come in, Grip. I'm sure that we have a lot to discuss."

"I'm sure that we do, Mister Ellis," Grip replied as he followed the attorney back into his private room and closing the door behind him.

After taking a seat in front of the large desk that was almost bare of paperwork, which surprised Grip, Mister Ellis sat behind the desk and smiled.

"That rather rotund example of manhood was Horace Berber. He was one of your father's competitors a few years ago, but your father bought his company. Mister Berber thought he'd duped your father because his company was in sad shape, but it turned out that his land was worth more than the factory. He wasn't happy that none of his own people had mentioned it to him and he suspected that your father had bribed them to keep that secret."

"So, he was pleasant to me because my father died?"

"I assume so. It was a terrible thing, Grip."

"Tom Truax, his driver, told me what happened, and Richard mentioned that none of the gang that set fire to the carriage had been apprehended."

"Alas, that's true. It's most likely that none will be punished for the murder as each of the suspects had an alibi for the night."

Grip nodded sadly but wasn't upset at all. He had to play his part as the grieving son as well as possible. He was sure that Mister Ellis knew much more about him than he did about the lawyer. It was just a question of how honest his father had been with the man and suspected that his father probably used the attorney for more than just legal documents. Mister James Ellis just had that look about him that reeked of dishonesty.

Before he could ask his first question, the door opened, and the clerk entered with a thick folder then set it on the desktop before quietly leaving again.

Mister Ellis opened the flap on the folder and slid its contents onto the desk.

There were about twenty sheets of paper of various sizes, two thick envelopes and a heavy ring holding six assorted keys.

As he turned the pages to face him, Mister Ellis said, "As your father's only relative, you are the sole heir to your father's estate. It's an extensive and complex holding that might take a while to review. I think you'll get a better idea if you visit Mister Stone at the Merchantmen's Bank. Do you know him?"

"Yes, sir. I'll go there after we finish."

Ellis smiled and said, "Excellent. The two envelopes contain lists of all of your father's major assets. All of these pages are legal formalities, such as his will."

After a short pause, the lawyer looked at Grip and asked, “So, have you made any plans yet? You’ve been away for so long that you’ll need some time to get a good feel for all of it and someone to guide you through the maze. You may want to appoint someone to manage these disparate operations until you learn the ropes.”

“You’re right about that, Mister Ellis. I just returned yesterday, so I’m still somewhat overwhelmed. It’ll take me at least a week or two to determine which path to take.”

“Please call me, James. You’re my boss, now.”

Grip smiled then replied, “Thank you, James. I don’t feel like anyone’s boss and I’m not sure that I ever will. Do we need to sign anything?”

“Just a few things, but when you’ve decided what you will do with this almost unfathomable industrial empire that your father left you, please let me know. I’ll do all I can to help.”

“Thank you, James. I’ll do that. Can we get the paperwork done? I need to head over to the bank and talk to Mister Stone.”

“Of course,” James Ellis said with a comforting smile.

Grip could almost see the dollar signs dancing in the lawyer’s brown eyes and managed to keep his laughter in check as he smiled back. James Ellis may have had a few other clients, but his father had provided almost all of his business and income and he now obviously believed that his income would greatly increase after his father's death.

Signing all the papers to close the probate took almost fifteen minutes and Ellis had filled each second of that time with a continuous offer to help Grip manage his father's businesses.

When he finally left the office with his copy of the legal papers, the two envelopes and the key chain in a fancy leather satchel, he was anxious to get away from the man. He had been close to just telling Mister Ellis to jump into the Mississippi and swim to Illinois.

———

Ten minutes later, he dismounted Pitch before the impressive edifice of the Merchantmen's Bank. It wasn't much larger than the office building that he'd just left, but it was much more elegant. The building itself was constructed with large granite and limestone blocks. It had six enormous columns supporting a Romanesque façade above the entrance. The dozen wide steps that granted entrance to the shrine to capitalism were marble, which was actually a bad idea. They may have been impressive, but only when they were dry as even a light dew would turn them into a slippery nightmare. The bank had soon discovered the problem and had to deface the surfaces with a pattern of grooves that defaced the marble but did reduce the liability presented by the smooth surfaces.

He strode up the wide stairs one at a time because they were more than two feet deep. If he'd taken them two at a time, even if they were dry, he'd probably find himself in an awkward and painful position on his fanny.

Grip entered the wide doors and crossed the lobby's smooth marble floor and headed to the executive offices on the right of the cashiers' windows. He was just fourteen when he'd first met Warren Stone, His father had brought him to his bank to set up a bank account for him. At the time, Warren was a clerk, and it wasn't as if he was a friend of his father. When they entered the bank, his father looked for an open desk and told the clerk, who happened to be Warren Stone, that he needed to open an account for his son, then his father had disappeared into the executive offices.

The young Grip had taken a seat and when Warren had made a somewhat snide comment about Mister Lawrence Preston Taylor for leaving his son at his desk, Grip knew he'd found a friend.

Over the years, he had come to trust Warren more than anyone else in the St. Louis business world and wasn't surprised when Warren made his way up the banking chain because he was good at what he did. Warren A. Stone was now a vice president at the powerful bank and Grip was sure that he was the only man who could handle what Grip needed to be done; to dismantle his father's empire.

He opened the outer door to the executive offices and entered the wide hallway lined with frosted glass doors emblazoned with the names and titles of the financial wizards within.

He closed the door behind him and headed for the second door on the right. When he read Warren A. Stone, Vice President, he smiled then turned the knob.

“Good morning,” he said as he smiled at Warren’s secretary.

“Good morning, sir. What can I do for you?” the man asked.

Grip hadn’t met him before, so he glanced at his desk looking for a nameplate but didn’t find one, so he replied, “I’m Grip Taylor and I was wondering if I could see Mister Stone.”

“Of course, sir.”

Grip had his hat in his hands and didn’t bother to sit down as the man stood and walked to the inner door and tapped on its paneled oak surface.

He opened the door and said, “Mister Stone, there’s a Mister Taylor to see you.”

Grip wasn’t surprised but still grinned when he heard Warren say, “That no-account? Tell him I have my wife with me, and I am not to be disturbed for at least another two minutes.”

Grip could tell that his secretary was shocked by his reply and was about to close the door when Warren started laughing then said, “Send him in, Al.”

Al visibly relaxed before he turned and smiled at Grip and waved him inside.

As soon as Grip entered, his secretary closed the door then Grip smiled at the banker and asked, "Two minutes, Stone? Really? I would think that Portia deserved much more than just two minutes.”

Warren laughed as they shook hands then each took a seat.

“I thought you’d be stopping by. Do you have any more details about what happened to your father?”

“I’m pretty sure that his carriage was set ablaze by some of his laid off workers. I’m surprised that the insurance company paid off so quickly when the arson was fairly obvious.”

“I was surprised myself. I guess that they didn’t want to lose the policies from all of your father’s other enterprises.”

“Well, that’s what I need to talk to you about, Warren.”

“When I heard about your father’s death, my first thoughts were to wonder what you’d be doing with his kingdom. I can’t see you riding to work each morning in a carriage and a three-piece suit, although I'll admit that you'd be an impressive sight."

"I have no intention of running even one of his companies, the legal ones or those that aren't. I'm leaving St. Louis as soon as I can get things organized and I'm going to dump a lot of responsibilities on you before I leave."

Warren leaned back then asked, "What kind of responsibilities?"

"I don't want to use Ellis for any of the legal work. The bank has attorneys on staff, and I'll need you to find one who can be trusted."

"I'll use John Vernon. He's helped me in the past when I needed absolute secrecy."

"Good. I'll want him to draw up a power of attorney so you can act on my behalf."

"What do you need?"

Grip slid the satchel on the desk, then opened the flap and extracted the two envelopes. He slid the deeds that he'd removed from the safe that morning from his jacket pocket and added them to the paper pile.

"These envelopes contain the listings of all of my father's businesses and other enterprises. These deeds I discovered yesterday in my father's secret vault. What I want you to do is to sell it all. There's no rush and the price that you get for each of them is unimportant to me. I just want to be rid of the lot."

"I can understand why you'd feel that way," Warren said as he glanced at the deeds.

"I have only a vague idea about my father's bank balance. Can you give me a rough amount?"

"I'll have Al get you an exact number, but if I'd have to put a dollar figure on the balance, I'd estimate it to be somewhere between three and three and a half million dollars and maybe close to four million. Your father was the second wealthiest man in St. Louis, but I imagine that you knew that."

Grip knew his father had accumulated a vast amount of wealth, but he was still stunned by the amount. His father had been born into money, but he had been growing his financial empire for almost thirty years and much of it was probably illegitimate. He'd do what he could to reverse that course.

He nodded and said, "Yes, I was aware of that. What I plan to do is to put two million into a trust fund that you will manage for various charities, and I may move most of the rest after I settle into a routine. I imagine that you'll be able to donate quite a lot just on the interest. I know that it will occupy a lot of time and I would suggest that you create a board to oversee the disbursement. I'll let you decide who should sit on the board. I'd recommend at least one woman be on it. Maybe Portia would enjoy handing out money."

"You're right about that. It'll take a while to set it up properly. Do you have any specific charities in mind?" Warren replied calmly although he had been shaken by Grips apparent ease about giving away such an enormous fortune.

"I'd prefer that the gifts go to families who are in need rather than institutions. When my father's assets are sold, just add those sales into the trust fund. We can include the legalities in the power of attorney. My father's estate is the only exception, at least for now."

"Why is that? I know you hate the place."

Grip then slipped the birth certificate from his pocket and as he unfolded it, he said, "I found this in my father's safe with those deeds and a few stacks of currency."

He handed it to Warren who quickly read the old document then looked back at Grip.

"Who is this and why would your father keep it?"

"I have no idea why he kept it, but I know that the mother, Charlotte Marley, worked for my father when I was six years old. He fired her and I'm pretty sure that the girl she bore, Julia Marley, is my half-sister."

"Are you sure?" he asked as he studied the birth certificate.

"No, but why else would he keep it? The reason that I don't want to sell the house yet is that I want to find Charlotte

Marley and her daughter. I know it will be difficult after all these years, but neither name is common, so a simple check of official records might provide the answer as to their whereabouts. If they're found before I leave, then I'll talk to them. If they're discovered after I'm gone, I want you to give them the house and a large settlement. They can sell it or live there. It'll be up to them. If they aren't found in six months, then you can sell the mausoleum. By the way, when we create the trust fund, call it the Julia Fund in my sister's honor."

"Are you going to hire a detective, or do you want me to handle it?"

"I'll do it. I want to meet the man they assign to the job. I figured I'd use the Pinkertons because they have a lot of resources."

Warren handed the birth certificate back to Grip and asked, "If this detective finds them, will you have him send them to see me?"

"Only after I've left St. Louis."

"Do you have a destination in mind?"

"Ogden, Utah."

"Utah? Have you become a Mormon while you were at that college?"

Grip grinned as he replied, “No, sir. I have a much more practical reason for the selection. It’s the railroad hub of the West.”

“Why is that important?”

“I’m going to try to make amends for all the harm that my father brought to society.”

“He wasn’t any different than other rich and powerful men, Grip. I know quite a few of the kings of industry and I don’t know any who wouldn’t sell their own mothers if they could get a good price.”

“I know, but that doesn’t mean that I’ll follow in his footsteps.”

“You never were going to do that anyway, Grip. He just left this world sooner than he’d planned.”

“He brought it on himself, Warren. Create a new account for the trust fund and transfer the money. Have those power of attorneys drawn up giving you authority over the fund and then go through those envelopes and deeds to prepare for their sale. I’ll stop by in a couple of days to review them all and sign what’s necessary.”

“You should give me at least three days, Grip. This is going to be a lot of paperwork.”

“Alright. As long as we keep everything quiet, then you can take as much time as you need.”

“Thanks for that, at least.”

Grip grinned and said, “You’ll have to set the salary for the fund manager, Warren. I think at least twenty thousand a year would be appropriate.”

Warren smiled and replied, “Well, I’m sure my wife will thank you. I don’t know if she’ll want to be on the board or not, but I suppose if I paid each of the board members five thousand dollars a year, she might agree.”

Grip stood and after sliding the birth certificate into his pocket, he shook Warren’s hand then left the office.

He had placed an enormous burden on his banker friend but knew that he’d handle it. He felt the twenty-thousand-dollar salary was probably a bit undervalued even if his wife did accept the lesser paying position on the board.

———

It was close to noon when he stepped down before the Pinkerton Detective Agency office. It was a separate, narrow building that was sandwiched between two much more impressive structures. The one on the right was a furniture store and the building on its left was a mortuary. He noticed that both shared the same owner, P.M. Dodge. He was snickering when he entered the Pinkerton office.

He scanned the busy office and one of the less busy detectives stood and walked toward him as he stood near the door.

"May I help you, sir?" the Pinkerton man asked.

"I need to have someone found after an almost twenty-year absence."

The detective grinned and replied, "That sounds right up my alley. My name is Joe Trimble. Come over to that mess that I call my desk and you can tell me what you need."

Grip removed his hat and walked behind the man to his desk. He hadn't exaggerated the disaster that the wooden surface supported. There were folders and stacks of papers spread across the desktop along with pencils, two pens and three bottles of ink, but only one seemed to contain any liquid.

As he sat down, Grip hoped that the man's skills as a detective were better than his administrative abilities.

"So, who do you need me to find, Mister…?"

"I'm Grip Taylor. It's short for Agrippa, and I won't mind any snickers or amusing comments. I've heard them all by now."

Joe didn't snicker, but he did smile as he replied, "I've heard worse. My parents named me Joseph, so I never had that issue. Who do you need me to find, Mister Taylor?"

“Call me Grip. Mister Taylor was my father, and I was never fond of the man.”

“Was your father Lawrence P. Taylor?”

“He was.”

“I hope that you aren’t here to have us find those responsible for his death. The St. Louis police department is never pleased when we investigate one of their active cases.”

“No, not at all. In fact, I hope that they never charge anyone with the crime. My father’s behavior had earned him that fiery death and by now maybe he has discovered that it wasn’t as hot as the burning pain that he is experiencing in hell.”

Joe didn’t comment about Grip’s father because he had never had a good opinion of the man and others like him who walked through those doors to engage their services. His son seemed like an entirely different sort.

“So, who do you need me to find?”

“Will it be you who does this job?”

“It will if you want me to do it. If not, we can see my boss in his private office behind me. Walk-in clients are usually assigned to the agent who greets them.”

“Good. You seem like the kind of man I need.”

“What gave you that impression?”

“You didn’t argue with me about not wanting to find the men who roasted my father in his carriage.”

“Oh.”

Grip then slid the birth certificate from his pocket and handed it to the detective.

Joe read the sheet and then looked back at Grip with raised eyebrows but didn’t ask a question.

“I discovered that birth certificate in my father’s secret vault. I’m sure that he didn’t know that I had found the vault years earlier. Anyway, I believe that the mother was one of his maids or housekeepers but was fired when I was six years old. She gave birth after leaving the house and her daughter is probably my half-sister.”

“It happens a lot more often than you realize.”

“I suspect that if anything, I overestimate how often it occurs. I know it’s been a long gap in time since she gave birth, but that certificate is local, and I would suspect that a thorough review of the county records might point you in the right direction.”

“That would be a good place to start as it usually is. I’ll need to write down more information including your current address.”

Grip nodded, then picked up one of the scattered pencils as Joe slid a blank sheet of paper onto one of the few bare sections of the desktop.

Grip wrote his address and after adding more information he handed it back to Joe Trimble.

"You're leaving St. Louis?" he asked as he looked at the page.

"After I settle some things. I hope to be gone within a month, and the sooner the better. If you show up at the house and I've already gone, see Mister Warren Stone at the Merchantmen's Bank. He knows everything, but I do need all of this to be kept confidential."

"We'd be a terrible detective agency if we didn't protect our clients' information. Do you want to know our fee schedule, or with your inheritance, don't you care?"

"I imagine that it will be reasonable, and I'll trust your reputation. But no, I really don't care unless it's totally outrageous and maybe not even then."

Joe grinned and shook Grip's hand. Before the handshake ended, Joe said, "That's quite a grip you have there, Grip."

Grip rolled his eyes before he stood and said, "That's almost beneath you, Joe."

Joe snickered as Grip turned and left the office. Grip was sure that he'd found exactly the man he needed to hire and hoped that Joe would find Charlotte and Julia Marley before he left. He wanted to meet his half-sister and had a lot of questions for her mother, too.

After mounting Pitch, he was going to return to the house, but it was just after noon, so he headed for a small café that he favored when he was in town. He knew that his father would never even consider going to the place which was one of the reasons he enjoyed eating there. The other reason was much more reasonable. The food was always delicious and very plentiful. The fancy restaurants his father preferred seemed to skimp on the quantity and tended to make the entrees look better than they tasted.

It was shortly after two o'clock in the afternoon when Grip left Molly's Place and rode down French Street. He had one more stop before heading back to the house and it was one of the few locations that he and his father both enjoyed visiting.

He soon pulled up before Charles Bainbridge & Sons Gunsmiths and Firearms. It was a very large operation as the owner had four sons working for him and had provided most of the weapons in his father's gun room.

He tied off Pitch and hopped onto the sidewalk before entering the shop. The smell of gunpowder, oil and cleaning fluid was pervasive, so he took a deep breath and strode toward the counter.

He had almost reached the counter when Fred Bainbridge, the oldest of his four sons spotted him and broke into a grin.

"Good afternoon, Grip."

"Afternoon, Fred."

"Sorry to hear about your father. It was a pretty gruesome way to go."

"It was but he's at peace now."

Grip wasn't sure how the Bainbridge men evaluated his father and wasn't about to react as he did with either Warren Stone or Joe Trimble.

"What brings you here today, Grip?"

"I need some work done, but I don't want to use any of the guns in the house."

"That's fine. What do you need?"

"I want to buy a Remington 1875 revolver and have it seriously conditioned. Then I want the factory grips removed and replaced with ebony. Do you have any of that wood?"

"Nope. But we can get some from the lumber yard. They have a whole section of exotic woods."

"Good. Get as much as you can, and I'll buy the excess."

"Okay. Is that all?"

"No, sir. I spotted a Sharps-Borshadt on the back wall when I entered, so I'll buy that one, and I'll want the stock replaced with ebony to balance the weight. It's a bit front heavy."

"It's not that bad, Grip."

"It will be after you mount a Malcolm telescopic sight on it. I want one of the eight power versions. Do you have any in stock?"

"We do. So, now you'll have a black-handled Remington and a black-handled Sharps-Borshadt. Are you sure you don't want to put one of those ebony stocks on a Winchester?" he asked followed with a surprisingly girlish giggle.

"Actually, I do. I want a Winchester '76 chambered for the .45-75 WCF cartridge with a thirty-inch barrel. If you don't have any in that length, go to thirty-two inches."

"I can do the thirty. All of this is going to take some time, Grip."

"How much time?"

"At least two weeks."

"That's fine. I'd like to have the pistol done first. When can I pick it up?"

"We can have that done in just a few days. Say next Friday."

"That'll work. I need to get a gunbelt for the pistol, then I'll be right back."

"Grab that Sharps-Borshadt on the way."

"I was going to do that, Fred," Grip replied as he walked away from the counter.

He pulled the heavy rifle from its perch and then continued to the back of the store where they kept their leather accessories. He didn't take long making his gunbelt selection after finding a black rig hanging at eye level. It had eight loops for spare cartridges and a matching sheath for a knife on the left side. What made it perfect was that it didn't have any shiny adornments. It was completely black and even the buckle was blued as if it was a rifle barrel.

He was about to return to the counter when he spotted another holster and even though it was a deep brown, he slid it from its hook and added it to his purchases. His next purchase wouldn't need black grips, but he might add them later after he was set up in Ogden.

When he returned to the counter, he set the gunbelts and the Sharps-Borshadt on the counter and Fred asked, "What are you going to put in that shoulder holster, Grip?"

"I was thinking about the Webley, but I might do something different."

"You can use one of the Colt Storekeepers. It's about the same weight and length as the Webley. It's not a double action, but it does have six shots."

"Do you have any chambered for the same cartridge as the Remington?"

"Yes, sir."

"Okay, sell me one of the Storekeepers and before you ask, I won't change the grips, so I can take it and the shoulder holster with me. I'm sure that I have enough cartridges at the house but give me two boxes anyway."

"Happy to oblige, Mister Taylor," Fred replied as he pulled two boxes of the .44 cartridges from under the shelf and set them on the counter.

He didn't bother asking Grip to pay for the cartridges or the Colt pistol he set on the counter beside the shoulder holster. He would just give him his massive bill when he returned to pick up his ebony-enhanced weapons. He was sure that Grip was good for the payment.

Grip took off his jacket and after setting it on the counter, he strapped on the shoulder holster, loaded the Colt and slid it into its new leather home before donning his jacket again.

"I can't even see it, Grip," Frank said as Grip pulled on his hat.

"You wouldn't tell me if it stuck out as if I had a howitzer under my coat, Fred," Grip said before he took the bag with the cartridges and left the shop.

As he rode back to the house, he wondered if he had missed anything on his first day back in St. Louis. He still had much to do and wondered how long it would take Joe Trimble to either find Charlotte and Julia Marley or discover that they were either dead or gone off to some other place. If she had married after being tossed out of his father's house, then Miss Marley might be happily married, and his half-sister could already have a family of her own, too. If that was true, then he'd have to at least determine how much their husbands knew about how Julia had been conceived before he even let them know who he was.

He found it difficult to believe that if they were still in St. Louis, that they didn't know that Lawrence Preston Taylor had died. His death had been front-page news in every newspaper in the city for three days. But if they had heard the news, then he was curious why they hadn't tried to contact him. If nothing else, they could demand some form of restitution, if not blackmail.

He had Pitch moving at a medium trot as he made his way back to the big house. He'd spend some time with his gelding's equine family when he returned. It would be a peaceful break in what could be a tumultuous couple of weeks. But first, he'd use the keys he'd gotten from Mister Ellis to see what was in that locked bottom drawer.

Grip turned the gelding down the long, graveled drive and headed for the large carriage house. He could see some of the horses grazing in the expansive, fenced pastures beyond the squat building that housed them in inclement weather.

He didn't see Tom Truax outside, but assumed he was in the carriage house with the mare who was about to foal. He did a quick count and calculated that there were three other horses inside as well.

His father may have loved his guns, but the horses were just there to pull his carriage. It was Tom Truax who cared for them like the children he and his wife, Jenny never had. Tom had convinced his father years earlier that it was more cost efficient to raise his own horses rather than try to find similar animals in one of the many stables in town or the horse farms that surrounded the big city. He knew that it wasn't exactly true, but the fact that he'd been able to keep a steady supply of all black horses which served as a matched team for the master's carriage had reinforced his position.

Pitch was one of the offspring of the first stallion that Tom had brought onto the estate, but Grip hadn't taken possession of him until his third year at Michigan.

He pulled up outside of the carriage house and dismounted. He led Pitch through the wide doors, and as expected, he found Tom Truax examining the swollen mare.

Tom turned when he heard Grip enter, then stood and said, “We were wondering if you hadn’t gone off to Utah already.”

Grip grinned and replied, “It’ll be a while before everything starts happening. I met with Mister Ellis, then went to the bank. I stopped at Bainbridge’s after lunch which is what took so long. How’s our lady friend?”

“She’s healthy and should produce a fine foal in about six weeks. We’re due for a colt after having three fillies in a row.”

“The odds are still fifty-fifty, Tom, although I think the number is closer to 51-49, but I don’t think it matters.”

“You haven’t seen last year’s crop. We have three yearlings out there, but like I said, they’re all girls.”

Grip laughed and replied, “Well, let’s hope you’re right about a colt. We’ll leave him as a stallion if he’s a boy. I think Edward is getting ready to give up his crown as the Black Prince.”

“He’s still happy to help his ladies provide us with more youngsters, but if Betsy here has a boy, we’ll let him keep what nature gave him.”

"Can you take care of Pitch for me? I need to check something in my father's office."

"That's my job, boss…I mean, Grip."

Grip just smiled and pulled the bag of ammunition from his saddlebags and the satchel from the hook on the side of the saddle before he left the carriage house and walked to the house. He'd use the front entrance because it was closer to the office.

When he entered the house, he was surprised to find no one in sight, but could hear bustling in the kitchen as someone was preparing to come rushing down the hallway.

"I'm just going to the office," he said loudly to forestall their need to take his hat and coat.

His father had been a stickler to have them perform such mundane tasks, and he was sure that it was ingrained into the staff. He knew it would take some time to eliminate the urge to run to the front of the house whenever he entered. Even though they wouldn't be living in the mansion much longer, he didn't want to be treated as the master of the house for another minute.

He hung his hat and coat on their hooks then walked through the parlor and entered the office. He closed the door and strode to the desk where he took a seat. After setting the bag of cartridges on the floor, he placed the satchel on the desk and opened the flap.

Grip removed the ring and examined each of the keys. Each one was charred to one degree or another, but there was only one that was small enough for the drawer. He inserted the key and turned the lock before setting the key ring back on the desk.

He pulled the drawer open and pulled out just a few sheets of paper.

The top page made his eyebrows shoot up and his eyelids spring open.

It was a handwritten note from his father that he had obviously hadn't had a chance to deliver and it was troublesome.

He read:

M.M. –

Here are the names of those that confronted me. I don't want to see them again. I gave those ingrates a job and now they dare to threaten me!
Make them pay for their arrogance.

Terrance Dooley
Harry Anderson
Peter M. Smith
John R. White
James M. White

The letter wasn't signed, and Grip wondered if the mysterious M.M. had actually been given the names in some other form. He had no idea who the man was, but obviously he handled the strongarm part of his father's empire. Grip suspected that he was far from the only one, and M.M. probably had an entire crew of thugs to carry out his father's wishes.

He flipped to the second page and found another note to M.M.

M.M. –

Keep an eye on those rabblerousers. I don't want them anywhere near my house. If threats aren't enough, use whatever means you feel are necessary.

I've found that threats against their families are often more effective than trying to scare them with bodily harm.

Grip found his already low opinion of his father sinking to new depths. He not only bullied his workers; he threatened their families. He must have discovered how effective it was as a bullying tactic that even M.M. might not have understood.

The third and last page just had M.M. scribbled along the top as if his father had been interrupted in his preparation of another set of instructions for his personal thug.

He returned them to the drawer and closed it but didn't bother locking it. He dropped the key ring into the middle drawer and shoved it closed as well before he leaned back in the swivel and rocking chair.

His plans for a quick departure for Utah were beginning to shift. He suspected that within a few days, he'd be paid a visit by M.M., so he needed to at least be able to identify him. He wasn't afraid of the man but wanted to be prepared.

After a minute of silent contemplation, he stood, snatched the bag of ammunition from the floor and walked to the gun room. He set the two boxes of .44s into one of the ammunition drawers, then hung his new shoulder holster on an empty hook before he left with the empty bag.

When he entered the kitchen, he found Richard and Wilma Bennett at the table and Jenny Truax at the cookstove pouring a cup of coffee.

Richard stood and asked, "How did the meeting go with Mister Ellis?"

"He expects me to take over my father's empire eventually, but he offered to run it until I was ready."

Richard chuckled then asked, "Did you start the process of divesting yourself of that empire?"

"I did. I met with Warren Stone at the bank and left most of it in his capable hands."

When Jenny handed him the cup of coffee, Grip said, "Thank you, Jenny. Please have a seat. I need to ask you some questions."

Jenny nodded and sat in one of the eight chairs surrounding the large table before Grip joined them.

"Richard, you are the most likely person to answer this one. Do you know of a man with the initials M.M. who might have helped my father out with some of his shadier dealings?"

Richard glanced at his wife before replying, "I imagine that would be Mister Mooney. I'm not sure of his first name and I've only seen him on two occasions. Tom might have seen him more often because he drives the carriage."

"What does he look like?" Grip asked before taking a sip of his coffee.

"The most noticeable thing about him is his size. You aren't a small man by any stretch, Grip, but that man is a giant. He's probably at least five or six inches taller than you and I imagine he outweighs you by more than sixty pounds. He has dark hair that he lets grow over his collar and wears a full beard. I can't tell you the color of his eyes because I didn't dare look at them. He had the appearance of a true brute of a man."

"Do you know if he works alone or does he have partners?"

"I have no idea. I wish that I'd never met him in the first place. I don't think your father was happy when he showed up here, either. When he appeared at the door, I almost lost control of my bladder. He just told me to tell your father that Mooney was here. When I did, your father was very displeased that he showed up at the house and ordered me to go to the kitchen and to keep everyone else there. The second time I saw him was just three weeks ago when I caught sight of him talking to your father by the carriage house."

"Thank you, Richard. I hope that you don't see him again. I contracted with the Pinkertons to find Charlotte Marley and her daughter, so we'll see how that works out. I told the agent to have them see Warren Stone at the bank if they didn't find them before I left for Utah. That's something else I need to talk to you about. I may be leaving all of you here for a month or so to find a new place to live in Ogden. I hope to be able to leave within ten days, but I'll leave you more than enough money when I go."

"We'll be fine, Grip. What changed your mind about us coming with you?"

"When I was at the gunsmith, I suddenly realized that I needed to do a lot of preparatory work in Utah before you arrived. I'll just take Pitch and some new guns that I ordered."

Richard smiled and asked, "Aren't there enough weapons in the gun room?"

"Not what I needed, Richard. I want to establish a persona when I get to Utah."

"A persona?"

"I want to be perceived as a gunman, and one who couldn't be avoided."

"Whatever for?"

"Because I want to weed out the troublemakers. I don't expect to actually get into any real gunfights, but once I have them identified, I'll use some of my father's resources to solve the problem."

"You'll have to clarify all of that one of these days."

"I'll do that over the next week while I prepare for the move and wait to see if Mister Trimble can find my half-sister and her mother. I'm curious to see if Mister Mooney shows up, too. I don't believe he will unless it's to offer his services. That might be a difficult situation."

"What do you want me to do if he shows up at the door?"

"Just show him in if I'm in the house. If I'm not, then politely tell him where I am."

Richard nodded, but hoped that Mister Mooney stayed in the shadows.

———

Mickey Mooney wasn't in the shadows but was playing poker in the bright front room of Mason Street Hall and Billiard Parlor. The boss had given him carte blanche to the cathouse and he extended that offer to his three cohorts without a word of complaint from either Lawrence P. Taylor or Francine Ballard, the madam for the establishment yet was still a working prostitute. She enjoyed the work.

Cajun Al Darnell asked, "So, how long before we get the word?"

"I ain't sure," Mickey replied, "That kid of his just got in town yesterday. Ellis said he's workin' his angle, but it was just one visit and he ain't sure yet."

"Is he gonna let Ellis run everything or not?" asked Bill Jones before he tossed his cards onto the table in disgust.

"How the hell should I know?" Mickey snapped before snorting and dropping his hand onto the table.

"Why don't you go and talk to him to find out before Ellis does?" Cajun Al asked.

"I scare the hell out of everybody, and I don't wanna scare the kid, but I reckon he might not trust that damned lawyer any more than we do."

Then he turned to John Schuler who had been winning too many hands already and said, "John, you ain't as scary-lookin'. So, why don't you go and pay the kid a visit tomorrow and introduce yourself as a trusted personal employee of his father. Try and get what you can out of him. We might be able to get a leg up on Ellis."

John grinned before he even looked up from his cards and said, "I'll do that. I'll be a genuine polite feller and maybe I'll even kiss him on the cheek."

The other three men all laughed before John showed them his full house.

———

After leaving the kitchen, Grip stopped in the foyer to retrieve his jacket then headed for the gun room.

After donning his shoulder holster, he pulled on his jacket and left the gun room to visit his father's room for the first time since his return. He had never even been inside the room since he was sixteen when his father had shown him the full-length mirror inside of the door of the large wall closet and explained its secondary use. After the night with Mary Duffy, his father obviously had expected Grip to be amused if not impressed.

He opened the bedroom door and slowly stepped inside unsure of what he might expect to find. He should have known that it would be almost sterile. The maids would have ensured that there was no evidence of his peccadillos or other failings before they left the estate.

He stepped to the big closet and opened the left door and stared at his image. The Colt Storekeeper wasn't invisible, but unless he turned to his right or pulled the jacket tight, it wasn't noticeable. After Richard described Mister Mooney to him, he felt that having the pistol might be necessary after all. He wondered how many of those .44s it would take to put down a man that large even at close range. He hoped he'd never have to find out the answer in practice.

He took a few minutes searching the room and found nothing of interest. What wasn't there was even more demonstrative of his father's nature than what was. There wasn't one photograph of his two wives or anyone else. He hadn't expected to find anything that would let a stranger know that Lawrence Preston Taylor had a son, but not finding a single piece of evidence that his father had even married said a lot about the man.

Grip didn't know what his reaction would have been if he'd found a treasured packet of love letters from his mother to his father or another sign of humanity in his father. In the twenty-five years that he'd been the son of Lawrence Preston Taylor, he had never seen one moment of tenderness displayed by his father.

He sat in the chair by his dressing table and did the math, trying to calculate just how much time he had spent with his father after he had gone off to St. Michael's. He found it surprisingly uncomplicated and when he finished just two minutes later, he came up with the figure of seven months and twelve days. But even in that amount of time, Grip would have expected to see some form of humanity in the man. In all that time, Grip couldn't even recall seeing his father just smile. He'd laugh for all sorts of reason, like when he'd seen Grip the day after his night with Mary Duffy.

Mary Duffy. Grip sighed and felt a curtain of sadness descend over his mind. Three days after his playful pseudo lovemaking with her, his father had fired her. His father had only mentioned it casually as if he'd tossed an old pair of worn socks into the trash bin.

He's heard that she had fallen on hard times after that and had died in suspicious circumstances three years later.

But Mary's dismissal was just another example of his father's callous disregard for people who didn't matter to him, which was just about all of them, including his only son. If Lawrence P. Taylor couldn't benefit from you, then you had no right to exist.

It was what made that birth certificate even more troubling and mysterious. *If his father had a total change in character and loved Charlotte Marley, then why didn't he at least provide for her and their daughter?* If she had been blackmailing him, then he would have just sent M.M. to crush her and probably have thrown her and Julia Marley into the Mississippi River.

Grip finally stood, slid the chair back into position and left the room, knowing that he would never visit it again.

Later that night as he lay in his bed, he spent an hour reviewing all that he still needed to do before he left for Utah. His first journey wouldn't require much as it would be a trip for exploration and preparation for the permanent move. He wanted to get a feel for the West and how to blend in. To look the part, he'd have to buy a new wardrobe, but wasn't about to visit one of the finery shops that his father favored. He'd do his shopping where the working men bought their clothes that weren't made by their wives. He may not look like a man of the West when he departed St. Louis, but he wouldn't have the appearance of an urbane gentleman either.

CHAPTER 3

After making his bed and taking a bath the next morning, Grip had breakfast with the staff and then saddled Pitch and rode out of the estate. He would start his transformation this morning, but his first stop wouldn't be a clothing store. He was sitting on an Eastern riding saddle which was much smaller and lighter than a Western saddle. It was what was appropriate in the cities where riders never ventured more than ten miles, but he was planning to ride much further and needed the heavier saddle even beyond the need to blend in.

It took him fifteen minutes before he dismounted in front of Robert and Alan Willoughby Saddlery and Tack. It wasn't the closest shop where Grip could have purchased the saddle, but it was the largest and he wanted a good selection. He could have had one made to his specifications but didn't want to waste the time. If he didn't find exactly what he wanted here, he'd just check some of the smaller places.

After tying off Pitch, he entered the store and was greeted with the pleasant odor of tanned leather. There were saddles of all types mounted on wooden supports that didn't look anything like a horse. The walls were covered with bridles, whips, saddlebags and just about anything else that could be attached to a horse.

The two salesmen were busy with customers, which suited him because he knew what he wanted, and no amount of salesmanship would get him to change his mind.

He slowly walked down the first row of saddles which were all of the Eastern style, which was to be expected. He reached the back of the store and after walking past the next aisle, he found a long row of Western saddles. Most were a tan or medium brown but as he strolled down the aisle, they began to grow darker. Grip reached the first black saddle, but it was too ostentatious for his taste and his intended use. It had fancy silver inlays and even a silver plate on the saddle horn.

He sidestepped to his right and after two more saddles he found one that was perfect. It was simply a heavy, black Western saddle. Even the stirrups were dark. The saddle maker had sewn the steel support under a thick pad of black leather.

Once he made his selection, he scanned the wall of accessories and spotted a matching bridle but couldn't find any plain black saddlebags. Unlike the saddle, it wouldn't take long for them to make a large set of saddlebags. It was the saddle that was important. He tapped the saddle's seat with his left hand and strode toward the counter. Both salesmen were still dealing with customers, so he decided to do some browsing. He headed for the back of the store and turned down the accessory aisle. He passed the bridles and saddlebags and wasn't surprised to find a display of gunbelts. He already had the one waiting for him at the gun shop, so he didn't need one. But when he saw something very different, he stopped and removed it from its peg. It was a black gunbelt much like the one he'd already bought, but there was something that marked it as unique. He'd never seen one like it before.

It wasn't the holster, the loops for the spare cartridges or the belt or buckle that made it odd. It was the attached sheath. Every gunbelt he'd ever seen that had a sheath for a knife, it had been attached with the point dropping straight down. This one had a wide attaching strap at a forty-five-degree angle and immediately saw the practicality of the design. Most uses for an attached knife were utilitarian and didn't need to be withdrawn quickly. The angled sheath allowed for a knife to be not only pulled more quickly, but at an angle that readied it for almost instantaneous use. A talented knife fighter could even pull and throw the knife in one motion. Throwing a knife was always a desperate move, but if it was that bad, then this angled sheath made that drastic attempt much more likely to succeed. He thought it was a less obtrusive way to mount a knife as well.

He turned and headed back to the front of the store, already visualizing the line of knives in the gun room to make the best selection for the unusual setup.

When he reached the long counter, one of the salesmen who was now free of his long-winded customer, stepped close.

"Will that be all, sir?" the man asked.

"No. I need a few more items you have on display and need a set of matching saddlebags, but I don't see anywhere."

"Let's see what you need, then I'll check our storeroom for the saddlebags. We don't have enough room to put everything on display."

Grip nodded before they headed for the Western saddle aisle. As it turned out, they did have a matching set of saddlebags in the large storeroom and they were even more voluminous than he had hoped. After paying for everything, Grip left with only the gunbelt, but would have everything else delivered to the house that afternoon.

He set the new gunbelt into Pitch's much smaller saddlebags and after mounting, turned him north to find an appropriate clothing store. He was fortunate that he had met a few men from the West while he was at the University of Michigan. He'd befriended men from the Dakotas, Wyoming, Colorado and even Texas. While they may not have dressed the same and their accents varied wildly, he had a good idea of what he needed to buy. While none of them wore a gunbelt and pistol on campus, he knew at least three who had them in their rooms. They may not all have worn similar headgear, but the Stetson or something like it seemed to be the most popular. What did seem to be almost universal was their choice in footwear. Even if they were wearing a proper suit to class, each of them wore Western-style boots rather than buttoned downed high-top shoes.

So, as Pitch trotted along the cobblestoned streets of St. Louis, Grip Taylor had a good idea of what he'd need to buy to avoid stares when he journeyed past the Missouri River and tried to think of anything else that he'd need for his first trip to Utah.

The stop at G.W. Gantry's Men's Clothing didn't take as long as he expected, but he did buy enough items that the order required another delivery.

It was almost noon when he turned Pitch down the gravel drive and spotted a man mounting his brown horse in front of the house. Grip slowed his black gelding to a walk and watched as the man wheeled his horse around. The man didn't have the look of a businessman or a lawyer, so Grip wondered why he had stopped by. He knew that his father had surprisingly few visitors to the house and the man riding away from the front steps was hardly the type who would merit an invitation.

Grip kept Pitch at a walk but pulled his horse to a stop when the stranger was just fifty feet in front of him.

John Schuler couldn't believe his luck. He'd just been told by Richard Bennett that the kid had gone off to do some shopping and he thought he'd have to come back tomorrow, but there he was riding in all by his lonesome. If he'd found him in the house, it probably wouldn't be a private conversation, so this was perfect.

"Mornin'," John said loudly as he pulled his horse to a stop just six feet away.

"Good morning," Grip replied.

"Are you Mister Preston's boy?" John asked.

"I am. What can I do for you?"

"My name is John Schuler and me and some other fellers did a kinda bodyguard work for your father. We figured after what happened to Mister Preston, you might need protection against those bad men who killed him."

"Where were you and the other fellers when his carriage was set on fire?"

"We wished we was there, but he sent us home 'cause he wanted his privacy. Me and the boss told him it was a bad idea after all those workers caused a ruckus. When we heard what happened, we felt real bad."

"I imagine so. Who is your boss?"

"Didn't your father tell ya? His name is Mooney, Mickey Mooney. He's a giant of a man and if he'd been there that night, you're pa would still be alive, and those bastards would all be dead."

"Well, I'm not worried, Mister Schuler. I can take care of myself and I haven't done anything bad to anyone."

"Those hotheads will still blame you 'cause you're a Taylor and once you take over, they'll likely come after you. You are gonna take your pa's place, ain't ya?"

Grip sighed then said, "Listen. I've only been back for a couple of days and have a lot of meetings with all sorts of people to figure out what's going on. If I feel threatened at all, I'll let you know. Do you have some way for me to contact Mister Mooney?"

"Sure. I got a paper with all of our names and where to find us. The boss said to tell you that we'll do anything you need, no matter what."

John pulled the folded sheet from his jacket pocket and had to walk his horse forward a few more feet to give it to Grip.

Grip smiled as he accepted it before saying, "Well, it's been a pleasure meeting you, Mister Schuler. I'll be in touch."

John grinned and then gave Grip a short wave before nudging his mare into a trot and heading down the drive.

Grip didn't bother watching him leave but stuffed the paper into his coat pocket then set Pitch to a slow trot toward the carriage house. He had no idea of what, if anything, he would do about Mister Mooney, but the single sheet of paper at least provided him with the number and whereabouts of his father's henchmen. He assumed that if he just ignored them, they'd eventually find another unscrupulous employer. He'd be in Utah soon anyway and they would become irrelevant. But the odd part of the conversation was that simple, almost innocuous question about whether he was going to take over his father's business. It could have just his way of having reassurance that Mooney's boys would still be on the payroll, but it was still an odd thing to mention.

As he headed for the barn, he wondered if Mooney and his crowd really did provide some form of bodyguard protection for his father and if that was so, *why weren't they there on the night the mob torched the carriage?* He hadn't asked Tom Truax about Mooney yet, but he'd ask him in the next few minutes.

He rode Pitch into the carriage house where he spotted the mare who looked as if she wasn't going to wait another six weeks to drop her foal. Tom wasn't there, and the mare was the only horse in the stalls. He guessed that the rest of them were on the other side of the carriage house because he hadn't seen them outside.

He dismounted and began unsaddling Pitch. He'd just removed the bridle when Tom walked through the doors.

"I'll get that for you, Grip," he said loudly as he stepped toward the stall.

"I'll handle it, Tom. I need to talk to you anyway."

"Sure. What about?"

"Did you see that man who just left?"

"I saw him. He looks familiar, but I don't know his name."

"His name was John Schuler and he's one of Mickey Mooney's boys. He offered their services as protection against the mob who set fire to my father's carriage."

"Really? You didn't agree to that; did you?"

"No, sir. He said that they served as bodyguards for my father, but he had dismissed them for that night. He even claimed that if Mooney had been there, the giant would have killed every one of that mob. Did they ever really act as bodyguards?"

Tom snickered as he shook his head, then replied, "Nope. I only saw them when your father had some nasty business he wanted done. He didn't want them to come to the house and he didn't ride on his own, so I'd drive him to one of his secret businesses and I'd wait outside. I'd see Mooney and the others leave first and then your father would usually spend another hour or so inside before leaving the place. I only recognized them because Mooney is so easy to spot. The others were all normal-sized and looked about the same. You know, height and hair color and such."

"That's what I thought. I know that you'll only be able to give me a guess, but do you think that they'll just look for another employer if I ignore them?"

Tom scratched the right side of his neck as he replied, “I never so much as talked to any of them, but if you don’t pay them, I can’t see them sticking around.”

“I wonder how much my father was paying them. I haven’t seen any secret log books that had listed his expenses, but then, I haven’t found any ledgers at all. I did find a list of those he bribed and how much he paid them and when, but that made sense. He was keeping it as insurance and to keep them in line. I guess he just paid Mooney cash under the table. He kept a large amount of cash in his secret safe in the house.”

“He had a safe in the house? Where was that?”

“In a hidden room behind the gun room. I found it accidentally a few years ago and even figured out the combination he used for the safe. He never told me about it, of course, but I don’t think that Mooney knows about it, either. I don’t believe that anyone except my father even knew that the room existed.”

“None of us knew about it, that’s for sure.”

Grip had finished stripping Pitch and said, “I’ll let you take care of my friend now. I ordered a new set of tack that was more suited to Utah than what he’s wearing now. It’ll all be delivered this afternoon, so just store it wherever you have space.”

“Okay, Grip.”

Grip smiled then asked, “Want to see something really different?”

“Is it going to scare me?” Tom asked with a grin.

“Maybe,” Grip replied as he slid the gunbelt from his saddlebag.

“What’s so strange about that?”

Grip strapped the gunbelt around his waist, not bothering to remove his jacket, then smiled at Tom.

“See the knife’s sheath? It’s at an angle, so I’ll be able to pull a knife and have it in the air in a fraction of a second if necessary.”

Tom shook his head and said, “I’ll admit that it’s different, but I hope you never have to resort to a stunt like that.”

“So, do I,” he said before popping Tom on the shoulder, removing the gunbelt and heading out of the carriage house.

He appreciated that Tom seemed to be adjusting to his new role faster than Richard or their wives, but he needed Richard to quickly adopt to his new position as mentor, confidant and planner. If he was going to have his Western plans work, he needed their support.

After entering the office, he removed the gunbelt, then sat behind the desk and pulled out the paper that John Shuler had given him. There were only four names and he noted that all of their addresses were on Albion Avenue, which was near the ruins of his father's foundry that had caused all the turmoil.

He assumed that it had been at least one of those names on the sheet who had set the foundry ablaze. It wouldn't be hard to commit the act of arson as there were mountains of coal in giant bunkers in the main foundry. But to get that coal to burn the way it did, the coal would have to be less compact so the air could get to the fire. Coal fires in a big pile didn't burn like a lot of folks thought it did. It smoldered more than blazed. The fire would have needed more fuel and be spread more widely. He hadn't seen the report from the fire marshal, but he was sure that the word 'arson' had appeared often. His only interest was if Mooney and his three boys had been the ones to set the fire. An arson job on a normal house or small business wasn't difficult but getting a big factory to burn down took expertise. He doubted if John Schuler knew how to do it and doubted that the others would have the ability either. If they did put the place to the torch, they had to have help.

He slid the paper into the center drawer and knew that it really didn't matter who had set the fire, even if it was Mooney. Within the month, he'd leave St. Louis and Mickey Mooney and his boys behind.

He stood, picked up his new gunbelt and walked to the gun room. He had his new Remington being modified and his shoulder harness with the Colt Storekeeper, but now that he had a second gunbelt with its angled sheath, he figured he may as well select another pistol.

He walked down the line of revolvers and snickered as he picked up the Smith & Wesson Model 3.

"You've got a Colt and a Remington, so why not?" he asked himself aloud before sliding the gun into the new holster and pulling the hammer loop into place.

He then turned around and began scanning the row of knives. The length and width of the blade had to be right for the sheath, which limited his selection to just four knives.

It wasn't a difficult choice. He picked up the dagger with a sharkskin-wrapped handle and rotated it slowly in the sunlight coming through the windows behind him.

It was a smaller knife with an eight-inch blade, which would leave more than an inch of empty space at the end of the sheath. But the two razor-sharp edges of the dagger made it a lethal weapon. He wasn't concerned about its practical uses. He had a good pocket knife for the simple cutting tasks, and he'd have the heavy Bowie knife in the other gunbelt as well. This was a killing blade, and its balance was perfect. It was the same knife that he'd used to impress his father when he was sixteen. It would fit well into the angled sheath and he'd practice the quick pull and throw when he spent some time on the target range his father had built on the western edge of the property.

He slipped the dagger into the sheath and then left the gun room. He may need to do some target practice, but he felt the urge to take a long run.

Grip returned to his bedroom, left his new gunbelt on one of his dressers and then stripped. When he ran, he wore some short pants and a cotton shirt so he wouldn't offend anyone. He hoped the folks out West weren't so prudish. The men he'd met from the land west of the Missouri River didn't seem as easily offended as those from the Eastern side of the Mississippi. On his feet, he wore socks and a pair of heavy wool coverings that looked almost like slippers but had laces to keep them attached. He always had several extra pairs of the odd footwear because he went through them so often.

He never ate before he went on a serious run, so he soon left the house and after a few minutes of fast walking to loosen his muscles, he set off at a fast jog to start.

It may only have been in the low eighties, but the humidity was thick and after just a minute at the slower pace, the sweat was already dripping from his pores. At least the estate was far enough from Old Man River that there weren't as many Old Man Mosquitoes to make life miserable.

Grip always felt so alive when he was running, and his mind seemed to match whatever pace he chose. That pace kept increasing as he ran. The property encompassed one hundred and sixty acres, so each border was a half a mile long. It made it easy to mark distances, but Grip never cared how far he had run. He ran for the pleasure as well as the exercise. He ran until it was no longer enjoyable and then pushed it until it became almost painful. For him, that was around thirty minutes or so at a fast pace. He could push it much longer if he wished, but he preferred to run as fast as he could for those thirty minutes. If he had measured the distance, it would have been over six miles.

When he felt it was time to stop, he slowed his pace until he reached a fast walk but never stopped until his breathing had returned to normal.

He didn't enter the house but walked into the carriage house where he dumped two buckets of cold water over his head. After drying himself with a towel, he headed for the house but removed his footwear on the porch. He finally entered the house then quickly climbed the stairs. Before returning to the first floor for lunch, he took a bath and dressed casually.

———

"You think he's gonna stay and try to run everything?" Mickey asked.

"It sounds like it. He said he's gotta talk to a bunch of folks to figure things out."

"You don't think that Ellis will try to turn on us; do you?" asked Bill Jones.

"I don't trust that bastard, but he wouldn't risk it. The kid's only been back for a couple of days, so I don't reckon that Ellis has to feel the kid out like we do. What good would it do him to tell the kid? He's in this deeper than we are."

Cajun Al said, "Mickey, you gotta figure that if Ellis tells his police friends what happened, they ain't gonna believe a word we tell 'em."

Mickey tugged at his beard as he thought about it. It was a problem that had been gnawing at him as well, but he hadn't voiced it to the others. Ellis was just too damned sneaky to be predictable. It had seemed like such a good plan at the beginning, but now the thought that the lawyer might take over the Taylor empire and then use that power to get rid of them was a real danger.

Under his breath, Mickey quietly said, "Maybe we ought to get rid of him just in case."

The other three at the table all turned their eyes to their big boss as none of them had heard him clearly.

He saw their confusion and in a slightly louder voice, he said, "We should make sure he doesn't have a chance to screw us."

Cajun Al asked, "When do you figure we should do it?"

Mickey hadn't taken the idea that far yet, so he replied, "Give me a minute. It sounds like the kid doesn't know much, but after what he told John, I reckon it won't be much longer before Ellis has his way. He knows all of the old man's businesses and rackets and the kid doesn't know a damned thing. If Ellis gets to spend much longer with the kid, then he'll become his best pal and then we might be in trouble."

The others remained silent as they watched Mickey think. None of them trusted the lawyer any more than their boss did and the one thing they knew how to do well was to end people's lives.

Mickey was good at intimidation and brutal enforcement, but planning wasn't his strong suit. Usually, their jobs required almost no planning or stealth, but he knew that getting rid of the lawyer would require both. Ellis was a shrewd and untrusting man, and those two traits would make it difficult to get the job done.

It would have to be done under the cover of darkness as most of them were, but it couldn't be on the streets. Mickey knew where the lawyer lived with his wife. That would be the best place to kill him. He knew that they'd have to do it without him because it would be easy for anyone who spotted them approaching the house to identify him just because of his bulk.

His hurried plan had taken him less than five minutes while his three men had watched in silence.

He then nodded and said, "Alright. Here's what I want to happen."

As Mickey quietly outlined the method for eliminating James M. Ellis, Esquire, John Schuler, Cajun Al Darnell and Bill Jones just nodded and listened. He explained why he couldn't join them, and they understood his reasoning. None of them thought he was a coward.

"After you're done, feel free to ransack the place and steal what you want. Make it look like a robbery gone bad."

It was John Schuler who spoke for the other two when he said, "Okay, boss. When do you want us to get this done?"

"After midnight tonight. I don't know the layout of his place, so you'll have to figure it out when you get there. Split up and each of you take different bedrooms. Kill the wife, too. I don't want any witnesses."

John nodded then said, "We'll make sure he doesn't cause us any problems, boss."

"I know you'll do the job right, boys," Mickey said before ordering a round.

At his home on Allison Street, James Ellis was sitting at the kitchen table sipping a cup of lukewarm coffee. His wife, Isabel, was already in their bedroom waiting for him. He knew which book she was reading and didn't care for the author.

Since he'd paid Mooney to arrange for Lawrence Taylor's death, he'd been expecting them to attempt to blackmail him. He had convinced them that once Taylor was gone, the kid would return from college and would then grant him control of his deceased father's empire. He knew that Grip had no business background and had no ambitions other than his interest in academic or engineering endeavors. He didn't know the kid well, but James trusted his own ability to win the confidence of men, including Lawrence Preston Taylor.

The attorney had been bilking the industrial magnate for years and it had allowed him to live in much better circumstances than others in his profession. The fact that the untrusting businessman hadn't even noticed the losses spoke more about James' own talents than Taylor's ineptness.

But even the large amounts that he'd taken from Taylor's enterprises weren't enough to satisfy James Michael Ellis. He wanted more than just money. He wanted the power that Taylor possessed and the only way to take it was to eliminate the man at the top and then manipulate his naïve son.

His plan was working well so far, but his one concern had been the four men whom he'd paid to betray their employer. He could have hired some other thugs who were common enough in the city, but he had been concerned that Mooney and his men would either stop the attempt or seek revenge on him after the deed. So, he'd spent some time convincing Mooney to be the agent to rid himself of Taylor.

Now he was worried that the four thousand dollars that he'd paid them for the job wouldn't be enough. Once he started paying them for blackmail, he knew that it would never end. He simply didn't know how he could deal with them on their level. He knew some ruffians, but not one of them would dare go after a monster like Mickey Mooney.

Not for one moment had he suspected that Mooney and his small band of cutthroats would do anything to hurt him because he was their cash cow. Now that Taylor was gone, he was their best source of income. If anything, they would have to protect him.

But that didn't mean that he hadn't taken precautions. In the locked bottom drawer of his desk back in the office, there was an envelope addressed to his clerk, who had the only other key to the drawer. In the envelope, he had written what was tantamount to a confession. He wrote that if he died violently, it would be at the hands of Mickey Mooney, John Schuler, Al Darnell and Bill Jones. He hadn't provided a motive for his own murder, but if he was dead, he wouldn't care if Mooney then blamed him for Taylor's murder.

He silently cursed as he tried to think of some way out of the maze he'd created. He couldn't even turn them in for the murder because they hadn't been with the mob that had set fire to the carriage. They had just convinced the men to do it for a small payment to each of the unemployed workers and told them that there would be no consequences for their actions. He couldn't get one of those men to point the finger at

Mooney knowing that the man would hang just by confessing that he'd been part of the mob that had burned the carriage.

It was a horrible situation that seemed to have no solution, so he stood and dumped the dregs of his coffee into the sink then blew out the last lamp in the kitchen and headed down the hallway.

After extinguishing the lamp in the parlor, he quietly made his way up the stairs to the bedroom. He'd figure out what to do about Mooney after he had a better understanding of Grip's plans.

———

Grip was sound asleep when three men walked down the gaslit sidewalk bordering one of the city's main streets. Each man wore a pistol at his waist but their preferred weapon for the night were the large knives that hung on sheaths on the left side of their gunbelts.

It was well after midnight but even at that hour, the streets of St. Louis weren't empty. There was some street traffic, but most of the movement was by greedy men who prowled the night for prey or disoriented men who had spent their last nickel on liquor and were trying to find a bed for the night.

But Allison Street was one of the quieter parts of the city, so after they turned onto the roadway that led to the lawyer's home, the sidewalks and the cobblestones were empty.

They didn't talk and they didn't walk quickly so as to not attract the attention of any patrolling policemen.

They had to walk four blocks before they reached the attorney's house and turned down the gravel drive that ran alongside the large home. They planned on entering through the back door for the same reasons that they had avoided drawing attention on the long walk to Allison Street.

After they softly stepped onto the porch, John Schuler tried the back door hoping that it was unlocked but wasn't surprised to find it secured.

It was no problem for Cajun Al, who was a gifted burglar in his earlier criminal life and just thirty seconds after John had found it locked, the three men quietly entered the kitchen but left the door open for their escape.

In the dim light of the waning moon, they made their way down the hallway. John was in the lead and glanced into each of the rooms but finding just the functional rooms of a house: the bathroom, dining room, a den and a library.

They entered the parlor and began to slowly climb the stairs. They stayed close to the wall to minimize the possibility of a squeak, and the carpeted steps made even their light approach almost impossible to detect.

They reached the second floor and stopped before entering the dark hallway. They had already decided that John would go to the end of the hallway and Cajun Al and Bill would start their search in the first two rooms. Each would open the door quietly and look inside for the lawyer. They assumed he would be with his wife, and once the occupied room was identified, they'd rejoin outside the bedroom.

John tiptoed down the hallway and headed for the window in the far wall that provided just enough light for him to see the darkened doors.

There were six doors, three on each side. He reached the last pair and then chose the one on the right for his first inspection. He turned the knob and slowly opened the door.

He almost giggled when he spotted two lumps under the quilts in a large four-poster bed.

He then turned and waved to let Cajun Al and Bill know that he'd found the lawyer but had to wait until they each had finished their brief looks into the first two rooms.

When they saw him, they hurried as quickly and as quietly as possible to John before each man slid his knife from his belt and the three stealthily entered the bedroom.

Cajun Al circled around to the other side of the bed where the wife was sleeping, but his left foot kicked one of Isabel's shoes that she always set on the floor at her feet. The shoe only flew a few inches, but the heavy heel created a loud pop that awakened Mrs. Ellis.

She saw Al's shadowy outline against the window and screamed as she bolted upright. Then chaos reigned as the stunned assassins were shaken by her banshee-like shriek.

James Ellis was shocked out of his sleep by his wife's wail but before he could even reach a sitting position, John's blade rammed into his left shoulder. As his scream joined his wife's continuing screeching, the tip of Bill Jones' knife punched into his gut, just below his ribs. He began to writhe in pain and didn't hear his wife's cries as Al panicked and pushed her onto the floor, slicing her forearm in the process.

Blood was everywhere as John and Bill kept stabbing their intended victim as he screamed, thrashed and raised his arms to ward off his attackers.

Isabel was on the floor in a ball just sobbing as she held onto her arm to staunch the bleeding, but Cajun Al had already turned to race around the bed believing that the wife would bleed to death.

His two partners were satisfied that they had done their job as well and had stopped stabbing. But just before he died in the suddenly silent room, James had looked at John Schuler and even though he couldn't recognize him in the dark, he used his last breaths to utter, "You're all going to hang…I wrote…a letter…they'll know…they'll know…"

John had been stunned by what the dying lawyer had said, but the echoes of his wife's screaming left each of them unnerved and none of them wanted to stay to ransack the big house.

John shouted, “Let’s get the hell out of here!”

Cajun Al and Bill Jones weren’t about to argue. The job they had been sent to do was done.

They left the house through the open back door and had calmed by the time they reached the sidewalk.

John was still mulling over the lawyer’s dying threat as they slowed to a walk to return to Albion Street.

———

“What did he say?” Mickey asked as he stared at John.

“He said that he wrote a letter and that they’d know. He didn’t say what they’d know, only that we’d all hang.”

“Son of a bitch!” Mickey exclaimed, “We need to figure out what he meant.”

“He coulda been bluffing, boss,” Cajun Al said.

“Not likely. A bluff don’t matter if you’re dyin’. He musta left a letter somewhere sayin’ that we had Taylor killed.”

“Do you want to go lookin’ for it?” asked Bill.

“We ain’t got time for that and it’s gonna be daylight soon. We only got a day or two before the law starts lookin’ for us.

We've got all that money that he paid us for the job, but we can't work here anymore. We need to get the hell out of St. Louis."

"Where can we go? Do we head for Chicago?"

"Too many cops and too much competition. I figure we're better off heading west. I reckon Kansas City would work better than Chicago."

"We don't know anybody in that town, boss," Cajun Al complained.

"We don't know anybody in Chicago either, Al. It don't matter much. We have enough cash to last us a couple of years, but I'm sure we can find some greedy bastard who could put us to good use."

"I'll go, boss," John said quickly.

Bill agreed and then Cajun Al acquiesced, although he wasn't overly enthusiastic about Mickey's choice for their destination.

"Let's get ready to get out of this burg and get on the next train to Kansas City," Mickey said before he stood which put an end to the discussion.

Less than an hour after they had invaded the Ellis home, the house was heavily populated with policemen. Isabel's wound had been sutured and she had been kept at the hospital.

James Ellis' body was already removed from the house by three o'clock in the morning and the manhunt for their murderers was already underway before dawn.

Three miles away, Grip slept peacefully in his bed as the chaos created by the murder of James M. Ellis, Esquire wound down just before sunrise.

CHAPTER 4

By the time the sun broke over the horizon, Mickey Mooney and his three men were already forty-five miles west of St. Louis on the westbound train. They had hurriedly packed their relatively few belongings that mattered and barely made the early morning express train to Kansas City. The train was scheduled to arrive in just eight hours, so they should be able to relax in a nice hotel by nightfall. They'd scan the St. Louis newspapers for news of the headline-making story of the assassination of the prominent lawyer so soon after his boss was murdered and try to get an idea if they were considered suspects.

As the train rolled west, Mickey wondered if their sudden departure wasn't almost as condemning as the mysterious letter that Ellis supposedly left behind. It really didn't matter in the long run as he was sure that they would have been primary suspects anyway. While Lawrence Taylor had done all that he could to keep their relationship hidden, Mickey didn't doubt that the staff knew about it and he was equally convinced that the lawyer's clerk was aware of the connection as well.

But even as the train rocked its way across Missouri, he was already thinking that Kansas City might not be far enough away. It was still in Missouri, so maybe they should go further west where nobody cared what happened east of the Missouri River.

———

It was midmorning and Grip was having coffee with Richard, Wilma, and Jenny while they talked about his decision to go to Ogden earlier to start preparing for the permanent move. He had just finished asking them what they wanted in their new houses when there was a loud knock on the front door.

He stood and waved them down as he said, "I'll get it."

Normally, he wouldn't have minded much if someone else had answered the door, but he wanted them to become accustomed to being his friends and not his employees, even if he was paying their salaries.

He walked quickly down the hall and after passing through the parlor, he reached the foyer and opened the door. He was more than mildly surprised to find two uniformed policemen and one other man in a suit who was probably a detective.

"Mister Taylor?" asked the detective.

"Yes. Please come in," he replied as he stepped aside and let them enter.

After closing the door, he guided them into the parlor, waved them toward the chairs and as he took a seat, he asked, “What can I do for you gentlemen?”

“I’m Detective Lieutenant Mike Nall. Last night, James Ellis was murdered in his bed.”

Grip was startled but quickly recovered before he asked, “What happened?”

“He was stabbed to death while he slept. His wife, Isabel, was cut but she’ll be all right.”

“Why have you come here? Am I a suspect?” he asked while looking at the two uniformed officers.

“Hardly, sir. There are other reasons for our visit. The first was that Mister Ellis was your father’s attorney and practically his only client. His murder occurred just days after your father’s violent death and even though the methods use in the murders are completely different, it would be irresponsible not to determine if there is a link between the two.”

“I agree that there is a strong possibility that they are connected and even though I can’t see a motive, I have a strong suspicion who may be the most likely suspects.”

“We already have suspects, Mister Taylor. Do you know a man named Mickey Mooney?”

"I've never met the man, but yesterday when I was returning to the house, one of his men met me on the drive. He asked if Mister Mooney's crew would continue to serve as protection for me as they had with my father."

Detective Nall glanced at the officer to his left then asked, "They worked for your father?"

"I'm sure that they did. I'm also convinced that he used them as muscle for shady jobs. The man I met yesterday, John Schumer, even gave me a sheet of paper with their names and addresses."

The detective's eyebrows popped up before he quickly asked, "Can you get it for me before we leave? We've been hunting for them since daybreak but haven't found hide nor hair of any of them. Men like that can go to ground just about anywhere."

"I'll do that. What are your other reasons for coming?"

"I guess it's not really a reason as it is a question. How well do you know Mister Ellis?"

"I hardly know him at all. I wasn't very fond of the man, but I didn't care for my father either. Mister Ellis didn't impress me as a very honest man."

"Do you know why they might have wanted to kill him?"

"No, sir. I've been wondering about that myself."

"Hopefully, we'll find the bastards and be able to figure it out."

Grip nodded as he stood and said, "Let me get that paper for you."

He quickly walked to the office and was more confounded than the police probably were in trying to figure out a motive for the lawyer's murder. He had no doubt that Mickey Mooney's crew had committed the crime, but the reason for them to invade the house and kill Ellis made no sense. *Had his father arranged a posthumous murder as some form of revenge?* It was the only thing that made sense to him. If his father was concerned that Ellis was plotting to kill him for some reason, he could have arranged to have his lawyer murdered in the event of his own assassination.

He took the sheet of paper with the names and addresses from the drawer and headed back to the parlor.

After handing it to Detective Nall, he sat down again.

The detective quickly read the page then handed it to the officer on his left and said, "Get a flying squad together and check these places."

Both policemen quickly stood and without saying a word, hastily left the parlor and the house.

"They're probably not there anymore if they were the ones who committed the murders," Mike Nall said.

"I can understand why they would run. I know this might sound bizarre, but the only motive that I can imagine is if my father was worried about something that Mister Ellis was doing or planning to do. He might have arranged with Mooney to assassinate his lawyer if he was murdered."

"That's not so strange, Mister Taylor. I was thinking along those lines myself. It may have just been a burglary that had gone wrong, but I hate coincidences, and this is one enormous coincidence if they aren't linked."

"Just to let you know, Mister Nall, I've already notified the staff and the bank that I'm planning on leaving St. Louis within a month."

The detective's eyebrows lifted slightly before he asked, "May I ask why you're leaving?"

"It doesn't matter now, I suppose. I was most concerned about Mister Ellis discovering what I was planning to do. I want nothing to do with my father's businesses, legal or otherwise. I've already instructed Warren Stone at Merchantmen's Bank to sell all of his assets. I've created a charity trust fund and arranged to deposit more than half of my father's wealth into that fund. I plan to move to Ogden, Utah and start a new life where no one has ever heard of Lawrence Preston Taylor."

"Why didn't you want Mister Ellis to know of your plans?"

"If you'd been in his office when I settled my father's estate, you would have understood. It was obvious that he expected me to step aside and let him run all of my father's enterprises. As I said earlier, I didn't like the man, and my distrust was much greater than my dislike."

Detective Nall stood, shook Grip's hand and said, "Thank you for your help, Mister Taylor. I'll keep you advised of our progress."

"Call me Grip. My father was Mister Taylor and I'm seriously thinking of having my name legally changed to Smith."

"If you're still going to move to Utah, I don't believe it will be necessary or even smart."

Grip escorted the detective to the door and after he'd gone, he turned and quickly walked down the hall to the kitchen. He was sure that everyone had heard the conversation but needed their opinions.

He entered the kitchen and wasn't surprised to find that Tom had joined them in his absence.

"I'm sure that you all heard what the detective told me, but nothing about that murder should affect us. His wife will inherit the estate and I believe that they had two adult sons and a few grandchildren, so they'll be fine."

"I agree that there has to be a connection between the two murders, but I can't figure it out," Richard said.

"I can't either, but I hope that his sons aren't like him. If they are, then I wouldn't be surprised if they don't institute a wrongful death suit just to extract something from their father's death."

Wilma quietly said, "Not all sons are like their fathers, Grip. Your character should have been molded by the harsh discipline of military schools, yet you seemed to have emerged into adulthood unscathed."

Grip smiled at her and replied, "I refused to let my father win, Wilma. If I had let those hard men force me to become like them, then I would have lost. It was what gave me the strength to avoid falling into that behavior. I discovered that the best way to defend myself was to find humor in whatever they did in their attempts to mold me into a copy of themselves."

Richard said, "I was always impressed that you seemed so cheerful when you were home. For a while there, I began to think you were simple, but those grades you earned put the lie to that thought."

"Don't give up on that notion yet, Richard. I'm still at a loss about whatever is happening around here. I'm anxious to leave St. Louis and all its intrigues behind. But for now, I'm going to visit his clerk and ask if he has any idea of why his boss was murdered."

"I'll go and saddle Pitch, Grip," Tom said before asking, "Do you want me to use the new saddle that arrived yesterday?"

"No. I'll save that for when I head off to Utah. I'll meet you in the carriage house in a few minutes."

Tom rose and as he headed for the door, Grip turned and walked down the hallway. He may not have wanted to use his new saddle, but he did want to start wearing his shoulder holster now. He suspected that Mickey Mooney was still in town somewhere and after murdering Mister Ellis, the giant thug would want to eliminate his old boss's son next just to cut the last loose end.

When he reached his bedroom to strap on the shoulder holster, the giant thug and his three men were just twenty-six miles east of Kansas City.

No one had seen them leave St. Louis because, even in their rush to escape, Mickey understood that his bulk would be noticed by workers at the station. He'd remained in the shadows and had instructed John to buy two tickets and then let Cajun Al and Bill drift in five minutes apart to buy theirs. It was still a bit unusual for three men to buy tickets on the express to Kansas City at that time of the night, but Mickey suspected that if the police came asking questions, they would only ask if a giant of a man had bought tickets out of town. He was familiar enough with the way that they operated to realize that it would be nothing more than a cursory check.

Ten minutes later, Grip gave Tom a short wave and wheeled Pitch around to make the ride down the long drive.

He was scanning the traffic as he turned onto the street, expecting to see Mickey Mooney or one of his men preparing to take a shot. He may only have been able to recognize John Schuster or the giant, but he didn't want to miss spotting someone taking aim at him, either.

But nobody gave him more than a passing glance as he trotted his black gelding though the busy byways of the big city.

He still planned to go to Utah within two weeks but wished the situation with Mooney was resolved before he left.

When he stepped down before the brick building that housed the Ellis law offices, he did one last scan down both sidewalks. If Mooney's boys were still in town, they'd be watching the building. It was possible that the lawyer's murder was unrelated to his father's death but had something to do with the relationship between the thugs and his father's attorney. Hopefully, his clerk would know of any dealings that his boss would have with the Mooney gang.

As he climbed the stairs to the second-floor offices, he wondered if the clerk was even there. He was certain that the police had paid him a visit but wasn't sure if he would remain in the office. He was also curious if there was some kind of legal limitation on what the clerk could reveal to the police. He hadn't taken any law courses in his years of education, but many of his history courses had included an in-depth study of the Constitution which was the foundation for all of the country's laws.

He didn't need to open the outer door when he reached the offices and could already see the clerk at his desk poring over papers. He still didn't know the man's name, but he'd find out soon enough.

Grip walked through the open doorway and the clerk immediately looked up from the pages in his hands.

"Mister Taylor! I was hoping that you'd stop by," the clerk said with obvious relief.

"I have many questions for you, and I suspect you have at least as many for me," Grip replied.

Before Grip was near the clerk's desk, the man popped to his feet and said, "Please come with me into the inner office."

Grip nodded then followed him into the late Mister Ellis' office and closed the door as the clerk seemed to want a private meeting.

The clerk walked around the large desk and took a seat as Grip sat in the client's chair before the desk.

"I never did catch your name," Grip said.

"Oh, I do apologize for that omission. My name is Roger. Roger McCall."

"Do you mind if I call you Roger? I prefer to be addressed as Grip, by the way."

"Roger is fine. I knew your first name, of course but, well, propriety precluded my use of your Christian name."

"It may be my first name, but it's hardly Christian in nature or origin."

Roger laughed lightly as he unlocked a drawer and pulled out an open envelope.

"I found this after the police left this morning. I suppose I should have been shocked by the news of the murder, but I was only saddened to hear that Mrs. Ellis had been injured because of her husband's questionable behavior."

Grip didn't ask why the clerk wasn't surprised and wasn't sure how much Roger knew about his boss' 'questionable behavior'.

Roger handed him the envelope and Grip removed the single folded sheet.

He glanced at the clerk before reading the page and was stunned by its revelation. Ellis had written that if he died violently, it would have been at the hands of Mickey Mooney and his three accomplices.

Grip read it a second time before returning it to Roger and saying, “We need to give this to the police. Is there some legal reason why we can’t?”

“No. I only found it an hour ago and if you hadn’t arrived, I would have visited you before going to the police,” he replied as he slipped the folded sheet back into the envelope.

“But the letter only points the finger at Mooney’s bunch. Why would you need to show it to me first?”

Roger sighed before he replied, “Mister Ellis had met with Mooney a few times in the month before your father died. I didn’t know why they were meeting and I’m sure that Mister Ellis wasn’t aware that I knew who they were. In the aftermath of your father’s murder, I suspect that it had been Mister Ellis who had somehow arranged for your father’s death though Mister Moody. It’s probably why he was murdered last night.”

Grip lapsed into silent thought as he began to tie the pieces together. It really didn’t matter if Ellis had been behind his father’s death or even if Mooney had somehow arranged for the mob to burn his father’s carriage. The letter he’d just read was proof that it had been Mooney who had murdered Ellis and they’d hang for that crime if they were captured.

He looked at the clerk and asked, “Do you want to join me when we take this to the police?”

“I can. Do you want me to tell them about the meetings between Mooney and Mister Ellis?”

"It doesn't matter to me, but I'm sure that Detective Nall would appreciate the information."

"Okay. Will you be needing another attorney? I haven't passed the bar yet, but I do know an honest lawyer who could protect your interests."

"Mister Stone at the Merchantmen's Bank has already selected a good lawyer to help me with my legal needs."

"That's a relief. I expect that the outer door will be darkened by crowds of eager lawyers wanting to take charge of Mister Ellis' office and you as a client."

Grip stood and smiled before saying, "Good luck with that. I plan on being in Utah within a month."

Roger stood and didn't ask about the pending move or the reason behind it before they left the inner and outer offices. Roger grabbed his valise and hat before he closed and locked the outer door. The two men strode down the hallway and then descended the stairs.

The visit to the police office didn't take long as Detective Nall wasn't in, but another detective assigned to the case was very interested in both the letter and Roger's theory about the possible motive for the double homicide.

The meeting with Warren Stone took much longer and was still in progress after the bank closed its doors for the day. John Vernon, the bank's attorney whom Warren had selected to handle Grip's myriad of legal issues was present for most of the conversation and even agreed to take on Roger as a clerk until he passed the bar.

It was early evening when Grip returned and rode Pitch into the carriage house. He unsaddled his gelding and brushed him down without seeing a sign of Tom Truax but after he finished, he spent another five minutes examining the mare.

When he entered the kitchen, he found everyone at the table and was pleased when none of them left their seats as Richard asked, "How did it go with the clerk?"

"I'll tell you what happened in chronological order beginning with my visit with Roger McCall, Mister Ellis' clerk. He gave me a letter that he'd discovered in a locked drawer of Mister Ellis' desk. In the letter, Ellis wrote that if he died violently, then his murderer was Mickey Mooney and his gang of thugs. I gave the letter to the police. When I visited the police, they told me that their search for Mooney had been fruitless. They'll continue the search, but I believe that they aren't in St. Louis any longer.

"After Mister McCall and I left the police office, we went to the Merchantmen's Bank to meet with Warren Stone and John Vernon, the bank lawyer he had chosen to handle my affairs.

That meeting took much longer than I expected as one issue after another kept popping up."

Richard then asked, "Are you still planning to go to Utah soon?"

"I am. As soon as things calm down and I think it's safe for me to go, I'll take the train to Ogden and do the groundwork for our new home."

They spent most of the rest of the day discussing the startling murder of James Ellis, the move to Utah and what Grip was planning to do when he was established in Ogden.

———

That night, as he lay on top of his bed in the humid warmth of the late spring night, the murder of James Ellis had created a new concern about leaving St. Louis. He didn't believe that Mooney and his small gang of thugs were in the city any longer, so he didn't expect them to come bursting through his bedroom door. He was worried that other hard men who might have worked for his father might visit the mansion in his absence and harm those he'd leave behind. The next time that he talked with Joe Trimble, he'd ask him about providing protection for the estate. He may have given away more than half of his father's money, but there was still enough to hire the entire Pinkerton staff for a century or two.

CHAPTER 5

That morning after breakfast, Grip was the only one in the house after the others had gone to church. Tom had bought a new carriage the day before after clearing the purchase with Grip.

He used that time to go to the gun room and take the Sharps model 1874 and a Winchester '76 that used the same .45-75 WCF cartridge as the one he was having modified then strode out to the gun range. He was wearing the new black gunbelt with its angled sheath and dagger. He'd do some target practice with each weapon, including his Colt Shopkeeper. He was curious how much range the pistol lost with the shorter barrel. He'd gotten fairly good results at fifty yards with a normal length barrel on the same model. But he thought he'd be lucky to get satisfactory results at half that with the Shopkeeper. But the range wasn't the purpose of the pistol anyway.

He spent more than an hour firing the guns, and the Shopkeeper had outperformed his poor expectations. He'd finished with the Sharps and even though it didn't have the Malcolm scope that the Sharps-Borshadt would have, the pop-up vernier rear sight was more than adequate to put six .45 caliber rounds through the bullseye at four hundred yards. He'd taken four more shots at eight hundred yards but had only managed to put one of them into the bullseye, despite the calm winds. He knew that it was far better than most shooters, but he had been disappointed. He expected that having the telescopic sight would provide a noticeable improvement. He'd used one before he even left St. Michael's and it was mounted on a much less capable rifle that was already well worn. But the lessons in its use would serve him well.

By the time he reentered the house, everyone had returned, and he spent another hour cleaning the guns before returning to the kitchen to continue the previous evening's conversation. He didn't want to leave any details uncovered.

———

Two-hundred-and-fifty miles away in Kansas City, Mickey Mooney was sitting at a table in Dinah's Diner with his three subordinates. They'd just finished lunch and were on their third cup of coffee.

"This ain't a bad town, boss," Cajun Al said.

"Nope. I reckon it's a lot better than Chicago woulda been. None of those stories in the St. Louis papers even mentioned our names, not that it matters. None of the local law knows who we are."

"You figure they know it was us who killed that bastard?" asked Bill Jones.

"I'd be real surprised if they didn't. They seemed mighty upset about it. Well, at least the newspaper writers thought so. That wife of his is still alive, but she ain't talkin', so it don't matter that you didn't kill her."

When they'd read that tidbit of news, they'd expected Mickey to explode, so his apparent dismissal of the mistake was an enormous relief.

"But why didn't they put it in the papers if they knew we did it?" asked John Schuler.

"I guess they didn't want us to know they were searchin' for us. By the time they figure out that we're gone, it won't even be on the fourth page of any of those papers. The law will give up lookin' in a couple of weeks and nobody will care anymore."

Bill asked, "So, what are we gonna do?"

"For a week or so, we're just gonna spend some of that money our friend paid us to kill Taylor and relax. We'll check out the local boys and see where we can fit in. I don't think they'll let us take over one of their operations, so we'll probably have to start our own."

Cajun Al said, "There's a lot of money to be had around here, boss."

"I'll agree about that and the best part is that there's even more out west where all that gold is. I hear that they've got piles of it in burgs like Denver that don't even have much law."

John, Bill and Cajun Al all grew grins as they picked up their cups in unison and slurped some of their thick coffee.

The fact that they even considered Denver a 'burg' was evidence of their total ignorance of anything beyond the city limits of St. Louis. Their education would begin soon and it would take many lessons before they adapted to life in the West.

———

Later that afternoon, Grip went upstairs to his room and changed into his running outfit.

He was able to leave the house without notice and after warming up, he took off at a slow jog toward the front of the house where he usually began. He'd go to the end of the drive and turn left, then run across the southern border before heading east.

By the time he made that first turn, he was already sweating, and his shirt was soaked before he reached the next turn. He had accelerated to a fast run by the time he made that turn and had to avoid the small holes left by groundhogs and rabbits as well as the many mounds of manure left by the horses. One mistake could break his ankle while the other could ruin his day.

Grip ran as if he was alone on the estate because in his mind, he was running through the large empty woods outside of Ann Arbor where he had to dodge the trees and branches.

But those quick jagged runs had been much more entertaining and as he ran across the cleared ground of the estate, he wondered what the land looked like in Ogden.

When he went there in another week or so, he'd choose property that proved more impressive. He knew that the altitude was much higher, but it was just another challenge. He had more than enough money to buy a substantial amount of land outside of town which was what he wanted. He'd buy at least a full section and he really didn't want any existing buildings. If they were there, he'd see what he could do with them, but he wanted to design and build his own. He was an engineer, for goodness sake! If the first Agrippa could design and build giant marble buildings, roads and aqueducts, then he didn't want to embarrass his namesake by having someone else design the houses and other buildings on his new property.

He finished his run about forty minutes later and began to slow as he sucked in every bit of oxygen he could. It was grateful that the humidity wasn't bad today, so he had been able to run faster than he had the last time.

When he entered the carriage house, he found Tom standing by the mare with a concerned look on his face.

"What's wrong, Tom?" he asked as he continued to breathe heavily, and the sweat still rolled from his brow.

"Oh, nothing much. I figure I might have been wrong about when she was going to drop that foal, though."

"I thought she looked almost ready. When do you think she'll let her baby walk?"

"It could be another two weeks or so."

"Well, all we can do is wait. I'll leave you with our soon-to-be mama, but I need to get cooled down a bit first."

"You're pretty wet, Grip, but I'll help you get wetter."

Grip laughed before he and Tom each picked up a bucket and walked to the inside pump. The stone floor in the carriage house was perfect whenever he had to douse himself and he added that feature to his design for the one that he'd have built in Utah.

After being drenched by several buckets of cold water, Grip felt renewed and as he dried himself with one of the towels from the nearby shelf, he and Tom left the carriage house and headed for the back porch.

The remainder of the day was filled with routine, which Grip knew would soon end.

Tomorrow was Monday and he'd begin his preparations for the trip halfway across the country. He still had to pick up his guns and find out what the Pinkertons had found so far. He'd mentioned the Pinkerton protection idea to Richard, but both he and Tom said it would be more of a nuisance than anything else.

It was very early in their investigation, but he thought that they might at least have found some basic information in the review of the official records. He'd give them until Thursday and if he hadn't had a preliminary report from them by then, he'd pay Pinkerton agent Joe Trimble a visit.

He closed his eyes and tried to imagine what his half-sister would look like, but never was able to put a face to the name on the birth certificate. He still had no idea why his father would even keep the record. Lawrence Preston Taylor wasn't the kind of man who was susceptible to blackmail, especially by a young woman claiming that he was the father of her illegitimate daughter. There was no father listed at all, so it wouldn't even serve the purpose of blackmail and Grip knew that his father couldn't care less about any spawn of his, legal or not.

It was a much bigger mystery than that posed by the murder of the James Ellis. In that case, all he had lacked was a motive, but Roger McCall's suggestion about collusion between the attorney and Mickey Mooney's bunch to kill his father rang true.

He wasn't sure that he'd ever have his answer to his remaining question and if the Pinkertons couldn't find Charlotte Marley or her daughter, it would stay a mystery that would haunt him for the rest of his days. Finding his sibling was even more important than solving the mystery. He felt that he owed it to her and her mother for how his father had treated them. He couldn't set things right with Mary Duffy, but he could help Charlotte and Julia Marley.

Now that the Ellis problem and the Mooney situation were both over and done, he'd be free to concentrate on finding Charlotte and Julia Marley until he made the permanent move to Ogden. If he hadn't found them by then, he might have to return to St. Louis in the future. He wouldn't return until he felt that he believed he had done enough to balance the damage his father had done during his life. He acknowledged that he may never return because it might never be possible to achieve his goal.

The first three days of the week were a blessed respite from the tumultuous few days that had preceded them, and Grip used the quiet time for more target practice and to continue to improve the level of comfort with Richard, Wilma, Tom and Jenny. He wanted them to feel like family and not hired help. He hoped to cement the new relationship by simply giving Richard the cash to pay them for a couple of years. He'd have to give him enough to pay for any household expenses before they left for Utah as well.

As he laid awake that night, Grip spent a lot of thought about what he would be doing in Utah. He still planned to go to

Ogden and use it as his base to help people. *But how long would he do it before he was satisfied that he'd done enough?* While his father was a greedy, unscrupulous man, he had provided work for men who would have starved if he hadn't kept those factories and businesses running, even in their poor condition. Grip was an engineer and could do a lot of good with his talents. He knew that he wasn't responsible for his father's misdeeds, but he hadn't stood up to his father either.

When he reached that facet of his behavior, he understood why he felt that he had to go to Utah. It was because he had not only ignored what his father was doing, he had run away. That wasn't an issue when he was a boy and had been sent to St. Michael's, but when he had the opportunity to at least raise loud objections to what his father was doing, he had run off to Michigan rather than fight with his father. He wasn't afraid of the man, but he had still used the excuse that he wanted to further his education to leave St. Louis. He'd even stayed at the university after he'd received his two undergraduate degrees and his master's degree just to avoid returning to his father's world.

Once he began exploring his reasons for staying away, he had to admit to an even more shameful character flaw. He wasn't staying away because he was a coward; he was avoiding conflict with his father to prevent from being disowned. He may have lived the Spartan life of a military student for most of his formative years, and even when he was in college, his lifestyle was more plebian than patrician. Unless another student knew that he was the son of Lawrence Preston Taylor of St. Louis, there was anything that marked him as special other than his classroom performance and athletic achievements.

Agrippa Samuel Taylor realized that he did care about the money after all and it wasn't a pleasant revelation.

It was well after ten o'clock but there was a half-moon in the sky, so Grip slid from under the covers, then pulled on his short pants and then his socks and thick wool foot coverings. After tying the laces, he quietly left the room and after silently leaving the house, he crossed the wide porch and stepped down to the front yard.

He began running without warming up and raced to the end of the drive where he turned right rather than his customary left.

Grip was running faster than he'd ever run before, wishing that the sweat would wash away the sin of selfishness. He knew it wouldn't, but he wanted to run. He needed the hard introspection that came when he was punishing himself physically.

He made the turns when the fences came close but didn't slow. He didn't know how fast he was running because it was night and he enjoyed running in the dark. It was always quieter outside, and the loudest noise was always his heavy breathing as his padded feet made little sound as they pounded the ground. He wasn't worried about gopher holes or even piles of manure tonight. He had to think.

He had finished two complete circuits of the estate before he reached the level of pain and exhaustion that pushed his mind into the expected higher plane of thought.

He no longer felt his legs moving as he let his mind concentrate on his perceived failing. *Why had he not confronted his father when he was more than able to stand against him? Had he been so worried about losing his rights to his father's money that he had stayed away?*

It was the race along the dark ground that gave him the answer and it almost made him stop to laugh. It was absurdly simple. He continued to run to make the last trip around the estate's perimeter but began to slow as he made the final turn.

His focused mind had revealed one of the rare discussions he'd had with his father. The one they had when he'd told his father that he was going to Michigan. It had been a heated debate as his father had expected him to stay in St. Louis, but Grip had adamantly refused and had even said those dangerous words, 'go ahead and disown me' before he left the room.

The reason he'd decided to go to Ann Arbor was for the only reason anyone should pursue advanced study. He loved engineering and knew that unless he wanted a career in the army and went to the Military Academy at West Point, the best engineering school in the country was at the University of Michigan.

His father had been furious but hadn't disowned him. At the time, Grip assumed that his father still believed that his only son and heir would change his mind and return. But soon realized that it was really his cold heart that allowed him to simply dismiss his son as he had his maids and other hired help. He hadn't disowned him because he had other, more important things to think about and almost thought of himself as immortal.

Once Grip had started his undergraduate studies, he found a whole new world that had swallowed him whole. He couldn't take enough classes as he filled his ignorant void. He had no social life to speak of as he was either in class, studying or engaged in athletic contests or training. He loved the life and wasn't about to return to his father's world. There was a strong urge to avoid the tense environment that awaited him in St. Louis, but the main reason he stayed was because he liked it.

Grip was walking down the moonlit drive toward his father's mansion that cast an enormous shadow across the darker ground and wondered why those thoughts had suddenly possessed him. Whatever the reason, he was grateful that they wouldn't return.

He had to enter the dark carriage house and dump some cold water over his head but didn't towel himself dry as he walked back to the silent house. Once he reached the front porch, he sat on the wide swing to let the light breeze take away the moisture.

He rocked the swing as he looked out at the night. The porch faced west, and in a few days, he'd board a train that would take him in that direction to Utah. When he arrived, it would be the start of a new life for him and the people in the house who were his responsibility. He found himself growing excited about the move for the first time since he'd returned to St. Louis.

CHAPTER 6

No one had noticed his nighttime run, or at least nobody had commented on it that morning during breakfast.

It was shortly after eight o'clock when he left the house, saddled Pitch and rode out of the estate.

He decided that he'd visit Detective Nall in the St. Louis Police Department after he met with Joe Trimble. He expected that he'd get at least some information from the Pinkerton agent, but not much.

He pulled Pitch to a stop before the Pinkerton Agency office and dismounted. After tying him off, he crossed the sidewalk and entered the busy office.

After closing the door, Grip stopped and had to hunt for Jim Trimble, but didn't see him at his slightly cleaner desk.

Another detective stood then stepped towards him and asked, "May I help you, sir?"

"I'm looking for Joe Trimble, but I don't see him."

"Are you Grip Taylor?"

Grip nodded and the detective said, "Joe is working on your case but should be back within an hour or so. Do you want to wait?"

"No, I'll stop back in a little while. I have to visit the police on a different matter."

"I assume it's related to the murders of Mr. Ellis?"

"Yes."

"Don't be surprised, Mister Taylor. We are good at what we do, and that case raised a few eyebrows in the office."

"It raised eyebrows everywhere in St. Louis and I believe that interest forced the murderers to flee from the city."

"I'm sure that you're right. The police haven't been able to find Mister Mooney or any of his boys yet."

Grip smiled and said, "You are well informed. Please tell Joe that I'll be stopping by to ask if he'd found anything yet."

"I'll tell him, but I can at least let you know that he is making progress in your case."

"That's good to know," Grip replied before nodding, turning around and leaving the office.

He mounted Pitch and was soon trotting along the busy streets toward the main police offices wondering what progress Joe Trimble had made. He assumed that the agent had found the legal records of both Charlotte and Julia Marley but hoped that he had discovered more information. He would have been pleasantly surprised if Joe had found both women so quickly. It was possible, of course, but because his father was involved, Grip suspected that neither woman was even in St. Louis any longer.

Ten minutes later, he was walking down the hallway of the large police building and entered the office of the homicide and assault detectives. It was a newly created position, and he wasn't sure if they were that good at finding the murderers, but they were learning new tricks almost daily.

The vast majority of murders and assaults were easily solved as the killers were usually family or friends, unless it was part of a brawl, which was even more common. Cases like his father's or the Ellis murder required a lot of time and resources and the police weren't about to go overboard in solving the crimes even if the victim was as powerful as his father had been. That would have changed if Grip had expressed even the slightest interest in having his father's killers prosecuted because money would always have influence in the application of justice.

He passed through the open doorway and spotted Mike Nall talking to another detective near a large file cabinet.

When Grip was close, the other man nudged Nall who turned and asked, "Mister Taylor, what can I do for you?"

“I just stopped by to find out if you had any more information on the whereabouts of the Mooney gang.”

“We think that they took a train west out of town shortly after the murders, but it’s a vague report.”

“I’m a bit surprised that they didn’t go north to Chicago where they’d be more comfortable.”

“They might have gone in that direction. The only reason we even think that they might have headed west was that one of the ticket agents said three men bought tickets on the express train to Kansas City in the middle of the night. He didn’t pay much attention to them and if Mooney had been with them, he would have noticed.”

“You’re probably right about that. Everyone who has seen him commented on his enormous size. I guess that I’m fortunate that I never met the man.”

“I’ll be honest when I tell you that I was hoping another officer would be the one to locate and try to arrest Mooney.”

“He’d need one of those giant bear traps to keep him under control, though.”

Detective Nall laughed as he and Grip shook hands before Grip turned and left the office. As he headed for the main entrance, he suspected that the search for Mooney and his boys had ended. He should have asked if they had sent telegrams notifying surrounding law offices of the escaped killers, but thought it was unlikely. As far as the St. Louis police department was concerned, both murder cases were essentially closed. If they found Mooney or any of his men in the future, they'd arrest them and charge them for the crimes, but the police were probably just as happy that the thugs were no longer their problem and it had been reflected in the detective's honest comment.

But even their suspicion that the Mooney gang had headed west gave Grip a new focus for his constantly revising plans. If they had gone to Kansas City, he might bump into them. What he would do if that happened was a big question. His father and Mister Ellis didn't deserve justice. They had already received their sentences for their crimes.

When Grip entered the Pinkerton Agency for the second time that morning, he found Joe Trimble at his desk. He'd barely crossed the threshold when Joe looked up and waved him over.

When he was near the desk, Grip pulled off his hat then took a seat.

"I found some interesting information for you, Grip. I haven't found your sister, but I can tell you where her mother is."

"Did you talk to her?"

"That's not possible. She's buried at the Northside Cemetery. I found her death certificate in the same folder with her birth certificate in the county records office. She died eight years ago due to pneumonia. But you need to understand that unless you have enough money to see a doctor before you die, the coroner always lists pneumonia as the cause of death. She was still Charlotte Marley when she died at the age of twenty-five and they didn't list a next of kin anywhere in the file."

"So, there was no record of her daughter?"

"I didn't say that. No one was listed as a next of kin in her records, so I visited the address where she'd died and talked to most of the folks that lived in the apartment building. Two of them remembered Miss Marley and her daughter. One of them recalled Charlotte mentioning that she was sending her girl to live with her sister."

"Is she still in St. Louis?"

He shook his head and replied, "No, she hasn't been in the city for a long time. I revisited the county records office and found that her sister, Emily Marley, who was five years older than Charlotte, had married a man named Steve L. Albert on April 10, 1858. According to the marriage certificate, Mister Albert reported a home address of, and I'm not making this up, 176 Charlotte Street."

"That is ironic, but that was twenty years ago. Is it likely that he's still living at the same address?"

"I wired our office in Kansas City, and I'm having an agent stop by the address. He won't identify himself as a Pinkerton agent but will use some cover story that seems plausible depending on the situation. I gave them instructions to ask about a young woman named Julia, but not to press the issue if it became difficult. We've found that if we aggressively question people, they tend to slam doors in our faces."

"How long will it be before you get a reply?"

"It shouldn't take long. I'm pretty sure that I'll have your answer by tomorrow afternoon. It may not be the one you're expecting, but we'll at least know if Mister Albert is still living at that address."

"Thanks, Joe. I'll stop by tomorrow afternoon."

"I can bring you the results when the telegram arrives."

"No, that's okay. I need to visit Bainbridge to check on the progress of some work that I needed done."

"I've heard tale of your father's gun collection, so why on earth would you need more guns?"

"It's a long story, Joe. I'm having a Remington pistol and a Winchester '76 and a Sharps-Borshadt all modified with ebony stocks or grips to make them all balanced and give them a certain look."

"You have my interest now, Grip. So, if you don't mind spending a few minutes, can you tell me why you're going that route?"

Grip nodded then had to spend more than just a few short minutes explaining what he planned to do and why.

When he finished, Joe Trimble slowly shook his head then said, “That’s a waste of your time, talent and money, Grip. You won’t change that many lives by going out there and you’ll be risking your own. For what? Let the law handle those problems.”

“There isn’t much law out west, Joe. That’s why I’m heading that way. That and I want to get far enough away from St. Louis to where no one has heard of Lawrence P. Taylor.”

“Don’t you worry about having a problem with the law yourself if you go that route? You’ll be sticking your nose into places where the men who wear badges are the same ones who are causing the problems. We have enough of those bent lawmen in St. Louis to fill a riverboat, but out there, you’d be alone and facing hard men who will kill you for a lot less than Mooney was paid to do your father’s dirty work.”

“I know the risks, Joe. I’m not even sure that I’ll ever feel that I’ve done enough, but I’m going to go to Ogden to find out.”

Joe sat back and then said, “Then let me help you to avoid being arrested and thrown into the local hoosegow.”

“How can you do that?”

"My brother is a Deputy United States Marshal. He works for the Missouri U.S. Marshal, Abner Guest. His office is just two blocks south of here. I'll talk to my brother and see if his boss will make you a volunteer deputy marshal. You won't be paid, but I don't believe it matters to you. You'd probably pay them for the badge, but it doesn't work that way. If he agrees, you'd have to follow their rules, but you're the kind of man who does that anyway. If you're in Utah, he'll have to notify the territorial marshal that you're there, but you won't have to report to him."

"Do you think that he'd agree to do that?"

"I give it at best a fifty-fifty shot. You do have one big advantage, though."

"I'm rich?"

"Nope. Your greatly disliked father is dead, and you're dismantling your father's empire."

"*How the hell did you find out about that?*" Grip exclaimed.

"Good Lord, Grip! We're detectives.""

"I guess that it doesn't matter now that Ellis is dead. Anyway, I'll stop by tomorrow afternoon and hopefully we'll find out if Mister Albert is still in residence on Charlotte Street in Kansas City."

"I'll talk to my brother tonight, too."

Grip nodded then shook Joe's hand as he stood and said, "Thanks for your help, Joe. Be sure to add a healthy bonus to your bill."

Joe grinned and replied, "I had intended to do just that."

Grip laughed then pulled on his hat and headed for the door. It had been a very productive meeting.

He had Pitch moving at a slow trot as he was stuck behind a big freight wagon but didn't mind. He was grateful for Joe's help with one of the issues that had nagged at him. He wasn't about to break any laws in what he needed to do, but he knew that it didn't matter when dealing with men who had already crossed that line. If they were men in power in their small fiefdoms, they would follow their own rules. If Joe was able to convince the marshal to swear him in as a volunteer deputy marshal, at least he'd have some measure of legal authority and that would be critical to his soul.

The other news about Charlotte Marley's death and the dispatch of her daughter to stay with her sister's family in Kansas City created more questions. He had no idea of the situation that Julia Marley was in now. She was probably already married herself and may even have had a baby or even two. She'd been gone for at least eight years, so she could have a new name and a new life now. He may have more information about his sister, but there was still a thick fog surrounding her.

He could have just forgotten about the birth certificate entirely and gone on with his life, but the mystery would nag at him even if he was able to forget that he had a sister somewhere. She could be like his father and be an angry, vengeful woman, but he refused to believe it. He began to picture his sister as a compassionate, pretty young woman with a big smile simply because it was a comfortable image.

When he reached the estate, he turned Pitch into the carriage house and when he was unsaddling his black gelding, he heard hoofbeats outside and turned to see Tom quickly stepping down from one of the blacks.

"Did you find your sister?" he asked.

"I found where she might be, but the detective said he'd have more information tomorrow."

"Where is that?"

"Kansas City."

"Are you going to see her when you go to Utah next week?"

"Maybe. A lot depends on what the detective tells me."

Tom nodded then patted Ebony's neck as he said, "I hope you find her. That would be special; wouldn't it? Finding a sister who you didn't even know existed until a week ago."

"It'll be awkward if I do find her. I don't expect her to be overjoyed to find that she has an older brother who is the spawn of the evil Lawrence Preston Taylor. She's just as likely to shoot me as welcome me with open arms. She's probably already married and has a child or two. We'll see."

"Will you ask her to join us in Utah?"

"I have no idea yet. I had planned on giving her and her mother this whole estate and a chunk of money, but I have a feeling that she wouldn't want to return. If she's happily married, I'll probably just give her and her family some money and let her know that if she needs anything to send me a telegram."

Tom nodded before he began to unsaddle the gelding. The horses were almost bare when Grip decided to do some more target practice.

Two hours later, he returned each cleaned gun to its proper location and then left the gun room. He spent some private time in the office as he thought about the possibility of finding his sister in Kansas City. He hadn't exaggerated when he said to Tom that it would be an awkward meeting. *How does a person say, "Hello, I'm your half-brother, Agrippa? You know, the son of the man who abused your mother and then tossed her out of the house when he learned that she was carrying you twenty years ago."?*

The more he thought about it, the more he questioned the whole process of finding her and then going to see her. If he was a coward, he could send her a letter with a bank draft to make amends, but he knew it was much more than just meeting her. He had so many questions that even she may not be able to answer. Her mother may have been so ashamed of the manner in which Julia had been conceived that Charlotte had never even told her of the violation. *What if his unexpected arrival turned into a disastrous revelation to his sister and destroyed her happy family life?*

He finally just exhaled and figured that it was better to at least wait until he talked to Joe Trimble tomorrow. If they found her, then he'd probably get a better idea of her situation.

He stood and left the office and walked out to the kitchen which was the source of all of the noise in the house. He could hear both couples chatting about what their lives would be like in the wilds of Utah. He smiled and thought he might have some fun and tell them that they were moving to northern Montana Territory instead.

The next morning just after nine o'clock, Grip mounted Pitch and rode away from the carriage house.

He soon reached the Pinkerton office and dismounted before he looped Pitch's reins through the hitching post then stepped through the open doorway.

Joe saw him enter and waved him over as soon as Grip caught sight of him.

Grip could tell that the Joe had news and he hoped it was good.

"What did you find, Joe?" he asked as he took off his hat and lowered his butt onto the nearby chair.

"I have some very interesting information for you, Grip. I received a telegram from our Kansas City office this morning. Mister Albert still lives at that address with his wife and four children. But he isn't sure if your sister lives there.

"When our agent arrived at the door, he acted surprised and told a very pregnant Mrs. Albert who came to the door that he was looking for a nanny for his daughter, but he must have been given the wrong address. Mrs. Albert then asked what the position paid, so our man said it was fifty dollars a month and included room and board. Mrs. Albert quickly said that her niece did a marvelous job helping her with the children and would make an excellent nanny but wasn't at home. She was about to ask him to return later when her husband showed up and angrily told our agent to leave them alone and slammed the door."

"That's an unusual reaction. It sounded as if Mrs. Albert wouldn't mind having her niece gone but her husband was of a different mind."

"That's what it sounds like. We can keep an eye on the house if you'd like to at least get a better idea of the situation."

"No, that's not necessary. I think it would cause more problems than answer any more questions. I'll be heading that way next week anyway, so I'll visit the house. What was the place like?"

"Our agent's description of the house was 'typical for the area'."

"Okay. Thanks, Joe."

"Don't you want to ask what the marshal said when I asked him?"

"Oh, that's right. I almost forgot after you told me about my sister."

Joe snickered then said, "My brother asked me to talk to him directly, so I did. He wants to meet you today before he even thinks about it. Your father's reputation almost prevented me from asking the question, but after I explained what you were planning to do, he said that he wanted to meet you. I believe that he's of the same opinion that I was when you told me about your plans."

"There seems to be a general consensus that I'm off my rocker."

"That's because you are, Grip. Here's the address for U.S. Marshal Abner Guest and his merry band of lawmen and the reports from our agent in Kansas City including the address.

He even included directions from the train station. I guess he figured you could afford the extra words in the telegram."

Grip laughed as he accepted the papers and replied, "I'd check with my accountant if I had one."

"You don't have an accountant?" Joe asked in surprise.

"My father let his different businesses do their own accounting. As long as the money rolled in at an acceptable level, he let them handle the numbers. I thought that was a lot crazier than what I plan to do, but I guess he thought he had everyone terrified."

Grip stood, shook Joe's hand again then said, "I'll let you know what happens in Kansas City, Joe."

"We're all waiting to learn all the details, Grip."

Grip folded the papers and slipped them into his light jacket's right pocket before heading for the door and pulling his hat back on.

He mounted Pitch and made the short ride the U.S. Marshal's office. He wasn't sure that it was even necessary, so if Marshal Guest just laughed at him, it probably wouldn't make that much difference. It was just an insurance policy and as he pulled up before the office, he wondered if he just shouldn't start a private detective agency himself. It normally took a while to grant the agents legal powers, but he'd learned long ago that money greased the skids better than grease itself.

He dismounted and after tying off his gelding, he stepped across the sidewalk and as he was reaching for the doorknob, the door swung open and he almost flattened a small man whose nose was at his chin level.

"Excuse me!" Grip exclaimed as he stepped aside.

The man looked up at him and asked in an unexpectedly bass voice, "Are you Taylor?"

"Yes, sir. Grip Taylor. I apologize for almost running into you."

"My fault. I was in a rush. Come on in," the short man said before wheeling around and reentering the office.

Grip removed his hat and walked inside, closing the door behind him.

The man then looked back and said, "Come into my office, Mister Taylor."

It was only then that Grip realized he had almost run over United States Marshal Abner Guest. It wasn't a very good way to greet the man.

He passed through the empty outer office and followed him down a long hallway before turning into his private office at the end of the hall. When he entered, he was surprised by how utilitarian the room was. There were two inexpensive straight-backed chairs sitting before a cheap pine desk that sat before a slightly more upscale armchair. None of the chairs were padded and there was nothing hanging on any of the walls. He'd seen barn lofts that were more elegant.

The marshal dropped onto his chair and waited for Grip to sit rather than ask him to park.

After Grip took a seat, the marshal said, "I had a chat with Joe Trimble, the civilian brother of one of my deputies. He told me what you wanted and gave me the gist of your reason, but I'd like to ask for the real reason."

"Excuse me?" Grip asked, "What real reason?"

"Oh, please! It sounds like you either want to go off playing sheriff and outlaw or you want me to give you a badge so you can go riding off to get revenge for your father's murder. Which is it?"

"If I found the men who had murdered my father, I surely wouldn't turn them over to the police. I wouldn't give them a bonus, but my father had pushed those men to that point. I didn't spend much time with my father and it was more out of choice than design. I'm sure many people, including the late Mister James M. Ellis, Esquire, believed that I was going to take over his empire and run it as he did. But I plan to rid myself of every Taylor enterprise and leave St. Louis. In a decade, I don't want anyone in this city to remember that he even existed."

The marshal had studied Grip as he gave his answer, then asked, "Okay, I'll believe that, but what about the sheriff and outlaw motive."

"I guess that's not far removed from the truth, but to be honest, I don't expect to have to use any of my guns to solve the problems I find out West. I'll use the power of my father's wealth, which is now under my control, to fix things. My only concern was if some men might believe they will be able to take more of that money by force or other means. They'll resort to violence and if I defend myself, there would be a good chance that I'd be the one blamed just so the local lawman with jurisdiction can fill his pockets. If I was a volunteer U.S. Deputy Marshal, then that threat would evaporate…well mostly. The crooked sheriffs and town marshals wouldn't be able to arrest me if I told them I'd notify the U.S. Marshal in Utah of their actions. I'm sure that there would still be a risk, but I think it would eliminate most of them."

"Mister Taylor, after I agreed to talk to you, I spent most of this morning thinking about it. The more I did, the more it sounded like a waste of my time, so I changed my mind a little while ago and was on my way to tell Trimble to just send you home. Do you know why I changed my mind?"

"No, sir."

"When you almost ran me down outside, you apologized. You couldn't see my badge, so I could have been a regular citizen. You're a good six inches taller than I am and you are a very rich and powerful man. Men with a much smaller bank account or of smaller stature would have just pushed me aside and entered the office, much less apologized. I was almost shocked when you did. It was in that moment that I decided to give you a chance to explain your motives. I still doubted that I'd agree to your request, but if you had enough character to apologize even when it was mostly my fault, I believed that you had earned the time."

"Thank you. It was just a question of courtesy, Marshal."

Marshal Guest snickered and replied, "I doubt that's the only reason, Mister Taylor."

"Call me Grip, Marshal. Mister Taylor is the man they buried before I returned to St. Louis."

"Okay, Grip. Call me Abe. So, give me more details about what you plan to do in Utah."

Grip's plans had been modified yet again after he'd talked to Joe Trimble about his sister. But his overall goal hadn't changed, so he was able to clearly state his objectives and his methods to the marshal.

When he finished, Abner said, "Well, I'll give you credit for having done a lot of planning, Grip. I didn't think you had a prayer of convincing me even after you apologized, but you're beginning to make sense. Are you any good with your weapons?"

"Yes, sir. I'm not going to pretend to be modest and tell you that I'm adequate because that's not true. I've been shooting since I was eight and I'm familiar with everything up to and including cannons and the Gatling gun. My father had an enormous collection of weapons, and I'm having new ones modified. I'm very good with knives as well. I was a boxing champion in college but I'm not ignorant of the less genteel ways of fighting."

"I'm glad you didn't try to give me an 'aw, shucks', answer. I hate phonies. I'm kind of surprised that a boy who grew up in a mansion could be so normal."

"I didn't grow up there, Abe. I spent my childhood at St. Michael's Military Academy and then I left to go to the University of Michigan. It was my determination not to be anything like my father that set my path."

"Well, I'm still impressed. Have you ever killed a man, Grip?"

"No, sir. I've never even shot at a man or intentionally tried to hurt one. I've done some serious damage in the ring, but that was only because my opponent refused to yield when he should have. The referees had to stop the bouts on four of my fights."

"If I swear you in as a deputy marshal, volunteer or not, you'll have to follow the rules. But I believe that you already would before you even knew what they were. At least you won't be burdened by the mountains of paperwork or the administrative duties that take up most of our time. Sometimes I wish that I had been a sheriff out West and just had to chase outlaws."

"I can understand that. Is there a manual that I'd have to read?"

"I have three copies, so you can take one with you. I'll swear you in shortly and give you a badge. Joe Trimble was right in that you don't have to report to me, but you'll have to notify Marshal Iggy Palmer in Salt Lake City if you have any issues. When you get there, let him know that you've arrived. I'm sure that he'll appreciate the help. The last time I heard, he's only got three deputies for the entire territory."

As the marshal opened one of his drawers and reached down for one of the manuals, he said, "There's one more thing that I have to tell you."

He set the manual and the Deputy U.S. Marshal's badge on the desktop and said, "If you do get into a situation where you're facing a gun, you can't hesitate. Killing a man can be a soul-destroying sin even if it's justified. You'll know that even as you start to aim your sights on the shooter. But you cannot, under any circumstances, let that sudden realization delay your trigger finger. If you do, you'll be dead. You have to make that decision long before you face that moment."

"Have you had to kill a man, Abe?" Grip asked quietly.

"Twice. The first time, I was caught off guard and it almost got me killed. I had a man named Jack Thomas under my Colt Walker. My hammer was even pulled back, and I thought I had everything under control. I was about your age. I hadn't had Jack drop his gunbelt, which was my first mistake, but when I was about to get him to mount his horse, he just looked past my ear and grinned. He didn't say a word, but his look was obvious, so I whipped around expecting to see his partner, but there was nobody there. By the time I looked back at Jack, he had his own pistol in his hand and that muzzle looked like a cannon's mouth. My sights were off to his right and I was a dead man. He pulled his trigger, but nothing happened. It was a misfire. He was cocking his hammer to get a hot round in position when I shot him. If his percussion cap hadn't failed, I wouldn't be here. I learned a lot from those mistakes. The second man was just an exchange of Winchester fire at forty yards. You'd be surprised how many rounds flew back and forth before one of mine caught him in the neck."

"How did you feel after each of them?"

"The one with Jack was a lot different. My heart was still pounding after Jack fell when I realized how close I had been to being shot. Then I threw up when I saw that he was dead. After that, I felt guilty and dirty for a while, but I was much more ashamed of my failures than anything else. The second man, a bank robber named Pete Brown, wasn't so bad. I felt bad that I hadn't brought him in, but he could have surrendered."

"Thank you for telling me, Abe. I've already faced that moral dilemma in my mind, but you put more teeth into the issue. I still don't plan to get into any gunfights, but if it happens, then I hope that I don't hesitate."

"It's a good thing that you have already thought about it. Too many men who put on a badge think that getting into a gunfight is a manly thing, but it's still just killing. I wish you could just stay and join us as a full-time deputy marshal. I could use a man like you, but I guess we couldn't pay you enough anyway."

Grip laughed then replied, "It's not about money, Abe."

"Not for you, anyway."

He then swore Grip in as a Deputy U.S. Marshal and had to get his personal information to put him on their personnel roster before he handed him the manual and the badge.

"Good luck, Grip. Be sure to let us know what happens out there. I don't want to keep pestering Iggy with telegrams."

Grip stood, shook his hand and replied, "I'll be keeping Joe Trimble informed, so I'll just have him tell his brother."

"Good enough."

Grip slid the badge into his jacket pocket, then walked out of the marshal's private office clutching the manual and soon exited the building and stepped onto the sidewalk. The relatively short time he'd spent with the short lawman had been very valuable. He'd learned a lot in that brief visit and was determined not to do anything that would make Marshal Guest regret his decision.

He mounted Pitch and headed him in the direction of Charles Bainbridge & Sons Gunsmiths and Firearms. He knew that his Remington should be done, and the Winchester might be, but he didn't expect the Sharps-Borshadt to be ready simply because of the amount of work it needed.

When he entered the shop five minutes later, Fred Bainbridge saw him come through the open door and waved him over, which was a good sign.

"I've got your Remington and Winchester done, Grip," Fred said before turning and entering the workshop area behind the counter.

Grip set his palms on the counter and leaned forward expectantly. He was curious what the guns would look like with the ebony.

When Fred emerged with the two guns, Grip broke into a big smile. They had even used the ebony on the Winchester's forearm. It gave the repeater an almost sinister appearance.

Fred set the weapons onto the counter and said, “I have to admit that I like the look, Grip. What do you think?”

“They’re perfect, Fred. How long before the Sharps-Borshadt is done?”

“We just started on it, so it won’t be ready for another four or five days.”

“That’s okay. I may not be here when it’s done, so can you send it to the house? I’ll pay for the entire order today.”

“We can do that. Do you want the spare ebony today? We’ve already selected the amount we’ll need for the Sharps.”

“Sure. Is it enough for another rifle stock?”

“You might be able to get three stocks and forearms out of the extra wood. We cleaned out the lumber yard rather than be short in case we screwed up the Winchester’s stock. Ed found that the ebony wasn’t as hard to work with as he’d expected.”

“Good. How much is the damage?”

Fred already had the bill ready, so even as Grip asked the question, he was sliding the paper across the counter.

Grip slipped his wallet from his jacket pocket and peeled off the bills but before he stopped laying them onto the counter, he asked, “I’m going to need some scabbards for the

Winchester and the Sharps-Borshadt. Do you have any in stock?"

"Toss on another ten dollars and I'll get them for you."

Grip pulled one more bill from the wallet and set it on the others before he picked up the Remington and slid it into its black holster then buckled the black leather gunbelt around his waist, but under his jacket. He was still in St. Louis, after all. He was wearing his Western boots to get them broken in before he left for Utah, and they were already comfortable.

He was admiring the Winchester when Fred set the two scabbards on the counter along with three two-inch thick, four-foot long ebony boards.

"The bigger scabbard should have plenty of room for the scope on the Sharps, and they're both lined with wool to keep the guns from moving too much."

Grip slid the Winchester into the smaller scabbard and was pleased to see the black stock jutting out from the black leather. It added a touch of elegance to the sinister appearance. It was exactly the look he hoped to create.

"Thanks, Fred," Grip said as he picked up the second scabbard and the stack of ebony then headed for the door.

"Good luck, Grip," Fred said as he watched Grip leave.

The ebony was heavier than the Winchester and getting the boards secured behind the saddle was awkward, but he managed. Mounting was odd but once in the saddle, he set Pitch to a slow trot to return to the house.

———

Grip soon turned Pitch onto the estate's long graveled drive and headed for the carriage house.

After his visit with Joe Trimble, he had made a major modification to their plans. He decided that once he reached Ogden to start setting up their new home, he would only return if it was necessary. He'd given Warren Stone power of attorney to handle most of the financial affairs and he'd give Richard and Tom instructions about how to set up the move. It was the possibility of finding his sister in Kansas City that had prompted the major change, but once he decided to stay in Utah, it seemed more logical anyway. So, even if he didn't find Julia Marley in Kansas City or if she was antagonistic towards him, he'd stay in Ogden getting everything prepared. He wanted to be part of the building process and make sure that the work was done to his specifications.

He soon walked Pitch into the carriage house then dismounted and began to strip his black gelding.

Before he removed the saddle, he glanced across the stall to the shelf at his black Western saddle the slid the heavy ebony boards from behind the saddle and set them on the shelf alongside the saddle. He left the two scabbards and the Winchester there as well, then removed his new gunbelt and after rolling it into a ball, slid it into one of the mammoth saddlebags that he'd be taking with him.

After stripping Pitch, he brushed his gelding and then when he was finished, he finally left the carriage house carrying the manual.

When he entered the kitchen, he was greeted by everyone as they sat at the table sharing coffee.

He pulled off his hat then set the manual on the counter as Jenny asked, "We haven't made lunch yet, but did you get anything to eat before you returned?"

"No, ma'am. I will grab some coffee, though."

He quickly snatched a cup from the shelf, then used a towel to pick up the hot coffeepot and pour his coffee. He had seen each of them automatically start to rise as soon as he'd said that he wanted some coffee and he had to stop that kind of thing from happening. He still made his own bed each morning and wasn't about to change the habit.

When he sat down, Richard asked, "How did it go? Did the Pinkertons find your sister?"

"I think so, but they're not sure. I have the address where they think she's living, but circumstances prevented them from asking the residents."

Wilma tilted her head slightly and asked, “Are you going to give us more details, or are we going to have to start our own Inquisition?”

Grip smiled, took a sip of his hot coffee, then said, “They found that her mother died eight years ago, and I guess that she knew she wasn’t going to survive whatever disease had taken hold of her, so she sent her daughter, my half-sister, to live with her older sister who had moved to Kansas City years earlier. I have her address and as I’ll be passing through the town on my way to Ogden anyway, I told the Pinkertons that I’d take it from there.”

As Grip took another sip, Richard asked, “Do you think that she’ll accept you as her brother?”

Grip shrugged then replied, “I have no idea. The agent who approached the house had said that he was looking for a nanny and would pay her a good salary. Charlotte’s older sister, Emily, had seemed more than willing to have her niece leave their home to take the imaginary position, but her husband appeared angry and even slammed the door in the agent’s face. The agent described the house as ‘typical for the area’, whatever that means.”

“Are you going to offer her the house and money as you first thought?” asked Wilma.

“If I even get to meet her, a lot will depend on her reaction. I’m not sure that I’ll even let her know my real name until I at least understand her situation. There's still that possibility that she's not my half-sister at all. It's a slim chance, but it's still there. I just don't know why my father would keep that birth certificate at all."

Jenny said, "Maybe he was keeping it as insurance in case anything happened to you and he still needed an heir."

Grip shook his head and replied, "My father thought he'd outlive us all and he couldn't have cared less if his entire empire went up in smoke after he died. I just wish that I could come up with some logical explanation for that birth certificate being in the safe."

Richard then asked, "This is off topic, but I've been thinking about this since your father died and I was wondering if it would be alright if everyone called me Rich."

Grip grinned and said, "I like it better anyway, and I assume that there's a reason you prefer Rich to Dick."

Rich smiled and replied, "I like it better."

Grip's grin faded before he said, "I also visited the United States Marshal's office and Marshal Guest swore me in as a volunteer deputy marshal. I have the badge in my pocket and the manual I need to study in on the counter. It's just to make sure that whatever I do is legal."

"That's a smart thing to do, Grip," Rich said.

"I also made a significant change to my plans. When I go to Ogden next week, probably on Monday or Tuesday, I'll be staying there preparing our new home. If you have a problem that only I can handle, then send me a telegram and I'll take the next train back. Warren Stone at the Merchantmen's Bank as the power of attorney to handle all of the sales of my father's enterprises and this house if necessary, but you can see him if you encounter any difficulties. What I'll need you to do is to choose what you want to bring with you and arrange for the shipping. Rich, as the household manager, you already have the authority to do all that.

"I want to take the contents of the gun room and the books, which will take some time to properly crate and we'll bring all of the horses. After that, it'll be your choice on what you want to move to Utah. I'll still be furnishing your new homes before you leave, so take that into account. I'll be taking Pitch and I'll buy another horse to use as a packhorse because I don't want to use any of the blacks in that role."

Grip could see a look of mild surprise in their faces, but there wasn't any sign of genuine concern. It was almost as if they'd expected it.

Rich said, "I was wondering why you thought you'd have to make that trip back, Grip. You'll have a lot of work to do in Utah, and we can handle what needs to be done when you're ready for us to join you."

Grip smiled again as he said, “I guess that I’m not as smart as I thought I was. I have a lot of things to do before I leave, but I have the rest of the day and the weekend to get it done. If any of you can spot anything I missed, let me know.”

They continued to discuss the many other tasks that would be necessary to affect the move including those that Grip needed to handle before he left St. Louis. Grip finally had to take out his notebook and pencil from his jacket pocket to create a list for himself.

After he was satisfied that he hadn’t missed anything, he stepped to the counter and grabbed the manual.

“I’m going to take this to the office and see what wisdom is hidden within,” he said with a grin before leaving the kitchen.

Once behind his father’s mammoth desk, he glanced at the table of contents before continuing to the first page. Grip found the manual to be very easy to read as it had been written at a third-grade level and rarely used words longer than two syllables. The exception was the repeated use of the word Constitution.

He finished the manual in less than fifteen minutes. He’d always been a very fast reader and was able to extract the pertinent information quickly from anything he read. It was one of his gifts that enabled him to do so well in his studies.

He closed the manual and then returned to the kitchen to share lunch with everyone.

"What are you going to do this afternoon, Grip?" Rich asked.

"I'm going to open my father's secret vault and empty his safe. I'll leave it open so the new owner can make use of it and change the combination if he wishes. I'll write the current combination down and leave it on one of the shelves in the safe. I'm going to leave a few stacks of cash in the safe for expenses while I'm gone, Rich, but I won't lock it or even close the door to the vault."

"Alright, but don't leave so much that I'd be tempted to snatch it and run off to New Orleans with some young lady," Rich said before Wilma smacked him on the arm.

Grip joined each of them in laughter before Wilma and Jenny began serving lunch.

After he finished eating, Grip made another trip down the hallway to the office.

When he reached the gun room, then used the secret method to access to the hidden vault for the last time. After today, it would be an open secret.

Once inside, he set the lamp's wick afire and closed the chimney before walking to the safe and spinning the dial.

He swung the door wide then began removing the packets of bound banknotes. He left two bundles of twenty-dollar bills on the shelf then turned and headed for the exit.

"Let's go into the light and see how much we have," he said aloud.

He set the money on the worktable but before he began his count, he pulled out his notebook, found an empty page and wrote the combination before returning to the vault and setting it on the top shelf in the safe near the remaining cash. He then blew out the lamp and exited the vault, hopefully for the last time.

He had twenty-eight thousand dollars on the bench and would take it with him to Ogden. He wasn't worried about being robbed but might need the large stockpile of cash to give to his sister, if that became the best solution.

After dumping the small fortune into the brown saddlebags that his father had used to bring ammunition into the room, he hung them over his shoulder and walked out of the gun room. There was enough time in the day to start his preparations in earnest.

———

That evening, two hundred and fifty miles west, in the small house at 176 Charlotte Street in Kansas City, Emily was putting four-year-old Teddy to bed as Julia tucked in two-year-old Mary.

Sixteen-year-old Billy was still at work on the docks and eleven-year-old Millie was staying at her friend's house after a birthday party. Steve had just left the house to spend some time with his friends, and it was the first opportunity she had to talk to her niece without offending her husband.

“Julia, we had a stranger stop by the door earlier. He must have had the wrong address, but he was looking for a nanny and was willing to pay fifty dollars a month plus room and board. I was about to tell him that you would love the opportunity, but Steve heard me talking to him and slammed the door. What do you want me to do if he comes back?”

Julia kissed Mary’s forehead then turned and asked, “Do you think he will?”

“I don’t know, but do you want to write a note, so if he does, I don’t have to say anything?"

"That’s more than twice what I get paid at the diner, including tips. I’d love the chance, so I’ll write a note in case he returns when I’m at work. Just make sure that Steve doesn’t find it.”

Emily nodded then said, “I’ll miss having your help, Julia, but I think it would be best for both of us if you lived elsewhere.”

“Somewhere where Steve couldn’t find me. He hasn’t done anything yet, but I think he’s just waiting to see if you live though another childbirth.”

Emily straightened and arched her back before she smiled at her niece and said, “I hope this one will be my last. I’m getting tired of always carrying this load every other year. I suppose I should be grateful that so many of my babies are still with me.

Julia kissed her aunt on the cheek before she said, “You’re a lucky woman, Emily. You have four beautiful children.”

“With Steve as their father, I’m a bit shocked.”

Julia laughed then said, “At least they’ll know who their father is.”

“Now don’t start that again. It doesn’t really matter to you now; does it?

“I guess it shouldn’t, but it still nags at me. I could have another family back in St. Louis and they wouldn’t even know that I exist.”

Emily took her niece’s hand as they left the small bedroom and said, “Maybe one of them will appear at our door one day and welcome you to their big mansion full of servants who will wait on you hand and foot.”

Julia giggled before saying, “You’re the one who needs to be waited on hand and foot, Emily.’

“That’s the truth,” her aunt replied as they slowly walked to the kitchen to have some tea.

———

The house was quiet as everyone had turned in for the night. Grip had already selected the clothes that he would be taking with him and the ones he'd wear on the train. He wasn't going to go 'all-Western' until he left Kansas City. It would an almost gradual shift in appearance as he journeyed westward across the country.

It was a long, sixteen-hundred-mile journey, but it would all be by rail, which is why he had selected Ogden. He'd take the express train to Kansas City, see if he could find his sister, then he'd continue across Kansas and Colorado, but the tracks would require a long detour through Wyoming before they reached Utah. He estimated that the trip would take three or four days after his stop to find his sister in Kansas City. It was still the big unknown for him. He was now convinced that his sister was living with her aunt on Charlotte Street in Kansas City. It was her reaction to his arrival that was the looming question.

With the agent's report, he was no longer concerned about causing disruption to her family as it appeared that she hadn't married yet. He hoped that she would be happy to see him and even ask if she could come with him to Utah. It was a long shot, but he suspected that given the agent's description of the house as 'typical for the area', she would be more than willing to take his offer of the estate and a large bequest. She may hate him for being the son of Lawrence P. Taylor, but he would be shocked if she turned down an opportunity to benefit from his father's death.

Tomorrow, he'd ride to Fuller's Horse and Mule Sales to buy his packhorse and a pack saddle. After that, the rest of his preparations would be in the house, so he should be able to board the train on Monday.

Saturday morning, he bought a handsome gelding at Fuller's along with a pack saddle on Saturday and after he returned, Tom admired the new horse; the first one on the estate who wasn't black. He'd christened the animal Brick because of his dark red coat.

He spent a few hours in the carriage house preparing the pack saddle to carry his excess baggage. The ebony boards would be coming with him along with the Remington and the Smith & Wesson in its own black gunbelt. He had switched the two pistols so the Remington would have the unusually angled sheath for the knife and had spent some time perfecting the way to make the best use of the configuration.

It wasn't a smooth or simple task to quickly draw the knife and in the same motion, launch it tip first across the gun room and then have it lodge in his target. It had taken him six throws to even get the knife to stick and another hour to improve his speed and accuracy. But by the time he rolled the pistol and dagger ensemble and put it into his black saddlebags, he was confident that it would work. He knew that if he ever had to reach for the dagger, it would be a desperate situation and he hoped that it never had to leave its sheath for any other reason than cleaning and sharpening.

———

On Sunday morning at eight-thirty, everyone left the house to go to church. It gave him time to do some tidying up before he boarded tomorrow morning's express train to Kansas City. It left the station at 5:20, and he could have taken a later train, but the urge to find his sister made the question moot.

He had totally forgotten about Mickey Mooney and his boys as not a whisper of their whereabouts had surfaced since the murder. He had even let Detective Nall's comment about the possibility that they'd gone west to Kansas City fade into his unconscious mind. As he made his final travel plans. he had no idea that he would be taking the same train that they had used to make their escape and that they were still in Kansas City.

While the house was empty, he rode to the massive St. Louis train station and bought his ticket and transport for his two horses. He didn't even think about buying a first-class ticket and it wasn't just to avoid the possibility of meeting one of his father's cronies. He simply felt more at home with regular people.

The churchgoers had already returned when he rode Pitch into the carriage house and after he dismounted, he began stripping his gelding.

"This will be the last time you feel this nice, light saddle on your back, son. Tomorrow, you'll feel a real piece of leather up there. It'll be a bit uncomfortable at first, but you'll get used to it. I've got to see how you like having a gun go off so close to your ears, too. I don't think that'll happen, but I'd rather not be thrown off your back if I have to fire one of my weapons. The Sharps or the Sharps-Borshadt are pretty loud."

He chuckled and patted his neck then continued to clear him of his tack.

Brick was in the corral outside, so after he left the carriage house, he checked on the newest member of their equine family and just talked to him for a few minutes so the horse would become more accustomed to his voice.

He had the black saddlebags over his right shoulder as he walked to the back porch. He'd pack his traveling clothes on the right side with the bundles of cash beneath them. He'd be keeping the saddlebags with him, so the other side would hold his toiletries and the two gunbelts. He'd be bringing the new ebony Winchester and the Sharps '74 that he'd used in target practice just to fill the second scabbard. He'd still bring spare ammunition for each of the guns, but just one box of each caliber except for the Sharps. He'd bring all of the long cartridges because he wasn't sure that he'd be able to find any in Ogden. The rest would come with the shipment in the final move. He'd buy more of the more common ammunition in Ogden for target practice after he found their new property.

When he entered the house, everyone was in the kitchen, so he poured himself a cup of coffee then joined them.

"I bought my tickets for tomorrow's express train, so I'll need to leave the house by four o'clock," he said before taking a sip.

"Have you finished your list?" Rich asked.

"Yes, sir. I'm a bit anxious to be on my way and I'm trying to think if there's anything that I've forgotten."

"Well, you have a few more hours to remember," Wilma said with a smile.

"I'll probably remember what it is when the train leaves Jefferson City station."

Everyone laughed lightly as Grip set the heavy saddlebags on the floor.

"The packs are filled and in the carriage house, so I'll move the Sharps and ammunition out there in a little while. All I need to do now is pack the rest of my things in the black saddlebags."

They spent a few more minutes in discussion over what he might find when he arrived in Kansas City and each of them had different guesses.

Twenty minutes later, he took his black saddlebags to the gun room to add the ammunition and had to adjust the balance before he returned to his room to complete his packing.

Grip was ready to go before sunset and in the dark hours of the morning, he'd just have to dress and carry the black saddlebags to the carriage house. Tom said he'd get Pitch and Brick ready while he had breakfast.

The ladies had baked a large chocolate cake and even frosted it for the occasion, so it was a cheerful group that last evening that they'd spend together for a few weeks.

As they enjoyed their cake and coffee, Wilma asked, "Do you think your sister will want to come to Utah or will she accept your offer and come back to St. Louis?"

"I have no idea, but if she does decide to take the house and the money, I'll send a telegram to give everyone at least a day's warning."

"We weren't going to turn her away, Grip," Rich said with a slight smile.

"I know and it never entered my mind anyway. But do you know what's unusual about her name?"

"Marley was Ebenezer Scrooge's partner in Dickens story; wasn't he?"

"I am impressed, Rich, but no, that's not what's unusual. It's her first name, Julia."

"That's not an unusual name. I know a few ladies with that name." Jenny replied.

"And what is my full first name, ma'am?"

"Agrippa."

"Marcus Vipsanius Agrippa was one of the most noble Romans who ever lived. If it wasn't for Agrippa, who had been a friend to young Octavian since he was a boy, Octavian would never have become Emperor Augustus. Anyway, his last wife was named Julia. That's what's odd about her name."

Wilma laughed lightly before saying, "That is an unusual coincidence. Maybe you should ask for some sort of dispensation so you can marry her anyway."

Grip grinned as he replied, "That's assuming that she's not a shrew or a conniving woman like many of the Roman patrician ladies."

"They did like their poisons; didn't they?"

"Yes, ma'am, but they usually just paid a slave to do the dirty deed then they'd have the slave killed for doing as she had ordered."

"Don't give her any ideas, Grip," Rich said quickly.

Wilma was grinning at her husband as everyone laughed.

Grip was still smiling as the conversation left the topic of Julia Marley and shifted into the move to Utah. It lasted longer than Grip realized, and it wasn't until Wilma said that it was getting late and Grip had to wake up in just five hours that the pleasant evening came to a close.

He said his goodnights, climbed the stairs and soon entered his bedroom. After stripping to his underpants in the muggy heat of the night, he laid atop his blankets and closed his eyes. He had his pocket watch's alarm set for three o'clock but suspected that he'd already be awake when it went off.

He knew he should sleep, but his mind was popping with thoughts about what awaited him in Kansas City and then Ogden. So much change would be happening in the next few weeks and the possibilities rattled around in his mind faster than he could track them.

Grip didn't know when he finally drifted off, but it seemed like just seconds before the dinging from his pocket watch reminded him that the next stage in his life was about to begin.

CHAPTER 7

The express train rolled out of the St. Louis station five minutes late, but the engineer wasn't concerned. Driving the express meant that he had priority all the way to Kansas City and if he pushed the throttle up a bit, no one would object. He was the senior man on the Missouri Pacific Railroad and knew every inch of the two hundred and fifty miles of track between the two largest cities in the state. There were more than a few areas where the posted speed limit was actually too high, but he knew that most of the line's rails could handle at least an extra five miles per hour. He loved his job.

The Missouri River was on the right side of the train as it hurtled along the Show Me State's countryside and Grip sat against the window on that side as the sun rose. He had brought one of his many Roman history books on the trip to pass the time. He was wearing his shoulder holster with its Colt Shopkeeper under his black leather vest, but he had a more urbane light tweed jacket over it, so he didn't attract attention. He had divested himself of his city slicker hat in favor of the new Stetson but didn't feel out of place as he'd seen two other men wearing similar headgear, although he was sure that they were just cheap imitations.

His black saddlebags sat on the seat beside him as the car rocked and clacked its way westward. The train was scheduled to arrive in the Kansas City station just eight hours after it left St. Louis. It only had to stop for coal and water and those stops were in the larger towns along the route.

After the sun climbed higher in the sky, he had enough light to read. He'd read this history twice before, but always liked to keep his mind fresh. He liked all history, whether it was Roman, Greek, English or American. There weren't many books on Oriental or other histories, so when he found one that wasn't mostly fiction, he bought it. It wasn't because of his name that he preferred Roman history, it was because of the lessons that could be learned from its rise and fall.

He wasn't as tired as he had expected to be after such a small amount of sleep, but he found it hard to concentrate on his reading, so he just watched the scenery slide past for an hour or so.

The passenger car wasn't even half full as most folks didn't want to spend the extra six dollars to ride the express, but when the train stopped in Jefferson City to take on coal and water, many of the passengers left the car. It was still too early for lunch, so Grip stayed on the train while it was in the station. He was just another four hours from Kansas City, and he planned to get a room at the nearest hotel then tomorrow morning, he'd swing by 176 Charlotte Street.

From what he had read in the report, he wouldn't even have to ride to the house but thought he might make a quick reconnaissance after dinner. With the calendar so close to the summer solstice, he would have at least another four of hours of daylight which would give him time for at least a walk past the house and make his own judgement of what ‘typical for the area’ meant.

The train rolled out of Jefferson City after just twenty minutes and was soon racing westward. Shortly after the sun reached its zenith, the express was only fifty miles from its destination and soon entered Jackson County, the last county in the state before the tracks entered Kansas. By then, he’d be riding the rails owned by the Kansas Pacific Railroad.

When he’d seen the extended railroad map to determine his route, he’d asked if it was affiliated with the Missouri Pacific and told that it was a totally different company. He found it more than mildly amusing that neither the Missouri Pacific nor the Kansas Pacific didn’t have one mile of track beyond their states’ borders. At least the Atchison, Topeka and Santa Fe touched most of the towns in the name. They hadn’t reached Santa Fe yet and he wondered if they ever would. Maybe they should have just named it the Atchison, Topeka and Pacific Railroad. It seemed to be a trend. There were the first ones, the Union Pacific and the Central Pacific and the equally long Northern Pacific. He was sure that there were many more, especially on the West coast. Maybe they were pointing to the tranquility of the ride offered by their trains and not the ocean at all.

Those light thoughts kept him smiling for the last few minutes of his first day’s journey and as the train pulled into the Kansas City station, his growling stomach suggested that he should have grabbed something to eat when the train had stopped at Sedalia. He pulled out his pocket watch and checked the time. It was almost two o'clock in the afternoon, but that was the time two hundred and fifty miles away. It might be different here, but his stomach was on St. Louis time.

He'd still get his room and get Pitch and Brick into a livery before he satisfied his gut's demands. He'd already decided that he'd be Sam Taylor until he reached Ogden. He expected that even on the other side of Missouri, his unusual first name might be recognized. He'd wanted to be addressed by his middle name when he was a boy, but the staff had always called him Master Taylor and his father called him boy. When he was sent off to St. Michael's, they called him Cadet Taylor, or mister. It was only when he had his first class on Roman history and its legions that he learned about the multi-talented and impressive deeds of Marcus Vipsanius Agrippa. After that discovery, he had his friends call him Agrippa. They were the ones who had shortened it to Grip by the time he was ten.

So, for the first time in his twenty-five years, Sam Taylor would make his appearance.

The train lurched and banged to a stop, so Grip pulled on his Stetson and hung his heavy saddlebags over his shoulder. The only gun he had on his person was the Colt Shopkeeper in his shoulder holster. Before he left that morning, he'd moved his two gunbelts and ammunition to the packs after he realized how unbalanced the saddlebags would be even after rearranging the load. He used the additional space for more clothes and moved half of the cash into the other side as well. He had two hundred dollars in his wallet and another sixty in his pants pocket, so he shouldn't have to dig into the bundles of currency in the saddlebags until he reached Ogden. That was unless he gave them to his sister, even if she wasn't his sister. It was still a subject open to debate, but she should be able to provide the answer. He was sure that her mother had told her the name of her father before she sent her across the state to live with her sister.

The eighteen other passengers in the car were already beginning to exit when Grip joined the queue. Kansas City was a good-sized yet still a growing town, and he had seen a lot of new construction out the window as the train arrived.

He left the car, hopped onto the platform and made his way through the crowd to the stock corral to wait for his horses to be unloaded. This would be the first lesson of what he considered his Western training. He wasn't sure of the protocols for leaving his weapons and supplies that were being carried by his horses. When he found his hotel, he'd have to ask the desk clerk when he got his room.

He imagined that they would have a livery associated or attached to the hotel and that his things would be secure if they were left in the livery. The hotel's reputation would depend on providing assurance to its guests that their things would be safe. He was going to keep the saddlebags with him, though. He wasn't going to use the hotel safe simply because he didn't want anyone knowing he was traveling with the enormous amount of cash.

As he waited at the corral, he thought about money. It was an unusual topic for him because he never really thought about it much. He had never been paid a salary and he always had money in his personal account to pay for his bills at college. He wasn't ignorant of the costs of daily life or the salaries paid for most jobs, but his father had accumulated so much wealth that it was difficult for him to understand the almost desperate feeling that most people had trying to scratch out their living.

He may have given two million dollars of his father's money to charity through the Julia Fund, but he still had almost a two-million-dollar balance at the Merchantmen's Bank, and he couldn't come close to spending it in his lifetime, even if he lived in extravagance. He still felt incredibly guilty for having so much money without earning a dime of it. He wasn't about to give it all away but had a driving need to at least feel he was a value to society.

He was in such deep thought that he hadn't even seen Pitch and Brick being led down the ramp from the stock car.

It was only when the stockman walked them close to him and asked, "Are you waiting for your horses, mister?" that he snapped into the present.

He grinned and replied, “Yes, sir. Here are my claim tickets.”

As he handed him the stubs, the stockman said, “They’re a couple of mighty handsome boys. Looks like they can run with the wind.”

Grip replied, “They are, but they have a couple of more days to spend in a stock car before they get to stretch their legs.”

The stockman opened the gate and handed Pitch’s reins to Grip.

“Where’s a good hotel?” he asked as he put his foot into the stirrup.

“Don’t bother with the Railway Hotel. It’s too noisy with folks comin’ and goin’ at all hours. Two more blocks down on the corner of Fourth and Vine on the left is the Merritt House. I’d go there if you don’t mind spendin’ another fifty cents a night.”

“I’ll do that. Thanks for the information,” Grip said as he mounted.

He walked Grip out of the corral, hung his black saddlebags behind the saddle and then headed down Vine Street. He studied the townsfolk as he made his way and noticed some changes in their appearance from the residents of St. Louis. There were more men dressed like cowhands and some were wearing sidearms. They didn’t make up a large percentage of the population, but because no one seemed to pay any attention to the armed men, he thought that maybe he could wear one of his gunbelts when he left Kansas City. He just didn't know when he'd be leaving yet.

He spotted the Merritt House just two minutes later. It was an impressive building and he noticed that there was a large brick livery attached to the hotel which answered that question. The livery had no name above its doors, so it was probably just for hotel guests.

Grip pulled up in front of the hotel, dismounted and pulled the saddlebags from Pitch before stepping onto the brick sidewalk and entering Merritt House.

The lobby was nice, but not ostentatious as some of the fancier hotels in St. Louis.

As he neared the front desk, the clerk smiled and asked, "May I help you, sir?"

"I'd like a room and I have a question that will announce my ignorance."

"I doubt if it would, but if you'll sign the register, I'll get your key."

Grip signed *Sam Taylor, St, Louis, Missouri*, on the next available line and as he put the pen back into its holder, the clerk handed him his key.

"You'll be in room 212. The room costs two dollars and twenty-five cents a day."

Grip pulled his smallest wad from his pants pocket and handed the clerk a twenty-dollar bill to pay for the week.

After giving him his change, the clerk asked, "And what was this question that you seem to be embarrassed to ask, sir?"

"I've never traveled with my horses before and was wondering if it was safe to leave their supplies and weapons in your livery."

"That's understandable, sir. We have two men working in our livery at all times and your tack and anything that the horses carry will be stored on large shelves in their stalls. There is a fee of fifty cents a day for each horse to cover the cost of the service."

Grip smiled and pulled out another five-dollar bill and slid it across the narrow, polished counter.

The clerk gave him more change, annotated something beside his registration line then gave him two small tokens before saying, "Just give these to one of the liverymen."

"Thank you. You've been very helpful," Grip replied before turning and heading back across the lobby noticing the entrance to the hotel restaurant on the left.

He dropped off his horses in the remarkably clean livery and spent a few minutes chatting with the two liverymen on duty during daylight hours. He didn't wait to watch them remove their saddles but left the livery to go to his room. He needed to at least wash his face before finally getting some food into his stomach.

When he reached his room, he was pleased with the furnishings. It wasn't elaborate, but it was tastefully decorated. The bed was larger than the one in his room back in St. Louis and as he set the saddlebags on the floor, he promised himself that when he furnished his new house, he'd buy himself a bed at least as large as this.

He scrubbed his face in the wash basin then after drying it with a towel embroidered with the hotel's name, he decided it was time to eat. He looked at the saddlebags and debated about leaving them in the room, then just shrugged and stuffed them into the middle drawer of the large dresser. If someone decided to ransack the room, they'd most likely find the saddlebags and be ecstatic with their discovery, but he knew it was an incredibly remote possibility.

Grip trotted down the stairs and crossed the lobby. He could have eaten at the nice hotel restaurant, but he was going to walk to Charlotte Street anyway, so he thought he might as well do a little exploring on the way. He'd stop at a nice café or diner when he spotted one that appealed to him.

Most of the businesses were to the north on Main Street, but Charlotte Street was on the south side of town, so when he reached the intersection of Vine and Fourth Streets, he turned and started walking south. He'd just reduced his chances of finding a nice eatery to satisfy his ever more annoying stomach, but he was anxious to see the house where his sister lived.

It was just after three o'clock in the afternoon, so there was no real reason to rush, but he still walked quickly along Fourth Street. He had just reached the intersection with High Street which was just three blocks north of Charlotte Street when he saw a reasonably nice restaurant named Claudia's Café. He smiled and even if it was an embarrassment to the culinary trade, he knew that he would have to partake of his long-delayed lunch at one of its tables. Claudia was Agrippa's second wife before he married Julia, so the establishment couldn't be ignored.

He was still smiling as he stepped through the open doors and the powerful scents of recently cooked food created a low growl of appreciation from his stomach.

He had his choice of a dozen empty tables as he had arrived in the dead time between lunch and dinner. That was a double-edged sword as it meant that he'd get better service because he was the only diner, but he'd probably be served with lunch leftovers.

He removed his hat and took a seat at the closest table, then set the new Stetson on the chair beside him. There wasn't a waitress visible, but he didn't want to be annoying and announce his presence, so he didn't rap his knuckles loudly on the table or even clear his throat as he waited to be discovered.

After another minute of silently sitting, he was about leave, Claudia's name on the outside of the café notwithstanding. He ran his fingers through his long black hair in preparation for putting on his hat when he heard voices from the kitchen. He couldn't interpret their words, but when they ended, he heard hurried footsteps from the back room then the waitress popped into the dining area.

She seemed harried, but Grip didn't pay much attention to her distress. She was an incredibly pretty young lady with reddish-gold hair and bright blue eyes. Her hair was wrapped in a tight bun and she was wearing an unflattering gray dress, but despite the almost frumpy nature of her attire, he could tell that she possessed an impressive figure.

When she spotted him looking at her, her face transformed from annoyed to positively angelic as she smiled and slowed to a more elegant gait.

Grip wondered why such an amazing creature was working at as a waitress. He imagined that she probably received a dozen marriage proposals a week from customers. He guessed her age to be about twenty, so she should have been married long ago.

She approached his table and said, “I apologize for the delay, sir.”

“That’s alright, ma’am. I’m in no rush,” he replied even though he had been in a hurry to get to Charlotte Street until he saw the young lady emerge from the kitchen.

“Thank you. What can I get for you?”

“Well, I know that I’m in between normal meals, so what do you have available that won’t kill me?”

She laughed lightly and her blue eyes danced as she replied, “My safest recommendation is the roast beef. It was our lunch special and it may be a bit overcooked, but I’ll have the cook cut deeper into the meat, so it won’t be so dry.”

“That’s fine. What do you recommend accompany the not-so-dry beef on my plate? I’m sure you have something equally safe.”

She continued to smile as she answered, “We always have at least two baked potatoes ready to serve, so I’ll add a baked potato and some carrots. Is that acceptable?”

“Yes, ma’am. I’ll need about a gallon of black coffee as well.”

"Coffee is always available. I'll bring you the coffee then I'll return with your food shortly."

"Thank you."

She smiled at him again before turning and walking back to the kitchen.

Grip was mesmerized when he watched her leave and wished that he'd be able to have her join him at the table just to get to know her better. He was already thinking of spending an extra day or two in Kansas City before boarding the train to Ogden. He'd almost forgotten about his sister after seeing the handsome young woman.

He was surprised by his reaction. He'd met many very handsome young women in his six years at the University of Michigan and quite a few of them had set their caps for him, but he hadn't been interested. He wasn't sure if it was because they all knew who he was that had created the attraction, but until he laid eyes on the young waitress, he'd never experienced this level of instant fantasy.

She soon exited the kitchen carrying a coffeepot in one hand and a cup and saucer in the other. Grip tried not to stare but was sure that she noticed his attention and it bothered him. He didn't want her to think of him as another one of the lechers who probably ogled her daily.

She set the cup and saucer on the table, flipped the cup into its upright position and began to pour his coffee.

"I haven't seen you before. Are you from Kansas City, or just passing through?" she asked.

"I just arrived an hour or so ago from St. Louis and I'll be leaving soon for Utah."

She set the coffeepot on the table, smiled and said, "Utah? I've never met anyone from Utah before."

"I haven't either. I just decided that's where I want to go, so I'm moving to Ogden."

"Why would you do that?"

"It's a very long and complicated story and most of the people who hear it believe that I'm out of my mind. I'm close to agreeing with them myself."

She laughed again before she replied, "You don't have the look of a madman."

"I've met a few men who were borderline crazy, and I couldn't tell just by looking at them."

"What are you going to do when you get there?"

"First, I need to find someplace to hang my hat. After that, I'll continue to do crazy things."

She glanced back at the kitchen before asking, "How long did you live in St. Louis?"

"That's a very debatable question, ma'am. I was born there and spent the first seven years of my life there, but after I was sent away to military school, I haven't spent more than a few months there until I had to return a few weeks ago."

"I was born and raised in St. Louis and only came to Kansas City when I was eleven because my mother had sent me to live with her sister before she died."

Grip stared at her with new eyes for ten disbelieving silent seconds. This wasn't possible. He desperately wanted to be wrong, but how many other young women had left St. Louis in that time frame to come to Kansas City when her mother died?

She noticed the sudden change in his demeanor, but she wasn't concerned because he seemed to be stunned for some reason and not anything close to being a threat.

He finally quietly said, "That must have been hard for you."

She nodded then replied, "It was. She was everything to me and I wasn't even there when she died."

Grip took a breath before saying, "And now you live on a street that bears her name."

It was Julia's turn to be stunned, but his quiet statement seemed almost malevolent. *How did he know about her mother? Was he stalking her? Was he some kind of detective?*

She quickly said, “I’ll get your food,” then whirled around and quickly walked away before disappearing into the kitchen.

Grip was still shaken by the extraordinary coincidence. He tried to calm down enough to think but was finding it difficult to get his thoughts in order. It wasn’t that much of a coincidence if he looked at it logically. He had come to Kansas City to find his sister and her house was just three blocks away. If she wasn’t married, then she’d be working and one of the few jobs open to women was waitressing.

But now he had frightened her and wondered if she’d even return to the table with his food. She might convince the cook to bring it to him rather than face him again.

Julia stopped in the kitchen and ignored Gary as he told her that the lone customer’s food was ready. She had enjoyed talking to the young man until he’d made that eerie connection to her mother. The only ones who knew her mother’s name lived in her uncle and aunt’s home on Charlotte Street. *How did he know? Why did he know? Why was he here?*

Gary reminded her more loudly that the food was ready and if the young man had presented a more threatening appearance, Julia would have told Gary to take the food to their only diner himself. But it was his pleasant nature that made her pick up the plate. She wanted her questions answered.

She had been gone for more than a minute and Grip was about to walk into the kitchen to at least attempt to explain why he was there when she reappeared carrying an overloaded plate.

Her blue eyes were afire as she strode towards him and before he could say a word, she set the plate on his table and sat down.

Before he could start his explanation, she hurriedly asked, “How did you know that? Have you been stalking me or investigating me?”

Grip ignored the food as he quickly replied, “It’s part of that long story that I mentioned, and it’s a real mystery to me. I apologize for scaring you. You are Julia Marley; aren’t you?”

“Yes. Who are you?”

“My full name is Agrippa Samuel Taylor. Does that help?”

Julia stared at him as she searched her distant girlhood memories from St. Louis but couldn’t remember his name. She was sure that she would have recalled hearing it before.

“No, it doesn’t help at all. Should it?”

“Maybe not. My father was Lawrence Preston Taylor. Is that name familiar to you?”

Julia slowly nodded. Her mother had talked often about the unkind man who had thrown her from his house when he'd discovered that she was carrying a child.

"Yes," she answered, "I remember that name. He was the bastard who sent my mother into the streets because she was pregnant with me."

"Yes, he was. His despicable nature finally caught up with him when he was murdered last month. I was in Michigan at the time and didn't exactly rush back to St. Louis for his funeral."

"Why are you here? Are you looking for me for some reason?"

Grip reached behind his jacket and pulled out his wallet. He opened it, slid the birth certificate from its folds and handed it to her.

"I discovered this in my father's safe in his secret vault that he thought no one knew about. There was money and some deeds in the safe, but this was inside the batch of papers. It's your birth certificate but the father's name is blank. I have no idea why my father kept it because it didn't benefit him in any way."

Julia was staring at the old document as Grip continued, saying, "I remember your mother. I was just six when my father sent her away, but I do remember her. I hate to tell you why, but I was a boy and called her Charlie Marley. But my father was more than just a cruel man, he was aggressive in his behavior to his female staff members. He'd hire pretty young women and use them like prostitutes. If they became pregnant, he'd usually send them to a woman to eliminate the possibility of a bastard child. He wouldn't rehire them, either. I didn't realize it at the time, of course, but I do remember how upset your mother was when she was sent away."

She raised her blue eyes to look at him from across his untouched food and softly asked, "Why did you come here?"

"I'm sure that you're my sister, Julia. We may have had different mothers, but I believe that we shared the same bastard for a father."

Julia was finding it difficult to believe because her mother had instilled such a hate for the man yet had never even suggested that he might be her father. The thought of being sired by such a vicious, monstrous man made her queasy.

"Are you sure? I don't want to be associated with him. The thought is abhorrent to me."

"I felt the same way for my entire life, Julia. I did more than dislike my father; I hated him. He wanted to mold me into a duplicate of himself and had hoped that sending me to a military school would make me hard and unfeeling. He even sent a note to the commander of the school to treat me more harshly than the other cadets."

"Why didn't it work? You seem to be a very nice person."

"I saw it as a challenge. I could either become the soulless monster that he hoped me to be, or I could fight him every day to become a man who understood and valued people. I could have turned into a rebellious student and been tossed out of the school, but I didn't want to give him that victory either. I pushed myself to excel at every endeavor just to prove to myself that he wasn't going to own even one tiny sliver of my soul.

"You seem to have a good sprit as well, Julia. I have no idea how you were raised but it sounds as if your mother was your guide to becoming a good person."

"She was," Julia replied, then said, "You'd better start eating before your food gets cold."

Grip nodded then as he cut his roast beef, he said, "Call me Grip. It's short for Agrippa and I hope we have enough time to talk so I can explain it to you."

"I'd like that, but I'd better get back to the kitchen or Gary might fire me. He threatens to do that fairly often, but he keeps me around because I attract so many customers."

Grip was chewing so he held up a finger until he swallowed, then said, "Don't worry about Gary. You won't have to serve another diner for the rest of your life, Julia."

Her eyebrows peaked as she asked, "What do you mean?"

He smiled then replied, “You seem like a very smart young lady, Julia, so your question is somewhat disappointing. I just told you that you’re my sister and before that I told you that I was the son of Lawrence Preston Taylor. So, do I really have to give you an answer?”

“But just because you believe I’m your half-sister doesn’t mean that you’d be willing to help me. You could just be looking for me to make sure I didn’t make any claim against your father’s estate.”

Grip set his knife and fork on the plate before saying, “Now I am even more disappointed in you, Julia. If I wanted to do that, why would I even tell you who I am? All I have is that birth certificate and it doesn’t even list the father. I could have burned it and then stayed in St. Louis. As it is, I’m going to Ogden and never returning to St. Louis because I don’t want to be known as the son of Lawrence Preston Taylor. Before I left, I arranged to have all of my father’s assets sold so the only place his name will be seen in the city will be on his gravestone. I have no intention of ever visiting his grave either.”

Julia stared at Grip as he returned to eating his cooling meal. Just a few nights ago, Aunt Emily had joked about a mysterious relative appearing at their door and taking her away. He may not have found her at that door, but he was sitting across from her now. But beyond all of the incredible beneficial possibilities he represented, she was saddened by one facet of his arrival. He was her brother and that relationship destroyed any possibility of a romantic involvement.

She'd never met any man with his combination of appearance, nature and intelligence. Even before he'd identified himself, she wished that he would be staying in Kansas City long enough for her to know him better, but now, she'd get to know him better, but as an older brother and nothing more.

Grip was clearing the plate faster than he normally would, so after he swallowed his last bite of potato, he started to say something to Julia but instead of a profound utterance, a loud belch escaped from deep within his throat.

Julia was startled out of her reverie and as she looked at Grip's distressed red face, she began to laugh.

Grip soon echoed her laughter and after just a few seconds of jollity, Gary emerged from the kitchen with a scowl blanketing his face.

"Julia, you know the rules. You can't sit down with customers even if the dining room is empty."

Julia began to stand when Grip snapped, "Sit down, Julia!"

She saw the power in his gray eyes and as she lowered herself back to the chair, Grip shifted his now menacing gray eyes to Gary.

"As of this moment, Julia is no longer working for you. She is my sister and not your waitress. I suggest you hurry to find her replacement before the dinner crowd arrives."

Gary's mouth mimicked a large-mouthed bass having a hook removed from its jaws as he stared back at Grip.

He glanced at Julia before spinning on his heels then quickly returning to the kitchen.

Grip's visage instantly transformed when he smiled and said, "That was fun. I've never had to order someone around before."

"Really? Not even in military school?"

"Nope. I never wanted to be in charge. They kept trying to make me a captain of cadets, but I thought it was a silly thing. Besides, I'd watched my father order everyone around for years and it was part of my personal challenge not to go down that road."

"I'm glad that you didn't, but you still put Gary in his place. I think he was ready to wet his britches if you'd said anything else."

"I just didn't want you to leave, Julia. We have a lot to talk about and I'd rather not do it here. Where do you want to go?"

"There's a small park a block west of here with some benches."

“Okay. Let’s go,” he said as he stood, dropped fifty cents on the table and then after Julia stood, he hooked his arm through hers.

They left the diner and turned right on Cherry Street.

Grip was extraordinarily happy to have found Julia so quickly and was even more pleased to discover what an amazing young woman she was. He had created so many different potential Julia images, but none had come close to the real Julia. She was taller than any of his imaginary Julia guesses too, just four inches shorter than his height. He had many questions to ask her and she probably had even more to ask him, but now they had time. He just wished she wasn’t his sister.

That thought must have been foremost in Julia’s mind when, shortly after they left the café, the first question she asked was, “Are you sure that you’re my brother?”

He glanced at her and hesitated before he answered, “I’m pretty sure. Aside from the timing and my father’s deviant behavior with the young women on the staff, the most critical piece of evidence is the birth certificate itself. Why would he keep it if you weren’t his daughter?”

“But he’s not even listed as the father. It was no proof of his paternity and from how my mother described him, he was far from the sentimental type who kept mementos.”

"I know. He didn't even keep a copy of my birth certificate. The only personal record of any kind in the house was your birth certificate. His motive for keeping it has been driving me to the brink of insanity and I was hoping that either you or your mother could have provided an explanation."

As they strolled west to the park, Julia said, "I wish I could help you, Grip. My mother never told me who my father was and made it clear that I wasn't to pursue the matter. But she didn't seem to have any difficulty in telling me about your father."

"Did it seem as if she was afraid to tell you? That would make sense if you knew my father."

"No, she wasn't afraid at all. It was, I don't know, a combination of shame and longing. It was as if she'd met a man she loved and was ashamed of loving him. I'd find it hard to believe that she could have loved your father."

"Nobody loved my father. I'm not even sure if my mother did but she died when I was a toddler. I've never even heard him say the word 'love' in the context of men and women. He did love his guns, though."

"Then there's a chance that I'm not your sister?"

"I suppose there is, but I'm not going to just ride off to Ogden and leave you in a sad situation. Besides, I just managed to have you fired from the diner."

She laughed and squeezed his arm as they entered the small park and took a seat on one of the three benches.

"What are you going to do now that you found me?"

"My plans depended on many factors. If you were married and had a family, then I'd do one thing. If you weren't married, but a mean-spirited lady, then I'd do another. To be honest, I thought it was the least likely that I'd find someone like you. You seem to be so well-balanced and I'll tell you without ulterior motives that you are a strikingly handsome woman as well."

"Thank you for the complements, big brother, but now that you've met me how do you plan to deal with your little sister?"

Grip laughed then replied, "You're hardly little and I wish you weren't my sister at all, but that being said, I have several offers for you, Julia."

"And they are?"

"If you were unmarried and a bit of a harpy, I was going to offer you my father's estate in St. Louis and fifty thousand dollars. You can still do take that option, but I'd probably give you half of what remains of my father's fortune rather than just fifty thousand dollars."

"How big was his fortune, if you don't mind my asking?"

"His bank balance was over almost four million dollars."

Julia gaped as she slowly repeated, “Four million dollars?”

“I had two million dollars put into a charitable trust fund, so that’s gone. I gave a friend the authority to sell all of my father’s properties and add them to the fund and told him that I might move more to the fund depending on what happened when I found you.”

Julia had never closed her mouth as the revelations kept arriving to her stunned mind.

Grip could see the impact the news had on her, so he continued, saying, “Right now, my father’s mansion is occupied by the household staff. They’re preparing to make the move to Ogden to join me as soon as I’ve prepared the new property. So, if you don’t want it, it’ll be sold along with the rest of my father’s empire.”

Julia finally recovered and replied, “I don’t want it, Grip. It’s not my favorite place in the world.”

“I can understand why you’d feel that way. Before I make any more suggestions, can you tell me about your situation?”

She nodded and replied, “I live with my Aunt Emily and Uncle Steve, but I assume that you already know that. They have four children and she’s heavy with her fifth. She lost three other babies and had one miscarriage, so it seemed that she was almost always pregnant. She’s convinced that this will be her last and I hope she’s right. I help her as much as I can when I’m not working as a waitress.”

"What does Steve do for a living?"

"He's a stevedore on the docks. He used to be a deckhand and that was how he met my aunt when his boat was drydocked in St. Louis for a month. He goes to work sporadically, so I don't think that he actively pursues work anymore. I give my pay and tips to Emily to pay for the food and other necessities, but I know that Steve expects her to give at least half of it to him. Their oldest, Billy, is sixteen and is working on the docks but gives all of his pay to his father. When Billy started working there is when Steve began staying more at the house."

"Does he hurt Emily or the children?"

"Not excessively, but he does give me the chills sometimes. When I first arrived, he treated me just like another one of his children, but that changed three years ago when I began to become more developed. He hasn't touched me at all, but he gives me these suggestive looks that Emily has noticed."

"I had the Pinkertons searching for you and their agent described your house as 'typical for the area'. Do you want me to help them financially?"

Julia bit her lower lip before replying, "I was wondering about that stranger who showed up at our door recently. It seemed odd that he was looking for a nanny in our neighborhood and was offering much more than most. I assume he was the Pinkerton you engaged to find me. But if you gave them money, Steve might even leave them, and they'd be in worse shape."

"You won't desert your aunt even if I did give you the financial ability to leave, would you?"

Julia smiled and shook her head as she answered, "If the Pinkerton agent had been a genuine father looking for a nanny, I would have willingly accepted the position if offered. But only if it was close enough to Aunt Emily's house so I could still check on them, and I'd still give half of my salary to her."

"Let us both think about it for a little while to come up with a solution. Money isn't the problem. Your biggest problem may be if your uncle discovers that you have access to almost unlimited funds now. We can help your aunt and cousins regardless of what your uncle does. I know that legally, he has total control over his family and that no powerful lawyer can change that. If it was just a question of giving him a few thousand dollars, I'd be happy to do that, but he sounds like the sort who would take the money, spend it and then demand more."

"You've got a good measure of the man without even meeting him. But I can't return to the house for another four hours because I'm supposed to be at work. Then when I do return, I need to give Emily my tips for the day."

“I know this sounds like an odd question, but are you hungry?”

Julia smiled and replied, “No, I’m fine. I nibble while I’m working. While we decide how to help my Aunt Emily, can you tell me why you’re going to Ogden? We have those four hours to fill.”

“Alright. I suppose I should start when I was in my dormitory room at the University of Michigan. I was reading a chart on ballistics when my roommate entered and…”

Grip’s hands and fingers danced as he narrated the tale that he’d already told so often. He skipped some of the details because there were still many questions that he needed to ask his sister.

Julia listened and was in awe of the extraordinary sequence of both horrifying and redemptive events that he'd experienced over the past few weeks. He spoke so calmly and methodically as he followed his memories in chronological order. It was as if he was reciting an epic poem.

Yet in each word and sentence, she recognized his compassion for those who had suffered at his father’s hands and the disgust for those who were in league with his father. She stayed focused on his dark gray eyes as he gazed back at her. It was an almost religious experience for her, and she wondered if he was actually hypnotizing her. He was certainly having that effect on her even if it wasn’t his intention.

Grip spoke for more than fifteen minutes with only short pauses to catch his breath, but when he finally finished, he believed that Julia had a solid understanding of what had happened, what he was planning to do, and most importantly, why he was almost driven to make amends for his father's behavior.

As soon as he stopped, Julia quietly said, "I want to come with you."

Grip blinked and replied, "To Ogden?"

"Wherever you go. I want to come with you."

Grip didn't even think about arguing but asked, "How can we help your aunt?"

"You said that one of your possible offers was to give me your father's mansion and fifty thousand dollars?"

"Yes," Grip replied before asking, "You want me to give it to your Aunt Emily and the children?"

"Would you?"

"Of course. I don't expect to have the new property ready for at least another month, so they could go to St. Louis and meet everyone. They'd help her and the children to get settled, and your aunt wouldn't need to buy anything. I'll have Rich Bennett hire a housekeeper and cook then arrange for a midwife for your aunt. It's summer, so her children will have a few months to get adjusted before school starts."

Julia smiled then said, "That sounds wonderful. But Billy doesn't go to school, so you'd have to come up with something else for him to do."

"I'll leave that up to him and Rich Bennett. I guess we'll be sending telegrams and letters back and forth almost daily if we can convince your aunt to leave Kansas City."

"She won't object at all, but Steve will be the problem."

"I know, but you said that if I gave him money, he'd probably just leave her and the children. Do you believe that it's likely that he'd really do that, or is it just a personal wish?"

"I think he would leave, but I believe that he'd try to get me to come with him and that could be dangerous. He's a strong man, Grip. He's not as tall as you are but he's probably heavier by twenty pounds."

"I'm not concerned about that, but I'm beginning to feel the wisps of a plan forming in the recesses of my brain."

"Let the wisps escape and tell me what you're thinking."

"The Pinkerton agent said that Steve slammed the door in his face, but it was after your aunt had told him that you would be interested in the job. Is that right?"

"Yes."

"He wasn't angry about the offer. He was upset because you'd be leaving."

"You're right again."

"What if I was to show up as an attorney representing your long-lost father and that I need you to come to my hotel room to sign some papers to claim his two-thousand-dollar bequeath. What would he do?"

"He'd start dancing."

"But you, Miss Marley, would be hesitant to go to a stranger's hotel room unescorted. He would offer to come with you to protect you; wouldn't he?"

Julia was smiling as she nodded and replied, "Yes, I'm sure he would."

"When we get to my room, I'll have you sign a legal-looking document that I'll create and then I'll hand you the two thousand dollars. You'll look at the stacks of bills and tell me that you're now afraid that you might get robbed on the way back to the house. He'll offer to take it back for you and you'll gratefully accept his offer."

"I'm not sure that he'll believe me that I'm suddenly afraid of just walking back to the house with the money. He'd be escorting me anyway."

"Once he sees the cash, he won't even think of anything else. After he puts the money in his pocket, I'll offer to take you both to dinner, but he'll decline and tell you that he'll meet you at the house. He'll scurry home and without a word to your aunt, he'll pack and then just disappear."

"That's expecting a lot out of a man you've never met, Grip."

"I've met dozens of men like Steve. They surrounded my father like moths flittering around a lamp on a hot summer night. If he does hold the money for you when he gets to the house, then it won't hurt. If he's gone by the time that I escort you back to the house, then we'll talk to your aunt. Don't tell her anything until after he's gone. She needs to believe my story."

"I had no intention of ruining your devious plot, sir."

He pulled out his pocket watch, flipped open the cover and read its hands before snapping shut and sliding it back into his pocket.

"It's not quite five o'clock. I'll have to spend some time making the fake legal document, so we can start our plan tomorrow afternoon. Do you have to work tomorrow?"

"I normally do, but I can use a woman's excuse that no man would ever question for missing a day on my feet. I'll be at home when you arrive."

"What is the possibility that Steve will be at work?"

"Not very high, but it is possible."

"Okay. I'll show up around four o'clock and we'll see what happens."

"Alright," she replied then asked, "Why didn't you argue after I told you I wanted to come with you?"

Grip grinned and answered, "I like you, Julia, and there's always that chance that you aren't my half-sister."

She smiled back as she said, "There is that chance; isn't there?"

He then asked, "Do you know how to ride?"

"I've never ridden a horse, but I think that's about to change; won't it?"

"If you come with me to Ogden, that will be one of the many changes you'll be making."

"I'm coming with you, so learning how to ride will be one of the first lessons you'll have to teach me."

"Aside from being a waitress, what other skills do you have?"

Julia sighed and answered, "Not many, I'm afraid. I can cook and do housework and take care of children, but that's about the extent of my talents."

"You're a smart woman, Julia. Now that you have every option available to you, there is no limit to what you can do."

"That's almost scary, Grip."

"It can be, but it can be exciting and incredibly fulfilling, too."

Julia nodded and wished that the earth would slow in its rotation so they could just sit on the bench for another ten hours before the sun set.

"Tell me about your childhood, Julia."

"It's not as exciting as yours, but my mother..."

Grip was amazingly content as he watched Julia's face recount her personal history. The mystery of her father's identity already hung over him much more than it had when he'd left St. Louis. Now even if as much as he wished that she wasn't his sister, there would be almost no way to prove otherwise.

He knew that most men who found themselves in a situation when they met a very desirable young woman of unknown pedigree, would choose to ignore the possibility of marrying a sister or first cousin. But Grip was still so sure that the only reason that his father kept the birth certificate was because he was the father of Charlotte Marley's child, that knew that he could never choose to simply dismiss the likelihood. He wished there was some way of discovering whose name should have been entered in the empty space on her birth certificate.

When Julia finished her much shorter life story, Grip said, "That wasn't very boring, Julia."

"It's not much different from everyone else's, Grip. People like you are rare. Even your name is very unusual. My name is pretty common."

Grip shook his head before saying, "That's where you're wrong, Miss Marley. I'll admit that my name is strange, but your name isn't common at all and it's very appropriate, I might add."

"Because?"

"Marcus Vipsanius Agrippa was a famous Roman of many talents who was the contemporary and best friend of Emperor Augustus. He had three wives and the last was named Julia."

She smiled and said, "So, he was tired of the other two and wanted a younger wife?"

"No, ma'am. Romans were very odd when it came to families. They adopted left and right and often adopted adults. Julius Caesar adopted his nephew Octavian who became the Emperor Augustus courtesy of his friend, Agrippa. They also married and divorced for almost any reason, but the patricians did it mostly for wealth and power. Love didn't matter at all to the ones at the top of the pyramid. Fathers would order a daughter to divorce a husband she may have loved to marry some old codger as a political favor or to gain access to his wealth. It was a strange society in that respect, but if you keep it in context of the times, it wasn't so odd.

"I'm sure in a hundred years or so, people will think that we all lived in log cabins or ran around with pistols and rifles shooting each other. They'll probably think that we're all quaint and polite, too. Look at how the men and women dress in the cities like St. Louis and even here and they'll think that we're all prudes."

"You don't strike me as a prude, Grip."

"I'm far from being a put into that category, ma'am, and I don't think that you would meet those standards either."

"I'll admit to having quite a few rather lurid fantasies when I'm in my bed at night."

"I think most people do. Anyway, that's a nice coincidence about your name. There is another one that turned me into your café. Agrippa's second wife was Claudia."

Julia laughed then said, "Claudia is Gary's wife and she's hardly what one would call a noble Roman, but she is a prude."

"I'm sure the original Claudia wasn't. I don't think the Romans even knew what a prude was. They were a particularly rowdy bunch."

They continued to talk for another two hours before the café where they met closed its doors for the day.

Just as their time together neared an end, Grip asked, "Did your mother give you anything to remember her when she sent you to her sister?"

Julia nodded and replied, "She gave me her copy of *Jane Eyre*. It was her favorite book and I read it often."

"Did she write anything on the pages to give you an idea of your father's identity?"

"No. All she wrote was on the title page. She wrote, '*Books provide more than just knowledge. They can give us peace and happiness when we need it most.'*. If you're familiar with the story, it makes sense."

Grip smiled and replied, "It's not a genre that I would normally read, so maybe I should buy my own copy."

"I think you'd be surprised when you enjoyed reading the book."

"Then I'll do that," he replied before saying, "I suppose that it's time to escort you to the corner of your street before I head back to my hotel."

"Thank you for everything, Grip. I hope your plan works tomorrow. If it doesn't, I'm sure you'll come up with another one."

"I promise," he said as he stood.

After Julia rose, he just presented his arm and she wrapped hers around his forearm before they started walking south. It was a pleasant late summer day, and the crickets were in good voice as they strolled along the sideway.

Grip noticed that the houses were growing less fashionable as they continued south and when they reached Charlotte Street, they stopped.

"I'll be at your door at four o'clock, Julia."

Julia just smiled and nodded before turning away and walking west along Charlotte Street toward #176.

Grip watched her fade into the setting sun and hoped that the first step of the plan to get rid of her uncle worked. He didn't have any idea of what he'd do if it didn't.

He wheeled about and walked at a brisk pace to return to his hotel room. He'd get something to eat at the hotel restaurant later that evening but there was no rush to create his fake document. He had most of the day tomorrow to get it done.

Before he entered the hotel, he paid a visit to Pitch and Brick and spent a few minutes chatting with the two liverymen about horses. He was doing more than just being friendly, although he did enjoy the conversation. Each moment he spent with men like them was another lesson in his education of life in the West.

He entered his room twenty minutes later and immediately opened the drawer to make sure the saddlebags were still there. He pulled them out and the weight confirmed that nobody had burglarized his room in his absence.

He almost giggled at the idea, but its loss wouldn't be the problem; it would be the delay in replacing the money to almost bribe Steve Albert to desert his family.

He headed downstairs to the restaurant and had a perfectly cooked ribeye steak for supper before returning to his room.

By the time he had undressed and slid beneath the covers, the previous night's lack of sleep, the long, monotonous train ride and then the excitement of finding Julia all conspired to quickly drive him into deep slumber.

CHAPTER 8

When Grip struggled to open his eyes the next morning, the first thing that came to his attention was his excruciating urge to empty his bladder. The bathroom was at the end of the hallway, but there was a chamber pot near the bed. and he came close to filling it halfway.

He wrapped himself in one of the hotel's bathrobes and carried his sloshing chamber pot and shaving kit out of the room and down the hallway. He emptied the chamber pot in the drainage sink that was there for that purpose, then set it on the floor before stepping to the bath and opening the valves to let it fill with hot and cold water. There were four bathtubs in the men's bathroom, and all were separated by a thin wall. He was the only one in the bathroom, so it really didn't matter anyway.

After a quick bath, he shaved then quickly returned to his room, passing another man who was quickly trotting to the bathroom rather than using his room's chamber pot.

He dressed quickly, set the saddlebags back into the drawer, then left the room to have his breakfast.

As he was sitting at the table waiting for his food, he checked his pocket watch, then wound the stem and slid it back into his pocket. It was already nine-forty, and he wasn't surprised by the late hour.

The pretty, smiling waitress brought him his enormous breakfast of eggs and sausage with toast and a private small pot of coffee and he returned her smile. He couldn't help comparing the young woman with Julia and despite her attractiveness, he didn't think that she held a candle to his sister.

Grip made short work of the smorgasbord that managed to fill just one big plate, left his payment and a large tip on the table and as he left the restaurant, he pulled on his hat and soon exited the hotel.

He stopped on the sidewalk and scanned the nearby businesses before he smiled and walked west for a hundred feet then made a zigzagging cut across a busy Vine Street without being run over before he hopped onto the other sidewalk. He continued walking west past shops and stores before he reached the corner shop and entered Carpenter's Stationery and Books.

He normally would have browsed their book collection, but this time, he headed for the stationery side of the shop. He selected a box of linen stationery and then bought a pen and two nibs along with a bottle of indigo ink. He didn't see anything else he needed, so he headed to the counter and paid for his selections.

Grip could have returned to his hotel and used the room's desk, but the shop provided a row of desks for use by their customers, so he headed for the end desk and took a seat.

He wasn't that concerned with the wording, but he needed to make it neat and officious in appearance.

He set a sheet of the expensive paper on the table then attached a nib to the pen before opening the bottle of ink and dipping the nib into the dark blue liquid.

He started writing, *"Being of sound mind and body…"*

He knew that he had precise penmanship due to his years of closely monitored instruction at St. Michael's. Sloppy handwriting was not acceptable when writing orders to subordinates. That didn't apply to generals, of course.

He wrote carefully and had to pause many times before reached the bottom of the page and had to sign and write the name of her unknown father.

Grip held the nip of the pen over the paper for a few seconds before he smiled and wrote, *James M. Ellis*. Using the crooked lawyer's name seemed to be appropriate for a fake document.

He let the page dry for a few minutes as he read what he'd written. It wasn't close to being a legal document, but he didn't think that Steve Albert would even glance at it after he saw the bundle of cash on the desk. He should have asked Julia if he could even read. The percentage of men who were illiterate in the country as a whole was about twenty percent and he suspected that Steve may be in that number.

Satisfied that his document was dry, he carefully folded it into three parts, then returned it to the box with the blank paper. He closed the ink and then put it all back into the sack that the sales clerk had given to him.

He was about to leave when he stopped, then turned and walked to the back of the shop and selected a thin leather satchel. If he was going to be an attorney, then he'd need a satchel. He really should have more papers and maybe a book or two inside when he extracted the phony will.

He hunted the shop and found a copy of Missouri Laws and Ordinances that wasn't too hefty and then he was surprised to find a binder with preprinted legal documents. He shook his head when he realized that he could have saved some time but bought it as well. After paying for the new items, he left the shop and headed back to the hotel. He had to change into more lawyerly clothing, but only had the Stetson now and wasn't about to buy a bowler for just an hour. He may be wealthy, but he hated waste in any form.

After entering his room, he set the bag and the satchel on the bed which he had automatically made before he left, probably confusing the maid when she arrived to tidy the room. It looked as if it hadn't been occupied at all, but there was a fortune in the saddlebags in the dresser that would have proven otherwise if she had looked.

He extracted the saddlebags and rummaged through his clothes. He pulled out his tweed jacket that he'd worn on the train from Michigan and set it on the bed. He wasn't wearing the denim britches he'd bought in St. Louis, so his lower half was all right. He removed his black leather vest but left his shoulder holster strapped in place.

Next, he pulled out four bundles of cash and had to replace all of them before taking out another three and finding two packets of ten-dollar notes. He could have used one of the twenties, but he wanted to impress Steve with the added bulk.

After returning the saddlebags to the drawer, he took the bag and the satchel to the desk and sat down.

He felt like a little boy pulling a prank as he arranged his props. He slid the two thousand dollars into the satchel, then opened the binder with the legal papers. He found the preprinted will and then compared it to his and decided that although the printed version was more legally correct, his looked more realistic. So, he took a few of the printed pages and then had to fold the additional sheets to match his homemade will. Satisfied that it was good enough, he slid the new multi-page will into the satchel and then finished by putting the law book inside.

He set the pen, nibs and ink onto the desktop, but put the sack and the remaining paper and the binder into an empty dresser drawer.

Grip then leaned back and stared at the ceiling. He began an imaginary walk to Charlotte Street where he knocked on the door and greeted whoever opened it as Samuel A. Taylor, Esquire. He'd explain how his client, who had just died in St. Louis, had included a Miss Julia Marley in his will, leaving her the sum of two thousand dollars. If he was telling Julia, he'd have to speak loudly for Steve to hear, but he suspected that it would be Mister Albert who answered the door.

He began rehearsing his role, first just mentally before then he stood and started acting the part until he felt it was as good as he could make it.

He left everything in the room but donned his tweed jacket to hide his shoulder holster before he went downstairs to the restaurant for his lunch. He wasn't that hungry after the massive breakfast, so he just had a ham and cheese sandwich and a beer.

When he returned to his room, it was just after one o'clock. He had another two and a half hours before he began his walk to 176 Charlotte Street. He had to kill some time, or he'd go crazy, but as he was a volunteer U.S. Deputy Marshal, he decided he may as well read the Missouri Laws and Ordinances book.

He sat at the desk and began reading. It was a dry, humorless tome but it was what he had expected. There were some laws that tickled his sense of humor because of their absurdity, though. He didn't know that it was illegal to serve beer to hogs in the state.

Grip's ability to read and grasp concepts quickly proved to be a curse as he finished reviewing the book after just an hour and a half, leaving him another hour to fill.

He closed the book then pulled out his Colt Shopkeeper. He pulled the hammer to the load position and began removing the cartridges. Once the pistol was empty, he released the hammer and began dryfiring the revolver for ten minutes. But when he slid the reloaded pistol back into its holster, he appreciated the delay it had provided.

He checked his pocket watch once again and even though it was only three o'clock, he decided that he had to start moving, even if it was early. He'd take the long way to Charlotte Street to use up the time.

He crossed the street after leaving the hotel and headed for Main Street to do some window shopping. He wasn't going to buy anything, but it was a good way to keep him from rushing to Julia's house.

Grip spent another twenty minutes passing by stores and shops without even seeing their displays and had made a loop on both sides of the business district. He finally figured he was close enough to the appointed hour as he turned south on Fourth Street.

After he switched sidewalks, he soon passed two men walking in the opposite direction and chatting loudly. He stepped aside to let them pass without paying them any attention.

But after he'd continued past, the slightly shorter man turned and looked back at him as he and his partner continued to Main Street.

"What are you lookin' at, John?" Bill Jones asked.

John Schuster glanced back again before replying, "That feller we just passed looked like Taylor's kid. The one that Mickey sent me to talk to when he got back into town."

Bill then stopped and looked at the receding pedestrian and asked, "Are you sure? What would he be doin' here?"

"I could be wrong, I guess. Do you think I should tell the boss?"

"It won't hurt to let him know."

John nodded then they started walking again and soon turned onto Main Street.

Grip passed Cornelia's Café a few minutes later and wondered if Gary had hired another waitress or already had another one working with Julia. He'd ask her later, hopefully when they were rid of Steve.

He turned onto Charlotte Street and began counting the numbers. Only about one in three had a number scrawled somewhere so the postman would know where to leave their letters, but it was enough for him.

He passed 174 and took a deep breath before turning onto the packed dirt path to the front of the Albert house.

After stepping onto the short porch, he knocked loudly on the door and waited.

He heard Julia's muffled voice shout, "I'll get it."

But just a second later, he heard a man's much louder voice yell, "Stay put. I'll see who it is. It had better not be that same feller from last week."

Grip could tell by the tone in the man's voice that he wasn't pleased about being interrupted and prepared to face an angry Steve Albert. At all costs, Grip had to prevent him from just slamming the door in his face as he'd done to the Pinkerton agent.

He barely had time to work up a smile before the door was ripped open and he faced the stormy eyes of Steve Albert.

“What do you want?” he snapped.

“Mister Albert?” Grip asked politely, “My name is Samuel Taylor. I’m an attorney from St. Louis and I’m here because of a bequeath made by a client.”

“A bequeath? What the hell is that?”

“It’s something that people leave in their last wills and testaments to friends and relatives after they die. In this case, my client, God rest his soul, left a sum of money to a Miss Julia Marley. I was told that she lives at this address. May I speak to her please?”

Steve Albert’s anger evaporated but there was a short pause before he asked, “How much is this bequeath?”

“I’m not at liberty to reveal the amount to anyone but Miss Marley. Does she live here or not? She was difficult to track down and my office needed to engage the Pinkerton Detective Agency to find her. They reported that it was most likely that she was here but didn’t have the opportunity to meet her.”

“Yeah, she’s here. Come in and you can talk to her.”

“Thank you,” Grip replied as he followed Steve Albert into the house.

It was a remarkably tidy house considering the condition and the presence of four children. He attributed it mainly to

Emily because Julia worked most days. In her advanced condition, she must collapse each night in exhaustion.

Before Steve had a chance to bellow for Julia, Emily and Julia entered the front room, leading twelve-year-old Millie, who was carrying her two-year-old sister Mary, while four-year-old Teddy walked slowly behind everyone almost for protection.

"Julia, this here's a lawyer from St. Louis. He says that he has some money for you 'cause one of his customers died."

Emily had taken a seat, and her children all either sat near her or stood beside her. Grip was surprised by the advanced stage of her pregnancy even though Julia had told him and hoped she didn't go into labor for at least the rest of the day. Her condition also caused him concern about his plan to have the family go back to St. Louis.

But that was a future issue. For it to get that far, the first act had to work when Steve Albert took the bait.

Julia looked at Grip and asked, "Who are you and why would you have money for me?"

"As I told Mister Albert, my name is Samuel Taylor, and I'm an attorney from St. Louis. I represent the estate of a recently deceased client who left a bequeath of two thousand dollars to a Miss Julia Marley. We had her birth certificate, but little else. We hired the Pinkerton Agency to track you down, but before we go any further, Miss Marley, I'll need you to answer a few questions to verify that you are the valid recipient of the bequest."

"Alright."

"What was your mother's full name?"

"Charlotte Mary Marley."

"What is the date of your birth?"

"The eleventh of October 1859."

"Finally, what is the name of your father?"

Julia stared at Grip for three heartbeats before quietly answering, "I don't know my father's name."

Grip smiled and said, "I'm sorry about that last question, Miss Marley, but I needed to be sure for another reason that will become obvious when we do the paperwork."

"You ain't gonna give her the money?" Steve asked sharply.

"Of course, I am. I am obligated by law and the orders of the probate judge. I surely didn't take a train across the state for no reason. I'll just need Miss Marley to accompany me back to my hotel room to sign a receipt before I give her the bequest."

Julia glanced at Emily before looking back at Grip and asking, “You want me to come with you to your hotel room alone?”

“You may be escorted if you wish, Miss Marley. Mrs. Albert could come with you, but I don’t believe she is in any condition to make the long walk. Perhaps Miss Albert would like to accompany you.”

Julia looked at her cousin and asked, “Millie, do you want to come along?”

On cue and before she could answer, Steve quickly said, “I’ll come along. I don’t trust this character.”

“Alright,” Julia replied.

Grip could see the excitement and greed in Steve Albert’s eyes as he waited for Julia to start toward the door.

He smiled at Emily before turning and walking behind Julia and could almost feel Steve Albert’s hot breath on his neck as the man strode behind him.

Once they reached the sidewalk and started walking east, Grip said, “I’m staying at the Merritt House on the second floor. This won’t take long.”

“That’s good because I need to return to help my aunt. I normally work as a waitress at a café just down the road, but

I'm off today for personal reasons. You're fortunate to find me at the house."

"I hope that it's nothing serious, but the large bequest should help you and your family considerably. You could even buy a new house with that much money."

"Who was your client?" she asked.

"That's one of the oddities of this situation. My client made it clear in his will that his identity must remain secret when processing his bequest to you. That also made it necessary for the bequest to be made in cash rather than a draft which would leave a paper trail back to him. If you knew the circumstances, then you'd understand."

"Your client was my father; wasn't he?" Julia asked as they turned onto Fourth Street.

"I'm not at liberty to answer that question, Miss."

"I understand."

They had kept their voices at a sufficient volume for Steve Albert to hear every word, but Grip suspected that even if they had whispered, he would have strained to listen. He had taken the hook and now Grip was almost literally reeling him in. He wasn't sure if the man was going to run, but all the indications were that he'd rush home, pack his things and disappear.

As they continued north on Fourth Street, Grip began making idle conversation about his imaginary law office in St. Louis to pass the time and to build his bona fides for Steve Albert. It wasn't difficult as he was sure that the man had never even been inside a law office, but Grip used his experience with James Ellis and Roger McCall to fill in any gaps.

Julia played her part even better than he'd expected and those had been high standards. She hadn't given a hint that she had met him before, or that she knew what to expect when they got to his hotel room. She hadn't even hesitated when he'd ask her cousin to join them rather than Steve. Julia had a very quick mind.

They turned onto Vine Street and soon reached Merritt House, then passed through the lobby and climbed the stairs to the second floor. Grip opened the door to his room and let Julia and her uncle enter before closing the door. The curtain for the second act in the play was rising.

"Please step over to the desk and we'll get this process completed quickly," Grip said as he stepped past the bed.

When he reached the desk, he pulled out the chair, then smiled at Julia and said, "If you'll have a seat, Miss Marley, I'll get the paperwork."

He opened the bottle of ink and set the pen on the desk before picking up his new valise and setting it on the nearby dresser.

He could feel Steve Albert's eyes burning a hole in the back of his head as he slid out the folded sheets of his homemade pseudo will, then pulled out the two bundles of bank notes.

Grip glanced at Steve before setting the two packets on the desk and unfolding the sheets of paper.

"As I've already explained what is in my client's will, Miss Marley, I feel that all we need to do now is to have you sign the bottom of the document as a receipt and then you can have your bequest."

"Alright."

Grip then slid the papers before Julia who dipped the pen's nib into the ink and then waited until Grip placed his finger beside a blank line on the page.

"Sign here, Miss Marley."

Julia signed and then set the pen near the bottle of ink before looking up at Grip and smiling.

"You may count the money before you leave if you'd like, Miss Marley."

"That won't be necessary. Surely, an attorney wouldn't cheat a client, even one who is no longer able to file a complaint."

Grip grinned before he answered, "There are some of my fellow lawyers who might take advantage of such an unusual situation, but I am not one of them."

Julia picked up the two bundles and said, "I didn't bring my purse."

"I only brought one of my lawbooks with me, so why don't I let you have my valise? I can buy another when I return to St. Louis."

"Are you sure, Mister Taylor. I don't wish to be an annoyance."

"You are hardly that, Miss Marley. In fact, I'd like to take you both to dinner in the hotel restaurant to celebrate your windfall."

Julia continued to play her part in the tradition of a great stage actress when she replied, "I wish that I could, but I do need to return to help my aunt."

Steve quickly said, "I'll help her, Julia. Why don't you go along with Mister Taylor and have a good time for a change? I'll take the satchel back for you 'cause some bad sort might see you with it and rob you."

Grip was almost surprised that he was so transparent. He had expected that Julia was going to have to at least suggest that he take the valise back to the house because she would be uncomfortable carrying that much money. His sudden response only confirmed Grip's belief that Steve Albert would be gone by the time he escorted Julia home.

Julia nodded then said, "Thank you, Steve. Tell Aunt Emily that I'll be home as soon as possible."

"I'll do that."

Grip then slid his Missouri lawbook from the valise and slipped the two bundles of ten-dollar notes into its empty spaces before closing the flap and handing it to Steve Albert.

Steve was all grins as he just turned and left the room holding the valise against his chest like a newborn babe rather than holding it by his side. He opened the door then quickly closed it behind him.

Grip could hear his hurried footsteps fading from the hallway when he turned to Julia and said, "That was surprising. I thought that you'd have to ask him to carry the money."

"I was about to do that, but he must not have wanted to give me the chance to use the money to leave town."

"He doesn't know you very well; does he?"

"He sees me but doesn't know me. Not even after all this time."

"Do you want to go to the restaurant at all? It's pretty early and I'm a bit worried about what he might do when he gets to the house. Emily might try to stop him from leaving, and that could put her in danger."

Julia grimaced slightly before replying, "Um, about that. I did manage to let my aunt know that odd things would be happening today and not to worry. I told her that if I left with a stranger, it would probably be with Steve and if he returned alone, just be nice and don't worry about what he did. I'm sorry, but I was worried about her."

Grip smiled as he said, "That's alright. It was a good idea, and it takes a weight off my shoulders. I know that you said she was in the late stages of pregnancy, but I was still taken aback by how close she must be to having the baby. Do you think that she'd be able to handle a long train ride in her condition?"

"That's another thing that I thought about last night after I talked to her. I know that I said that I wanted to come with you, and I do. But if Steve does leave, then I can't leave my aunt. She'll need my help more than ever. Do you understand?"

"I do and I'm pleased that you feel that way. It only increased my respect for you, Julia. We'll spend a few minutes talking about how to help your family before we walk to the house and find out if your uncle is still there."

"Okay. Are you going to sit down first to ease my neck strain?"

"Yes, ma'am," Grip replied before he pulled over the chair from the dressing table, set it four feet in front of her chair and sat down.

"Are you still going to go to Ogden?" she asked.

"I have to start my preparations. I'll stay around until I'm sure that everyone is safe and settled. If Emily says that she can handle the train trip, will you go with her?"

"I have to, Grip. But if she accepts your offer, once she's settled in her mansion, I'll join the others when they leave for Utah."

"You should stay with her even after the others leave until you're satisfied that she is happy and her children, including the one who hasn't made an appearance yet are at least content. Once everything is stable, if you still want to join me in Ogden, just get on a train."

"It sounds as if I'm breaking a promise and deserting you, and I don't want to sound like an ingrate, Grip. But I admit that I feel an obligation to my aunt. She didn't have to take me in when my mother was deathly ill. She'd never even met me and could have ignored my mother's letter, but she didn't.

"Even though she already had children of her own and was living in a small house, she gave me refuge. She had to convince Steve to let me come, and I don't know how she managed it. I was old enough by then to help around the house, so I guess that helped with her arguments. But it was my Aunt Emily, as much as my mother, who gave me hope. I have to do whatever I can to help her."

He took her hands and said, "You aren't breaking a promise nor are you deserting me, Julia. You're not even acting out of a sense of obligation or debt. You are doing this because you love your aunt, and you have an enormous sense of compassion. Now, for the first time in your life, you have the resources to provide help to someone you love. It's a wonderful feeling; isn't it?"

Julia's blue eyes moistened as she smiled at Grip and squeezed his hands.

"It is a very new sensation for me, Grip. I wish it would never leave."

"Well, in a little while, we'll go to the house and you can watch Emily's face when I make the offer. Is there a chance that she'll turn it down?"

"I don't think so, but she might want to move out of that mansion if it's as gaudy as you claim it to be."

"It's a mausoleum, Julia. It has sixteen large bedrooms on the two floors. At least it doesn't have a separate house for the servants like many of them do. If she sells the entire estate, she'd probably add another twenty thousand dollars to her bank account."

"She could buy a nice place for that much money. I don't know if she'd want to buy one in St. Louis, though. She's not fond of city life."

"After the baby's born, you could escort her and the rest of the Albert family to Ogden."

Julia quickly said, "I hadn't thought of that. I'll have time to discuss all of that with her after you've gone."

"There is a lot of the unknown in the future for all of us, Julia. But do you know what would make my life a lot better?"

"I can think of a few things but go ahead."

"I'd be ecstatic if I discovered that the name that's missing from your birth certificate was anything other than Lawrence P. Taylor."

She smiled and said, "So, would I. I don't suppose that we could assume that it was Santa Claus or maybe Emperor Augustus, can we?"

"I wish I could, Julia. It's such a frustrating omission. The twenty-year gap from when it was created makes it almost impossible to get that answer. The doctor who signed the certificate died seven years ago according to the Pinkertons."

"I still want to be close to you, Grip, even as a brother."

"I'd miss having you with me too, Julia. I wish it wasn't as a sister, but I can live with it. Just promise me that if you meet a man you want to marry, just tell me and I'll give you an enormous dowry, but I won't want to meet him."

She smiled as she said, "I promise. I hear that Mrs. Claus is seeking a divorce."

Grip laughed before saying, "I know it's only been a few minutes, but do you think we can start back now? We can take our time and go down Third Street."

"Okay. "Let's start our slow stroll."

He released her hands then they stood and headed for the door.

———

As Grip and Julia left the Merritt House, in an even nicer hotel on Delaware Street which ran parallel a block north of Main Street, four men huddled in room 222.

"Are you sure, John?" asked Mickey Mooney.

"I only saw his face for a couple of seconds, but it sure looked like him. He's got these gray eyes that are kinda spooky and he's pretty tall, too. I looked back at him but that didn't help. He was walkin' south on Fourth Street, but he wasn't searchin' for anything. He was thinkin' pretty hard, though."

"If it is the kid, why would he be here and not back in St. Louis spending his father's money?" asked Cajun Al.

Micky pulled on his right ear lobe as he slowly replied, "I don't have a clue, unless he's here tryin' to find us."

John quickly asked, "Why would he do that? He hated his old man and I figured he'd be happy to have him dead and gone."

"Maybe it has something to do with Ellis," Mickey mumbled.

Cajun Al asked, "Why would he care about him? Besides, he's just a damned book learner. He has enough money to send an army battalion to hunt us down."

A frustrated Mickey Mooney snapped, "Maybe he's just on vacation! *How the hell do I know?*"

John then said, "Want me to go look for him, boss? I'm the only one who knows what he looks like."

"Let me think about it for a minute," he replied, then said, "Just when things were workin' out, too."

The room was silent for two minutes before Mickey said, "Alright, here's what I want you three to do. Head south on Fourth Street and check out any hotels that way. If it is the kid, he's probably staying in one of 'em. John, you look out for the kid, but Al, you and Bill go into the liveries and inspect the horses. We've all seen those blacks that Taylor liked and they're easy to spot. If you see one in a hotel livery, get what you can out of the liveryman. Slip him a buck or two if you have to. If he's here, then we'll have to figure out why and if he's gonna be a problem."

As the three men nodded, Mickey stood then exclaimed, "Get going! We need to find out if he's here before he sees us."

"Yes, sir," John replied as each of them bounced to their feet and hurried out of the room.

Less than five minutes later, they were turning onto Fourth Street.

Grip and Julia had extended the twenty-minute walk to more than half an hour, but as they approached 176 Charlotte Street, Grip was concerned because they hadn't seen Steve Albert.

He looked over at Julia and said, "I thought we'd see him heading to the train station."

"Maybe he went to a saloon to celebrate."

"Or he could still be in the house. It's only been a little over an hour."

Julia just nodded, because she suspected that the last act of the day's performance wasn't going as they'd scripted.

They turned onto the dirt walkway and approached the house.

"I don't have to knock," Julia said before she reached for the doorknob.

She opened the door and each of them expected to hear Steve Albert's bellow as they stepped though the doorway, but they didn't.

After their eyes adjusted to the shadows, they saw Emily sitting on the couch with Mary on one side and Teddy on the other. Millie was standing with her arms folded looking at them.

Emily asked, "What took you so long? Why is the lawyer with you and not Steve? What's happening, Julia?"

Julia quickly asked, "Steve didn't come back an hour ago?"

"No. He went with you to the hotel and I was beginning to get worried because it was taking so long."

Julia looked at Grip who then said, "Mrs. Albert, I'm not an attorney. My name is Grip Taylor and I'm the son of Lawrence Preston Taylor and possibly Julia's half-brother."

Emily stared at Grip for a second before looking at Julia and asking, "Did you know all this?"

Julia nodded slowly as she replied, “Yes, Aunt Emily. Grip asked me not to tell you, so I disobeyed him and tried to prepare you for what might happen today. I’m sorry that I couldn’t give you more details.”

“I’m not upset at you, Julia. But what is happening? Where is Steve?”

“When we got to the hotel room, Grip gave me the two thousand dollars that was supposed to be the bequest from a man who didn’t even exist. Steve said that he’d take the money back to the house for me, but we expected him to come home, pack his things and just leave. You know that he’s threatened to do that more than once.”

“If he has that much money, then I think he’s already gone. He had nothing here of value, least of all his wife and children. He could already be halfway to Topeka by now.”

“Mrs. Albert,” Grip said, “I don’t want you to worry in the least about his departure. I have an enormous fortune left to me by my recently murdered father, so I’ll provide for you and your children.”

“Your father was murdered?” Emily asked.

“It was almost inevitable given the way he lived his life and the many enemies he made. I’ll let Julia give you the details, but we have a lot to discuss before we get to that point.”

He then smiled at Millie and said, “You may as well sit down, Miss Albert. This could take a while.”

She returned his smile and sat down in a nearby chair.

Julia then pulled a straight-backed chair to the center of the room facing the couch and almost pushed him onto the seat before stepping to the chair beside Millie and sitting down herself.

With all of their eyes focused on him, Grip started his explanation with the circumstances that had first made him want to leave St. Louis and then his discovery of the birth certificate, which had driven him to find Julia. He even explained the vague sibling connection between them because of that blank space on the record of her birth.

He had planned on just making the offer, but as soon as he'd seen the look in Emily's eyes, he felt that she deserved the same full explanation he had given to Julia.

He paused often to listen for the unexpected return of Steve Albert, but no one asked any questions as he narrated the story. Of course, the only two Alberts who understood what he was saying were Emily and Millie. He didn't believe that Millie would say anything without her mother's permission. He finally reached the point in his narration where Steve left the hotel and felt it was time to make his offer.

“Emily, I told Julia when I met her yesterday that, depending on her personality and situation, I might offer her my father's estate in St. Louis and fifty thousand dollars. She declined the offer, even after she'd told me that she wanted to join me in Ogden. I've described the property to you and I probably minimized its grandeur. It's almost like one of those English castles you see in storybooks.

"Anyway, as she turned the offer down and I have no intention of keeping the place after those I left behind join me in Utah, I'll make the same offer to you. If you'd like, I'll arrange for you and your family to take the train to St. Louis. I'll give a letter to Julia, who will be accompanying you, to instruct my banker to sign the deed over to you and put fifty thousand dollars into an account for you. The property would be yours to do with as you please which includes selling it. I can buy you a nicer home here if you'd like and still create a bank account, but understand that as your husband, if Steve found out about it, he'd be legally entitled to the house and the money."

Emily sat in stunned silence for more than two minutes as she tried to digest the incredible promise that had just been set before her. She absent-mindedly stroked her swollen belly as she thought.

She finally said, "I don't know if I'd want to live there, Mister Taylor. It would be a totally alien life for me and the children. Have you met my son, Billy?"

"No, ma'am. Julia described him to me, and he sounds like a fine young man."

"He is, but I don't know if he'd want to leave. I don't think we'd be safe here either. Do you have any other suggestions?"

Grip glanced at Julia then replied, "I talked to your niece before we left the hotel and I still believe it would be safer for you to go to St. Louis and live in the mansion with whom I now consider my family. If you think your condition would allow for an eight-hour train ride, then once you arrived, you'd be able to relax in complete safety and when your time comes, your baby can be delivered by an excellent doctor. When you and Julia think the baby can travel, you can have them sell the mansion and join us in Utah. I'll even have a new house built for you before you arrive."

"I like that idea much better. Can we do that, Julia?"

Julia asked, "Do you think you'll be all right for the journey to St. Louis, Aunt Emily?"

"I think so. I'm not due for two more weeks, but I have a feeling that I'm harboring more than one infant. I wasn't this big even for Billy."

"If you can handle the train ride, then we'll start the arrangements tomorrow. Can you help, Grip, or will you be leaving for Ogden?"

"I'm staying until the last one of you steps onto the train. I'll buy first-class tickets on the express so it will be a lot more comfortable."

"Thank you, sir," Julia replied with a smile before asking, "Are you going to stay for dinner and meet Billy?"

"I want to make sure that you are all safe before I leave and I'd like to meet him, too."

"Good. I'll start supper and you can chat with Aunt Emily and Millie, if you can get her to talk. She's a little shy and you have very scary gray eyes."

Grip laughed before saying, "Only when I need them to be, ma'am."

Julia smiled as she stood then left the front room and headed for the kitchen.

———

While Grip was trying to coax Millie out of her shell, Cajun Al and Bill Jones entered the livery of the Merritt House. Their search at the Windsor Hotel on the next block had been fruitless, and they had greater expectations of finding the black gelding at this one because there weren't any other hotels close to Fourth Street.

They walked down the long, wide center of the livery and Bill headed toward the liveryman to talk to him and distract him while Al checked the horses.

Al let him go and began scanning the stalls for Taylor's mount. If his father hadn't been so insistent on having only completely black horses as a symbol of his wealth and position, it would have been much more difficult to spot the kid's horse. But after passing four stalls, he stopped and grinned. Pitch had his nose buried in his feed bag but there was no mistaking the animal. He would have been a perfect model for a legendary king or general and didn't have a speck of discoloration to mar his black coat.

He quickly joined Bill Jones who had just said something to the liveryman that elicited a belly laugh.

Cajun Al kept a disinterested façade as he reached his partner and smiled at the liveryman.

"I reckon my pal told you about the time he tried to shoot a rattlesnake and the ricochet nicked our big boss's right butt cheek."

Igor Titov laughed again then shook his head and said, "No, sir, but that sounds pretty funny, too."

Al then said, "I really like that black over there in the fifth stall. I've only seen a few others like him, and they were all back east in one feller's place. I didn't figure I'd ever see another one."

"You mean there are more beauties like him?"

"Yes, sir. They're owned by a friend of mine named Taylor. I wonder if the man who rode in on this one bought it from Mister Taylor."

"I don't figure he bought him, mister. That horse belongs to a Mister Sam Taylor. He has that handsome red gelding in the next stall, too. He's stayin' in the hotel if you want to talk to him. Do you reckon he's your friend who owns those others or just a relative?"

"Maybe we'll go and see him. Is he alone? I don't want to bother him if he is in the company of a lady."

Igor snickered then replied, "He showed up alone, but I saw him walkin' past with a real handsome filly a little while ago, so he might be, um, occupied."

Al laughed before he said, "Then I reckon it'll be better if we check in with him later. Do you know how long he's gonna stay in town or why he's here?"

"He's paid up for the week, but I don't know where he's headed. He said he was from St. Louis, so he might be headed back that way."

Al popped the liveryman on the left shoulder then handed him a silver dollar before saying, "This is for your help, my friend. I'm glad we saw the horse and appreciate lettin' us know about Sam Taylor."

Igor was grinning at Al as he slid the coin into his overall's center pocket and then waved to the two men as they left the livery.

As he watched them exit the doors, he was happy to have the dollar in his pocket, but there was something about the two men that bothered him. They weren't guests and they hadn't even asked about the livery itself or the rates, so they weren't planning to get rooms in the hotel. There was something wrong about their interest in Mister Taylor's black gelding. They didn't have the look of lawmen or even Pinkerton agents, either. Mister Taylor had seemed like a right nice young feller and had already tipped him five dollars to take extra care of his horses and gear. He'd also given the same amount to Elrod White, the other day shift liveryman.

He walked to the other end of the stalls where Elrod was mucking out a mess left by a tan mare.

The two liverymen discussed the unusual behavior of the two men and agreed that the best course was to tell Mister Taylor about them when they saw him again.

Before Igor returned to the desk near the middle of the livery, Elrod said, "I'd rather be on good terms with Mister Taylor anyway, Igor. Did you see those guns he's got with him? I ain't never seen a Winchester with a black stock like that and that Sharps looks almost new."

"I reckon that Mister Taylor can deal with the likes of those two, but I wish I'd been smart enough to ask their names to let him know who they were."

"Bah! They woulda lied to you anyway."

Igor nodded then waved and headed back to his desk to write a note for Mister Taylor in case he didn't stop by to visit his two horses.

Grip finally met Billy Albert at six-fifteen and after being introduced by Emily, Grip shook his hand.

"Your mother has a lot to tell you, Billy. I'm going to go into the kitchen and help Julia with the cooking."

"You can cook?"

"I'm a bachelor, Billy. If I couldn't cook a steak at least, then I'd be as skinny as Millie."

Millie laughed then said, "I don't think so, Grip. You'd have to lose about fifty pounds to get close."

Grip smiled at Millie then waved and headed for the kitchen.

Billy watched him leave, then looked at his grinning younger sister, wondering why she had been so friendly to a stranger as walked across the room and sat down near his mother.

While Emily explained the enormous change that Grip had brought to their lives, Grip helped Julia prepare their supper. It wasn't exactly a culinary wonder, but there was plenty of stomach-filling food and he got to spend more time getting to know her.

As he slid the tray of warmed biscuits from the oven, he asked, “Do you think you’ll be safe tonight?”

“I think so. If Steve had just gone to a saloon to celebrate his sudden wealth, he’d be too drunk to walk back, but I don’t think he’s in Kansas City anymore.”

“At least he doesn’t have a gun. Did you want me to leave one with you before I go?”

“You aren’t armed, Grip. How could you leave me a gun, even if I knew how to use one?”

He opened his tweed jacket and showed her the Colt Shopkeeper before saying, “I can show you how to fire it before I go. It’s not hard to learn and you’re a smart lady.”

“No, that’s alright. I’d probably just shoot my toe off anyway. We’ll be fine.”

“I like what I saw in Billy. He wasn’t shaken by my appearance or the absence of his father.”

“You’ll like him better the more time you spend with him.”

“I won’t have much time because you’ll be on the train heading east on Thursday. The eastbound express leaves late at night but arrives in St. Louis in the morning.”

“That might be difficult for Mary and Teddy. Is there another time?”

"There is a normal passenger run that departs on Thursday morning and arrives in St. Louis at six in the evening. It stops more often, but the departure and arrival times may suit the youngsters better."

"Can you get us tickets on that one?"

"I'll do that tomorrow, Miss Taylor."

———

Grip left the Albert home just before eight o'clock. Billy was excited about the opportunity for a new life and expressed his thanks to Grip before he left. Grip told him to notify his boss that he was quitting and then return to the house to help with the move on Thursday.

Emily and Millie had kissed him on the cheek before he had just smiled at Julia and told her that he'd see her in the morning. It had been an awkward moment for both of them.

He made a point of scanning the streets searching for Steve as he walked back to the hotel. He had thought about visiting the closest saloon to see if he was there, but realized it was pointless. If he was tossing the cash at the bartender, then he'd be on the floor and the two thousand dollars would be lifted from the valise by the first sober man who could reach the leather satchel. It was the valise that made it more likely that he'd just boarded a train out of town. He was technically a thief and even Grip could arrest him, so once he decided to keep the money, he had to escape from the law. Grip wondered if Steve thought that because he was Julia's uncle, that he was legally entitled to the money.

———

Steve most definitely knew he could be arrested and thrown in prison for a long time if he was caught. The last place he wanted to be was at 176 Charlotte Street, and he didn't want to stay in Kansas City for a moment. Luckily, he knew just the place to go where no one would be able to find him and soon, he'd be out of Missouri altogether.

———

Grip was still wondering where Steve had gone when he entered the hotel. As he crossed the lobby, the desk clerk called out to him and then waved him over.

Grip stepped close to the window and the clerk handed him a folded sheet of paper as he said, "Igor Titov, one of the liverymen, left this for you."

Grip nodded then opened the note, which he was sure the clerk had read, then silently turned and headed for the front doors.

He soon entered the livery and as soon as he passed through the wide doorway, Igor spotted him then began to approach.

"You wanted to see me, Igor?" he asked as he held out the note.

"Yes, sir. It's probably nothin', but earlier today, two fellers came in lookin' at the horses. One of 'em started talkin' to me and tellin' me funny stories while the other one looked at the stalls. Then he came over and asked me about your black gelding. He said he knew about more horses that looked the same and were owned by his friend named Taylor.

"They were both tryin' to be like my pal, but there was somethin' about 'em that bothered me. They asked if you were alone and I told 'em that I saw you with a young lady. I probably shouldn't have done that. They asked me how long you were gonna stay here and I told 'em that you had paid up for the week. I'm awful sorry that I told 'em so much, Mister Taylor."

Grip tried to think of anyone who would ask about his horses but the only one he could think of was Steve Albert, who might have picked up a friend to join him, so he asked, "Was one of them a man a couple of inches shorter but much heavier? He had a full black beard, too."

"No, sir. Neither of those boys looked like that. They were both about the same height but kinda slim, and both were clean shaven with brown hair and eyes. They were both packin' iron, too."

"They were wearing pistols?"

"Yes, sir. Looked like they knew how to use 'em, too."

"Well, don't worry about what you told them, Igor. I'm very grateful that you told me about their interest. Did they comment on my guns?"

"No, sir. I don't reckon that they even noticed 'em."

"Okay. I'll keep an eye out for them."

As Igor nodded, Grip pulled his loose bills from his pocket and handed Igor two twenty-dollar bills as he said, "Give one to Elrod just so he doesn't get jealous. If you can hide my rifles and saddlebags, I'd appreciate it."

Igor stared at was almost a month's wage and was more than pleased that he'd written the note as he grinned and replied, "We'll keep 'em outta sight, Mister Taylor."

Grip smiled then turned and before he left the livery, he stopped at his saddlebags and pulled out his black gunbelt with the Remington and the angled sheath. As he walked back to the hotel, he was trying to think who it was that had been searching for him. His father had made many enemies over his lifetime, so there was a very long list of men who might wish to cause him harm just out of spite. Yet not many of them knew he was in Kansas City. Since he'd returned from Michigan, he had expected to be besieged by his father's sycophants trying to get close to whom they assumed would be the new Emperor Taylor, but that hadn't happened. He guessed it was because of the timing and circumstances of his father's death, but whatever the reason, he was grateful for the relative privacy. The only one of his father's cronies he'd met was James Ellis because he had no choice but to meet with the man.

As he passed through the lobby and ascended the stairs, the appearance of the lawyer's name in his mind triggered the connection to Mickey Mooney and his three thugs. Detective Nall had passed along the rumor that they might have gone west, and that three men had bought those tickets to the Kansas City express the night of the murder. *Had Mooney's men deserted him?* The report of the Ellis murders had listed just three men in the house, and none were big enough to be Mickey Mooney.

Grip wondered if Mickey had divested himself of his three men in the wake of the murders and they had gone to Kansas City. It made more sense than anything else he could come up with.

So, as he entered his room and began to strip, he tried to recall the descriptions of the two members of the gang whom he hadn't met. John Schuler met all of those physical characteristics, and Tom Truax had mentioned that the others were of the same average height and build.

But what he would do from now on would be to wear his holster with his black-handled Remington and its angled knife sheath. The Shopkeeper would become his backup weapon as it was more difficult to extract. He'd start carrying his Deputy U.S. Marshal's badge as well.

Regardless of who those two men were, he'd try to avoid them until Julia and her family were on the train heading for St. Louis.

He removed his hat and jacket and tossed them onto the bed before he sat at the desk and after taking some of his paper, opening the bottle of ink and dipping the nib inside, he began to write a letter to Rich Bennett.

———

"He's at the Merritt House?" Mickey asked.

John nodded and replied, "Yes, sir. I had to give the clerk a couple of bucks to look away while I read the register. He signed in as Sam Taylor from St. Louis."

Mickey then looked at Cajun Al and asked, "He has two horses in the livery? Why did he have two?"

Al shrugged before he answered, "The liveryman said that he was with some young woman and I reckon he was gonna take her out ridin'."

"You should have asked him."

"I figured I was pressin' my luck already. What do you want to do about him, boss?"

"I'm not sure yet. He's four blocks away, so if he's searching for us, then he'll show up here in the next couple of days."

"*We're gonna just let him find us?"* Bill Jones asked in astonishment.

Mickey didn't like the idea even as he'd said it. He hated being on the defensive and not even having a clue to the reason that the kid was in Kansas City was driving him crazy.

"Yeah, I don't like it either. Let me think about it."

"Maybe he's plannin' on putting the law onto us," John suggested.

"That still doesn't make any sense. I reckon he might even give us a bonus for makin' him rich."

Cajun Al asked, "What about Ellis?"

"What do you mean? He probably hated that lawyer more than he hated his father."

"If he ain't here for revenge, then why is he here at all?" asked John in obvious frustration.

"That's the mystery. I don't want to have a bunch of lawmen bust into the room with their guns drawn," he said then looked at Bill Jones and said, "I want you to keep an eye on the hotel and see what he's doin'. Follow him at a distance and keep outta sight. If he goes to the law, get back here and let me know. We'll have to get out of here as fast as we can. If he gets on a train back to St. Louis, then we'll be able to start our action here."

"Okay, boss," Bill replied, "I'll be over there first thing in the mornin'."

Mickey nodded but knew that he wouldn't be completely at ease until the kid was long gone and maybe not even then. Maybe they'd have to get out of Missouri altogether and head even further west where the number of lawmen dropped off to almost nothing.

Since they'd been in Kansas City, they had tried to strike up friendships or even just alliances with elements of the criminal community but hadn't made even a small penetration into the local world of crime.

The presence of a large sheriff office and a healthy police department modeled after the one in St. Louis had already planted the seed of moving west into Mickey's mind. They still had a good bankroll and the possibility that Taylor might be searching for them added the final touch of fertilizer to that seed, and the thought blossomed until it was fully grown in his mind.

He'd let Bill keep an eye on Taylor, but he'd start his plans for them to move west to Colorado where the gold was.

———

While Mickey was planning his own departure on tomorrow's train heading west, Steve Albert wasn't having to plan anything. After taking the cash-filled valise, he quickly made his way to the docks. He knew most of the crews on the riverboats that plied the Missouri, so after he glanced at the chalkboard schedule, he walked along the wharf and crossed onto the deck of *The Dakota Queen.*

It wasn't difficult for him to get a bunk in the crew's quarters as a deckhand, but he'd get off the boat when it docked in Omaha and then he'd enjoy his unexpected windfall. He'd be as free as he was in his bachelor days, but he'd have the money to make this second go around a lot more interesting.

Grip's letter of explanation and instructions to Rich Bennett had taken him six pages to write and he still wasn't sure if he'd missed anything.

He finished the letter and after letting it dry, he folded it and slid it into the envelope he'd already addressed. He'd mail it tomorrow at the train station's post office and then send a telegram to Rich letting him know of the letter and the arrival of the family on Thursday evening's train from Kansas City.

By the time he blew out the lamp and crawled into his bed, he had a difficult time trying to put the day's events into chronological order. As an engineer, he hated disorder in anything, and his brain was in chaos.

The one thing he could focus on was the surprise appearance of two of Mickey Mooney's boys at the hotel livery. He expected that they'd be watching the hotel tomorrow, so he'd use the rear door to leave the building. It was going to be a cat and mouse game until he escorted Julia and her family to the train. After that, he had no idea what he'd do about them.

He never even gave a thought to visiting the local law. He suspected correctly that they wouldn't be interested in crimes that had happened on the other side of the state. He still didn't think that Mickey Mooney himself was in Kansas City, and maybe if he had, he would have at least mentioned it to the police. Having a known murderer in your town who could be easily identified might be worth their attention.

CHAPTER 9

Grip awakened early, then bathed, shaved and dressed in a fresh set of clothes. He didn't wear his tweed jacket, but after strapping on his shoulder holster, he donned his black leather vest and then wrapped his gunbelt around his waist. He studied his appearance in the large mirror and admitted it was an impressive look for him, even without Pitch and his black saddle. He had intentionally selected a medium gray Stetson and wore a gray shirt that was close to the shade of his hat. The shirt was tucked into a new pair of blue denim britches.

He slid the letter into his black saddlebags, then left the room and after a quick breakfast, he strode down the hallway to leave the hotel.

Grip exited the back door and stepped into the shadowed alley before he turned left and headed for the next alley before he headed south. He finally stepped onto Fifth Street and was reasonably sure he hadn't been seen. He still checked the street behind him and even though it was well-trafficked, he didn't spot anyone paying him any attention.

He reached the Albert house and knocked on the door, hoping that Steve wouldn't be the one to open it.

Julia opened the door and Grip thought his heart had stopped as she smiled at him.

"Come in, Mister Taylor," she said cheerfully before he remembered to move his feet.

She hadn't affected him this badly even when he'd first seen her as a pretty waitress at Claudia's Café. He had no idea why she had such an impact but admitted that he had thoroughly enjoyed the unexpected rush.

"No sign of Steve?" he asked as he entered and closed the door.

"Not a whisper. Billy went to the docks to tell his boss that he wouldn't be back. I told him not to make a big deal about the pay that they owed him."

"When will he be back?"

"Soon, I would think. You look decidedly different this morning. No tweed jacket and you're wearing a pistol. Is it because of Steve?"

"No. I'll explain in a minute. How are things going?"

"A lot smoother than I had expected. It makes a big difference if you don't have to worry about taking things like furniture or cookware."

Julia started walking toward the kitchen and Grip followed, pulling his hat from his head as they entered the hallway.

When they entered the small kitchen, he found Emily sitting at the table spooning something brown into Mary while Teddy sat behind his bowl of oatmeal shoveling it into his busy mouth.

Millie smiled at him and said, “Good morning, Grip. You look very nice today.”

“Thank you kindly, ma’am,” Grip replied with a grin.

“I’ll pour you a cup of coffee and you can tell me why you’re wearing your pistol,” Julia said as she walked to the cookstove.

Grip waited until she handed him the cup then said, “One of the liverymen told me that two men were asking questions about me. From the descriptions he gave me, they sounded like two of Mickey Mooney’s men. I’m not sure, of course, but it’s the only thing that makes sense.”

“Are they following you?” Julia asked as she sat beside Emily.

“No, ma’am. They were long gone from St. Louis before I left. If it is them, then they might be thinking that I’m following them. That doesn’t make a lot of sense either, but I’m not about to go looking for them. I’ll keep an eye out for them and even left the hotel through the back door to avoid being seen.”

Grip quickly inhaled his coffee and set the empty cup on the counter then had to deal with the after effects of the hot liquid.

Julia saw his distress, but didn't smile as she asked, "Are you in any danger?"

"I doubt it. I'm going to rent a carriage tomorrow morning to get everyone to the train station. I'm going over there in a little while to buy your tickets and send a letter to the folks at the estate to let them know you're coming. I'll send a telegram, too. Tonight, I'll write another letter and give it to you in case the one that I post gets lost in the mail."

"We'll be ready to go by lunchtime."

"That's great. Oh, while I'm here, I have to remember to give you money for clothes and other things until you get settled in St. Louis."

Emily said, "We'll be fine, Grip."

"I like an even balance in my saddlebags, so I'll just give you a thousand dollars."

"Just a thousand dollars?" Julia asked with wide eyes and a smile.

"I know," Grip said as he dug in his black saddlebags and picked out a packet of ten-dollar notes and handed it to Julia.

She didn't protest, but just slipped the bundle into her dress pocket as if it were some loose change, then asked, "How long are you going to stay this morning?"

“I just stopped by to make sure that you were all safe and to see if you needed my help with anything. You seem to be doing fine and as soon as Billy returns, I’ll head for the train station.”

“Can you at least sit down until then?”

“Yes, ma’am,” Grip replied before setting his saddlebags on the floor then taking a seat in one of the two empty chairs at the table.

Emily had many questions that she’d thought of the night before, so Grip had little time to do anything other than provide her with answers. Each of his positive responses seemed to give Emily more comfort about being uprooted from the home where she’d raised her children.

He was in the middle of an answer when Billy loudly entered the front room. Grip quickly finished his reply before Billy popped into the kitchen wearing a grin.

“Mister Weston was mad when I quit but was happier when I told him that I didn’t need to be paid.”

He then looked at Grip and asked, “How come you’re wearing a gun?”

“Your mother will tell you, sir. But now that you’re here, I need to sneak over to the train station to get your tickets.”

“Sneak?”

Grip smiled then stood, hung his saddlebags over his shoulder and said, “Another question your mother or cousin to answer.”

He smiled at Emily and Millie then as he was about to look at Julia, she stood and took his arm.

“I’ll escort you from the house, Mister Taylor.”

“Thank you, Miss Marley.”

The couple wore smiles as they walked down the hallway with no room to spare on either side.

After they left the house, Grip turned to Julia and said, “I’ll be back tomorrow morning at seven o’clock with the carriage. The train leaves at 8:15. You might want to have Emily pack food for Teddy and Mary. It’s a good idea to carry some for the adults, too. You’d be able to leave the train at some of the longer stops, but I’m not sure Emily will want to hurry off, stuff food into her stomach and then hustle back.”

“I wouldn’t, either. I’ll make sure we have a basket of edibles.”

Grip nodded as he stared into her bright blue eyes without saying anything.

After thirty seconds, she softly said, “I’ll see you tomorrow, big brother.”

He nodded then after letting out a long breath, he pulled on his hat and left the small porch before Julia reentered the house.

He walked down Charlotte Street without taking a side street as he headed for the Missouri River. The river took a sharp eastern turn after Kansas City and he wondered why the state of Missouri claimed this side of the river when most state borders were formed by prominent rivers.

The rails ran alongside the river, so when he had the tracks in sight, he turned north on Third Street. He wasn't looking for the Mooney boys as the traffic was too heavy for him to pick them out anyway.

He'd already decided to rent the carriage today and after he dropped everyone off at the station in the morning, he'd drive the carriage to the hotel two hours before his westbound train to Denver was scheduled to depart. He'd have Igor and Elrod get Pitch and Brick saddled then he'd check out and ride to the station. He should be out of Kansas City less than four hours after the eastbound train for St. Louis had left the station.

He bought five first-class tickets for St. Louis and was able to arrange for hot meals to be provided to the adults, a service which had surprised him. He found that the earliest westbound train that he thought gave him enough time to get his tasks done departed for Denver at 11:40. So, he bought a ticket and two horse transports for the AT&SF train. After he reached Denver, he'd have to board a Union Pacific train to Wyoming then travel a couple of hundred miles west before the tracks twisted south into Utah. It would be a much longer journey than if it had been a straight line from Kansas City to Ogden.

With the tickets in his saddlebags, he entered the post office. When he reached the counter, he said, “I’d like to have this go out on the express and then delivered immediately upon arrival in St. Louis. How can I do that?”

“Just pay the express delivery charge, sir. That service is only available at our larger post offices. It’s kinda pricey, though. It’ll cost you two dollars.”

“That’s worth it to me,” Grip said as he pulled out some bills and handed him a five.

The postman gave him his change then Grip watched him stamp the letter with EXPRESS DELIVERY.

Grip thanked him then turned and left the post office wondering if the clerk wasn’t going to just toss it into the bag with the regular mail.

He’d be sending his telegram next and he’d give Julia a letter as backup, so he supposed it didn’t matter. It was only two dollars, but a man could feed his large family for a week on two dollars. If it didn’t arrive by tomorrow morning, he’d have Rich file a formal complaint with the St. Louis post office, not that they’d do anything about it. He suspected that if his father had filed a complaint, heads would roll, maybe literally.

His telegram was on the wire ten minutes later, so his next stop was to rent the carriage. It had to be big enough for six, but he hoped that Julia would ride with him in the driver's seat. He'd only have a short amount of time with her until everyone arrived in Ogden. Of course, that was all dependent on when Emily had her baby, or babies as she suspected.

He didn't want to go far from the station to rent the carriage, and only had to walk a block and a half to find what he needed. The carriage wasn't fancy or overly expensive, but it was roomy. He rented the two-horse rig for two days and told the man at Ridley's Carriage and Buggy Rental that he'd probably be returning it midmorning tomorrow.

It was past noon when he drove the carriage along Vine Street's cobblestones. He wasn't sure that he should return to the hotel yet even if he was driving the carriage. He didn't want to interrupt the Albert family's preparations either, so instead of staying on Vine, he turned right on Fourth Street and headed for the business district.

Without realizing it, he didn't have to worry about being spotted any longer. Mickey had been growing twitchier with each passing minute without news from Bill Jones about the whereabouts of the Taylor kid.

As Grip was walking east on Charlotte Street to the train station, Mickey had sent Cajun Al to fetch Bill and tell him that they would be leaving Kansas City shortly. When Bill entered the room, he was still surprised to find that all of their things, including his own, had been packed.

"Why are we leavin'?" he asked as he scanned their travel bags.

"I don't want to risk that kid running to the law if he spots us. He may not recognize you or Al, but he knows John and I'm easy to pick out. We're going to take the train west out of here in an hour."

"Where are we goin'?" Bill asked as he picked up his travel bag.

"Denver. It's where all the gold is, and nobody is gonna look for us out there."

"Okay, boss."

Each of them grabbed his large travel bag and soon left the room. They may have been hard men, but they had always plied their trade in St. Louis, and while Kansas City wasn't nearly as large nor as cosmopolitan in nature, it was still a city. Denver was growing rapidly and would soon match and eclipse Kansas City, but it was far from tame and unlike St. Louis, many of the residents were armed. None of them were skilled on horseback either, and to learn how to adapt to the more rustic environment that faced them, they'd have to either disgorge some of the money they'd made for killing Lawrence Preston Taylor, or they'd have to relieve other men of their horses. The other serious failing in their background was that none of them had ever even used a rifle. Each of them was reasonably proficient with his Colt or Remington, but not a long gun. The weapon of choice for each of them was the sharp, heavy blade they wore with their gunbelts, or in Mickey's case, the enormous fists he could make to frighten any man.

It would take some hard lessons for them to realize that to survive in the dark side of society west of the Missouri River, they would need to adopt a very different way of killing. But many of those lessons wouldn't be necessary after they arrived in Denver. They could use their knives and pistols in town, but once the law recognized their presence, their ignorance would force them to abandon their long-developed tactics to find new and better methods.

In an almost choreographed ballet of shifting paths, while Grip was in the post office, Mickey Mooney and his three men arrived at the station to buy their tickets for the same train that Grip would be taking tomorrow.

Grip stepped out of the post office, and if he'd looked right, he would have seen them standing at the ticket window in a short queue to buy their tickets. But he turned to his left to go to the telegraph office and none of the four men so much as looked his way.

By the time Grip left the telegraph office, he quickly turned left again to look for a carriage rental service. He wasn't in view long enough for Mooney's men to see him, so by the unlikeliest of chances, Grip had left the station behind to rent the carriage and the men who had arranged for his father's murder soon boarded the AT&SF westbound train for Denver.

———

Grip drove the carriage through the streets of Kansas City for another hour before he turned it down Sixth Street and after turning east on Oak Street and driving two more blocks, he turned north on Fourth Street. He scanned the sidewalks and windows across from his hotel and didn't see anyone watching the front door, so he continued until he reached the livery then drove it through the big doors.

He waved at Igor and grinned as he pulled it to a stop and after setting the handbrake, clambered down the side.

"You bought a carriage?" Igor asked.

"No, sir. I just rented it for a couple of days. Can you take care of it? I'll need it to be ready to go tomorrow by seven o'clock. I'm going to drop off some folks at the train station, then come back and check out. Can you have my horses saddled and ready to go by say, nine o'clock?"

"No problem, Mister Taylor. Those boys ain't been back, either. You figure out who they were?"

"Just a guess, but I won't know unless I bump into them."

"I reckon you'd rather not. I see you're packin' iron yourself now."

"No point in giving them an advantage, Igor."

"Nope."

Grip gave Igor a quick salute then turned and after a brief visit with Pitch and Brick, he walked out of the livery through the big doors facing Fourth Street. If there was a watcher, he would have seen him driving the carriage into the livery anyway.

After entering the hotel, he headed for the restaurant and after taking a seat and lowering his black saddlebags to the floor, he gave his order to the waitress, who didn't seem concerned about the Remington at his hip.

As he ate his very well-seasoned fried chicken, he ran through the tasks he'd need to do before he left in the morning to pick up Julia, Emily and her children. It wasn't much, but he didn't want to visit their house before then and risk being trailed by Mooney's boys, if that's who they were. They would be unprotected tonight, and he wasn't about to put them in danger by association.

He made short work of his lunch and after leaving a dollar on the table, he snatched his saddlebags and hat, then left the restaurant, crossed the lobby and climbed the stairs to the second floor.

Once in his room, he set his saddlebags near the desk then disarmed himself before taking a seat at the desk to write the letter for Rich that he'd give to Julia in case his other letters didn't make it in time.

Because he'd already written a similar letter last night, this one took less time and was a page shorter. After the ink dried, he folded it and slid it into one of the hotel's envelopes. He smiled when he noticed that there were six envelopes on the desk again after he'd already used one yesterday.

He still had the pen in his hand, so he slid another sheet of blank linen paper from the stack and dipped the nip into the bottle to write another, far more difficult letter.

Before he touched the tip to paper, he thought about how he should address the letter. It should have been a simple, *Dear Julia,* but it sounded so common and purposeless. He wished he could express much more of his feelings in those first few words, but he felt as if he was on standing on a log surrounded by quicksand. One misstep could be a disaster.

After almost three minutes of thought he finally dipped the pen in the ink again and began to write:

Salve Carissime Julia,

I was at a loss about how to address this letter, and I hope that you understand why it was so difficult.

When I first discovered your birth certificate just two weeks ago, I was shocked. For someone who had grown up without any real family, knowing that I might have a sister somewhere was a revelation.

Finding it also created a mystery for me as there seemed to be no logical explanation for its presence in my father's safe, But I knew that Julia Marley was the daughter of Charlotte Marley who had been sent away from my father's house when I was a boy. I was convinced that you were his daughter and I committed myself to finding you. I wasn't sure where you were or what you were like, but I hired the Pinkertons to search for you.

Once they reported that they'd found you, I knew that I had to be the one to tell you the secret. I wasn't sure if you knew and even then, I wasn't convinced myself that you were my sister. Regardless of your parentage, I felt an obligation to provide for you and your mother because of my father's ill treatment of her.

When I first saw you in Claudia's Café as a waitress and not my sister, I was in awe of your appearance as I'm sure most men are. But when I talked to you, I felt a closeness that I had never experienced with any woman before.

Then you said that one sentence that made every bone in my body shudder when I realized that you were my sister, and it was the strangest mix of emotions that I ever hope to experience.

Since then, I've become less convinced that you are my father's daughter, but still can't rule out the possibility. You have none of the physical characteristics of my father with your golden blonde hair, blue eyes and soft oval face, but as much as I wish to ignore even that remote chance, I find that I can't.

Tomorrow, you will be going east, and I'll be traveling west. I know that I'll miss you long before you reach St. Louis. If there was any way to fill in a name on that blank line on your birth certificate, I'd rush back to St. Louis and beg to be allowed to court you.

While we may have joked about the situation, I seriously have no intention of blocking your path to happiness. If you do meet someone who will make you happy, don't wait for a miraculous solution to our dilemma that will probably never arrive.

I can't tell you how I feel because it would be the first brick in the wall which could keep you from the happy life that you deserve. While you are in St. Louis, don't become a hermit or a wallflower. Go to parties at least as a chaperone for Billy.

Enjoy life, Julia.

Amica mea in sempiternum,

Agrippa

Grip reread the letter twice and was reasonably sure that Julia couldn't read Latin, but if she could, or if she had someone interpret it for her, at least she'd have the letter.

As he folded it and slid it into one of the new envelopes, he wondered if it wouldn't be better to make the break now. If he gave her the letter, she might not go to those parties, even as a chaperone.

He wanted to be the selfless, noble man who could honestly say that all he wished was for her to be happy, even if it wasn't with him. But what he really had written was, 'go ahead and have fun, but I love you and please don't find someone else'.

He stared at the blank envelope as he held the inked pen in his hand. He took a breath then set the pen back on a blank sheet of paper to keep any ink drops from staining the desktop.

After almost two minutes of silent contemplation, he left it unaddressed and set it on the desk next to the second letter to Rich.

He stood and checked the time on his pocket watch. It was still mid-afternoon, and he thought he was ready for tomorrow morning, so he needed something to pass the time. He wanted desperately to go to make the walk to 176 Charlotte Street, but even if the watcher wasn't keeping an eye on him, spending more time with Julia would have the same effect as the letter in the blank envelope. It was best that he'd just drive everyone to the station and see them off in the morning. He'd have to keep his emotions in check, too.

He paced the room for ten minutes before a smile spread across his lips and he returned to the desk. He took a stack of linen paper on the desk before he twisted and pulled the black saddlebags closer to the desk. He opened the left saddlebag and rummaged around with his fingers beneath the cash until he felt the thin wooden cylinder then pulled the pencil out from under its expensive covering.

He sharpened it with his pocketknife then took one of the blank envelopes and folded it over to use as a straightedge. It wasn't exactly a draftsman's table, but he wanted to start designing the new houses and buildings for their new home in Ogden. It would keep his mind busy and away from his Julia conundrum.

Grip was just going to set basic ideas on the pages rather than fully developed blueprints. It would have to start with how many buildings he'd need. The easiest was the carriage house. So, he began with the basic outline which was going to be even larger than the one on his father's estate. It was going to house more horses and he wanted enough stalls for all of their animals to protect them in the harsh winters. He added unusual touches for the stables including four large dormers to let in light with the doors closed and a heat stove to keep the horses reasonably warm.

Once that was done, he had to pause to decide how many houses he'd need. He wanted to live alone, so he added one for Rich and Wilma Bennett and a second for Tom and Jenny Truax. He wasn't sure about the Alberts. He decided that he'd just create one standard design for the other houses and have two built. That would give them plenty of living space and if he needed more, he'd add them. His own house would be very different, and he'd design that one on the train ride tomorrow. If he had the time after leaving the train station, he'd swing by Carpenter's Stationery and Books and buy better materials.

———

In the days after he'd left St. Louis, the two couples had many conversations about the move and with the arrival of Grip's wire, the two couples were anxious to find what Grip had discovered in Kansas City, but none of them could have imagined what was on that single yellow sheet of paper that Rich slid from the Western Union envelope.

Rich unfolded the telegram and read:

RICH BENNETT 14 ARBOR ST ST LOUIS MO

FOUND SISTER IN KANSAS CITY
SENDING HER AND FAMILY OF FIVE TO YOU
EMILY ALBERT CLOSE TO GIVING BIRTH
WILL ARRIVE ON THURSDAY EVENING TRAIN
SEND CARRIAGE
SENT LETTER EXPRESS MAIL WITH DETAILS
WILL GIVE HER COPY
GOING TO UTAH AFTER THEY LEAVE
HOPE ALL IS WELL

GRIP TAYLOR MERRITT HOUSE KANSAS CITY MO

He looked at Wilma and exclaimed, “This is a surprise!”

“It’s going to be a crowded house after they arrive. I wonder how old the children are?”

“Well, the Pinkertons said that Julia Marley left to live with her mother’s older sister eight years ago when she was eleven, so I believe that would make her aunt almost forty years old by now. Her children could be anywhere from twenty to, well, not born yet. We have a lot to do before they arrive.”

“We certainly do,” Wilma replied.

The telegram inspired a melee of preparation. Jenny had been a midwife at six births, so she would be able to help Mrs. Albert, but suspected that Grip would want them to have the doctor at hand when she went into labor.

The surprising news outlined in the telegram made everyone anxious to read the letter with the details that Grip had sent via express mail.

———

Grip began designing the house and was still working on it when he began losing his light and he realized how late it was. He set his work aside, checked the time and found it was 8:10.

Grip hastily put his work into the saddlebags before he left the room and after a brief visit to the bathroom, he headed downstairs for his delayed supper.

His decision to engage his mind with something more constructive had cost him more time than he had anticipated. After gulping down his dinner, he paid his bill, then left the restaurant, stopped at the front desk to let them know that he'd be checking out in the morning before he trotted up the stairs and returned to his room. He didn't ask for a refund and the clerk didn't offer one.

He stripped and set his clothes aside for tomorrow then packed what was still loose and set the two envelopes on top his saddlebags to avoid leaving them behind.

He set his pocket watch alarm for five o'clock then slipped beneath the quilts. Things would settle down after he boarded the train for Denver. In four days, he'd be in Ogden and he'd start building his new life. It would be a life of uncertainty and potential danger, but it was the same for many people and few of them had the resources that were available to him.

Tomorrow, he'd say goodbye to Julia, and he hoped that it wouldn't be the last time he saw her but had to admit to that possibility. For that matter, he really wasn't sure how many would be joining him in Utah. They had been enthusiastic about the move before he left, but he had been the source of that enthusiasm and that was before he sent the Albert family to join them. Things might change among the four he'd left behind after they arrived, especially when Wilma and Jenny met Millie, Teddy and little Mary.

Then there was the very different change for the Alberts. Emily and Julia had grown up in St. Louis, so she had a good idea what to expect, but none of them had lived as lavishly as they would when they moved into the mansion. It would be a revelation to each of them, and there was a chance that Emily would change her mind.

Grip realized that there was a chance that he'd eventually be living by himself on his new property with at least three new houses and a nice set of stables. He'd find the dogs that he and Tom had talked about, so he wouldn't be completely on his own. He'd have most of the blacks sent to Utah along with the contents of the weapons room and the books even if they stayed. He'd be a well-armed, well-read twenty-five-year-old hermit living with his dogs and horses.

He snickered at the idea, but he'd get a better read on the mood back in St. Louis from the letters that would flow between his old home and his new. They would have at least six weeks to make the decision of whether or not to leave what they knew to venture into the unknown West of Utah Territory.

———

Grip rolled the carriage out of the livery in the early morning sun. It had been Igor who had suggested that it would be easier to just take his horses and gear with him, so after realizing that the liveryman was right, he let Igor and Elrod saddle Pitch and Brick while he moved his cache of weapons and packs to the stalls .

As he turned onto Fourth Street, he didn't bother looking for any spies as he set the carriage southward. He was wearing his tweed jacket over his black leather vest because the jacket's pocket had room for the lone letter that stuck out from the left pocket. He didn't want to forget to give it to Julia. He expected that his mind might be elsewhere, and he could have left it in his saddlebags with the blank envelope if it wasn't so visible.

When he arrived at 176 Charlotte Street, he pulled the carriage to a stop, set the handbrake and climbed down. He trotted down the walk and before he reached the small porch, the door flew open and Julia stepped outside wearing a light blue dress and a warm smile.

He returned her smile as she said, "You're even a little early."

"Yes, ma'am. I didn't want you to miss the train."

She hooked her arm through his and had to sidestep to get through the doorway. Once inside, Grip noticed the lineup of new travel bags and one basket.

Julia turned to look at him as she said, "We did some shopping yesterday, but I made sure we didn't go overboard."

"I'm glad that you thought of it. The good news is when I bought your tickets, I found that they offered a meal service to the first-class passengers. I paid for the service, so you'll have hot food served to you on the train."

"That sounds wonderful. We only packed some snacks for the adults. Most of the food in the basket is for Teddy and Mary."

"I'm glad that it worked out. Let's get everything loaded."

Grip, Julia, Billy and Millie quickly carried the travel bags and basket to the carriage and after it was stowed in the boot or in the driver's seat, Julia helped Emily into the carriage as Grip carried Mary from the house.

Soon everyone was seated, so Grip climbed into the driver's seat and released the handbrake. He had set two of the travel bags on the wooden seat to remove the possibility of Julia sitting beside him. It was going to be difficult enough without feeling her sitting so closely.

He made a U-turn and soon had the carriage rolling into the bright morning sun. He had to avoid a collision several times as the traffic was already building up and he had a difficult time finding wagons or riders in the glare. But after ten minutes of hazardous maneuvering, he pulled the carriage to a stop at the station. He may have started out early, but there were only forty minutes before the train was scheduled to depart.

After Julia stepped out of the carriage and began to help Emily, Grip scrambled down and walked to Pitch, lifted the flap of the left saddlebag and pulled out the hotel envelope that he'd used for their tickets. He made sure it wasn't Julia's letter before he walked to the station side of the carriage. Everyone was already on the platform, so Grip hopped onto the wooden surface and handed the ticket envelope to Julia.

"Here are your tickets. Show them to the conductor and he'll help you board the first-class car. Why don't you and Emily have a seat with Teddy and Mary while Billy and I unload your bags."

"Alright," she replied as she accepted the envelope then picked up Mary and walked with Emily and Teddy to the nearest two benches.

Billy and Grip unloaded their bags and set them on the platform between the benches along with the basket. Emily sat on one with Mary and Teddy and Julia sat alone on the other.

Grip then said to Julia, "When the conductor announces that the train will be leaving in twenty minutes, call the porter over and he will carry your bags and the basket onto your car. All you'll have to do is to make sure Emily doesn't have her baby before you get to St. Louis."

Emily laughed and said, "Babies, sir. Not baby."

"I stand corrected, ma'am."

"Are you going to use me as a mailman?" Julia asked as she pointed to the envelope jutting from his pocket.

Grip smiled as handed the letter to her and said, "If you don't mind, ma'am. A copy of this letter should be arriving in St. Louis this morning. Rich Bennett would have gotten the telegram, so there will be someone there to meet you."

"Do I give him this even if he's already received your letter?"

"Yes, ma'am. It isn't an exact copy and there is some additional information."

"Then I'll play postman and deliver it this evening, sir," she replied as she smiled.

Grip wished she wasn't so incredibly nice or so overwhelmingly pretty as he returned her smile.

She slid the letter into her new purse and asked, "Are you going to stay and talk to me for a few more minutes before we have to board the train?"

He had already prepared to use the excuse that he had to return the carriage before catching his own train later, but he was too weak to resist and took a seat next to her on the bench.

She made it worse when she took his hand and said, "I can't wait to see Utah. I've never seen a mountain before. Have you?"

"Not a real mountain. It'll be a new experience for me, too. Do you know what I did last evening to pass the time?"

"I have a few ideas, but what did you do?"

"I designed houses for the new property. They're just crude drawings, but it kept my mind occupied."

"Why didn't you come to visit?"

"I was worried that whoever had been looking for me might follow me to your house and cause you trouble."

"Have you seen them again?"

"Not even a shadow. I'll be taking the train to Denver later this morning, so I won't have to worry about them anyway."

"How long will it take before everything is ready?"

"About six or seven weeks. I'll write to keep everyone abreast of the progress."

"Will you write to me?"

"Of course, I will, dear sister."

Julia laughed and squeezed his hand before saying, "Now there's a term of endearment that I hope to never hear again."

Grip nodded as he smiled then said, "If you are my sister, I'll still be very happy to have met you. You're a very likeable person."

"Likeable but not loveable?" she asked with a slight smile and laughing eyes.

"You are really making the most out of these last few minutes; aren't you?"

She laughed then replied, "I'm sorry, it's just that this whole 'maybe' brother and sister issue is almost silly if it wasn't so frustrating."

"I'll grant you that, but when you get to St. Louis, will you just relax and enjoy yourself. You'll only have to do what you want to do, so you'll have the time."

"Are you trying to tell me to socialize and meet other men?"

Grip sighed and as he looked at platform's dry pine boards, he answered, "Julia, I don't see how it's possible that we'll ever discover whose name should have been entered on your birth certificate. If I hadn't found it in my father's safe in his secret vault, it wouldn't have mattered. But I can't think of any other reason why he had saved it all these years."

"Maybe someone just mixed it in with the other papers by accident. How about that?"

"I already dismissed the idea because of the dates on the deeds and the different color of the birth certificate. It was too different to go unnoticed."

"So, you don't think that there's any chance for us?"

"Not much. When you return to St. Louis, you can see Pinkerton Agent Joe Trimble and tell him that I want him to search for your father's name. It may take a while and if he finds that you are the daughter of Lawrence Preston Taylor, then we'll go on as brother and sister."

"I'll think about it. Okay?"

"Alright. Anyway, I think your train is getting ready for boarding, so let's have the porter move your things."

She nodded, before they stood and stepped across the platform to the porter. He followed them back to their benches and loaded their bags onto a cart before wheeling it to the first passenger car.

Grip smiled at Julia, took her hands and said, "I guess you're in the first car."

"Unless he's stealing our bags."

Grip laughed and felt the urge to kiss her, but stepped over to the other bench and said, "Emily, let's get you rolled over to your train."

Emily smiled and slowly rose from the bench and Julia took her arm. Grip shook Billy's hand and kissed Emily then Millie on the cheek before looking at Julia and giving her a brotherly peck on the cheek as well.

"Say hello to everyone for me, Julia."

"I will. Goodbye, Grip."

"Goodbye, Julia."

Millie took Teddy's hand then Julia walked with Emily across the crowded platform as Billy carried Mary. Grip lost sight of them as the surge of passengers began queuing to enter the passenger cars.

He exhaled sharply, then turned and headed back to the carriage. By the time he reached Ridley's Carriage and Buggy Rental to rid himself of the conveyance, he heard the train's whistle shriek announcing its departure.

He mounted Pitch and trailing Brick, he rode west to make his stop at Carpenter's Stationery and Books before returning to the station.

After selecting a pad of large graph paper, he added a steel ruler, protractor and compass along with a dozen pencils and a proper pencil sharpener. He decided that he'd add some reading material for the long train trip, and when he scanned the large selection, he thought that he might take a break from his serious reading.

He added a collection of Jules Verne's works that he thought of as engineering fiction more than adventure stories. He stacked copies of *Around the World in Eighty Days, Journey to the Center of the Earth, From the Earth to the Moon* and *Twenty Thousand Leagues Under the Sea* onto his more constructive selections.

He knew that he could probably read all four of the novels in a day, so he would have to pace himself. With the rocking of the train, he knew that he'd have a hard time drawing even with the proper tools, but they'd pass the time as well.

He returned to the station before eleven o'clock and after leaving Pitch and Brick with the stock manager, he stepped onto the less crowded platform with his black saddlebags over his shoulder and his bag of drawing supplies and the four books in a large sack. He was wearing his gunbelt with the Remington and angled sheath when he sat down on the same bench he's just shared with Julia.

He tried to calculate where their train would be by now. It had left the station more than two hours ago, so even with stops, it would be at least fifty miles away, or a fifth of the way across Missouri. It was probably more than that because he knew it would arrive in St. Louis in seven more hours.

An hour later, he was sitting against the window with his saddlebags on the floor near his feet and the cloth bag with his drawing tools sitting beside him. He had started reading Verne's *From the Earth to the Moon* first because the physics intrigued him. After just twenty minutes, he noticed that the author had already committed many errors in the laws of physics, but it was fiction, so he let it go. Ballistics wouldn't allow an object to escape the atmosphere unless the amount of energy produced was beyond comprehension. But even if that was possible, he couldn't imagine that a human body could withstand the forces of the kind of acceleration which would result from being fired out of a massive cannon.

Even though he had promised to pace himself, he finished the book quickly because he found it enjoyable and a distraction. He left the train in Topeka for lunch and a visit to the privy before he returned and began a more detailed design for his own house.

As his train hurtled westward, Mickey Mooney and his boys were continuing to discover just how different life was in Denver. Even before they settled into their hotel room, each of them noticed the greater number of men who wore sidearms.

The second day in town, it was Cajun Al who noticed that many of the men rode horses to just travel a block or two and that each of them carried a Winchester.

As they sat at a table in Boomtown Saloon, Mickey said, "I think we're gonna have to get ourselves some horses and we'll need to buy some Winchesters, too."

John said, "I was talkin' to some fellers at the barbershop and they told me that the sheriff and the town marshal each have at least eight deputies. That's a lot of badge toters, boss."

"I heard that myself. I also heard that a lot of the gold comes from Leadville, just a couple of days' ride west of here, and that town is wide open. I figure we can stick around here and learn to ride better and shoot a rifle, then we can head to Leadville and see if the stories are true. We could hit it big over there, boys."

"Okay," Cajun Al said, "then I reckon we've gotta spend some of our money to get horses, saddles and rifles. How much do we have left, boss?"

"Just short of two thousand. We're doin' all right, but let's see about getting a real good price on those horses, like for free."

John, Bill and Al all laughed but each of them knew that stealing horses would be a lot harder with so many lawmen around. Besides, Mickey might need a strong plow horse to haul his massive bulk around.

———

Everything was ready for Julia and the Alberts arrival, so at five o'clock, Tom climbed into the carriage with Jenny. Jenny had convinced him to take her along because of Emily's advanced pregnancy, but he suspected she just wanted to satisfy her curiosity about Grip's sister.

Rich had been given many more instructions in his long letter, but none could be started until everyone arrived.

Wilma and Jenny had already prepared a sumptuous feast to welcome them and were timing its completion for seven o'clock.

As their train slowed before reaching the St. Louis station, Emily was noticeably tired, despite her frequent naps. The thickly cushioned first-class seats helped but Julia was sure that Emily was very happy to reach the end of their journey across Missouri. She wondered if she would be able to handle the much longer trip to Ogden in just six or seven weeks. If she delivered her child, or children, in another three or four weeks and everything went well, she would still be very tired. Emily was just a few months short of forty and this had been a hard pregnancy for her. She kept insisting that she was carrying twins, but Julia suspected it was her age more than the weight she carried that was having the impact.

Millie was obviously excited as she watched out the window as St. Louis flowed past and Billy was interested but trying to appear as if he was too mature to be smiling.

Julia was as curious about how she would be accepted. She wasn't sure how much Grip had explained to everyone in the house about their questionable siblinghood but suspected that Grip had told Mister Bennett about his doubts before he left.

The train was at walking speed as Julia scanned the platform trying to identify Rich Bennett or any of the others from Grip's adopted family.

Julia still hadn't spotted anyone when the train stopped, and she helped Emily out of her seat. Billy hefted Mary into his arms and Millie took Teddy's hand as they made their way to the back of the car.

When they stepped onto the platform in the muggy evening warmth, Tom had no problem identifying them and stepped quickly in their direction to greet them. Jenny walked beside him and was surprised to see that Julia was blonde with blue eyes. She already had doubts about her being Lawrence Taylor's daughter as she and her husband reached the Albert family.

Tom had relieved Billy of little Mary and said, "Welcome to St. Louis, Mrs. Albert. I'm Tom Truax and this is my wife, Jenny. Our carriage is just past the platform. Where is your baggage?"

Emily smiled and replied, "The porter said he'd bring it along shortly."

Billy then said, "I'll wait here and have him bring it to the carriage, Mama."

"Thank you, Billy."

She then said, "Mister Bennett, please call me Emily. This is my niece, Julia, my son Billy, my daughter Millie. This fine boy is my son Teddy and you're holding Mary."

"It's a pleasure to meet everyone, Emily. Please call me Rich. Grip insists that we treat each other as family, and I'm sure that you'll feel that way when you meet everyone."

"He's a remarkable young man; isn't he?"

"Very. He's about as far removed from his father as an eagle is from an earthworm."

Julia then smiled at Jenny and said, "Grip told me many things about everyone, Jenny. It's a pleasure to meet you."

Jenny smiled as she replied, "Thank you, Julia. It's nice meeting you as well."

Tom then took Teddy's hand and started across the platform, so Julia escorted Emily behind them leaving Billy to hunt for the porter.

Billy approached the porter who had just set the basket on the stack of travel bags then asked the porter to follow him as he headed to the waiting carriage.

After loading the bags into the large boot, the porter placed the basket on one of the seats, then Billy climbed into the driver's seat with Tom and Jenny sat beside Julia to start a mild inquisition. Tom snapped the reins and the carriage rolled away from the platform.

Julia was forthcoming in answering Jenny's questions and didn't hesitate to express her wish that she wasn't Grip's sister. Jenny admitted that she'd already come to that conclusion the moment she'd spotted her.

Before they'd reached the halfway point, Jenny was already offering suggestions about how Julia could find the missing name on her birth certificate. Unfortunately, none of them were new or helpful. Julia and Grip had already visited each possibility and found it wanting.

Julia would talk to Joe Trimble when she had the chance and maybe he could help her to find her elusive father.

———

As Julia and the Alberts were being welcomed to their temporary home in the Taylor mansion, Grip's temporary rolling home continued clicking its way toward Colorado.

He'd lost his light, so he couldn't read or work on his design that he'd started after leaving Topeka.

It was around ten o'clock when the rhythmic motion and repetitive clicks of the passing gaps between the rails lulled him into sleep. The train was approaching Russell, Kansas and the lurching stop awakened him. He blinked, yawned, and used his left foot to check for his saddlebags. He was startled when his boot swung a good foot without being stopped. He popped to his feet and without pulling on his hat he scanned the dimly lit passenger car.

He almost missed the shadowy figure exiting the back door of the car but when he spotted the man, he raced down the aisle, knocking over a small man who was just about to leave his seat.

He flew out of the car and saw the man hurrying across the platform with his black saddlebags in his hand. He was wearing a gunbelt, so Grip knew that this could be his first confrontation with danger, and he hoped it wouldn't be his last.

The man glanced behind him and must have been shocked that the sleeping man had seen him because he didn't look forward again for another three seconds as he raced across the platform.

Grip was reaching for his Remington as he flew across the platform that was just thirty feet across and before he even released his hammer loop, the thief reached the far edge and didn't realize where he was until his left foot didn't find the flat surface where his brain had expected it to be and his foot plunged unexpectedly to the ground eight inches lower. The man arced face forward with his arms flailing and slammed into the street's hard dirt.

He grunted loudly then quickly rolled over and was reaching for his Colt when he heard the click of Grip's Remington's hammer being drawn to the firing position.

"Don't even think about it, mister," Grip growled as he stared down at the man.

The would-be thief quickly yanked both hands away and showed his palms to Grip as he exclaimed, "Don't shoot me, mister! I didn't know it was yours! I just took it by mistake! Really!"

"I doubt if you thought my saddlebags were yours, but I'll agree that you made a big mistake."

Grip then opened his tweed jacket and showed him the U.S. Deputy Marshal's badge that he'd pinned there before he left just in case it became necessary. He wasn't sure that it was necessary, but it definitely had an impact on the man on the ground.

The man groaned and asked, "Are you gonna arrest me?"

"I have to get back on the train in a minute, so I don't have the time. But I want you to unbuckle your gunbelt with your left hand and toss it onto the platform."

The disheartened robber did as Grip had instructed, and after the gunbelt thumped onto the boards, Grip grabbed it then released his Remington's hammer and holstered his pistol.

"Now I have no use for another pistol, especially not one that's in such poor condition, but you can't be running around with it, so I'll remedy that problem."

The train's whistle sounded as Grip pulled the hammer to the loading position, emptied all of the .45 Long Colt cartridges, then yanked it all the way back and slammed the hammer against the platform, snapping the hammer in two. He stepped down next to the man, picked up his saddlebags, then dropped the useless revolver to the ground next to him before tossing its gunbelt on top of the cold Colt.

Grip turned and trotted across the platform and hopped onto the steel steps of his car and swung through the open door. He knew that the pistol could be repaired, but the cost would be more than the pistol was worth. The man may have been a poor thief, but he still should have taken better care of his weapon.

As he walked down the aisle, the other passengers regarded him with either awe, fear or just plain wonder.

He stopped at the seat where the small man sat looking at him and said, “I apologize for knocking you over, sir, but I couldn’t let that thief get away.”

The man smiled and replied, “I understand, sir, and there’s no reason to apologize. I’m glad that you caught up with him.”

“So, am I,” Grip said as he returned the man’s smile.

He soon reached his seat and sat against the window again. He’d learned a few lessons in that brief encounter. The first could be put into effect immediately, as he pulled out the leather straps that he used to secure the saddlebags onto Pitch and lashed them to his left boot.

The train began rolling again and Grip spent a few minutes reviewing the brief and bloodless encounter. Aside from letting his saddlebags be lifted without his notice, he hadn’t made any serious mistakes and hadn’t overreacted. It wasn’t much, but it was a good first step.

He wondered if any of the other passengers had seen the thief steal the saddlebags. He doubted if all of them had been asleep, but he could understand why they wouldn't have confronted an armed man when he wasn't taking something that belonged to them. He was a stranger to each of them, and why should they put themselves at risk for someone they didn't know?

That was a valuable lesson, and it had confirmed his original decision to go to the West where there wasn't the protection of the law and help those who weren't able to stop the wealthy and powerful or the just plain mean bastards who wanted to take what wasn't theirs. The thief who tried to relieve him of his very valuable saddlebags was far from a real threat. He was just a sneak who preyed on sleeping victims. The real bad ones were out there waiting. He wondered what Mickey Mooney's men were doing in Kansas City and if their giant of a boss was with them or still in St. Louis.

It didn't matter to him now. Kansas City was already far behind him and would soon be a thousand miles away.

CHAPTER 10

As Grip continued his journey on the rails of the AT&SF and then on the Union Pacific after transferring in Denver, the extended crowd in St. Louis was becoming more familiar with each other.

Julia had given the second letter to Rich and after Billy had talked to Rich, he had announced as his preferred form of address was now Bill, but Millie had giggled about it and ignored his request.

Grip's new Sharps-Borshadt had been delivered the day after their arrival and Rich had left it in the weapons room to be shipped with the rest of the guns, knives and ammunition.

One of Grip's instructions to Rich was that Tom should give Julia, Billy and Millie their own horses. He didn't need to mention that Julia deserved the best of the impressive animals.

The afternoon of their second day on the estate, Julia, Bill and Millie selected their horses from the small herd of blacks and even though Tom already had given names for each of them, he let them give them new ones. But when Julia asked him what her chosen gelding's name was, she was happy to retain Tom's choice of Ebony.

With the large amount of cash that she still had in her purse, Julia led a serious shopping expedition so everyone could add more clothes, including riding outfits for her and Millie. She bought clothes for Emily, who had remained in the house regaining her strength, and a large quantity of baby clothes, supplies, and even a crib. Despite all of the purchases, she hadn't made a dent in the wad of cash that Grip had handed to her so casually.

The shopping trip, while providing much-needed clothes and other necessities, had given Julia an inkling of just how much money Grip had in the bank even after giving so much away. He had casually mentioned that his balance was still close to two million dollars and she couldn't fathom that much money. She had over nine hundred dollars in her purse and thought she was well-heeled. It was an uncomfortable feeling for a young woman who had to hand over dimes and nickels each day she worked at Claudia's Café. Yet as rich as he was, Grip had none of the pretense and airs that she associated with those who had but a tiny fortune when compared to his.

As she sat in the parlor while Emily chatted with Wilma and Jenny about the pain and joy of motherhood, she found herself wondering if she was good enough for Grip, even if she did discover the identity of her father. He had to be one of the most eligible bachelors in the entire country, yet when she'd asked Richard, he'd told her that he never had any girlfriends as far as he knew. *Did the entire population of women in St. Louis or those who knew him at the University of Michigan not realize he was available?*

They had talked about many things in their brief time together, but she had never asked him why he was unmarried because of the tenuous nature of their relationship. Now she wondered about it, but no one in the house had ever been closer to him than Rich Bennett, and he didn't know. Not only did Grip not have any women acquaintances, he didn't seem to have any serious male friends, either.

Julia started to wish that she hadn't come to St. Louis. When she'd first told him that she wanted to come with him, he had readily agreed, but it was too late now. She knew that she had to be with her aunt until she gave birth but now wondered if she could leave before everyone else.

Before she even thought about leaving, she wanted to learn how to ride the black gelding. One of the first places she would ride would be to the Pinkerton Agency to talk to Agent Joe Trimble.

———

Grip's train finally rolled into Ogden, Utah, and he was more than happy to stay in one place for a while. The days had rolled past, and they had almost blended into one long day by the time he stepped onto the platform.

He stepped over to the stock corral and would have to apologize to Pitch and Brick for their long imprisonment and let them stretch their legs.

It was just eleven o'clock in the morning, so he could get a lot done today. After getting a room, he'd finally relieve himself of most of the cash in his saddlebags and then start his property search. He didn't expect to find anything today and wasn't sure who was handling open land sales.

He did know where he wanted to live. Northwest of Ogden, just past the Ogden River were heavily forested tracts of land, but the railroads ran through that area, so he wasn't sure if they had been given land grants.

He soon gathered his equine companions and mounted Pitch. He walked him into Ogden and pulled up near the Globe Hotel which seemed to be a comfortable establishment. He dismounted and pulled his black saddlebags onto his shoulder before stepping across the boardwalk and climbing the three steps to the entrance. He paid for a week in advance, then after taking his key, he left the hotel and strapped the saddlebags back in place before stepping up.

It was early, but he was already hungry, so he set Pitch to a slow trot heading north and soon stopped before the Ogden Restaurant to fill his stomach.

He was back atop Pitch forty minutes later with a satisfied stomach and decided to do a quick tour of the town. It was a lot cleaner than he'd expected and the streets were heavy with traffic.

Grip smiled when he spotted the large brewery as he wasn't sure of the Mormons' outlook on the consumption of alcohol. Like most people he knew, he had heard the sinister rumors about the Mormons, but had put it in the same catalog of ignorance that had included similar whispers about Jews and Catholics. The heathen Chinese and Indians had their own volumes. As long as no one tried to convert him to their beliefs, he was more than happy to let them practice their own. He was curious about the Mormons, though. He'd never met one and now he was living in a territory that was home to most of the Mormons in the country.

He spotted a Mormon Tabernacle, but then found a Methodist and an Episcopal church. There were schools attached to each of them and when he spied a Roman Catholic church, he found not only a school, but a convent nearby. At least the Mormons seemed more tolerant than some of the other religions.

He passed one shop that attracted his attention. J.M. Browning & Bros., Guns, Pistols, Ammunition & Fishing Tackle. It was a small shop but seemed to be very popular. He could see at least eight customers inside and two more about to enter. He had no plans to do any fishing but knew that he'd be paying the shop a visit soon.

He found a public school, then turned down another road and soon found the Ogden Bank. It wasn't as large as The Merchantmen's Bank in St. Louis, of course, but few were. But it was bigger than he had expected and imagined that it had something to do with the Mormon practice of tithing.

Whatever the reason, the bank seemed substantial and Grip pulled Pitch to a stop in front of the brick building and dismounted. He tied off the black, pulled down his saddlebags and entered the open double doors.

There were a number of customers in line, but he needed to see a clerk at one of the eight desks that lined the right side of the lobby.

Three of them were available, so he scanned their nameplates and picked Ford Garvey, just because he had an interesting name, and he might appreciate meeting a man with an even more unusual moniker.

When he approached the desk, Mister Garvey looked up at him and said, “Good afternoon, sir. What can I do for you today?”

“I just arrived in town and I’ll be living here, so I’d like to open an account.”

“Let me be the first to welcome you to Ogden. I’m Ford Garvey and feel free to wonder why I was christened with that name.”

Grip grinned, shook his hand and said, “Well, Ford, I’m one up on you. My name is Agrippa Taylor, but please call me Grip.”

Ford snickered before he said, “Have a seat, Grip. Was your father a fan of General Agrippa?”

“I have no idea. I never asked and he sent me off to military school when I was seven, so it came in handy after a while.”

“I’ll explain Ford later, but let’s get this process started,” he said as he slid two forms from his drawer and dipped a pen into his desk’s inkwell.

“Sounds good,” Grip replied as he pulled his saddlebags onto his lap.

“How much do you wish to deposit today?” Ford asked as he had his pen poised above the form.

“I’m not sure of the exact amount, but let’s start unloading some of this.”

Ford was disinterested until Grip began setting bundles of cash onto his desk.

He stared as Grip then shifted to the other saddlebag and built a second stack.

When he finished, Grip said, “Let’s make it twenty-two thousand. I’ll keep some with me.”

Ford swallowed and in a weak voice, he asked, “Um, Grip, I don’t mean to imply that you’ve acquired this money illegally, but could you tell me where you came into such a fortune?”

"I can't say for certain that it was honestly obtained, but my father is the one who accumulated most of it except for what his father left to him. I have around two million in the Merchantmen's Bank in St. Louis, and I'll be transferring some of those assets here as necessary."

Ford slowly lowered his pen as he hesitantly asked, "Two million? You have two million dollars?"

"I really hate to talk about it, and I hope that we can keep that information as private as possible. A lot of bad men would visit me if they found out about it."

Ford finally recovered and said, "You don't seem like a man who would have such an incredible amount of wealth. How old are you?"

"I just turned twenty-five and I was about to get my doctorate in engineering at the University of Michigan when my father was murdered. He wasn't a good man, so don't express any condolences. I'm trying to make up for all the harm he caused and already set up a charitable fund in St. Louis with half of his money."

"You're an engineer, too?"

"I'd rather build things than force men to work in horrible conditions just to care for their families. Anyway, I think we need to get this done so you can put it into your vault. I think some of your customers are already looking this way."

"Oh, of course. Let me handle this."

Grip let him do the necessary paperwork and after he finished and Grip completed and signed both forms, Ford stacked the bundles and carried them past the row of tellers' windows and disappeared into a hallway.

He reappeared with just a slip of paper a few minutes later, then sat back down and handed him the receipt.

"What else can I do for you today, Grip?"

"I need to buy some property to build some houses, but I don't know who to see about it."

"It depends on where you want to live and how much land you want to buy."

"I would prefer northwest of town."

"Most of that property is part of land grants owned by one of the four railroads that service Ogden. If you want a large tract of land, you might want to look at something to the northeast of town. In fact, unless your heart is set on an open plot of ground, you might want to talk to Ernie Upton."

"Does he handle real estate?"

"Not normally, but he has a problem that you could probably rectify. It almost got him fired and he still could lose his job if he doesn't fix it."

"What is the problem?"

Ford leaned closer and replied, "In April, John and Martha Wilkerson met with Ernie who is in charge of our mortgage department. They owned a ranch northeast of town and applied for a mortgage loan. Ernie knew the property and valued the ranch itself at four thousand dollars, but they asked for more and offered their four hundred head of cattle as collateral. So, Ernie, being a warm-hearted man, especially for a banker, gave them a six-thousand-dollar mortgage. The mortgage was for the land, buildings and cattle. The couple thanked Ernie and took the mortgage in cash, which wasn't unusual. They had six ranch hands working for them, and Ernie guessed that they hadn't been paid for a while.

"Everything seemed fine until last month when their first mortgage payment was due, and no one showed up. Ernie wasn't worried for another two weeks, then finally rode out to the ranch and found not only were John and Martha gone, but the bunkhouse was empty and even worse, almost all the cattle were missing. He found three old cows wandering the pastures and after notifying the sheriff, things got worse for Ernie.

"It seems that he had no legal recourse because in the mortgage, he had listed the collateral as the land, house and the cattle, but didn't specify the number of animals. The sheriff did check and told him that the couple had sold the entire herd to another rancher the day after the mortgage loan was given to them. The rancher hadn't broken the law and the cattle were legally his. After selling the herd, John and Martha had escaped with over ten thousand dollars and there was nothing anyone could do about it."

Grip couldn't keep from smiling as he said, "You've got to give them credit for a new way to steal without stealing."

"That's what Sheriff Johnson said. So, if you want to make a friend for life, you could buy the ranch for the cost of the mortgage. It's not a great price without the cattle and the ground couldn't support more than five hundred head anyway. He's been desperately trying to unload the place and he's close to panic."

"How big is it?"

"You'd have to talk to Ernie, but I think it's eight sections."

"Is any of the other area surrounding it available."

"I have no idea. The Greater Utah Property Management Company holds most of the ground east of town, but not all of it."

Grip grinned and said, "I guess I'll go and have a chat with Mister Upton."

Just three minutes after meeting with Ernie Upton, he and Grip left the bank and after Ernie brought his horse around to the front of the bank, they rode northeast down Fourth Street until they passed East Street which was the last roadway with a name before leaving the town. The street faded into a trail but just three minutes later, they passed between a pair of whitewashed stumps.

Ernie pulled up and said, “This is the center of the Wilkerson ranch. The property starts here and is a mile in each direction left to right and continues for four miles.”

Grip nodded and stood in his stirrups to inspect the landscape. While not having the thick pine forests on the northwest, the left side of the property was anchored by the Ogden River that flowed down from the mountains to the east and there were heavy growths of pines and deciduous trees along most of that side of the ranch. There was a large canyon in the distance that entered the mountains, but it was well northeast of the ranch. It would be fun to explore though. The terrain was a mix of flat and rolling ground with another, smaller forest of mostly pines covering the northeast corner. He could see another stream cutting across the property and emptying into the Ogden River.

He saw the ranch house in the distance almost straight ahead and a barn a hundred yards or so to its right. The only other structure he could see must have been the empty bunkhouse.

“It looks good, Ernie. If it doesn’t present any bad surprises, I won’t even dicker with you. I’ll give you the six thousand that you have outstanding on the place.”

Ernie wanted to giggle but managed to just smile before tapping his horse's flanks and putting him in motion again.

Grip's inspection of the ranch revealed nothing to change his mind. In fact, everything he found seemed to be a bonus. The house was good-sized and well built. The barn wasn't anything special, but it was a barn. The house was furnished, and the kitchen was stocked with cookware and dinnerware, so he could live here while the other houses were being built.

The bunkhouse was a bit of an oddity that actually suited him. It was an L-shaped structure with eight bunks aligned against the walls, but in the short leg of the L, there was a small cookstove, a small pantry, a fairly large kitchen table and eight chairs. He guessed that Mrs. Wilkerson didn't do their cooking and they didn't hire a cook either.

The bunkhouse could serve as a gun room until he built his house but having the small cookstove was a real plus, and the bunkhouse might have another purpose if he was able to fulfill the promise he'd made to Tom Truax. He'd ask Ernie about it when they finished their inspection.

When they left the bunkhouse, Grip said, "Okay, Ernie, let's get back to the bank and we'll end all your worries."

Ernie grinned as he shook Grip's hand before they mounted and headed back down the access road.

Grip still scanned what would become his new home and was already seeing many possibilities.

As they reentered the outskirts of Ogden, Grip asked, “Say, Ernie, do you know where I can get some dogs?”

“What kind of dogs?”

“Smart ones who could be watchdogs and still be friends with children.”

Ernie thought about it for a few seconds then said, “Let’s swing by and visit Jimmy Laughlin. He runs a sawmill and lumber yard just north of here and keeps some German shepherds around to keep the beavers away. He usually has a few excess puppies that he tries to give away. He should get rid of the bitches and it wouldn’t be his problem anymore.”

Grip snickered then replied, “Let’s go see Mister Laughlin.”

The stop at Laughlin’s Lumber took forty minutes, but mostly because he was a chatty type and loved to tell tall tales. But he did have more than just a couple of young German shepherds that he was more than happy to give to Grip. Grip had only wanted a pair but wound up accepting four curs who were all about three months old. He didn’t want a bitch because he wasn’t about to get into the dog mill business. He agreed with Ernie’s opinion and could already see the trouble it had created for Mister Laughlin.

Because Jimmy Laughlin was more than happy to get rid of the dogs, he didn’t ask for any payment, but Grip said he’d pick them up tomorrow. He’d sleep in the hotel tonight but move into the ranch house tomorrow.

It wasn't even four o'clock when Grip left the bank with the deed for his new home. He had a lot of things to do, but as soon as he registered with the post office, he'd be able to write letters with a return address of Ogden, Utah.

He left Pitch & Brick at the L&M Livery, which was the closest to his hotel before finally reaching his room. He'd left his drafting supplies in the packs along with his books which he'd finished three days into his trip. He expected to be asleep shortly after sundown.

He'd finished the rudimentary design of his house and transferred the carriage house and the standard house to the larger graph paper. He wasn't sure that the builders would need a full blueprint, but he'd ask Jimmy Laughlin about it tomorrow when he picked up his dogs. He was debating about letting them stay in the bunkhouse or the barn when he finally began to strip. He wasn't very hungry, but the bed was already calling to him and it wasn't even six o'clock.

———

In Denver, Mickey and his boys were a bit put off when they had to buy four horses and saddles, including a large, strong gelding for Mickey. Even the used tack had pushed the total bill to almost six hundred dollars. The Winchesters and ammunition had added another hundred, so by the time they had taken to the saddle with their repeaters, their stash had been reduced to almost a thousand dollars.

They had spent two days becoming accustomed to the new horses and Western saddles and both John and Bill had been thrown once. The Winchesters didn't pose nearly the same problems, but they had to ride out of town to become familiar with the rifle.

So, by the time that Grip was returning to his Ogden hotel room, Mickey Mooney and his three men were sitting in the Boomtown Saloon to prepare for their invasion of Leadville. They still hadn't realized that, despite their meanness and willingness to kill, they were still ill-equipped to be successful criminals in the world of the hardened men they would meet in Leadville. Those that discovered the gold and silver were not only capable of protecting it, they were extremely suspicious of strangers.

Mickey's enormous size which had proven very beneficial ever since he was a street bully in St. Louis would work against him in Leadville. The four murderers still had lessons to learn.

———

Earlier that day, Julia had ridden with Tom Truax to the Pinkerton Agency. She was still learning how to handle Ebony and Jenny had insisted that her husband accompany her on the ride.

When she entered the office, every agent at his desk looked at her, but Julia was used to the male attention, so she was able to ignore it as she searched for Joe Trimble.

Joe was one of the agents who had seen her enter, but recognized Tom Truax behind her, so he smiled, then stood and asked, “Miss Marley? I’m Joe Trimble.”

He even had a strong suspicion why she had come to the office the moment he had seen her.

Julia smiled and with Tom trailing, she stepped over to his desk.

Joe shook her hand and said, “Have a seat, Miss Marley.”

Julia sat and asked, “How do you know my name and that I’m not married? Did Grip tell you?”

“No, ma’am. He said he’d let me know, but I’m guessing that he headed off to Ogden and barely had time to notify Rich Bennett of your arrival. He had told me that if you were married with a family, he’d offer you the estate and some cash, but you wouldn’t be here if that was true. You’d be at the bank seeing Warren Stone, but I have a good idea why you’re here as well.”

Julia smiled before she asked, “And what would that be?”

Joe grinned then replied, “You want us to find out whose name should have been on your birth certificate.”

"How on earth did you figure all that out just because I came here?"

"I'm sure that you realize that you are a striking young lady, Miss Marley. So, if you weren't married, which is a bit surprising to be honest, then it's reasonable to assume that you found our friend Agrippa, who is also an amazing young man, to be at least very interesting. Is that right so far?"

"Yes. I found him to be more than just interesting and I know that he enjoys being with me."

"That being said, Grip had us find his half-sister, which we did. He told me that it was possible that you weren't his sister but wasn't sure because there was no father listed on the birth certificate. His reasons for believing that were sound. There was no purpose for his father to keep that document unless you were his daughter."

"I know that, but before we parted, he said that there was a strong possibility that we didn't share the same father."

"That was my other clue for your arrival. When I saw you with Tom, I noticed that you share none of the Taylor physical attributes. Grip and his father both had black hair and dark eyes, but you have reddish-blonde hair and blue eyes. Did your mother have blonde hair and blue eyes?"

"Yes. I always thought that brown eyes were dominant."

"You're a smart lady, too. I'm not sure exactly how that works, but I have found blue-eyed children when only one of the parents or even grandparents had blue eyes. That being said, I have a few cautions for you before you ask me to start the process of trying to find your father."

"What are they?"

"The most obvious is the difficulty. It's been almost twenty years since that birth certificate was created and the certifying doctor died years ago. Even if we could track down the midwife, I doubt if she'd know who your father was. If your mother didn't tell you, then I don't believe she would have told the midwife. There are no leads in this case, Miss Marley."

"So, there's no point in asking you to try?"

"It would be very difficult and time consuming. Your mother was fired by Lawrence Taylor almost twenty years ago and none of the staff who worked there at the time are still employed on the estate. If you want us to do this, our only real starting point would be to find someone who worked with your mother or find out about her life before she started working for Mister Taylor. Did she talk about her family or life?"

"No. She and my aunt didn't talk about their lives growing up much because they were raised in an orphanage and it wasn't a happy experience."

Julia then turned and looked up at Tom and asked, "Do you know anyone who worked for Mister Taylor back then?"

"I thought you might ask, but by the time I was hired six years ago, the only ones who were already there when I started working were Rich and Wilma Bennett. They were hired just four years before I was, so I'm not sure that they'd met anyone who worked at that time, but they might have heard a name or two.

"Mister Lawrence was very hard on his staff. Most quit after a year for one reason or another and he fired them for almost any offense. You can imagine why he fired the pretty maids he hired. Richard and Wilma are the longest-serving staff members and me and Jenny are the second longest. Mister Taylor wasn't getting soft in his old age, he just became more involved in his, um, less reputable enterprises. He stopped bothering the maids because of an incident five years ago."

"What was that?"

"A young lady named Abigail Fairfield walked into his office and confessed that she was pregnant. He didn't even look up from a paper he was writing and told her she was fired and to leave the estate within an hour. She left the office and he continued to write. She walked out to the kitchen, took a butcher knife from the block then returned to the office. I imagine that he heard her enter and was looking up when she stabbed him. It was just a glancing cut because he must have deflected it with his arm.

"He was bleeding when he picked her up and threw her across the office into a glass bookcase. No one knows if she died from one of the sharp pieces of broken glass or he stabbed her with the butcher's knife. The police didn't even bother writing a report on her death much less do an investigation. The only real impact of the attack was that he stopped using the maids as whores."

Julia shuddered then looked back at Joe and asked, "If I can find a name can you try to search for my father?"

"I'll do that, Miss Marley."

"Thank you."

"You know, most men wouldn't let something as vague as this to stand in the way. I'll be honest and tell you that I wouldn't care."

"That's what Grip told me, but I don't believe that he could ever do that. I'm not sure that it's a completely moral argument either. I think that he might be worried that if we married, it would be more likely that we'd produce another Lawrence Preston Taylor."

"Whatever the reason, ma'am, get me a name and we'll take it from there. But are you sure you want to know the answer?"

"I do, and I don't want you to falsify the report if it was his father. We'll face that when I get the answer."

"You may never get your answer, Miss Marley."

"I know. But may I ask you another question?"

"Certainly."

"I know that you haven't spent much time with Grip, but you did to an investigation for him, so you interviewed many people who knew him in his past. Is that right?"

"I did most of that."

"Do you have any idea why he never married? He never even mentioned a girlfriend."

"I wondered about that myself. Even before he went off to college, I imagine he was the target of more than half of the single young women in St. Louis. I have no idea why he didn't marry, but what impressed me most about him was that if you didn't know better, you'd swear that he was a lawman. That's an interesting story, too."

"You mean about the volunteer deputy marshal badge?"

"Yes, ma'am. Not that he carries the badge or even that he has the look. It's that Marshal Guest told my brother that he was about to toss him out on his ear without even talking to him because he had expected to meet a spoiled rich kid looking for adventure. Suffice it to say that the marshal not only talked to him but swore him in as well. Grip made that kind of impression on him."

Tom then said, “Julia, maybe you should ask Wilma about why he never married.”

“I asked Rich and he didn’t know.”

“Ask Wilma. She might be more likely to have a name for you anyway.”

“I’ll do that when we return.”

Joe then stood and said, “If you can find me a name, I’ll start the investigation. I’ll just give the bill to Mister Stone.”

Julia rose, shook his hand and said, “Thank you, Mister Trimble.”

“You’re welcome, ma’am.”

Julia and Tom then turned and left the office as every agent’s eyes watched her leave.

After they mounted and walked their horses away, Joe said, “I hope we don’t find her father because I agree with Grip. There was no other reason for his old man to keep that birth certificate. I actually was thinking about waiting a few weeks and then just plugging a name into a report, but I guess that would be unethical.”

“Write in Lawrence Taylor and then ask to visit her, Joe, or maybe I will.”

Joe laughed then turned and said, “Come on, Louis, do you really think that any of us ugly bastards would have a chance with a woman like her? Besides, I believe Lottie would probably take her own butcher’s knife to you and she wouldn’t stab you either. She’d geld you.”

Agent Louis Florissant snickered before Joe sat back down and continued writing his report on the Goodly adultery case.

———

After supper, Julia asked Wilma if they could talk in the office.

Once inside, she closed the door and sat in one of the chairs in front of the enormous desk and Wilma took a seat in the other.

“I went to the Pinkerton Agency and asked the detective who had found out where I lived to ask him if he could find out who my father was.”

“It’s because of Grip; isn’t it?”

“Yes. Until we know who he was, I’ll always be his half-sister. The detective asked if anyone knew the names of any of the employees who worked here at the same time that my mother did. That was twenty years ago, and Tom said that no one here has been employed for that long but if anyone could recall one of those names, it would be you.”

Wilma nodded, but didn't answer as she tried to summon the names of anyone who had worked on the estate at that time. The trouble was that there were so many names of employees who had come and gone during those two decades. Things had stabilized somewhat in the last ten years, but before that, those massive front doors may well have been turnstiles.

Julia could almost hear the cogs and gears in Wilma's mind whirring as she searched her memories.

After almost two minutes, Wilma shook her head and said, "Let me think about it for a while. There are just so many names."

"Didn't he even keep records of his employees? How would he know how to pay them?"

"He didn't keep records for the household staff. The household manager knew how much each staff member was paid and at the end of the month, Mister Taylor would give him the exact amount of cash for him to distribute."

"If you can remember a name, please let me know."

"I will."

Julia then said, "Wilma, Tom also said to ask you if you knew why Grip never married or had any girlfriends. Everyone, including me, finds that astonishing."

Wilma smiled as she replied, "So, did I. I do know why he hasn't even had a girlfriend, but I've never told anyone, not even Richard. Now that the mean old bastard is dead, I suppose it no longer matters."

"Why did it matter?"

"Because the woman who told me of the incident worried about reprisals from Mister Taylor. She died a few years after she left the house, but the subject never came up until you asked."

"What happened?"

Wilma told her the story that Mary Duffy had confessed to her the day after it had happened. Mary had been boundless in her praise for how Grip had treated her and was worried that somehow his father would discover the deception. She had extracted a vow from Wilma to keep her secret.

Julia asked, "How did that pretend coupling make Grip decide not to marry?"

"Mary said that before she left the room, she kissed him, and he said that he would never treat a woman so poorly and would only be intimate with a woman he loved. She thought it was just the emotional reaction of a boy, but he was also a boy who hadn't bedded her despite his obvious desires. Mary was a very well-figured, pretty young woman and even she was stunned that he had been able to keep his lust in check. I imagine that our Grip wasn't just passing off some excuse for not succumbing to his enormous teenage needs."

"I should have stayed with him to get to know him better. I couldn't let Emily take that long train trip in her condition, but I wonder if I shouldn't go to Ogden before everyone else leaves."

"Maybe. But wait until Emily has her baby. I think she'll need your support more than the doctor's. When he tells us his new address, you'll be able to write back and forth. It may not be as good as face-to-face conversation, but it'll help."

"I'll be writing a lot, and if you can remember a name, let me know."

"I will. As long as we're alone, let's talk about Grip. I'll tell you some stories that maybe will give you a better idea of the young man's character."

"I'd like that."

Wilma nodded then began one of her many Grip tales that she was sure he hadn't had time to tell Julia.

CHAPTER 11

When the sun rose to announce Grip's first full day in Ogden, he was already awake, dressed and shaved.

He checked out of the hotel and walked to the livery where he retrieved his two horses and asked the liveryman where he could buy a wagon and a team of draft horses.

Before he rode to Keeler's Wagon and Carriage Makers, he stopped at Goolsby's Diner for breakfast. He had attracted the attention of many of the other diners as he was a stranger and was wearing an ominous black gunbelt with a pistol that sported black grips. It was an effect he would appreciate later, but he made sure to smile often and when the young waitress took his order, he was sure that he'd drawn her attention for a very different reason.

He stopped at the carriage maker's and bought a large wagon that bordered on the size of a freight wagon. They had a small selection of horses in the corral behind the assembly room, but two of them were well-suited to pull the wagon, so by midmorning, Grip was able to stop at G.M. Smith's Mercantile to buy food and supplies for his new house. There was plenty of grass for grazing, but he'd need some oats and hay before long.

The beds all had linen, but he still bought sheets, blankets, quilts and pillows along with the food and basic necessities like kerosene. The wagon was almost half-full when he left it by the store and walked to the nearby post office. He rented a post office box and was assigned #25. He'd write a letter tonight to let everyone know about the property and what he would be having built.

After he registered the deed at the county land office, he finally climbed into the driver's seat of his new wagon and rolled north on Young Street until he reached First Street and turned right.

Pitch and Brick trotted behind the wagon as he had the team pulling it at a brisk pace along First Street until he reached Laughlin's Lumber and pulled it to a stop then set the handbrake.

It was an expansive operation, even if it wasn't the biggest sawmill in the town. There were large stacks of cut boards drying in the open air, so he hoped that he'd be able to help him by giving him business as a form of payment for the dogs.

When Jimmy spotted Grip, he broke into a grin and walked towards him.

"Come for your boys?"

"Yes, sir. But I may have some business for you, too. I just bought the Wilkerson ranch and I'll be moving into the ranch house shortly. But I had already planned to build a house and a large stable. I'll be building a couple of other houses after that, too. I already have the designs, but not in the form of full blueprints. Is there a construction firm in town who does good work and won't object to my guidance?"

"Well, sir, Ollie Jacobs runs a good operation. He's over on Second Street. He has two full-time crews but can add more if he has the work. I supply a lot of his lumber, so I'd appreciate the business, too."

"I guess I'll be visiting Mister Jacobs tomorrow. Let's relieve you of those four critters."

Jimmy was all grins as they hunted down the dogs and after putting simple cord leashes around their necks the four small canines were put into the back of the wagon and tied down.

They were a loud bunch and seemed to like Grip as they took turns ripping his face with their wet tongues while wagging their tails to express their doggy affection.

Grip soon rolled back along First Street before turning right onto East Street then a few minutes later he made one last turn onto his ranch. He wondered if he could call it a ranch if it didn't have cows or cow hands. As he thought about it, he wondered what had happened to the three old cows that the Wilkersons had left behind to satisfy the mortgage requirements.

He pulled up near the bunkhouse and released each of the young dogs into the small building, but they bounced out after just a few seconds.

"You boys are going to cause me trouble; aren't you?" he asked as they all stared up at him with active tails.

"I did buy you some meat, so I'll give you something after I get the wagon unloaded and take care of the big critters."

He stepped back into the driver's seat and rolled the wagon to the back of the house with the four young dogs trotting behind but leaving a safe space from the horse's metal clad rear hooves. They were smart dogs.

It took him twenty minutes to unload the wagon and Brick's packs, then put everything where it belonged before he was able to move the wagon to the barn and unharness the team and unsaddle Pitch and Brick.

The dogs were never more than six feet away after he stepped down from the driver's seat, but the horses wandered to the trough and were drinking as he returned to the house. He'd let them graze before moving them into the barn.

It took him much of the rest of that first day to put the house in order and didn't have time to fire up the cookstove for a proper meal, so he satisfied his hunger with a smoked beef sandwich. He cut some fresh beef roast into chunks for the dogs who had followed him into the house. He didn't risk a canine brawl, so he tossed one to each of the anxious young dogs until the meat was gone. He knew he'd have to figure out a better way to feed them as they would be growing rapidly.

There wasn't an office in the house, so he used the rather nice kitchen table as his desk. He wrote a letter to Rich giving him all of the details about the property and his immediate plans. He included the acquisition of four furry friends he had named Otto, Karl, Fritz and Max. He'd let Tom figure out why he'd given them those names. To identify each of them more easily, he'd used the cord that Jimmy Laughlin had used as leashes to make loose collars for each of them. Rather than write their names on tags, he just attached a different number of short cords to the collars. Fritz had one, Karl had two, Max had three and Otto had four. The alphabetical order would help. If they had more obvious differences in their coloration, the collars wouldn't be necessary. He'd be able to tell them apart after a week or so, but he wanted each of them to learn his name.

The four boys were curled together in one large furball near his feet as he wrote his letter to Rich and then started a second one to Joe Trimble because he'd promised to let him know how things worked out. He had decided to delay writing to Julia until he'd received mail.

He finished his day by baking two potatoes before he cooked two thick steaks. He would only have one of them and wasn't sure he'd be allowed to even finish it. At least the dogs wouldn't want his baked potatoes, or so he thought.

Over the next four days, Grip continued to make improvements on the ranch house, barn and bunkhouse. He'd been able to train the dogs, who were already learning their names, to stay in their new bunkhouse home. He'd bought a large supply of smoked beef and pork but also discovered that the dogs were avid hunters. They supplemented their diet with rats in the barn and any other small critter that dared to show his face or leave his scent for them to find.

He'd contracted with Oliver Jacobs Construction to build the large stable and his house and spent hours with his draftsmen who converted his designs into blueprints. He'd given them the design for the other houses and told Ollie that he only wanted two of them built but may need one more. His house and stables would be built near the northern border of the ranch just a hundred yards from the Ogden River. It would provide a ready source of water for the buildings.

The other two houses would be a hundred yards apart pointing to the original ranch house and barn which would still leave enough room for two more houses if they became necessary.

But it wasn't just the easy access to water that had driven him to have his house built in that location. The trees that lined both sides of the river not only acted as a good windbreak, but they also provided a spectacular view with the mountains just beyond. He'd have the front porch of the house facing the southwest to enjoy the incredible sunsets.

The construction would start tomorrow, and he'd already ordered everything that the houses would need for furnishings and the daily necessities of life.

He'd monitor the construction, but after he'd met Ollie Jacobs, he had complete confidence that the job would be done to his specifications and with fine workmanship.

While the work was ongoing, he had other things he'd need to do.

Grip's letter had arrived that morning and Rich had gathered everyone together in the parlor to read it aloud, as Grip had instructed in the first sentence.

It was a long letter, and in the first paragraph, Grip had explained why he had written just the one letter to Rich.

As he read the descriptions of the ranch, Ogden and the beauty of the landscape, Rich felt as if he was reading poetry and not a simple recitation of information. It increased his own desire to see their new home and he was sure that Wilma, Tom and Jenny felt the same way.

As he continued to read about Grip's plans, he paused, then looked at Tom and grinned.

"He said to tell you that he has four young boy dogs named Otto, Karl, Fritz and Max and that you could figure out the breed."

Tom laughed then said, "He asked me when he first got back if I liked dogs, but I thought he might have forgotten about them with all that he had to do. If they're German shepherds, then I'm a happy man. They'll probably be close to full grown by the time we get there."

Rich nodded then resumed reading the letter, flipping page after page until he finished.

"He said to let each of you read it if you'd like, just in case I misread something."

"It sounds as if Grip is making excellent progress," Wilma said, "He already has the contracts done for his houses and the stables as well."

"It does sound like a wonderful setting," Jenny said as she smiled at her husband.

"And he already has our dogs," Tom replied with a grin.

Julia had been listening but watching her aunt as well. Emily hadn't said much about making that long journey to Utah, but Julia wasn't studying her to look for the same display of enthusiasm that the others had, but more to determine how she was doing physically. She had been spending much more time resting than she had at this stage when she was carrying Mary, and Julia was growing concerned.

After the group began breaking up, she approached Wilma and pulled her aside.

"Can we have Doctor Morris stop by to examine Emily?"

"I'll have Rich stop by his office tomorrow and ask him to make a house call. He needs to see her anyway. It was only yesterday when we arranged for him to come when she goes into labor. I'm sure she's all right."

"That's what she tells me, but she's nearing the end of her childbearing age and that's a very dangerous time for a woman."

"I know. I've lost two babies at childbirth and the last one almost took my life when I was thirty-five. Of course, Mister Lawrence told Richard that I should be fired when I couldn't work for two weeks afterward."

"Thank you, Wilma," Julia said before walking to the office to write a letter to Grip now that she had his address.

She soon sat behind the desk that seemed almost like one of the navy's monitors, slid some paper from the box in the corner and dipped a pen into the open bottle of ink.

Wilma hadn't recalled a name and Julia was growing frustrated. She'd asked Jenny but she knew even fewer of the former employees.

She looked at the blank sheet of paper and suffered the same difficulty that Grip had confronted when he had begun to write the letter to Julia that was still in his black saddlebags.

After a minute of thought, she addressed it as, *My Dearest 'I hope you aren't my' Brother Grip*.

She smiled then began to write, avoiding any excessively emotional wording. She told him of her visit to the Pinkerton Agency and that Joe Trimble had explained the difficulties, especially without a name. She didn't hide her frustrations about not having even a starting point for an investigation.

Finally, she wrote an entire page about what Wilma had told her about Mary Duffy and how she had impacted his life. As much as she had tried to keep from expressing her feelings in the letter, when she'd written of Mary Duffy and how Wilma had described that night when she had been sent to his bedroom to 'make him a man', it was hard to keep her emotions in check. She wrote that she hoped that in the event she discovered that her father was someone other than Lawrence Preston Taylor, that he would be willing to accept her as the woman who could fill that gap in his life.

She finished the letter but didn't read it as she was concerned that she may have gone too far in the last page.

She quickly folded it and slid it into an envelope before addressing it to Grip Taylor, P.O. Box 25, Ogden, Utah Territory.

Her letter would be posted tomorrow with the others. Even Bill and Millie had written a few pages that Emily would include in her letter.

Mickey Mooney's gang arrived in Leadville two days after Grip moved into his house and were stunned by what they found.

It was indeed a wide-open town, but what had set them all aback was that almost every single man was armed. They had been moderately surprised to find so many men wearing sidearms in Denver, but it was difficult to find one without a pistol in Leadville.

They'd stayed in the town for two days and tried to use their strongarm tactics that had proved so effective in St. Louis when they followed two men leaving the assay office with a wad of cash. The two men had divided the bills as they walked down one of the dirt streets as if there was no danger.

Mickey saw their chance when they turned into an alley to cross over to the next street where there was an entire block of saloons and brothels.

Mickey had assumed that his size and their greater number would make the men just hand over their money without hesitation, but he was sadly mistaken.

Their biggest mistake was that they left their hammer loops in place when they quickly and loudly approached the two men with their big blades drawn.

The two miners heard their noisy approach and before they even turned to see who was rushing behind them, they quickly drew and cocked their Colts.

When they whipped around, Mickey and his boys found themselves staring at the two muzzles with nothing but knives in their hands.

"You boys want somethin'?" the shorter man growled.

For the first time in his life, Mickey felt the stab of fear race through him. He may have been a giant of a man, but at this range whatever caliber bullet shot out of that pistol would probably be the end of him. There was no excuse he could make, so without answering he quickly slid his knife home and began to backstep.

John, Cajun Al and Bill Jones followed suit and the gang of thugs hastily made their shameful escape from the near-death confrontation.

After they reached the boardwalk, Mickey said, "This place is crawlin' with gun totin' bastards. I figure we need to find a more peaceable place we can take over without any competition."

"Where do you want to go, boss?" Cajun Al asked.

"Let's go back to the hotel and talk about it. We need someplace quiet without a lot of law."

"There's a lot of places like that, boss," Bill said.

"And we gotta find one," Mickey said as they walked east along the boardwalk.

After they'd walked for thirty seconds, Mickey said, "I hear them Mormons are real peaceable. Kinda like a big flock of sheep."

John snickered before he replied, "I don't reckon they'll be peaceable for long after we get there."

"It won't be an easy ride 'cause we'll have to take the train through Wyoming, but maybe we'll find one of those peaceable towns on the way."

"Whatever you say, boss," John replied.

Again, it was their combined ignorance that would cause them grief when they equated Mormons with Quakers and believing that they refrained from shooting or even carrying firearms. They didn't realize that the only thing that the Mormons and Quakers shared in common was their firm beliefs.

They didn't have a clue that one Mormon who lived just four miles from where Grip now called home would become the most famous of all American gunmakers. John Moses Browning would patent more world-changing guns than anyone, including the already famous Samuel Colt.

They would have been shocked to know that Mister Browning would soon make the acquaintance of the son of the man whose father they had set up for murder.

While the Mooney boys were planning on leaving Leadville, Steve Albert had departed Omaha, but not in the fashion he had hoped.

He'd been mugged and robbed the night before and was lucky to have survived. He had a broken left forearm and bruises all over his body, but his loss of the money had given him few options but to return to his house in Kansas City.

He begged his way onto the *Sturgeon,* a tired sidewheeler but couldn't do any work with his broken arm. He knew that he was fortunate that he knew the first mate, because without the ability to help, not many of the boats would let him ride for free.

Steve expected that when he reached home, he'd just walk in the door and find a sympathetic wife and an angry niece. He'd already created a believable story for what had happened by the time the *Sturgeon* had pulled away from the

Omaha docks. He'd tell them that he'd been robbed in Kansas City on the way back from the hotel and then dumped onto a riverboat that was heading south. He'd spent the last few days recovering from his injuries and walking back home.

As the steamboat plied the Missouri heading for Kansas City, Steve was already anxious to reunite with his family. Emily would have her baby soon and he would be surprised if she survived the childbirth this time. She'd had a bad time with Mary and that was more than two years ago. Then Julia would have to stay to take care of the children and everything would be better. Maybe he should have just pretended to be robbed before he got on the boat to Omaha. He could have hidden the cash and had Julia and the money. It was too late now, but one out of two wasn't bad.

Steve was in a good mood considering all that had happened in Omaha. What he wouldn't realize for a while was that his worst injury hadn't been caused by the muggers who had nearly beaten him to death. The very expensive prostitute he'd paid twenty dollars for spending the night with him had left him with a gift that she presented to all of her clients.

He wouldn't discover the syphilis for another month, but he would find his other problems tomorrow when he walked through the door of his empty house with his broken arm.

It was officially the first day of summer and Grip had ridden from the ranch leaving the dogs in charge. There were four construction crews on the property creating a symphony of rasping saws and hammered nails sprinkled with crescendos of loud cursing.

He had visited U.S. Marshal Ignatius Palmer in Salt Lake City yesterday and the two men had formed an instant friendship as they shared similar values. The marshal had received a letter from his counterpart in St. Louis, so he wasn't surprised to meet Grip. They had shared stories for an hour and Grip had explained why he had asked for the badge and promised to keep the marshal informed. The marshal had told him that he'd appreciate any help he could provide because he only had three deputies for the entire territory.

On the day before that visit, he'd met with Weber County Sheriff Zeke Johnson and enjoyed talking about Ernie Upton's fiasco about the Wilkerson ranch. The sheriff explained how he had to avoid laughing when Ernie tried to convince him that they had defrauded the bank.

He's also spent a good amount of his time in Ogden just showing his face and meeting the townsfolk, so they'd be comfortable seeing him in their midst.

With his legal and recognition foundations settled, today was a much-welcomed break in the hectic weeks he'd had since his arrival.

He soon stepped down before J.M. Browning & Bros., Guns, Pistols, Ammunition & Fishing Tackle, pulled his unfired Winchester '76 from its scabbard and entered the busy shop.

There were three men behind the counter all talking to customers and another four men browsing the selection of weapons that filled the relatively small business.

He approached the counter just as two of the men turned then exited the shop.

"What can I do for you, sir?" one of the two freed gunsmiths asked.

He laid the Winchester on the counter and said, "I have a question about my '76. It's chambered for the .45-75 WCF, but I hear that they're offering the model in a .50 caliber bore. I'm not sure that the design can handle that large of a caliber, but I'm an engineer, not a gunsmith. I don't claim to know more than the boys at Winchester, but I wanted an expert opinion before I decided to buy one."

The man smiled, then turned to the other gunsmith and said, "You'll want to talk to my brother, John. He's a genius when it comes to guns of all sorts. He even designs his own."

Grip smiled at John who stepped closer to the Winchester and asked, "May I?"

"Please."

John picked up the repeater and examined it closely before setting it back on the counter.

“I noticed the unusual stock and forearm and I was wondering what other modifications you had made but didn’t see any.”

“The only changes were cosmetic for a specific reason.”

“I’d ask what that reason was, but I’ll answer your question about the Winchester first. I agree with you about the .50 caliber models, and I think that the .45-75 is the limit of its capability. They’re going to have to totally redesign the gun’s internals to give it the ability to handle more power.”

“I have an 1874 Sharps back at the house, but I ordered a Sharps-Borshadt with a Malcolm eight-power scope before I left St. Louis a couple of weeks ago. I had the stock and forearm changed to use the same ebony that I used for this stock and on the grips of my Remington.”

John said, “Come back into the workshop and I’ll show you a rifle that is better than both of those long guns. It’s something totally new and those boys from Winchester you mentioned are already interested.”

Grip picked up his Winchester and followed John around the counter then up some steps into the large workshop on the second floor. He could see rifles in various stages of completion, so he wasn’t sure what the gunsmith was working on.

John picked up a completed rifle and as Grip stood by his shoulder, John said, “This is a falling block design that is a lot different than previous types. This one is what I call the high wall version because the hammer completely disappears when you bring the lever forward to load the chamber.”

“It’s a single shot?”

“Yes, sir. But it’s a very robust design and the seal on the cartridge is better than anything else, so all of the power of the charge is used to send the bullet down the barrel. It has a floating forearm, so the sights won’t dance very much making the shots more accurate and consistent.”

“That is impressive. What cartridge does this one use?”

“I built this one to use the Sharps .45 caliber cartridges. They’re relatively easy to find. Is that what your ’74 uses?”

“Yes, sir. The Sharps-Borshadt uses the same caliber.”

“I think you’d be more impressed with one of these, Mister…?”

“Oh, I apologize. The name’s Grip. Grip Taylor. It’s short for Agrippa.”

John grinned then shook Grip’s hand before asking, “Did you want to buy one of my falling block rifles? I can have one built for you in two weeks.”

"I'd like that. If I drop off some ebony boards, can you use it for the forearm and stock?"

"I've never worked with that wood before, but one of my brothers is very good with woodwork."

"Can I have it chambered in the same .45 caliber? I'll bring the ebony by tomorrow."

"Good enough. It's an ideal platform for a telescopic sight because there are no obstructions. I can mount that same eight-power Malcolm scope on it if you'd like."

Grip grinned before he said, "Let's do that and now I wonder why I even bought the Sharps-Borshadt."

"It's a good gun, but mine is a bit better."

"Thank you, John. You have a real talent with weapons."

"As everyone keeps telling me."

Grip nodded and then headed for the stairs. He hadn't been given a price, but it didn't matter. He was curious how much better John Browning's new rifle would be compared to his Sharps. He had been putting rounds into the bullseye consistently at six hundred yards and had expected even better from the Sharps-Borshadt when it arrived with his other weapons.

He stepped out into the bright sunshine and mounted Pitch ending his recreational break.

He stopped at the post office and was enormously pleased to see three envelopes waiting for him in box 25. After unlocking the box and sliding the letters into his inner jacket pocket, he left the post office, mounted his black gelding and set off northeast to his ranch.

After checking with the construction crews, he unsaddled Pitch then walked to the house with his four German friends following.

———

Gray-haired and bespectacled Doctor Peter Morris finished his examination of Emily, patted her on the shoulder and said, “I’m sorry to disappoint you Mrs. Albert, but you only have one baby in there, but he’s a big child, so I’m going to have you admitted to St. Mary’s so I can keep a close watch on your progress.”

Emily suspected that the doctor was worried about her age and that there was a very real possibility she wouldn’t be alive much longer. She’d given birth so many times and survived when many other women hadn’t. Bringing Mary into the world had almost sent her into the next world, but Mary was now her two-year-old angel. But she knew that worrying wouldn’t help. She was happy that she’d be staying at St. Mary’s.

“Thank you, Doctor.”

“I’ll make the arrangements,” he said as he stood, picked up his black bag and left the room.

Julia smiled at her aunt then followed the doctor through the doorway.

Once they reached the parlor, the doctor turned to her and said, “Your aunt is carrying a very large child and while I do have concerns about her age, I found her in excellent health. When she’s at St. Mary’s, she’ll receive the best of care.”

“I was worried about her. She seemed more tired than before and I didn’t think it was because of her age.”

“She’s a very fortunate woman, Miss Marley. By coming here and being relieved of everyday chores and being on her feet so long each day, her chances of a successful delivery have become much better. I’m admitting her primarily because I will be nearby when she goes into labor but also to ensure that she rests as much as possible. The good sisters will see to her every wish.”

“Thank you again, Doctor. When I see Mister Stone, I’ll be sure to suggest that he provide a large donation to St. Mary’s from the charitable fund that Grip established before he left.”

“He’s an amazing young man and nothing like his father, which I find remarkable. It would have been much easier for him to just accept the path his father prepared for him, yet he took a far different direction.”

“How well did you know him?”

"I first saw him as a patient when he was nine and he cut his left forearm with a knife. It took a few stitches, but he never even shed a tear. The reason I can still recall that so vividly is because as much as I was impressed with his stoicism, I was stunned that he smiled at me and kept reassuring me that it didn't hurt while I was putting in the sutures. He even complimented me on my stitching and apologized for my having to make a house call because of his stupid, boyish mistake. It's not the kind of thing that one forgets.

"Over the years, I was pleased as I watched the rift between father and son grow. I only visited saw him three times over the years, and each time was for a relatively minor malady. I believe that he just wanted to talk to a friend."

"You were his father's doctor for that long?"

"I didn't see him that often because he believed he was invulnerable, but yes, I've been with him more than twenty years now."

Julia felt her pulse quicken as she asked, "Do you remember my mother, Charlotte Marley?"

"I know that I never saw her as a patient, but I recall the name. She didn't work in the household for very long, if I remember correctly."

"Was she pregnant when she showed up to work here?" Julia asked hoping the doctor had at least heard a whisper.

"I wish I could tell you, Miss Marley, but I simply don't know. I never was allowed to even examine any of his staff."

Julia sighed then asked, "Is it possible for a brown-eyed, black-haired man to father a child with my coloring?"

"If the mother has your coloring, it is, but it's less likely. I don't suppose my answer helped you either."

"I had already been given that answer but was hoping it was wrong. I'm desperately trying to find the identity of my father, but it was so long ago, and his name isn't on my birth certificate and the doctor who signed it is dead."

"And when did your mother pass?"

"Eight years ago. I'm going to visit her gravesite tomorrow."

"May I ask why it is so important that you find your father's name? You obviously don't need any financial support."

"It's because I don't want to be Grip's half-sister and he doesn't wish to be my half-brother. We'd prefer a much different relationship."

"I'm not surprised that he didn't choose to ignore that possibility. I wish I could help, Miss Marley. Anyway, I'll be sending around the ambulance to bring your aunt to St. Mary's in a couple of days."

Julia smiled and said, "I'll have her ready and I'll tell my cousins not to worry."

"Thank you, Miss Marley and good luck on your search."

Julia nodded then watched the doctor leave the house before she turned to go to the kitchen and talk to her cousins. Doctor Morris' soothing words had calmed her worries and she was very grateful that Grip had sent her aunt to his care. She'd have to thank Grip when she saw him again and hoped by then she'd know the name of her father.

———

Mickey Mooney's gang had spent a few days in Cheyenne and had continued to adapt to the very different lifestyle of the West. They'd been riding much more and had committed their first two crimes in the town. One was just a simple mugging that had only added forty-two dollars to their cache. The second was much more profitable when they rode to a nearby small town and robbed the dry goods store, the saloon and the greengrocer. They'd managed to ride away with three hundred and ten dollars after the extended day of thievery, but they had killed two citizens in Whitewater and instead of returning to Cheyenne, had ridden to the next stop on the Union Pacific's line and taken a train to Green River in Western Wyoming, just sixty miles from the Utah border.

———

While the Mooney boys were checking out prospects in Green River, Grip sat at the kitchen table with a cup of coffee and began to read his mail. The letter from Rich explained how well Julia and the Albert family was doing and that they were all pleased that he had found what sounded like a wonderful new home. The included letters from Wilma, Tom and Jenny all reinforced what Rich had written, but Wilma added that she had told Julia about Mary Duffy and hoped he wasn't upset with her.

Grip was actually pleased that Wilma had told Julia about Mary but was curious if Julia would mention it in her letter that he'd save for the last. He read Emily's letter and wasn't surprised when she hinted that she was thinking about staying in St. Louis after all but would decide after the baby was born. The included letters from Billy, who had explained his dismissal of the 'y' from his name and from Millie, who wrote more volubly than she spoke were both light-hearted and kept him smiling as he read them.

He finally opened Julia's letter and after the twisted salutation, he was almost disappointed when the first page was just an explanation of her meeting with Joe Trimble and her first riding lessons on Ebony. She expressed her growing concerns about her aunt and her hope that the expanded Albert family would be joining them when they left for Utah.

But when he flipped to the second page, her tone changed to what he had hoped to find on the first page. She did more than just let him know that Wilma had told her about Mary Duffy, she let her emotions free to express her desire to be the woman he needed to fill his soul.

When he finished reading her letter, he set it with the others. He was using the kitchen table as his desk, but wasn't about to keep the paper, envelopes and ink on the tabletop until they were needed. So, after retrieving them from the nearby cupboard, he sat down and slid the first sheet of blank paper before him. He'd write replies to Rich and the others first and reserve more time to respond to Julia's missive.

His writing was interrupted by a visit from one of the foremen with some questions about his house and then by a quick lunch which he ate standing at the counter, but by four o'clock he was ready to write his letter to Julia.

He'd already given Rich an update on the progress he'd made so he just needed this one to be personal. As he started to write the letter, he looked at his black saddlebags that he always kept in the house even though most of the cash was now in the vault of the Ogden Bank. He decided to include the first letter he'd written to her in Kansas City.

He didn't use a Latin salutation but mimicked hers when he wrote: *My Dearest 'Please Not Be My' Sister Julia,* on the first line.

He didn't allow himself to become excessively emotional but did retract his earlier wish that she enjoy her time in St. Louis and meet other prospective beaus. He also added some thoughts about how she might find her answer to the question that haunted them both. He suggested that she ask Joe Trimble to find her mother's grave, if she hadn't already and see if anyone had visited her resting place. If her mother had truly loved the man who had fathered her, then unless he was a heartless cur, he would have come to talk to her or leave flowers. He may be dead, but it was something.

He also thought that Emily may tell her more now that Steve was no longer there. Charlotte may have mentioned where she'd worked before she entered the employ of Lawrence Taylor in one of the letters that she'd written asking Emily to care for Julia. It wouldn't be much, but even if she had the name of the household where her mother had worked it would be a starting point for Joe Trimble.

He ended the long letter with as close as he dared to tell her that he loved her but avoided that four-letter word until he could tell her that he loved her as a woman and not a sister.

Before sealing the envelope, he took out the first letter and on the blank face, he wrote: *I wrote this in Kansas City but didn't want to put any pressure on you to stay.*

He folded it then slid it into the properly addressed envelope before sealing the flap. He picked up all of the letters and set them on a chair to keep them from getting covered in dog saliva. His boys were getting better at staying in the bunkhouse when they weren't out causing trouble for the workmen, who seemed to enjoy having the young dogs nearby anyway. He had gotten them into the habit of staying there by feeding them in the bunkhouse rather than the house. He'd also removed their collars as he was now able to identify them by their different markings and they were responding to their names.

The crews were packing up for the day and he hadn't eaten supper yet. There was still a lot of sunlight and he thought it was time to have his first long run on his new property. It wasn't fenced in, but the two-by-four-mile perimeter would give him a lot of space. He had ridden the property several times and had followed a path that would give him a good workout with several hills and a few streams that he'd have to leap across. The trick was finding ground that was reasonably clear of obstacles other than trees.

He changed into his running footwear and his cut-off britches and with no female eyes within five miles, he didn't bother putting on a shirt. The altitude was over four thousand feet, but the air was much drier than St. Louis, so he didn't expect any difficulties.

Grip left the back of the house and started jogging away from the construction. He soon picked up the trail he'd marked with Pitch and turned onto the path. He followed his usual process and began to pick up the pace as his muscles loosened.

He was in his element as he crossed the ground and leapt the first creek in his path. The addition of the three hills he'd need to climb added more strain to his muscles which was why he'd chosen his path to cross over their crests rather than go around them. The downslope was a bit dangerous and he thought about making a different course for his night runs.

But now he just ran, exploring his property in greater detail than he had from Pitch's back. As his feet pounded the ground, he found himself wondering what Julia would think of it. He thought it was an exquisite piece of landscape, even if it wasn't suitable as a cattle ranch.

He made a turn and soon entered the forest in the northeastern corner. He zigzagged between pine trunks and had to push aside branches as he kept his feet moving at a rapid pace. If he'd been on a horse, then he probably wouldn't have met another occupant of the forest. But as he shifted to avoid a three-foot diameter trunk, he had to abruptly end his run as he skidded to a halt.

Grip knew he had a serious problem when he looked at the three gray wolves just twenty feet away. They were staring at him with menacing eyes but weren't snarling or even moving.

He was sure that there had to be more of them nearby but didn't see any. He knew that most wolf packs numbered between six and eight and they always hunted in packs. He wondered if they were hunting him or if he had just entered their world uninvited.

He stood his ground and just stared back at the wolf he identified as the alpha. She was a handsome animal with powerful shoulders and looked remarkably like his young canine companions. They continued to stare at each other for another thirty silent seconds before she just yipped, then her two companions turned and all three melted into the trees.

Grip exhaled and wiped the sweat from his brow, uncertain if it was there more from the exercise or the brief interlude with the wolves. He knew that he should just turn around and head back, but the wolves had gone to his right and deeper into the forest, so he began to jog again along his path. He suspected that the wolves were the reason he hadn't found the three old cows that had been left behind.

He emerged from the trees and turned north. He saw other wild animals on his run, but nothing as frightening as the wolves. He knew that black and brown bears inhabited the area as well as coyotes, foxes and a wide variety of herbivores to keep the carnivores fed. The presence of so much water and forested cover provided a good habitat for all of them and he wasn't about to change that. He was sure that the sharp-toothed critters had been disappointed then the cattle were sold off. He also decided that the next time he ran, he'd be armed. He wouldn't bring a heavy pistol, but he'd buy another knife that suited his needs the next time he visited John Browning.

He'd dropped off the ebony the day after his first visit and struck up a longer conversation with the brilliant young gunsmith. He had explained the reason he'd come to Ogden, but not the amount of money he had. John had agreed with most of the other men he'd told about his plans and told Grip that he thought he might be short a few cards in his deck. He'd also bought a large basket from the Chinese laundry for his dirty clothes out of necessity. It had a sling to attach to his saddle, so he wouldn't have to use the wagon to drop off or retrieve his clothes.

He finished his long run and found that he hadn't had any problem with the higher altitude, but the hills had proven to be the challenge he had hoped that they would be. As he cooled down, he inspected the construction work on his house, the stables and the other two houses which Ollie had told him wouldn't delay the work on his house or the stables. The stables were the farthest along, and his house wasn't far behind. He was pleased with the progress and the original estimate of six weeks for the jobs should be met easily.

That night, as he lay on his bed with the window open allowing a cool night breeze to pass through the room, Grip thought that even though he wasn't quite settled yet, it might be time for him to begin his attempt to pay back the damage his father had inflicted.

He had thought that he'd have to remain on the property to oversee the construction, but after watching the crews work and the control the foremen had over the workers, he felt redundant. He'd check the *Salt Lake Tribune* and the other local papers tomorrow. The newspapers primary goal seemed to be the ongoing war between the Mormons and non-Mormons and disaffected Mormons in the state, but they still provided other news stories. He'd see if any of them would provide him with his first opportunity to put his plan into motion.

CHAPTER 12

Grip rode out past the two whitewashed stumps that marked the entrance to his property the next morning around nine o'clock. It had taken him longer to leave as he'd had to argue and then bribe the dogs to stay.

He'd stop by the book store which was next door to the sheriff's office to pick up a few newspapers. He might buy a few books to keep him occupied as well.

Ten minutes later, as he dismounted before Aubrey & Sons Books and Periodicals, he heard shouting from the sheriff's office. He tied off Pitch and his curiosity made him put reading newspapers to the back burner as he stepped onto the boardwalk.

He walked to the open doorway, but the irate shouting made him stop before he entered in case someone threw something.

A man's voice yelled, "Are you telling me you can't do a damned thing about this?"

"Al," Sheriff Johnson pleaded, "They're not breaking the law. If you had a proper deed to your place, then I could go out there and tell 'em to leave you alone. But they bought that land and you've gotta go. I'm sorry."

Grip took one step forward and peeked inside to see the beet red Al shaking a sheet of paper in front of the sheriff as he snarled, "This ain't right, Zeke! I've been on that land for ten years and nobody said a word. Now they're tryin' to kick me and mine out of our home and take everything 'cause they said I don't have any cause to be there. It ain't right, Zeke!"

"I know it isn't, Al, but my hands are bound by the law. That eviction notice is legal, and you've got another three weeks to vacate the property. It's the same for the Sandersons, Smiths and the Millers, too. All of you have to get off that land or they're gonna force you off."

"They'd better come with a lot of firepower to do it, Zeke."

"Now, don't go saying things like that, Al. You know that they've already got those four gunmen to do their dirty work, and you don't want to risk your wife and young'uns, do you?"

Al was by no means mollified but just continued to glare at the sheriff.

Grip realized that this might be exactly what he needed, so he stepped through the doorway and said, "Good morning, Zeke. Got a problem?"

Al Leibnitz turned and looked at Grip who had the appearance one of the gunmen that The Greater Utah

Property Management Company had hired and assumed that he was here on their behalf.

Before the sheriff could answer, Al snapped, “Are you gonna shoot me with your private sheriff watchin’, mister?”

Grip smiled as he shook his head and replied, “No, sir, and I’m sure that Zeke is an honest lawman, so you owe him an apology. My name is Grip Taylor and I moved here a couple of weeks ago. I just heard you ranting at the sheriff and thought I’d see if I could help you.”

“Help me? Why would you help me? Is this some trick to get me out there alone so you can shoot me in the back?”

“No, sir. Take a deep breath and calm down, then I’ll let Sheriff Johnson explain the issue to me.”

Al was about to protest, but Grip’s smile and calm demeanor had its intended effect, so he just nodded.

Grip looked at the sheriff who said, “The Greater Utah Property Management Company bought up a large part of Weber County east of your property. It includes the land that Al and three other families had built ranches or farms. The problem was that none of the families had a legal right to the land. They had built their homes on open land when there was nothing nearby. They’re squatters, whether they like the word or not. When the Greater Utah Property Management Company bought it, they had me issue eviction notices to each family. I hated doing it, but they had the law on their side and made it clear that I had no choice.

"Like Al mentioned, they hired some gunmen to push them off out of their homes if they don't leave willingly. I can't fight them legally or otherwise and even that badge you carry won't help."

"I know, but I do have something that might work. It'll be my first attempt at being useful, too."

"I hope you're right, Grip," Zeke replied then looked at Al and said, "If anybody can help you, Al, it's Mister Taylor. He's a good man and a U.S. Deputy Marshal, too. Like I just told him, the badge won't help, but it should at least let you figure out he's not a one of those gunslingers that the company hired."

"Where is the company offices?" Grip asked.

"Down in Salt Lake City, but they set up a small office in Huntsville. It's a small town about another ten miles along the Ogden River. Al can show you where it is."

"Is anyone there who can handle land sales, or is it just for their enforcers?"

"I reckon they can sell the land, or they wouldn't be there."

Grip wondered why they would have an office in a small town rather than the county seat but didn't believe that the sheriff knew the answer.

Grip nodded then turned to Mister Leibnitz and said, "Let's swing by my house so I can pick up some things, then we can go to Huntsville and have a chat with the boys. You can give me more details on the way."

Al glanced at Sheriff Johnson then said, "Alright."

Zeke was visibly relieved when he said, "Thanks, Grip. I appreciate the help. Let me know how things work out."

"I'll do that, Zeke," Grip replied before he and Al left the office.

Al mounted his brown gelding that looked like a workhorse as Grip mounted Pitch.

After he posted the letters to St. Louis, they headed east out of town and Grip asked Al to start providing him more details as soon as they started riding.

By the time they reached his property, Al had begun to trust Grip, even though he had no idea how he planned to fix the problem. He was surprised when he spotted the many construction projects but didn't ask as he didn't want to risk offending Grip if it was something unsavory.

Grip stepped down before his house and just entered as the four dogs raced from the bunkhouse. Al stayed in his saddle because Grip had told him he'd be out in a minute or so, but he smiled when the dogs sat in a row at the bottom of the porch steps waiting for him to emerge.

Grip soon exited his house carrying the Sharps cloaked in its scabbard then smiled when he saw the boys lined up.

"I need to get past, fellas," he said as he stepped onto the first step.

They popped to their feet as their tails began to beat the wind. He rubbed each of their heads in sequence, saying their names as he always did. He didn't bribe them this time but attached the Sharps scabbard to the left side of Pitch's saddle, then mounted.

"Keep an eye on everything, gentlemen. I'll be back in a few hours or maybe not until tomorrow depending on how things go."

He was still smiling when he turned Pitch away from the house and asked, "Can we pick up a road from here, Al?"

"Yes, sir. It's on the other side of the river, but there are a few fords we can use."

"I didn't see it before, but I guess those trees block the view."

"I reckon so."

Grip then looked across at Al and said, "You didn't ask about the construction."

"No, sir."

Grip then began to explain what he was having built, but not the full reason. He needed to pass the time now that he had a good idea of what to expect. He'd only picked up the Sharps to impress any of the company's gunmen. He didn't plan on using any of his firepower but was more than willing to use the power of the purse.

His only question was how much the Greater Utah Property Management Company would demand for the land. He could buy the entire expanse but didn't want to give them too much profit. If he made an offer to purchase it all, then they'd know how much he could afford and would overcharge him for what he needed to buy to allow the folks to remain in their homes.

He just hoped that he'd get the chance to enter the office and talk to someone who was interested in selling land. He almost thought about returning to the house and changing to a less threatening appearance, but he had decided to go down this road when he'd left Ann Arbor and it was too late to reverse course now. He'd soon find out whether it was a smart decision or not.

His biggest concern as he and Al Leibnitz rode across his property was that he'd be challenged by one of the gunmen who had been hired by the land company. He didn't expect that a hard man who sold his gun for hire would react the same way as the thief on the train.

They soon reached a ford and walked their horses across the Ogden River and picked up the road.

"We've got about another four miles or so," Al said loudly.

"Are you sure you want to come along? I might be able to just talk to them easier if they didn't see me with you and it might get dangerous."

"I can handle my Colt," Al proclaimed loudly before he asked, "You ever shoot anybody?"

"No, sir. That wasn't my plan, but I've already made that commitment in my head courtesy of United States Marshal Abner Guest in St. Louis. If one of those boys wants to cause trouble, I'll be ready, but I'd rather handle this peacefully."

"Good luck with that, Grip. I ain't sure what the company told them to do, but I hope you're right."

"Do you know how many of the gunmen are at the office?"

"There are four altogether, but most of the time, two or three of 'em ride around our places to let us know that they're serious."

“I was kind of surprised when the sheriff told me that they had the small office there and not in Ogden. Are you sure that’s where they can sell some land?”

“I never asked, but they got a sign over the door.”

“Okay. The sheriff said that there were three other families that have been served eviction notices. Can you tell me about each of them, including yours?”

“I have my wife, Bridget, my only girl, Rhonda, she’s nineteen, then I have two boys, Tad who’s fourteen and Jasper who’s eleven. Harry Sanderson is a widower, but has four young’uns, two barely teenaged boys and two older daughters. Jason Smith is a Mormon and has three wives, so they have a whole passel of kids but none of ‘em are older than twelve. Hanley and Mary Miller have four boys between seventeen and thirteen and a young girl. The boys are kinda scrappy.”

“Has there been any gunfire yet?”

“A few shots have been sent the gunnies’ way to let ‘em know they ain’t welcome.”

“Did you do any of that shooting?”

“I mighta let a few loose.”

Grip nodded and realized that this was already sounding more dangerous than he’d anticipated. He could visualize the land company's enforcers almost taunting the families to fire warning shots at long range almost as an excuse to take action. Men who received pay for shooting people didn't like to just ride around. The company may not have given them instructions to do any killing, but he doubted if they'd mind much. There was no law in Huntsville and once the first farmer or rancher was killed, all hell would break loose.

The rest of the ride into Huntsville was quiet as Grip continued to dwell on the problem. It all depended on what he found when he rode into the small town.

The first buildings appeared just minutes after he'd started to ask Al about the gunmen, and before he asked, Al said, "The office in halfway down the street on the left."

"Okay. Are you sure you don't want to just head home?"

"Nope."

Grip still thought it would be better if he went into town alone. Al had told him where the families lived, so they wouldn't be hard to find if he had been smart and gone back to his wife and children. But he could already see traffic on the main street and was trying to spot the one or two gunmen who had remained at the office. If they were inside, he'd be at a bigger disadvantage.

It didn't take long after they entered the main street before he found not only the office, but one of the gunmen who was already staring at him as he sat in front of the office on a bench.

He didn't need to have Al point the man out to him either. His hard eyes advertised his profession and Grip was sure that he had been identified as a challenger. The gunman stood as Grip turned Pitch to the seed and feed store which was adjacent to the office.

He didn't look at Al as he dismounted then stepped onto the dry boardwalk but heard Al's footsteps as he hopped onto the boardwalk behind him.

To change the gunman's perception, Grip smiled and started walking at a normal pace toward the small office of the Greater Utah Property Management Company.

When he was about fifteen feet away from the man, he asked, "Is there somebody in the office I can talk to about buying some land?"

The man made no pretense of courtesy, much less friendliness when he snapped, "Who are you, mister? And what are you doin' with that squatter?"

Grip glanced back at Al and then replied, "The name's Grip Taylor and I just bought some land along the Ogden River, and Al here told me that I might be able to buy some more nearby. Is there somebody in the office I can talk to about that?"

"There ain't nobody in the office. My name is Archie Wilcox and I'm tellin' you to get back on your horse and go back to your new place. This ain't no place for you, Mister Taylor."

"Why don't they have someone who can sell land if they have an office here in Huntsville?"

"I told you to forget about it and just get on your horse and ride away, or didn't you hear my name?"

"I heard your name, but it doesn't ring a bell. I was living in St. Louis last month."

Archie stared at Grip as he slowly asked, "Did those squatters hire you to try and face us down, mister?"

"I never met Mister Leibnitz until an hour ago or thereabouts. Why would they hire me to do that anyway? I'm an engineer, not a gunman."

"Ain't you kinda young to be drivin' a train?"

"Not that kind of an engineer. I build things. But if there's no one here who can sell me some land, then I guess I'll just have to ride to Salt Lake City and talk to the folks in the main office after all."

Archie's right thumb flicked the hammer loop off his Colt as he said, "You won't find anybody down there wantin' to sell you the land that those squatters are on if that's what you're thinkin'."

It wasn't difficult to sense the growing hostility and tension and he began to doubt that he'd be able to talk his way out of the situation.

Grip scratched his chin as he said, "That's plumb silly," but didn't bring his hand anywhere near his pistol. He knew he'd be a dead man if his fingers came within six inches of those ebony grips.

"Are you callin' me silly, mister?" Archie snarled.

"I'm not looking for trouble, but don't push your luck either. I may not be a hired gun like you, but if you keep acting with such arrogance, I'll be forced to respond."

Archie didn't give Grip a hint of warning as he suddenly grabbed his Colt's grips, but Grip knew that he'd pushed the hired killer too far and was already expecting him to go for his pistol.

But the moment that Archie's hand dropped to his revolver, Grip's right hand that had been scratching his chin whipped to his left side and snatched his dagger from its sheath.

As Archie's Colt was being cocked and brought to its firing position, the dagger flew across the fifteen feet and slid deeply into his gut.

Archie's eyes flew open as his index finger yanked his trigger and his left hand automatically reached for his abdomen to pull the blade free.

The .44 blasted through the dry boards at his feet before his Colt tumbled from his hand as he yanked the dagger from his gut.

Grip had pulled his Remington by the time Archie Wilcox dropped to his knees and stared up at Grip in shocked silence. The blood was pumping onto his tan shirt and oozing between his fingers as he struggled to breathe.

He finally gasped, “You bastard…you cheated…you…”

He then rolled onto his right side but was still breathing as Grip picked up his dagger and wiped the blade on Archie’s already bloody shirt.

Archie was rasping as blood continued to flow onto the boardwalk and Grip picked up his Colt, then turned and looked at Al and handed him the pistol.

“I’m going to need you to write a statement for me about what just happened.”

Al quietly said, “Alright,” but was still stunned by what he had just witnessed. It had happened so quickly, yet Grip didn’t seem affected at all. He said that he’d never killed a man before, yet he’d dispatched the notorious Archie Wilcox without hesitation.

Grip was far from unaffected by what had just happened. His stomach was doing backflips and his mind was reliving those horrible few moments. He knew that he could have avoided it by just going home and leaving the families to their fate, but that was why he had decided to come to Ogden in the first place. He'd have to live with what he had done and what he had to do in the future, but he had to keep faith with his mission.

Grip asked, "Who can bury him?"

"Um...Carl Borcher is the one who buries folks. He runs the butcher shop over there," he replied as he pointed across the street.

"Let's go visit Mister Borcher," Grip said before he stepped down from the boardwalk.

He was surprised that more folks hadn't exited their homes or businesses after hearing the gunshot but could understand their reluctance. Those in the street when he and Al had ridden into town had disappeared when he and Archie Wilcox had begun their tense but short conversation.

As he and Al crossed the street, he asked, "Was I supposed to know who Archie Wilcox was?"

"He had a reputation. The others do, too. The worse of 'em is Scratch Coppell. He's a string bean of a man about two inches taller than you but probably fifty pounds lighter. He's a blonde-haired and blue-eyed feller that looks real pleasant, but he's supposed to be as mean as a snake. He's usually hangin' around my place 'cause I reckon he has his eye on my

Rhonda. She's a mighty handsome lass and if Jimmy Miller was a bit older, I reckon he'd be beatin' a path to court her."

"Would he be there now?"

"More'n likely. Do you want to go to my place after we finish talkin' to Carl?"

"I'd like to meet all of the families, at least the adults, so I may as well do it at your place."

"Okay. My Bridget is a helluva cook, so she'll feed you while I round up the others."

"As long as Mister Coppell doesn't object."

They entered the butcher shop and after a short conversation with Mister Borcher who had watched the action through his window, they left his shop to make the two-mile ride to Al's house. Carl Borcher had assured Grip that he'd make sure to get the body at least hidden quickly so the others wouldn't find it.

When Grip mounted Pitch he saw the large pool of blood on the boardwalk and doubted if they'd be able to keep the secret for very long.

As soon as they cleared the east end of town, Grip could see a tall rider in the distance and asked, "Is that Coppell?"

"I think so. That's where we usually see him."

Grip nodded and this time, he released his Remington's hammer loop rather than getting into another almost hopeless situation. But the lack of a sales agent at the small office meant that his plan to simply buy their farms and ranches was probably not going to work.

He knew how good he was with the pistol but still had nothing to use as a comparison other than having just watched Archie Wilcox draw his Colt. He'd been able to get his dagger airborne before he even cleared leather but wondered if he could have gotten a shot off in that short of a time. He never worried about drawing his pistol quickly because he always wanted that little bit of extra time to be accurate. If Mister Coppell or the others were faster and still retained the accuracy, then he'd never be able to return to his house.

Scratch Coppell had been focused on the Leibnitz ranch house expecting the girl to show up again. He wasn't worried about being shot by anyone inside the house because they simply weren't that good. He hadn't seen Al ride away that morning or he might have paid the house a visit. The wife and the two kids wouldn't be a problem, but the girl was a real firecracker in addition to being an eye-catcher.

He was grinning as he stared at the house before he swung his eyes to the west and saw two riders approaching. At first, he thought that they were Smoke Talbot and J.M. McAllister, but neither one of them rode a black horse and they were south of where he was, not north.

He soon recognized Al's horse but had no idea who was accompanying him, so he continued to watch as they drew closer. When they were within four hundred yards, he slipped his hammer loop off then pulled his Winchester and cocked his hammer.

Al said, "It looks like you ain't gonna get a chance to talk to Scratch, Grip."

"I'll agree with you, Al. Instead of heading straight at him, let's cut across your land and head to the house. If he looks as if he's getting ready to fire, kick your horse into a gallop."

"What are you gonna do?"

"I'm not sure yet."

Scratch was watching intently as Grip and Al shifted their direction and headed for the house.

He was around four hundred yards away when they made the change, so he tapped his buckskin gelding on the flanks and began to cut the angle on the two men but was concentrating more on Grip. He knew that Al was no threat, but the stranger had the look of a hired gun.

Grip saw his move and slid his Winchester from its scabbard and cocked the hammer but didn't bring it level.

"Get ready to move, Al," Grip said loudly as he stared back at Coppell.

Al didn't reply but was already leaning closer to his horse's neck in preparation for the dash to the house still three hundred yards away.

Grip decided what to do, then said, "Keep going, Al," as he pulled Pitch to a stop and turned him to face Scratch Coppell.

Scratch was surprised by the sudden change but kept his horse moving at a slow trot to close the gap. He ignored Al who was continuing toward his house and began marking the decreasing gap between him and the stranger.

Grip knew he could pick off Coppell at this range but still kept his Winchester's muzzle pointing alongside Pitch's right ear. If the gunman suddenly brought his to a firing position, then he'd act. But he used his eyes to keep his imaginary iron sights on the tall, thin man as he drew closer.

Scratch began to wonder why the stranger was just sitting there with his rifle pointing in the wrong direction. It didn't make any sense. He was losing any advantage he might have if he was good with the repeater, but Scratch wasn't about to give up his. He just wondered how close the stranger would let him get before he tried to bring his rifle to bear.

Grip knew that the killer would have to take his shot soon but thought that it was likely that as soon as he let that first bullet fly, he'd either charge, change direction or even dismount.

He smiled, then quickly took off his hat and tossed it aside before he stepped down and walked ten feet behind Pitch.

Scratch had been surprised by the sudden movement and almost fired at a hundred and twenty yards, but after he saw the stranger toss his hat away, he was surprised again when he dismounted.

It was when Grip stood with his legs spread and his Winchester hanging muzzle down along his right leg that Scratch realized that he was being challenged. It was the last thing that he'd expected, but it suited him immensely. He was good with his pistol, but he was even better with his Winchester.

He kept his horse moving until he was another thirty yards closer then mimicked Grip when he tossed his hat aside, letting the bright sun reflect from his almost pale blonde hair then stepped down.

Grip could have shot him easily as he was dismounting, but he suspected that Scratch already knew that he wouldn't, or he would have stayed in his saddle.

Neither man spoke as they stared at each other across ninety yards of Utah soil. It was now a war of nerves to see who felt the need to fire first.

Scratch had been in several shootouts with his Winchester, but none had been like this. This was more like a pistol contest at fifty feet, and the difference left him a bit rattled. He almost wanted the stranger to fire to get it over with, but he just stood there looking at him refusing to appear weak by making the first move.

Grip could see the effect that the delay was having on Scratch Coppell. He'd lost the arrogant smile he had first displayed when he had dismounted. He had no intention of being the first to fire. The longer he was able to sustain the delay, the greater his advantage. He had spent most of his life learning discipline and self-control. He knew all of the techniques to avoid letting external situations or stimuli affect his mind. He doubted if his opponent had received similar training.

No matter how good he was with the cocked Winchester he held in his hand, the longer that Scratch Coppell stood facing him, the more likely it would be that he'd rush his first shot and miss.

It wasn't as if Grip was immune from fear about the very real possibility that he might die, it was just that he was able to deflect the emotion and let his mind remain focused on the man facing him.

The unusual stand-off had gone on for more than two minutes, but to Scratch, it had seemed like twenty. Taking off his hat had exposed him to the blazing summer sun and his light blue eyes were allowing too much light to pass through while Grip's dark gray eyes gave him another invisible advantage.

When the sweat began to slide down Scratch's face, he knew he had to act now. The tension alone was driving him into a place he'd never been before, and he didn't want his vision to be ruined by his salty perspiration.

He suddenly brought his Winchester level but didn't fire. He threw himself into a prone position and as he reacquired the stranger, he expected that he would try to reduce his profile as well and hit the dirt. But as soon as his eyes found his target, he was surprised yet again. The stranger was still standing and has his Winchester's sights on him.

Scratch quickly fired and after his repeater's butt banged against his shoulder, he rolled slightly onto his left side to cycle the lever. He didn't think that he'd missed, but it was second nature to have a live round in the chamber.

The moment Grip had seen the man drop to the ground he's set his sights on him and counted. As soon as he hit three, he took one sidestep just before Scratch fired. He quickly settled his sights again and squeezed his trigger. The .45 caliber round spat from his muzzle and as Scratch was bringing a fresh round from his magazine, the bullet rammed into his first thoracic vertebral body shattering his spine and ripping his spinal cord to shreds before punching into his lower gut destroying tissue and blood vessels as the lead chunks tumbled into his viscera.

Scratch screamed from the intense pain but all he could do was to flop like a fish out of water while he wailed, and blood began to fill his abdominal cavity.

Grip didn't fire again or even cycle in a new round but turned and walked back to Pitch and slid his ebony Winchester back into its scabbard then picked up his Stetson and pulled it on.

He glanced at the ranch house and saw Al standing on the porch near his horse before he mounted his black and turned him to where Scratch still cried out in pain. He had no idea how long the gunman had to live but suspected it wasn't going to be long.

By the time Pitch was close, Coppell's screams had diminished into sobbing. Grip dismounted then approached the gunman's handsome buckskin and took his reins before leading the horse to his rider.

Scratch looked up as Grip stepped next to him but never uttered a word. He just gurgled twice, then his left arm shook, and he stopped breathing.

Grip didn't feel as bad as he expected for shooting the man, but now he had to clean up the mess from the second killing he'd committed in less than an hour and it wasn't even two in the afternoon yet. He picked up his Winchester, release the hammer and slid it into his scabbard before looking back at the ranch house and saw Al riding towards him.

Grip removed Coppell's gunbelt, hooked the hammer loop in place and hung it over Pitch's saddle horn as Al arrived.

"Why'd you do it like that?" he asked as he stepped down.

"It just came to me. That's all. Where can we bury him? I suppose I should take him into Huntsville."

"That's okay. I'll have my boys dig a shallow grave in the family cemetery."

"Alright. I'll get him onto his saddle and bring him in. You can have everything he has with him. He has a pretty horse."

Al nodded as Grip hefted Scratch from the ground and laid him face down across his saddle. His wound and blood-soaked clothing were on his back, so the leather on the saddle wouldn't be stained.

He mounted Pitch and took the reins of the buckskin, then followed Al past his ranch house and soon reached the small family plot that already had two headstones. He wasn't sure why Al would allow a man who was probably expecting to kill his family to be buried here, but it wasn't his call.

When they reached the cemetery, Grip didn't even dismount but just grabbed Scratch Coppell's britches, slid it from the saddle and just let the corpse collapse onto the ground.

Al asked, “Are you gonna come in and meet the family? After I introduce you, I’ll go and get the other men for that meetin’.”

“No. The circumstances are much different than I had expected. I thought I could talk my way into a more peaceful solution, but I need to visit the other two gunmen. I assume they return to Huntsville each evening for chow?”

“Yes, sir. Sometimes they come back at night with torches to scare us.”

“I don’t want them to find their friends missing, but I don’t want you nearby when I find the other two. When this one spotted you, he knew I was trouble, but I want the others to see me as an ally.”

“Are you gonna stop by after you kill ‘em?”

“I don’t want to kill them, Al. But I’ll stop by on my way back to the house.”

“They’re probably at Smith’s ranch about four miles south of here. They seem to spend more time harrassin’ him ‘cause he’s a Mormon and has three wives. I’ll go tell the boys to start diggin’.”

Grip nodded then wheeled Pitch around and started him off at a medium trot heading south. He hoped that they were together just so this would be over sooner. His well-intentioned plans to avoid hostilities and simply use his father’s wealth to solve issues wasn't working at all. He had simply underestimated the joy that the hard men found in hurting people. He as sure that the first one in Huntsville, Archie Wilcox, had no intention of letting him ride away peacefully. He knew that the moment he turned Pitch around, he would have felt a .44 slam into his back.

But he had another method of dealing with the last two and then he'd see if he could use his money mountain to put a final end to the problem of eastern Weber County that had been created by the Greater Utah Property Management Company.

He crossed over a rise and saw the Smith ranch in the distance and wasn't surprised by the size of the house but had expected there to be more than one dwelling. He wondered how many children it took to make a 'passel' as Al had described it. While the concept of polygamy itself didn't bother him, he wondered how the practicality of the practice worked. *Did the husband have a schedule for his duties to his wives? How did he keep jealousies in check?* He found it difficult to believe that the first wife would be happy to meet the second wife and so on.

But that wasn't his concern now, but as Pitch trotted on the downslope, he spotted the two last gunmen, and they were surprisingly close to the large, two-story ranch house. He wondered if they were tempting Smith so fire at them to give them an excuse to unload into the house. He was sure that they'd heard the recent gunfire, but he hoped that they would consider it part of their normal activities.

Why they were being so aggressive when the families still had three weeks to leave was more than just an idle question like his polygamy thoughts. It was as if they'd been ordered to do more than just drive the families out of the area.

He was less than a mile out when both men began firing their Winchesters at the house. Grip had no idea where their bullets were going, and he almost reached for the Sharps but knew it would be a difficult shot and might make matters worse. He kicked Pitch into a fast trot, hoping that they didn't kill anyone before he was close enough to draw their attention away from the house.

———

Smoke Talbot and J.M. McAllister were enjoying themselves as they sent .44s into the house. They knew that it was unlikely that they'd hit anyone, but they wanted the entire family to be on the floor before they set the house on fire.

Smoke didn't have his nickname because he used the weed, or that he liked the smell of gunsmoke. He was a gifted arsonist, who also happened to be a talented gunman. He would use his skill with flame to make short work of the wooden structure. He had two canteens filled with kerosene and while J.M. kept the Smiths cowering in fear, he'd do his job. He loved to watch the small fires grow into a raging inferno and drew added pleasure by hearing the screams of anyone left inside the burning building.

J.M. had stopped firing to reload his Winchester when Smoke spotted a rider approaching from the north.

"Who's that?" he asked as he pointed.

J.M. had a .44 in his hand as he looked then replied, "I don't know. I've never seen that horse around before."

"Keep loadin' and I'll keep an eye on him."

"Okay."

Grip was less than four hundred yards out when they had spotted him, and he released his Remington's hammer loop because he'd probably need the pistol if they let him get that close. If he played his cards right, they wouldn't be suspicious about it, either.

When he passed the two-hundred-yard mark, he waved and kept riding at the same pace.

J.M. had finished his reload and looked up just as Grip waved, then asked, "What do you think, Smoke?"

"I ain't sure, but he looks like a gunnie. You reckon they hired somebody else without tellin' us?"

"Could be. He's better armed than either of us but we can put a couple of .44s into him before he can bat an eye."

As Grip approached, Smoke began shoving fresh cartridges into his Winchester's loading gate without taking his eyes off the stranger on the black horse.

When he was fifty yards out, Grip slowed Pitch to a walk and didn't show any emotion at all. He needed to be a hardened killer to make this work.

When he was close enough, he glanced at the house and loudly said, "They still here? I thought that they'd be gone by now."

Smoke glanced at J.M. before asking, "Who are you, mister? Hatcher didn't say anything about hirin' somebody else."

"That's because he wanted things sped up and knew I'm the man to do it."

"Who are you?"

"My name's Grip Taylor. I came all the way from Kansas City to get this done."

"I never heard of you," J.M. said as he studied Grip.

"Not many have, and I like to keep it that way. Why were you two just shooting willy-nilly into the Smith house? That's just a waste of ammunition."

J.M. replied, "We're just keeping their heads down. Smoke is gonna set fire to the place and we'll keep them inside."

Grip nodded then said, “That’s a plan at least. I just saw the Leibnitz place and talked to Scratch. He seems to have a thing for that daughter of his. I told him to quit worrying about things that don’t matter. Are you headed there next?”

Smoke quickly asked, “Why would we do that? They ain’t Mormons.”

Grip was surprised by his answer but replied, “Cover. If you burn one place and not another, then it looks bad.”

Smoke looked at his partner and said, “That’s a good idea, J.M.”

J.M. nodded then asked, “What are you gonna do?”

“I’ll stay here with my Winchester and keep them inside with you while Smoke sets his fire. They could make a break while he’s getting it going.”

J.M. smiled as he said, “We were kinda worrying about that.”

Grip then slid his ’76 from his scabbard and cocked the hammer. Before either man could react, he quickly brought the muzzle level just fifteen feet from J.M.’s chest.

“Drop the rifles, boys. I’m a United States Deputy Marshal and you’re both under arrest.”

Smoke thought he might have a chance but not with his Winchester, so he just dropped his repeater to the ground and watched Grip's eyes. His Colt sat free in his holster and he was a fast draw. All he needed was a distraction.

J.M. had the same thoughts, but his Colt was still held in place beneath his hammer loop, so he'd have to depend on Smoke. He knew that he had to attract the lawman's attention to give Smoke his chance.

Grip watched both Winchesters fall but in that brief interim between his order and their compliance, he'd checked their holsters and didn't see a strip of leather across the top of Smoke's Colt. If he had trouble, it would be with him.

J.M. then engaged Grip in conversation when he asked, "You any good with that pistol, Marshal?"

"I am, but before you say another word, I want each of you to use your left hand to unbuckle your gunbelts and drop them to the ground."

"If you say so, Marshal," J.M. replied as he slowly moved his left hand to his gunbelt's buckle.

Grip watched as Smoke followed suit and thought for a moment that they were actually both going to disarm themselves. Maybe they believed that they weren't going to actually see the inside of a jail. They were working for a rich and powerful man, so they might think that they had no worries.

Just as Grip had begun to believe he wouldn't have to fire his Winchester at all, J.M. coughed and bent over onto his horse's neck. Grip almost fell for the ruse, but as Smoke pulled his Colt quickly from his holster, Grip shifted his repeater's muzzle just two inches to the left and squeezed his trigger.

Smoke never even fully cocked his Colt's hammer when the .45 caliber slug of lead ripped through the left lower part of his chest, turning his heart into a useless pound of meat before it exited his back and eventually buried itself in the Utah soil.

As Smoke rocked twice on his saddle, J.M. realized that he was on his own and quickly pulled his hammer loop from his pistol and was about to draw it from its holster when he realized that it was too late. As soon as he'd fired, Grip simply dropped his right hand to his side and pulled his Remington. He had it cocked and pointed at J.M. before the last gunman even reached for his own pistol.

As soon as he realized he had no chance, J.M. ripped his hands into the air and leaned back in the saddle hoping that the lawman didn't shoot him anyway.

Grip didn't pay any attention to Smoke who had rolled off to the right side of his horse and crumpled to the ground awkwardly, not that he felt any pain.

"Now, mister, as your pistol is no longer secured, I want you to use two finger of your left hand and slide that Colt out of its holster and drop it to the ground."

J.M. was relieved that he hadn't been shot and carefully slipped his unfired pistol from his holster with his thumb and index finger and let it fall.

They were close enough to the house for Grip to shout, "Mister Smith! It's safe now. I need to talk to you!"

While he waited for the head of the household to show himself, he asked, "It sounded like you were supposed to kill the entire Smith family because they're Mormons. Why is that? Most of the territory is Mormon."

"There are folks in the territory that hate them and don't like it that they're taking over. I don't care myself. I'm just doing what they paid me to do."

"Who's Hatcher?"

"He runs the company down in Salt Lake City, but he doesn't own it."

"Who does?"

"I don't have any idea."

Before Grip could ask another question, Jason Smith cautiously approached with two women.

“Who are you?” he asked when he was near.

“My name is Grip Taylor. I’m a United States Deputy Marshal, and I’ll be taking this man into Ogden. Can you help me out and bind his wrists? I haven’t checked him for any hidden weapons, so be careful.”

“I didn’t bring any rope.”

“Pick up his revolver, cock the hammer and point it at him. I’ll take care of it.”

“Glad to help, but you need to be careful. There are two more of them.”

“No, there aren’t. They’re both dead.”

J.M. quickly turned to look at Grip. Believing that he at least had Archie Wilcox to count on had been his ace in the hole.

Jason Smith picked up the Colt, cocked the hammer and pointed it menacingly at J.M. as he snarled, “Give me any excuse to shoot you. You shot my home to pieces and almost killed my little girl. I’d have no regrets for putting a bullet through your face.”

Grip knew he wasn’t making an idle threat as he dismounted and pulled some cord from his black saddlebags.

“Is your daughter all right, Mister Smith?” he asked as he stepped near J.M.

“That bullet missed her by two inches. Two inches!”

Grip nodded then had J.M. dismount and after a quick search, found no more weapons, not even a knife. He bound his wrists and had him mount again, then tied his wrists to his saddle horn.

He then walked to Smoke’s body, stripped his gunbelt and then hoisted him onto his saddle. He didn’t care how much the leather was stained by his blood. He then tied a length of cord from his wrists to the ankles to keep him from falling off before tying the horse’s reins to J.M.’s saddle.

“I’ll take them both to Ogden, but I’ll swing by the Leibnitz place to let him know that they’re no longer a threat.”

“I appreciate that, Deputy, but what about those eviction notices. We still have to move in three weeks, or they’ll send more men.”

“Don’t worry about it. I’m not finished. I’ll take the train to Salt Lake City tomorrow and meet with Mister Hatcher. I’m sure we can come to an agreement.”

“I don’t think that’s possible.”

“We’ll see,” Grip said as he mounted and took hold of the handsome dark brown gelding’s reins with J.M. anchored to his saddle.

Grip headed back north and soon crossed the rise again. He was still adjusting to the massive change in direction his plans had taken and knew that it wouldn't change. Things were just different in the West.

He soon approached the Leibnitz ranch, and he wasn't surprised to see a crowd waiting on their back porch. The loud report from his Winchester would have let them know that he'd run into the last two gunmen.

He could see the fresh mound of earth in the cemetery and doubted if it was a very deep grave. He suspected that Al had instructed his sons to make it shallow so the wolves and coyotes could smell it and dig it up and had no moral qualms with his decision.

He approached Al and couldn't help but notice his daughter, Rhonda, standing beside him and his wife. He could understand why the oldest Miller boy was so disappointed that he was two years younger than she was. She was a very handsome young lady with shining black hair and dark brown eyes. She was smiling broadly as he neared which was a bit odd considering he was leading one horse with a bound prisoner and a second with a bloody body draped over its saddle.

"We heard the shot, Grip. They give you much trouble?"

"No, sir. I'm going to take Mister McAllister and the body of his friend into Ogden for Sheriff Johnson to keep in his cell. I'll ask him about whether or not he'll need your statements for the other two deaths that you witnessed. I'm going to have this one charged with attempted murder. They were going to burn down the Smith's home with everyone inside because they were Mormons. Does that make any sense to you?"

"You haven't been here long enough to understand that there's almost a civil war going on in the territory. Most folks get along fine, but there is bad blood among enough of 'em to make for a lot of trouble."

"I told Mister Smith that I'd be going to Salt Lake City tomorrow to talk to the man who hired the four gunmen. Don't worry about the eviction notices until I return. Okay?"

"I don't know how you can help, Grip."

"We'll see," he replied, then smiled at Rhonda Leibnitz and tipped his hat before he turned Pitch back toward Ogden.

At least he wouldn't have to ford the river again because he wouldn't be returning to Huntsville. The bridge he and Al had crossed after leaving the town didn't seem strong enough for both horses at the same time and he wondered how they managed to get a wagon across without it collapsing. Maybe he'd have a new bridge built if things worked out. He still had no idea what to expect when he visited the main offices of the Greater Utah Property Management Company.

He had already transferred another hundred thousand dollars from his St. Louis account, so he had more than enough funds to handle anything, but he wasn't sure that they'd be willing to sell at any price knowing that Mormons would still be living on the land. He assumed that was why the company had purchased the big tract on Weber County.

The ride was uninterrupted by any conversation as J.M. sat on his horse in a state of stunned silence. He had never seen the inside of a jail cell and had never expected to be in this situation. He was just too good. *How had this kid gotten the better of him?*

He was still making mental excuses for himself as they reached the outskirts of Ogden. Grip had intentionally swung along the edge of his property to avoid letting the gunman know where he lived. As far as Mister McAllister knew, they were still passing through open ground owned by the Greater Utah Property Management Company.

He led the horses into town and pulled up before the sheriff's office. It was late in the afternoon as he dismounted and tied off Pitch but didn't bother with the gunman until he talked to Sheriff Johnson or one of his deputies.

Grip strode through the open doorway and found Deputy Sheriff Henry Manning at the desk.

"Afternoon, Henry. Is your boss in?"

"Yup. He said that you went off with Al Leibnitz this morning. Run into trouble?"

"Lots of it. I have J.M. McAllister tied up outside and the body of Smoke Talbot stretched out over his saddle. They were about to burn down the Smith house with the family inside."

"You're kidding!" he exclaimed as he shot to his feet.

Zeke Johnson had caught Grip's last words as he left his office and as his deputy exclaimed, Zeke entered the office and asked, "What about the other two?"

"I'll explain in a minute, but I don't think you want to leave those two out in front of your office."

"Let's get them moved," the sheriff said to Henry as the three men left the office.

Henry led Smoke's horse away as Grip helped J.M. down from his horse and followed the sheriff into the jail.

After putting the gunman in one of the cells, they returned to the front desk and as they began to sit down, Zeke asked, "So, what happened?"

"When we arrived in Huntsville…" Grip began.

His verbal report took almost ten minutes and when he finished, he didn't have to wait long for the sheriff's reaction, and it wasn't as bad as he'd expected.

"Just write it up and we'll send it over to Ben Barber, the county prosecutor. I don't reckon he'll have any problems sending McAllister away for a long time for what he did just on your testimony, but he'll probably want to have Mister Smith on the stand to tell how he almost lost his little girl."

"I'm going to head down to Salt Lake City tomorrow morning, but I should be back by the evening."

"Just write your report and drop it off before you go."

"I need to get something to eat, but I'll write the report and leave it with you before I get back to the house."

Sheriff Johnson nodded, then quietly asked, "How are you doing, Grip? You said that you never even shot at a man before and you just killed three. Will you be okay?"

"I don't know how long it will stay with me, but I'll be fine. I really didn't have any other choice with any of them and I wish that I did. I guess that's why I don't feel as bad as I should. There was never any doubt that I had to act, or I would have died."

"If you need any help, let me know."

"I've got to tell Marshal Palmer about it when I get to Salt Lake City tomorrow. I do technically work for him."

"I'm sure that he'll tell you that you did a good job."

"Maybe."

Grip then rose, turned and walked out of the jail. He'd head over to Goolsby's Diner first then write his report before he returned to his house and took care of Pitch and his weapons. He'd need to check on the construction and the dogs, too. He needed to return to a routine.

It was almost ninety minutes later when he walked Pitch into the barn and stripped him. He brushed him down and after filling his feed bag, he brushed him down. After he finished, he patted his black friend on the flank, then picked up his two rifles and headed for the house.

He soon heard the loud yapping from his other four-footed friends and greeted each one by name as he scratched his head. They didn't follow him inside as he entered the kitchen and laid his two rifles on the table. He removed his gunbelt and set it on the tabletop as well before taking off his Stetson and just leaving it on the seat of the adjacent chair.

It took him twenty minutes to restore his weapons to a fully loaded, pristine condition, so by the time he finally finished, the sun was already setting. He hadn't even heard the sound of construction because his thoughts had been so distant.

He knew that he had to set his mind into a different mode now. If he was determined to continue to do as he had originally planned, he needed to expect even more violence.

———

As Grip sat at his kitchen table, in Green River, Mickey Mooney and his boys were on the run again. After their success in Whitewater, they had upped their game considerably. Even though they were well aware that they had come to the attention of the law in Wyoming, they decided to make one big score before leaving the territory and going to the more peaceful Utah Territory.

They had robbed the Green River Territorial Bank that afternoon and after shooting two tellers and one customer, had made off with over two thousand dollars. They had to avoid being run down by the large posse that had been sent after them and it was by sheer luck that they weren't caught.

The twelve-man posse was just a half a mile behind the escaping outlaws when Sheriff Horace Whitacre, who was in the lead as they passed through a narrow gap, pitched forward as if he'd been shot. The fifty-four-year-old lawman hadn't been hit by a slug of lead but had succumbed to the rigors of his hard life when his heart failed.

When his trailing deputy saw him fall, he quickly pulled his pistol, believing that the sound of the gunshot had been masked by their thundering hooves. He fired over the top of the sheriff's unmoving body at nothing in particular, but his action set off a barrage of gunfire from the others in the posse with no target in sight.

The air was filled with all calibers of bullets that ricocheted off of the granite slabs that had created the gap, and the combination of their own gunfire and the ricochets, only reinforced their belief that they were under attack.

Many of them leapt from their horses to seek protection from the rocks as others emptied their pistols and pulled their repeaters into their hands as Sheriff Whitacre fell to the ground.

It didn't take long before their own gunfire began finding a home in the posse itself, and it took another three minutes of wild shooting before the deputy who had initiated the melee finally realized that there had been no gunfire from their front. It took another thirty seconds of loud shouting to slow the firing until the last .44 was sent into the empty Wyoming air.

There were six wounded men, and one was serious, so the deputy had them load the sheriff's body onto his horse and it was only when he examined the bloodless body that he realized that there had been no reason for him to fire. He'd never admit to his mistake, but the posse had to return to Green River to see to the wounded. He'd send out a telegram to the surrounding law offices, including the United States Marshal in Cheyenne. He had a good description of the murderous robbers and he was sure that they'd spot the enormous man who'd done most of the killing.

When the gunfire had first erupted behind them, Mickey and his boys had all hurriedly dismounted and hid behind nearby boulders waiting for the posse to come charging around the rocky bluff, but as the firing intensified without getting any louder, Mickey had them mount and make good their escape. None of them realized just how close they had been to having their criminal careers end in the wilds of western Wyoming Territory.

Julia was sitting in Emily's private room in St. Mary's with Bill and Millie.

Emily smiled at them and said, "They're treating me like a queen. I don't know if I ever want to leave."

Julia laughed and replied, "You won't have any choice after your big boy makes his appearance. Doctor Morris said that he could show up any day now."

"I guess that I won't be disappointed to have another son. Do you think Grip would mind if I named him after him? He's the one who made this all possible."

"I'm pretty sure he'd be horrified, but I don't think he'd mind if you used his middle name. Sam is a good name."

"Alright. I'll name him Sam if he's a boy. I'll name him Julia if she shows up without external plumbing."

Julia smiled and didn't argue. She just hoped her aunt would be able to raise her new baby.

"Any luck with finding that elusive name?" Emily asked.

"None at all. I visited mama's gravesite and ordered a proper headstone for her, but I had hoped that there might have been something carved in the old one to give me a clue, but it was just a wooden cross."

"All you have to remind you of her is her copy of *Jane Eyre*."

Julia nodded before Emily said, "I know that all she wrote in the book was the short sentiment on the title page, but did you ever wonder why the book was so important to her? She didn't have it when I left for Kansas City. Maybe there's something significant in the book itself beyond just the story of lost and rediscovered love."

"I've read it dozens of times and nothing seemed to resonate."

"But that was in Kansas City. Why don't you study it again while you're waiting for me to have Sam?"

Julia laughed lightly then asked, "What do you mean study it? I can almost quote it word for word now."

"I'm not sure. Maybe it was one of the characters' names that was so important to my sister."

Julia had exhausted all other possibilities and Joe Trimble had come up with nothing either, so she said, "I'll do that when we get back."

"Any more letters from Grip?"

"Not yet, but I'm hoping."

She kissed her aunt on the forehead and waited for Bill and Millie to say their farewells. They had brought Teddy and little Mary to visit their mother yesterday, but Emily had asked that they limit her youngest children's visits, so they didn't catch any of the diseases from other patients.

Bill drove the carriage back to the estate in the twilight and Julia decided that she'd take Emily's suggestion, but didn't hold out much hope. She had been trying to avoid slipping into a somber state as the likelihood of finding her father continued to fade.

———

When Grip slipped beneath the covers that night, he expected to awaken with nightmares at least once during his sleep. He still was waiting for the effects of the killings to take their toll and he almost hoped that they would be fierce when they arrived. He may have had no choice in what had happened, and he had probably saved the Smith family with their passel of children, but he wasn't sure if it was enough.

CHAPTER 13

Grip was on the morning train to Salt Lake City by eight-thirty the next morning. He had enjoyed an uninterrupted sleep and the only dreams he recalled weren't about death and gunfire. The one that remained buried in his conscious mind was about Julia. He wished his pocket watch's alarm hadn't awakened him and ended the incredibly pleasant dream, but he had more work to do.

He wasn't wearing his gunbelt or even his black leather vest. He still had his shoulder holster under his tweed jacket, so he wasn't unarmed. He wanted to make a different impression on Reginald Hatcher. He'd stopped by the jail before boarding the train and the sheriff had passed on more information he'd gotten from McAllister.

He had two blank drafts in his wallet and two thousand dollars in cash. He didn't expect to part with any of the bank notes, but he needed to let Mister Hatcher understand that he wasn't a man to be ignored.

He planned to go to the offices of the Greater Utah Property Management Company first before meeting with Marshal Palmer. If all went well, he'd be able to put a proper ending on his report.

It was only an hour after boarding when the train slowed to enter Salt Lake City's station. He knew where the U.S. Marshal's office was located, but he didn't know where to find the Greater Utah Property Management Company. So, as soon as he stepped onto the platform, he walked to the closest porter.

The porter gave him directions and after thanking him, Grip quickly headed to the boardwalk and began taking long strides heading south.

Three blocks later, he found the offices of the Greater Utah Property Management Company and was disappointed. He'd expected to find an impressive building with ornate signage, but it was just a larger and slightly upscale version of the small office in Huntsville.

He entered the offices and found two men at their desks. One was reading a novel and the other was writing. Grip wasn't sure it wasn't an application for transfer.

The one who had been engrossed in his book looked at him and asked, "What can we do for you, mister?"

"I'd like to talk to Mister Hatcher, please."

"I'm Reggie Hatcher. Why do you need to see me?"

"Mind if I sit down, Mister Hatcher?" he asked as he approached his disorganized desk.

It may not be as bad as Joe Trimble's disaster, but it was close.

"Go ahead."

Grip sat at the only chair between the two desks and noticed that Hatcher hadn't even asked him his name, which was odd.

"My name is Grip Taylor and I just moved here from St. Louis. I bought a ranch outside of Ogden and was looking to buy some more land that adjoined my eight sections. I was told that your firm owned that land and most of the other property on the eastern half of Weber County."

"We do, but I don't think we're going to sell you any more land."

"Why not? Isn't that the purpose for your company?"

"It's not my company. I just run it for the owner."

"May I ask who the owner is?"

"His name is Ashcroft Milhouse and he's the eleventh Earl of Wickingham in England. He's across the other side of the ocean, so you can't talk to him."

"Why on earth would an English aristocrat buy such a large tract of land in Utah? It doesn't have contain precious metals or anything else of intrinsic value."

"It isn't about making money. One of his fellow lords bought a big piece of land down in Arizona, so Lord Milhouse wanted to outdo him. The Arizona land was about eight hundred square miles, so he bought a thousand square miles of Utah."

"And he isn't going to sell any of it?"

"He doesn't care now that he outdid his lordly pal, and I can do anything I want with it now. I have other needs for the land."

Grip wasn't surprised by the almost disdainful attitude of the English lord for the property as it wasn't any different than that of his American father. But it did open up an opportunity.

"Can you save me a trip to the county land office and tell me how much he paid for the property?" he asked.

Hatcher leaned back and after a few seconds, he answered, "Forty thousand dollars."

"And if I were to offer him fifty thousand for the land, he still wouldn't sell?"

Reginald Hatcher stared at Grip for a few seconds then asked, "You got that kind of money?"

"I have investors. What did you want to do with the land?"

"It ain't important, but I need to have some things done first. If you can make it fifty-five thousand, I'll sell it to you but only in a month."

Grip understood the reason for his delay, and it was time to put an end to the charade.

"Mister Hatcher, do you know how I came to learn your name?"

"I'm known around town."

"I first heard your name from a man named Smoke Talbot. His friend, J.M. McAllister explained a lot before I left him in the Ogden jail under the care of Sheriff Zeke Johnson. I had to write a report explaining why I had to kill Mister Talbot, Scratch Coppell and Archie Wilcox before I arrested McAllister."

Reggie felt his stomach twist in knots as he said, "You're lying! Nobody could beat even one of those boys except one of the other three. They were the best I could find."

"Ah, Mister Hatcher, you just admitting to conspiracy to commit murder and I'm sure that McAllister will be more than willing to tell the jury that he was acting under your orders when he and Mister Talbot were about to set fire to the Smith home."

Hatcher glanced at the other man in the office who was intensely avoiding eye contact.

When Grip saw his eyes return, he flipped open his jacket and showed him his U.S. Deputy Marshal's badge to put the final nail into Mister Hatcher's coffin.

Hatcher swallowed and said, “I’ll sell you the land for fifty thousand today if you’ll let me go.”

“No, Mister Hatcher. That offer is no longer on the table. I’ll pay your English lord forty thousand dollars and you’ll sign the deed over to me before I give you a draft in that amount made payable to Lord Ashcroft Milhouse, so it will do you no good. I assume you’ve already accumulated some amount of graft, so you have enough to make your escape. I don’t have any firm evidence on you yet other than your confession. But once McAllister starts talking, even this offer will evaporate.”

Hatcher couldn’t conclude the sale fast enough and in just ten minutes, Grip left the offices of the Greater Utah Property Management Company, which no longer owned a square inch of Utah.

He wasn’t sure if Hatcher would really send the draft to England, but he had given it to the other man before he followed Grip out of the office.

When he entered the nicer offices of the United States Marshal, he found Marshal Palmer talking to one of his deputies.

When the marshal spotted Grip, he broke into a grin and said, “I hear you’ve been up to mischief, Grip. I got a telegram from Zeke Johnson. Let’s go into my office and you can tell me what happened.”

"I just took care of the root problem for all those folks and have no idea what I'll do with the fruit of my solution."

Ignatius snickered as they walked down the hall and entered his office.

Grip spent twenty minutes explaining everything that had happened from the moment he'd found Al Leibnitz until he left the offices of the Greater Utah Property Management Company.

When he finished, the marshal whistled and said, "You did a lot more than I figured. I didn't know how you'd be able to handle the mess that Hatcher was creating up in Weber County. The problem was that he hadn't done anything illegal yet and if you hadn't shown up, I don't think that we'd ever know what happened to the Smith family or the others if they had witnessed it."

"I'll have to have the land surveyed and make sure that they have valid deeds to their property, but I'll probably donate most of what remains to the town of Ogden. I'll do some engineering work too and make the roads better. I will hang onto another eight or twelve sections, though."

"It sounds like you got a good plan going."

"Do you need a report, Iggy?"

"Nope. I'll send a letter to Marshal Guest to let him know what you've been up to."

“I appreciate it,” Grip said as he began to stand.

“Before you go, I figure you might want to read a telegram I received a little while ago from Green River. They had a nasty bank robbery and almost caught the thieves but had a problem. Anyway, I remembered the descriptions you gave me of those boys in St. Louis that killed the lawyer and probably set up your father and as far-fetched as it sounds, their descriptions matched yours almost word for word. Is that possible?”

“When I was in Kansas City, I thought that three of his gang might have been there after they escaped from St. Louis, but I wasn’t sure that their giant of a boss was with them or not.”

“Well, there’s something else, too. A few days earlier, in a small town outside of Cheyenne, four fellers matching the descriptions robbed a few businesses and killed a couple of citizens. I only found out about it when the deputy from Green River included the information in his telegram.”

“Did the deputy say which direction they were headed?”

“That’s why I thought you’d want to know. They were headed southwest, so they could already be in Utah by now.”

“Thanks for the information, Iggy. I’ll let Zeke know about it and I’ll keep an eye out for them. If it is them, one of them might recognize me but the others won’t. They’ll probably identify my horse, so I’ll start riding my red gelding.”

"I'll join you for lunch before you board the train back."

"I'll be happy with your company, Marshal," Grip said as he stood.

As Marshal Palmer left his seat, he said, "You're paying."

Grip laughed as they left his private office and soon exited onto the boardwalk.

———

Grip sat on the window side of the seat as the train rolled north to Ogden. The likelihood of finding Mickey Mooney and his men was almost beyond comprehension. If it hadn't been for the gang leader's enormous size, then he could have more easily dismissed the possibility. He did have the advantage that they had no idea that he was in Ogden but wasn't totally sure. They had talked to Igor in Kansas City and he couldn't recall if he'd mentioned his final destination when they'd chatted.

Regardless if they knew or not, they'd have to find him on his property and even though his dogs were still young, he didn't doubt that they'd react to men who appeared so menacing. He just didn't want to leave it to the dogs.

———

In St. Louis, Julia was writing a list of each of the characters' names from her copy of *Jane Eyre.* She had concentrated on the men, especially the focus of Jane's affection, Edward Fairfax Rochester. She underlined his name and after completing the list, she closed the book and began eliminating any common or unimportant names.

There were just six names on the list, and she'd bring it to Joe Trimble tomorrow. But before she let him see the list, she walked out to the kitchen and found Wilma and Jenny with Teddy and Mary, spoiling them with cookies and milk.

Julia smiled as she said, "My aunt is going to give you both a tongue-lashing when she returns with her baby."

"She'll be too busy trying to keep that big boy fed," Jenny said with giggle.

Julia smiled as she sat next to Wilma then slid her list before her.

"Do any of these names ring a bell at all?"

Wilma and Jenny both studied the list for a few seconds, but each of them shook her head.

Julia then asked, "What if you mixed up the names? Does that give you any ideas?"

Wilma then pointed to Edward Fairfax Rochester's name and said, "If you forget about the Rochester, then you might have a bit of a stretch with Farley Edwards."

"Who is he?"

“You don’t know?” Wilma asked in surprise.

“No, I’ve never heard the name before.”

“The Edwards family is in the same social circle as the Taylors. In fact, Farley’s father was one of Lawrence’s major competitors for the richest man in St. Louis for a while. About fifteen years ago, Amos Edwards, stopped fighting with Lawrence and even sold many of his business to him. The Edwards were still very wealthy, but Amos had lost much of his power. His son, Farley, didn’t enter the business world, but thought that the best way to get his revenge on Lawrence was to go into politics. He was elected to the state legislature when he was just twenty-two and is now a United States Congressman, a position he’s held for twelve years now.”

“Is his father still alive?”

“No. He died a few years ago, and his wife followed him the same year.”

“How big is his family?”

“I’m not sure, but I know he married just before his father’s humiliation at Lawrence’s hands.”

Julia nodded and said, “Thank you, Wilma. You’ve been a great help.”

She stood and as she started to leave, she stopped and looked back before she asked, "You don't know what he looks like; do you?"

Wilma smiled and replied, "Most women in St. Louis can give you that answer. He's fairly tall, about an inch shorter than Grip but has dark blonde curls and deep blue eyes. I'm sure that in his day, he would have given Grip a run for his money."

Julia smiled but felt her heart pounding against her chest as she walked down the hallway. Tomorrow she'd visit Joe Trimble and see if he could find out more details about Farley Edwards. It would be a delicate issue, but she began to believe that her best chance might be to don a proper dress and visit the Edwards home.

It was still a long shot, but it was something.

———

When he returned to Ogden, Grip spent thirty minutes with Sheriff Johnson and told him what had happened at the Greater Utah Property Management Company which made the lawman's face almost split in half with his grin. But the news that the violent four outlaws, whether or not they were Mickey Mooney's crew, coming into his area caused his grin to quickly fade away.

After he left, he stopped at the land office and registered the deed, which raised a few eyebrows, then checked for any letters in the post office before riding to his recently expanded land holdings.

He'd visit R. Smith & Sons Surveyors tomorrow to start the process of restructuring the land's boundaries and he'd have to visit the families as well.

As Grip entered his ranch, he was very pleased with the progress on the buildings. All of his orders for the things needed to fill the houses were waiting for delivery to the ranch in a large warehouse near the train station.

He was hoping to have found some letters in his mailbox, especially one addressed in Julia's smooth script.

He knew that she probably hadn't received his last letter yet but was curious if she had made any progress yet in her search for her father. He hadn't received any information from Joe Trimble either, but Joe had his address now.

It was early afternoon and even though he had other things to do, he decided he'd ride out to the families today and let them know that their homes could no longer be taken from them.

———

As Grip saddled Brick for the ride, Mickey and his three boys had just swung around the town of Evanston, the last large town before they entered Utah. They had hijacked a farm a few miles east of Evanston and after killing the entire

Marsden family, they'd eaten their fill, emptied the larder and taken as much as they could carry on the family's two horses. They didn't have a pack saddle, so they made a disjointed collection of pillowcases, empty burlap sacks and even two buckets to carry their loot from the farm. It didn't matter how long it would be before anyone found the family as they knew that they were now being hunted. No one would discover the tragedy for another almost a week.

But they had made one last error in assuming that just as it had been in St. Louis, the law wouldn't pay much attention to anything outside of their jurisdiction.

When they entered Utah before sunset, they believed that they would be safe.

Grip finally met with all of the adults and near-adults of the combined families in Al's main room. He doubted if there was a barn large enough to assemble the entire membership of the four families.

He noticed that Rhonda Leibnitz was paying closer attention than anyone else and could tell that Jimmy Miller was already jealous of her apparent interest.

After everyone was seated, he told them that there would be no more trouble with the Greater Utah Property Management Company because it no longer existed. He'd have the land surveyed and then once that was done, he'd give them the deeds to their land.

"How'd you do that, Grip?" Al asked in disbelief.

"I threatened Mister Hatcher with the consequences of what he had done when he ordered the men to do those evil things. He's probably halfway to Arizona now. The sheriff said that he won't need you to write any statements, Al, but he thinks that the prosecutor will want Mister Smith to testify how they shot up his house and nearly killed his little girl."

"I'll be happy to tell them what those bastards did," Jason Smith growled.

"Alright. It's not a lot of information, but I need to get back to my house. I'll stop by to keep you abreast of any changes but don't be alarmed if you see men suddenly start arriving in the area. They'll be using special tools to determine your property's borders. They'll probably stop by and ask you to tell them the four corners of your land, so feel free to put some stakes in the ground before they arrive. It would be a good time to add a few acres, too."

"Do you mean what you just said, Mister Taylor?" asked Harry Sanderson.

"Absolutely, but don't go crazy and please, whatever you do, don't start a new land war. I don't want to come out here and shoot anyone else."

They were all smiles and grins as he said, "I've got to get back. If you need to ask me any questions, I'm living on the old Wilkerson ranch."

"That's between here and town," Al said.

"It is and now maybe it's time to run a road that way. I imagine that they wouldn't let you do that before."

"No, sir."

"Well, it'll be a busy month coming up, folks. I'm glad that I was able to help."

"Don't you want to stay and join us for supper?" Bridget Leibnitz asked.

"I appreciate the offer, ma'am, but I still have a lot to do on my place."

"You're always welcome, Grip," Rhonda said with a big smile.

"Thank you, Miss Leibnitz," Grip replied before turning around and making a hasty retreat before Jimmy Miller tackled him or worse.

He had intentionally used a formal term of address to avoid any hints of interest. Julia may still be a pipe dream, but she was his only dream.

The next two days were almost routine in both Ogden and St. Louis. Grip's letters had arrived, and Julia had read hers in the privacy of her bedroom and was glad that she had when she read his earlier letter. She wasn't going to reply until after she met with the Mister Edwards and maybe it would be the answer that they both hoped to find.

The only other noteworthy event was when Julia met with Joe Trimble and asked him about Farley Edwards.

It wasn't surprising that he knew more about the congressman than Wilma had, and as he gave her more details, her hopes continued to rise. After advising her of the delicate nature of an investigation into the powerful politician's background, he'd asked if she still wanted him to pursue the matter. Julia had already planned on asking the questions herself because she knew it was far more likely that she'd be able to gain his attention more easily than Joe or another male Pinkerton agent.

Joe had told her that he was dedicated to his wife and their three children, so she wasn't about to lure him with her very impressive female temptations. She wasn't going to wear a dress that accented her curves or revealed the mounds of her breasts. She was going to be the sweet, lovely young woman who she really was and simply ask him if her mother had ever been in his father's employ.

He was now around forty years old, so he would have been the right age when she had been conceived.

As she rode Ebony back to the mansion, she began to create the scenario that would have resulted in the dilemma that was keeping her and Grip apart.

If her mother was employed as a maid or housekeeper at the Edwards home, it was possible that she fell in love with Farley and they had taken that love to its physical conclusion. If her mother had been caught in bed with the young Edwards, then his father would have banished her mother from the house. She didn't know how much power Amos Edwards would have had over his son, or if Farley was just taking advantage of her mother's affection. But if that were so, Julia found it difficult to believe that her mother would have continued to hide his identity after all those years. If she believed that she had been used, then she would have been happy to expose him.

But if she'd been sent away by Amos Edwards, *why had she been hired by Lawrence Preston and then fired so quickly? Why did Grip's father keep that almost useless birth certificate, even after Amos Edwards had died?*

By the time she returned to the house that evening, she knew that there was only one man who could answer her questions and planned to pay him a visit soon. She just needed to prepare herself for what could be an ugly confrontation.

Unfortunately, an expected event would intervene to delay that important visit.

The construction was going well, the surveyors were out on the land with their measuring devices to divide the land, and not a whisper had been heard of Mickey Mooney's gang. Grip had decided that it was easier to just identify them as Mooney's boys even if they weren't.

When he met with the surveyors, he had outlined his own property which crossed over the Ogden River. The new ranch would be sixty-four sections, eight miles by eight miles. It would make for an interesting run with the widely varied terrain. He even thought about building a proper bridge across the river to the other side of his property. He hadn't met with the Ogden city officials yet but would let them know of his gift after the surveyors were finished.

He'd only managed to squeeze in one run since his meeting with the families but had done other forms of exercise and added a few target practice sessions. John Browning had told him that his new rifle would be ready on the tenth of July and he was anxious to try it. He said that the added weight of the ebony even with the ebony forearm, made him add two inches to the barrel to maintain its balance, but agreed that the accuracy and range would both benefit from the added steel.

Yesterday, he'd seen his first bears, a small black female with a cub who was attached to her as if she had a short leash. The cub's father must be somewhere nearby, and he suspected there were other bears on the larger property now.

If he spent even an hour outside, he'd see some wild critter or another, and his biggest concern was that his dogs might have a confrontation with the wolf pack. They may have names and were becoming his trusted friends, but they weren't far removed from their bigger, wild relatives. They were at a disadvantage in size, but spent all of their time near the buildings, even the ones that were still under construction.

That night as he lay in bed, he wondered how much longer it would be before everyone was able to join him. He knew that the construction wasn't the determining factor anymore. It was Emily's delivery date. He just hoped that it would be soon.

He didn't know that even as he was eating his supper that day, Emily's delivery date had arrived.

While Tom waited outside in the hospital's hallway, Julia and Jenny were talking with her when her water broke and the nurse summoned Doctor Morris.

Even though Julia wasn't a midwife, she'd been with her aunt when she'd delivered Teddy and Mary, so she wasn't about to leave her side.

By the time that Doctor Morris arrived, Emily's contractions were well under way and he began giving instructions to the two nuns, although they were far from inexperienced and had already done many of the steps before he walked into the birthing room.

Julia tried to stay close to Emily, but unlike the last two times she'd given birth, this time the room was almost filled, and she found herself more than just redundant. She was in the way.

She smiled at her sweating, grunting aunt and said, "I'll be outside, Aunt Emily."

Emily tried to smile back but just nodded before Julia hurried around the nurse nuns and the doctor before she left the room where she joined Jenny and Tom.

Jenny said, "I'm glad that none of her children were here when it started."

"Bill and Millie were there when Emily was giving birth to Mary but didn't stay for very long."

"I imagine so."

Julie glanced back at the door when Emily emitted a particularly loud cry then said, "I'm still worried about her, Jenny. Could you and Tom return to the house and tell everyone that she's about to have her baby?"

"Alright. Do you want us to send you anything?"

Julia shook her head and replied, "I'll find someplace to rest and I'm sure that they can give me something to eat. I just hope she doesn't have an extended labor."

Tom said, "I'm still going to send Bill to stay with you, and he'll probably want to bring Millie with him. I'll just let him use the new carriage. That way I won't have to unharness the team."

Julia smiled as she said, "I guess that he'll almost demand to be here and I think that he and Millie should be here but wait until Teddy and Mary are put to bed."

"It's almost time anyway," Jenny said.

After watching them leave, Julia sat in the cushioned chair on the other side of the hallway just six feet from Emily's doorway. One of the nuns had closed the door for privacy, but she could still hear her aunt.

Bill and Millie arrived sooner than she had expected, and she told them that their mother was doing well, even though she hadn't been in the room or talked to anyone since Jenny and Tom left.

"Are we going to stay out in the hall?" Bill asked.

Julia rose from her chair and answered, "There's a big visitor's room at the end of the hallway. Let's go there and we can talk and wait. They even have some refreshments."

There was a loud cry from Emily's room, and Bill and Millie both glanced at the closed door as Julia said, "You've heard that before with Mary. She'll be fine."

"I don't want to lose mama," Millie said.

"You won't. She's a strong woman," Julia said before shepherding them down the hallway.

After taking seats in the visitor's room, Bill said, "How long do you think it will be before she has the baby?"

"Doctor Morris said that it won't be as long as her others because her contractions are coming so fast. That's why he stayed. Well, that and Grip is a very rich man. He said that it could be as short as six or seven hours."

"We can stay all night; can't we?" Millie asked.

"Of course."

Bill then asked, "Are you going to see Mister Edwards tomorrow like you said you would?"

"I may have to delay it for a day or two depending on how your mother is doing."

"I hope he's your real father, Julia. I really like Grip and I think you two should be together," Millie said with a smile.

"You have no idea how badly I want to hear Mister Edwards confess that he is my father. You know, I think that if I was still a waitress earning nickels and pennies, I'm not sure he'd admit it. He'd probably believe that I was trying to blackmail him or at least expect some form of compensation. But I need to show him that I'm far from destitute when I meet him, and I'll probably introduce myself as Cornelia Albert."

"Why would you use a different name?" Bill asked.

"I assume that I'll have to give my name to a butler or housemaid, and if he hears Julia Marley, he might panic and send me away without seeing me. I thought about using Julia Taylor, but after what Joe Trimble and Wilma told me, I don't believe he'd want to meet anyone with that last name. So, I'll use your family name and Claudia, who was Agrippa's second wife."

"I thought Grip never got married!" Bill exclaimed.

Julia laughed and said, "Not our Agrippa, the Roman general Agrippa. Grip told me about him, and he had three wives. Julia was his last."

"Was he a Mormon like the ones he wrote about in his letter?"

Julia was still smiling as she replied, "No, Millie. Let me tell you what he explained to me about the Romans."

The discussion of the very different way of life of the Romans was a welcome diversion from Emily's labors. It shifted to other topics as the hours passed, but soon each of them was dozing on chairs and couches.

Julia had no idea what time it was when Doctor Morris entered the visitor's room, touched her shoulder and said quietly, "Miss Marley?"

Julia's eyelids fluttered and after a short, confused delay, she quickly asked, "How is Emily? Is she all right?"

Doctor Morris smiled and replied, "She's fine and her baby boy wasn't quite as large as I'd expected, but he's a strong, healthy lad. She asked me to bring you to see her. She'll see her children later."

Julia was incredibly relieved as she stood and followed the doctor to Emily's room.

When she entered, she found just one nun with her aunt then walked around the nurse and soon reached the head of Emily's bed.

Emily's hair was matted down from perspiration and the constant sponging by the sisters, but her face was radiant as she smiled at her niece.

"Isn't my Sam a handsome baby?" she asked softly.

Julia looked at the little boy as he slept in the crook of his mother's arm and smiled.

"He is. How are you, Aunt Emily?"

"I'm tired, but very happy. I was worried that I might not live to see my baby, but here he is. Doctor Morris is going to keep us here for a few days because I'm an old woman."

"You look like a young bride right now, Aunt Emily."

"Before I see Bill and Millie, I wanted to tell you that you should do what you want and need to do. Don't act as my nurse and hover around the hospital. I'll have my children and Wilma and Jenny to give me everything I need. You go visit Mister Edwards and if you get the answer you hope to hear, then get on the train and go to Utah. Will you do that for me, Julia?"

Julia nodded and said, "Thank you, Aunt Emily. I desperately wanted to do both of those things, but I felt obligated to you ever since I arrived at your door. I'll never be able to repay you for what you've given me."

Emily kissed Sam's forehead before saying, "I don't think I would have Sam if it wasn't for you, Julia. You've repaid whatever obligation you feel you owed me many times over. Now go visit Mister Edwards and get your answer."

Julia smiled, kissed Emily and then Sam before turning and smiling at the nun then Doctor Morris as she left the room.

She wasn't surprised to find Bill and Millie waiting when she entered the hallway and said, "Your mother and baby brother are in perfect health, and she's given me orders to go home and visit Mister Edwards. So, I'll drive the carriage and Tom can bring it back."

Bill said, "I'll drive you back, Julia. I think Tom is sleeping now anyway."

"Alright," Julia replied before she began walking to the stairs.

The predawn was arriving as Bill turned the carriage into the Taylor estate and after dropping off Julia, he followed the long loop and was soon on the cobbled street to return to St. Mary's to meet his new brother.

———

Joe Trimble had given Julia the address to the Edwards home, so when she boarded the carriage later that morning, she was able to give Tom directions.

Tom was dressed in the driver's regalia that Lawrence Taylor had expected him to wear whenever his regal presence was in the carriage. He hadn't worn it since that night that the old carriage had burned with his regal presence inside, but this was different as Julia had explained the impression she wished to make.

Julia was wearing an exquisite, yet perfectly suitable dress that wasn't quite a gown. The difficulty for her was having Wilma help her with the corset, which she'd never worn before.

Congress was on their summer break, so Representative Farley Edwards would be at home with his family.

As the carriage clattered over the paved road, Julia rehearsed her lines from the short play she'd written in her mind. It was only a few lines as she realized that after she revealed her true identity, there was no point in predicting what would follow. She hoped that he wouldn't have her forcibly removed from his house as soon as she told him her real name, but if he did, then it would almost be confirmation of the truth.

But almost wouldn't matter to her or Grip. She wanted to hear him tell her what had happened twenty years ago. She knew that it was just as possible that he might look at her with a curious look and ask her what she was talking about, but in the deepest recesses of her soul, she knew she was right.

The carriage turned onto the grounds of the Edward estate, but it wasn't nearly as large nor as palatial as that created by Lawrence Preston Taylor. A few weeks ago, she would have been struck dumb just seeing the wealth displayed before her, but Grip had opened a new world for her, and she was able to see it as just a big house.

Tom brought the carriage to a stop before the front porch, then Julia waited for him to step down and open the door for her. She almost started to giggle as she waited. She didn't like the hat she was wearing any more than she cared for the strangling corset under her new dress. But it was only a small price to pay if it allowed her to finally have her answer.

Tom helped her from the carriage and pushed her giggle threat higher when, as he took her hand, he solemnly said, “Madam, we have arrived. May I escort you to the door?”

Julia kept the giggles in check and just smiled as she replied, “Yes, Thomas. You may escort me to the door.”

Tom nodded but released a quiet snicker before walking with her up the steps and onto the porch. He tugged the pull cord for the doorbell and waited.

When the butler opened the door thirty seconds later, Tom said, “Miss Cornelia Albert would like to have a few minutes of the congressman’s time. She apologizes for her lack of an appointment, but she has an urgent matter to discuss.”

“Please come inside, and I’ll notify his secretary. He has an office suite in the residence to conduct his official business.”

“Thank you,” Julia replied before she swept into the room with Tom following.

The butler closed the door and escorted them into the parlor before leaving to tell the secretary of her arrival. He knew that Mister Edwards rarely saw his constituents in his private offices, but he was sure that he’d want to meet Miss Albert. The family name wasn’t familiar to him, but she obviously came from the upper crusts of society and no politician could afford to ignore those who provided him with the means to stay in Washington City.

He entered the outer office and said, “Mister Howard, there’s a Miss Cornelia Albert waiting in the parlor to see Mister Edwards. Her driver said that she’s here on an urgent matter.”

“Did he explain the nature of this urgent matter?” Fred Howard asked.

“No, sir. But I’m sure that he’ll want to see her. Her family name is unknown to me, but she is not only a very handsome young lady in every conceivable way, she is very well situated.”

“Very well. Give me a moment and I’ll ask Mister Edwards if he’ll see her.”

“Thank you, sir.”

Fred stood and walked to the heavy oak door, rapped on one of the panels and swung it open.

He stepped before his boss who was actually doing official work as he edited a bill he’d present at the next session.

“Yes?” he asked as he looked up at his secretary.

“There’s a young lady named Cornelia Albert in the parlor wishing to see you on what her driver refers to as an urgent matter.”

"Albert? Do you know any families by that name?"

"No, sir, but he said that she is obviously well situated. She's also very young and extremely feminine, so it might be wise to have a chaperone during the visit."

"If she's well situated, what would she try to do in just a short visit that should cause me distress? Just have her enter and I'll hear her urgent issue."

"Very well, sir," Fred said before turning and leaving the office without closing the door.

Two minutes later a very nervous Julia entered the office and Fred closed the door behind her.

Farley Edwards rose from his chair and admitted that his secretary hadn't exaggerated her attraction, but he wasn't about to be unfaithful to Margaret, no matter who the woman was.

He said, "Please have a seat, Miss Albert and tell me what brought you here today."

Julia sat in one of the three comfortable chairs before the desk and said, "Mister Edwards, I've only been in St. Louis for a few weeks, so bear with me when I explain the reason for coming."

"I understand. I was wondering who your family might be as I couldn't recall any Alberts, so now that make sense."

Julia kept her eyes focused on him as she spoke, watching for his reaction that would dictate the rest of the conversation.

"I lived in Kansas City with my aunt's family for the past eight years. She had married a man named Steve Albert, but I never adopted her name. I still used my mother's name, but never knew my father."

She saw only curiosity on Farley Edwards' face, but expected it to change momentarily.

"I was born in St. Louis almost nineteen years ago. My mother's name was Charlotte Marley."

Julia had her proof when Farley Edwards' eyes expanded in shock, but he didn't say a word in reply to her stunning revelation.

"My real name is Julia Marley, and it's critical for me to know my father's name. Did you know my mother, Mister Edwards?"

Farley continued to simply stare at Julia for more than a minute as his mind raced and stumbled through distant memories that he had never expected to relive.

Seeing his turmoil, Julia finally said, "I'm not here for any form of retribution or to even an official recognition. I have a very different reason for my desperate need to know the truth."

Farley finally whispered, “Why do you need me to dredge up those painful memories?”

“Because if I don’t know the true name of my father, I can’t marry the man I love.”

“What? That doesn’t make any sense at all.”

“It will if I tell you that the man that I hope to marry is named Grip Taylor, the son of the late Lawrence Preston Taylor.”

Farley’s stunned appearance slid into one of anger as he spat, “That bastard almost destroyed my family, and I can’t tell you how happy I was when I read that he’d been roasted alive. I hope he’s still broiling in much hotter flames.”

Julia smiled and said, “That’s almost exactly what Grip told me when we first met. He hated his father more than I thought possible and has chosen his own way of life. Have you ever met him?”

“No. I never wanted anything to do with anyone named Taylor. But what I still don’t understand is why didn’t he tell you that I was your father? Why did you have to find me and confront me?”

It was Julia’s turn to be surprised, but she soon asked, “What do you mean? Why would he know that you were my father?”

Farley sighed and replied, “I suppose I’ll tell you the whole story and then you’ll understand.”

“Alright.”

“Your mother was hired as our housemaid in the spring of ’58. She was a very pretty young lady, and I was smitten immediately. Of course, my parents couldn’t know of it or they would have fired her immediately. It wasn’t as if I thought of her in the manner that Lawrence Taylor viewed his maids and housekeepers, but I fell in love with her and she loved me.

“It was a hidden, forbidden love and if I’d been a little older, I would have taken her away with me. We’d managed to become intimate on several occasions and thought we never would be exposed, but it was the butler who discovered our secret. He blackmailed me to keep the secret and I had to pay his blood money or lose your mother. That lasted for two months until my father noticed that the butler had too many fine things and it didn’t take long for him to point the finger at me and your mother.

“I was in school when they sent her away and he wouldn’t tell me where she lived. But I shamefully gave into my father’s demand that I never see her again. To cement the arrangement, they matched me with my future wife six months later and when I graduated from college, we were married. I know that I should have found Charlotte and at least given her enough money to make her life better, but my father was keeping a close eye on me and even advised the bank to let him know of any significant withdrawals.

“I was married and grew to love my wife very much, but it wasn’t the same passion I shared with your mother. I didn’t even know that you existed until my father called me into his private office in a rage. He told me that his hated rival, Lawrence Taylor had the birth certificate for a baby born to Charlotte Marley just seven months after she’d left our household. He had hired her because she was pretty, but soon discovered she was pregnant and fired her. He didn’t know that she’d worked for my father for years, but when he made that discovery, he was sure that I was the baby’s father. He then showed my father a copy of the birth certificate and threatened to expose the scandal.

“That was what triggered my father’s downfall and increased Lawrence Taylor’s power and wealth. He never recovered and blamed me and your mother for his lowered status. By then, I couldn’t even mention her name because it would destroy my marriage. It was the big family secret that only my father and I knew and after he died, I thought it would just disappear. I’m ashamed to admit that I didn’t even know your mother had died and I’ll have to live with that shame until I pass on. Please forgive me for all the suffering my neglect and cowardice has caused, but I beg you not to tell anyone, especially my wife.”

Julia was ecstatic, despite the horrible nature of the story, but said, "I don't understand why your father would have accepted Lawrence Taylor's word for your fatherhood."

"He showed him the birth certificate. He had no choice, but that's why I don't understand why you had to visit me."

"I needed to know that you were my father because the space for the name of the father had been left blank."

"*What?*" he exclaimed, "*Are you telling me that my father didn't even check the county records to verify my name was on the birth certificate?*"

Julia nodded then replied, "While you were telling me the story, I was wondering that same thing. But I wonder why Mister Taylor didn't fill in your name on his copy. That's what drove Grip to search for me. When he found the birth certificate in his father's safe, he was convinced that the only reason it was there was because I was his daughter. It was the only possible explanation for him to keep that one record and even that made little sense to him.

"He had the Pinkerton's find me then Grip arrived in Kansas City to meet his sister. By the time I left to return to St. Louis with my aunt's family, neither one of us wished that we were related, and only by finding you would we be able to fulfill our dreams. I still don't understand why he kept it."

Farley leaned back and after a few seconds, said, "He kept it to keep that threat alive and probably hoped to use it against me after I was elected to Congress. It sounds as if he was bluffing my father when he had his made his original threat. He must have showed him the front and was hoping that my father didn't demand to see my name on the back. That's probably why he hadn't filled in my name because the handwriting would be different. My father probably wasn't thinking straight in his rage and wasn't about to go to the county records to ask for your birth certificate."

"He could have hired a detective to do the search."

Farley shook his head and said, "My father would never even say your mother's name, so he wasn't about to have anyone else look. He gave up so much just for his pride and ignorance. I guess it's poetic justice when you think about it. He lost most of his power which he had earned in much the same way that Taylor had, and now Lawrence Taylor lost not only his power but his life. I may not be as wealthy as Grip, but like him, I'm determined to carve my own path. I still wish I'd met you sooner, Miss Marley. May I call you Julia?"

Julia smiled and replied, "You're my father. If you can't call me Julia, then who can?"

Farley visibly relaxed as he said, "I wish I could see you more, but it would be difficult."

"It would be, and I don't intend to suddenly barge into your life."

“May I come to the Taylor estate and meet Grip? I feel as if we may share a kindred spirit.”

“If you did meet and talk to him, you’d find that you’re probably right. He’s as different from his father as imaginable. Do you know what he did when he returned to St. Louis after receiving notice that his father had died? He not only began to dismantle his father’s empire, but he also created a charitable trust fund with more than half of his inheritance. As his father’s enterprises are sold, the proceeds will be added to that fund. He even named it after me before he left St. Louis while he believed me to be his half-sister.”

“Why can’t I see him?”

“He’s making a complete break from his father. After we left Kansas City, he went on to Ogden, Utah where he’s living now. He bought some land there and is planning to help people who are unable to defend themselves. He wants to do more than donate money to make up for what he perceives as his father’s sins. He wants to risk his own safety almost as penitence for the damaged done by his father and I’ll soon be joining him now that there is no longer an impediment to our being together.”

“That’s an unusual and an imbalanced thing to do, but I can understand it. But why didn’t he simply ignore that administrative oversight and marry you?”

"It's a measure of the man I am now free to love as a man and not a brother. He's an extraordinary man, and if you ever come to Utah, be sure to stop and visit."

"Do you need me to write a note to him?"

"Nothing specific, just write that something like 'my name should have been on that old piece of paper'. I know that he would probably believe me anyway, but I don't want to risk that he might take another step up that moral ladder."

Farley laughed and as he already had paper and pen on his desk, he quickly wrote the note and after setting the pen down, he said, "I'll let it dry and you can tell me more about your future husband and I guess, technically my son-in-law."

Julia spent much more time talking about Grip than it took for the ink to dry, but she did need to visit Emily and then start to prepare for her long journey to Ogden.

She had immediately decided not to let him know she was coming and would need to convince the others to keep it secret. She'd carry any letters with her, so unless they sent a telegram, her secret would be secure.

After slipping the note into her purse, Farley escorted Julia out to the parlor. Julia offered the polite and proper farewell expected from a visitor as Tom rose then they walked from the house and soon stepped close to the carriage.

Tom glanced back at the closed door and didn't have to ask his question he had prepared when he saw the look of absolute joy on Julia's face.

He helped her into the carriage and said, "I have to take you to the house, Julia. I don't think the horses could handle the drive to Utah."'

Julia was still riding the tidal wave of happiness as she replied, "We need to stop at St. Mary's on the way so I can visit my aunt and newest cousin."

"Yes, Miss Marley," Tom said as he closed the door then climbed into the driver's seat.

Emily was very happy for her niece and told Julia that she should leave St. Louis to see Grip immediately and not wait for her and Sam to leave the hospital. She had also said that after talking to Bill and Millie, she was now positive that she'd want to come with everyone else to Utah. Doctor Morris had told her that he'd visit the house every few days to check on her and Sam's progress but just on his initial examinations, he expected that she'd be able to make the journey in three or four weeks.

When Julia returned to the house, she jubilantly told everyone the news and extracted promises from each of them to keep her secret.

But it wasn't long after her announcement, that Jenny modified her traveling plans. She suggested that Tom escort her to Ogden. Tom would bring some of Grip's weapons, including his new Sharps-Borshadt, as well as some of the black geldings. Julia hadn't argued as she had been uneasy about traveling alone for such a long trip and would be bringing Ebony with her.

Once the new arrangements were set, Julia began her preparations for departure. She still had more than enough money for the trip but needed to pack much more as well. Luckily, there were still quite a few travel bags in the house.

As she began her hurried preparations, Tom started to complete his own plans for the departure. Julia wanted to be on tomorrow's express train to Kansas City, so the Taylor mansion soon became a madhouse.

CHAPTER 14

July 3, 1878

Grip had settled into a routine after the excitement of the previous week and was able to spend time with his dogs to see if he could train them to follow simple commands. They learned quickly as if each was in competition with his brothers to be the best.

The trial for J.M. McAllister wasn't very exciting, even with Jason Smith's emotionally charged testimony. He was sentenced to thirty years in the territorial prison and was probably grateful that he hadn't been sent to the gallows. His and Smoke's horses, gear and money were given to Jason Smith for the damage he and Smoke had done to his house.

He still hadn't written a letter to Julia or the others about what had happened with the land that was still being surveyed and marked on the maps because he was hoping to receive another letter from her soon.

Grip had been exploring his enlarged property and was pleased with the wider range of topography. As he rode Brick or Pitch across the landscape, he envisioned bridges and roads to make it possible for wheeled vehicles to pass more easily. His personal wild menagerie was adding new critters on each ride and now included wild turkeys, grouse and pheasants from the game bird column, hawks, eagles and an enormous barn owl in the flying hunter category. He'd spotted a large brown bear that had been feeding on a deer carcass, and the wolves could be heard as often as they'd been seen. The prey that the wolves and coyotes hunted were in abundance. He'd seen a few elk, but mostly white-tailed deer. A large family of beavers had created a large pond for their use on one of the new section's creeks, and he was impressed with their engineering skills.

As he discovered the creatures and the layout of the property, he wished that Julia was riding Ebony beside him so they could share the wonder and beauty of his new home. It wasn't exactly an empire or kingdom, but it was much better than the one his father had built.

He knew that many would think of him as an ingrate for not being thankful for the enormous wealth his father had unwittingly left him, but he had a solid argument for anyone who would suggest the idea. It was his grandfather who had laid the foundation for the Taylor fortune, and even though his father rarely gave him the credit he deserved, Grip had done research about his grandfather and had come to admire him.

He had done it right and had taken a single small operation and built it into a large collection of businesses in just twenty years. He'd taken enormous risks and almost lost everything twice before he died. Grip often wondered what his grandfather thought of his own son, and was reasonably sure that he was in a much nicer place now while his son, who had inherited the foundation for his empire, was roasting in hell.

He still was unsure what to do with the vast fortune he still had in his account in St. Louis, but having it more than a thousand miles away gave him the luxury of almost forgetting that it existed.

But this empire was his home now and he wasn't going to change much of it other than adding a few bridges and the one road from the ranches to Ogden.

He was riding along the far eastern border and could see the back of the Sanderson ranch. He saw riders moving cattle and was curious how much each of the families had added to their holdings. He'd check with the surveyors tomorrow.

He continued riding north when he spotted a rider coming towards him and knew who it was immediately and wished he'd taken a different route. But he couldn't race away as it would be rude, so he continued walking Pitch north as the rider drew closer.

Rhonda Leibnitz was riding at a fast pace and her long black hair flew out behind her. She was quite a sight and it was obvious that she was trying to impress him. She was wearing a white blouse that seemed almost transparent and he wondered if she had been wearing a jacket or sweater when she left the house. She may legally have been an adult, but he doubted if it would have mattered to her mother if she'd seen her daughter get on the horse dressed as she was.

He pulled to a stop and smiled as she slowed and walked her gelding closer. He was the same tired horse that her father had ridden when they first met, and he was already breathing heavily when she brought him to a much-needed stop.

"Your horse is exhausted, Rhonda," Grip said with a smile.

"I suppose I shouldn't have ridden him so hard, but I wanted to talk to you."

"Well, here I am, so what can I do for you?"

"I wanted to thank you for all that you've done for us. You didn't ask for anything in return but now everything is so much better and we're not afraid anymore."

"Your father and the others already thanked me, Rhonda. I just did what had to be done."

"But you risked your life doing it! You bought all that land and just gave it away, too. Why are you helping us? You didn't even know us until you met my father."

"It's just a promise I made before I came here. I wanted to help people who are being mistreated by the wealthy and powerful. Your family and the others certainly fit into that category."

"But why? I know you don't expect anything in return, but I feel guilty for not doing anything to stop those men. I can shoot a Winchester, but I didn't even take a single shot."

"You shouldn't have needed to take a shot, Rhonda. No one on those four ranches should have had to get into a gunfight to stay in their homes. You shouldn't feel guilty, either. I'm better equipped to handle men like that anyway."

"I know you have a lot of guns, but were you a gunfighter before?"

Grip smiled and replied, "No, ma'am. I was a student for most of my life and now I'm an engineer, the kind who builds things. It's just that my first twelve years of education were in a military school, so I'm very comfortable with guns and other weapons."

After a short pause, Rhonda asked, "Can I watch when you do some target practice? I'd like to learn to shoot better."

Grip saw the danger and replied, "I'll tell you what, Rhonda. We'll do that after the construction work is done in a couple of weeks. I don't want such a pretty young lady distracting the workers. You might cause one of them to hurt himself."

Rhonda smiled broadly as she asked, "You think I'm pretty?"

"Don't pretend that you don't know. Your father said that Jimmy Miller wished he was old enough to court you and when

I first met with everyone, he looked as if he was ready to put a bullet between my eyes."

"I know how he feels, but he's just a boy. How old are you, Grip?"

"I just turned twenty-five last month and before you ask, no, I'm not married."

Rhonda was getting excited as she asked, "Do you have a girlfriend?"

"That's a good question. I sent a very special young lady back to my house in St. Louis with her family and because of a very unusual set of circumstances, we're not sure if she's my half-sister or not. If she is, then she'll come here as my sister. If not, then she'll arrive, and I imagine that we'll be married within a week."

A deflated Rhonda then asked, "How will you know?"

"We may never know because the path of discovery is so twisted and old."

"Oh. How long will you wait to find out?"

"Forever."

"You mean if you never have the answer, you'll never even visit with another woman?"

"I can't because it wouldn't be right. If she finds out that she's my sister somehow, then I can move on, but not until then."

"That could be a terrible waste of your life, Grip."

"I'll agree with you about that, Rhonda. Anyway, I've got to get back and check on the construction."

Rhonda smiled and said, "I hope to see you riding again soon."

"If you do, please don't make your horse labor again."

"Maybe I'll convince my father to let me ride the horse that you gave him."

"I think your old boy could use a rest," Grip said with a smile before turning Pitch west.

Rhonda watched him ride away and wondered how committed he was to the woman who may or may not be his sister.

Grip wanted to kick Pitch into a fast trot as he made his escape and was now concerned that Rhonda might pay him a visit one night and that simply couldn't happen.

By the time he reached the barn and stepped down, he figured he'd better start locking his doors. He didn't think that she'd take the risk of a night ride but wasn't about to grant easy access to his house. He doubted if the dogs would have stopped her.

As Grip was walking to his house, his non-sister and Tom were in the first-class passenger car on the express train to Kansas City. Unlike Grip's journey, she had no intention of stopping in the city where she'd spend so many years.

Four of the blacks were in the train's stock car, including Ebony and another gelding. The other two were mares. Each of them wore a scabbard holding a rifle created by a different manufacturer. Ebony had the new scoped Sharps-Borshadt, while the other gelding had Grip's Winchester '76 with the standard stock. One of the mares carried a double-barreled twelve-gauge Remington shotgun and the other's scabbard held the father of all lever-action repeaters, the Henry. Tom had only brought it along because he wanted to get Grip to launch into his almost mandatory description of the faults of the rifle which Winchester resolved with its '66 model.

Each horse also carried a set of saddlebags with various pistols and ammunition, but also had their excess baggage hung from their saddles.

Julia and Tom each had one travel bag with them and as the train roared westward, she read her mother's copy of *Jane Eyre* with greater appreciation.

The reason that no news of the Mooney gang had surfaced was that they realized it was easier to make their way into Utah by visiting ranches and farms. They were now relaxing in the Spann ranch house just eight miles east of Coalville, the largest town in Summit County which bordered Weber County. The town still wasn't very large with just seven hundred residents, so as Mickey and his boys enjoyed the generosity of the late John and Fannie Spann, they were talking about the town.

"They only got a sheriff and one deputy, boss," John said before he shoved a piece of steak into his mouth.

"And that bank looks ripe for the pluckin', too," Cajun Al added.

Mickey nodded then replied, "I figure we just make one of those lawmen leave town, or maybe both of 'em, and then we move in while they're gone."

"How do you wanna manage that?" asked Bill Jones.

"Easy. We do a bit of scoutin' and find a town at the edge of the county. We have John ride into town and tell him that the gang that robbed the bank in Green River had just rode into the town and is goin' crazy. When they race outta town to try to stop us, we'll hit the bank and head west."

John grinned and said, "That sounds like a good plan, boss. Do we start our scoutin' tomorrow?"

"I have to stay here, or they'll know it's a trick. Once we're ready, I'll come with you and wait just outside of town for your signal."

There was a sense of excitement among the group as they started making their preliminary plans. They may still have had a good stash of money, but the thrill of robbing another bank was almost better than being with a woman.

———

Grip crawled into bed that night in his locked house and thought about the meeting with Rhonda. She was an inspirational young woman and almost the same age as Julia, but she wasn't Julia, not by a long shot.

But that short conversation had reminded him of the secondary reason why he'd never even had a girlfriend. Rhonda, like almost every other young lady who'd shown an interest in him, knew that he was at least well-off. What had made the almost instant connection he'd made with Julia so perfect was that she had already been attracted to him when he was no more than another customer at Claudia's Café.

He wondered if it would have been different when they'd first met if she'd known who he was and that there was no chance that they were brother and sister. It didn't matter as he still wrestled with that last hurdle that prevented him from being with her.

Even if she somehow discovered that he really was her brother, he knew that he'd just be friends with Rhonda, if she allowed him to be one and nothing more. He could just ride off to Wyoming or some other distant location and pretend to be just a cowhand to meet another woman, but he doubted if he'd do it. He had already concluded that he would either marry Julia or he wouldn't even bother looking elsewhere. He simply had no idea how she'd be able to discover what the Pinkertons hadn't been able to find.

As he drifted off to sleep, the woman who had a note from her father in her purse was sleeping on the express train from Kansas City to Denver. She wanted to get to Utah as quickly as possible.

Tom had visited the horses at every opportunity but was now snoozing in the same seat beside her. He was taking his role as chaperone and guardian very seriously. He was even wearing a gunbelt with a Colt '73 as a warning to any men who might take an interest in Julia. He assumed most of the other passengers believed him to be her father, but if they thought he was her husband, he wouldn't object.

When they had changed trains in Kansas City, she hadn't given one thought to her Uncle Steve who was sleeping in his empty house on Charlotte Street. His broken arm wasn't healing well, and he had been drinking heavily after finding the eleven dollars in house money that Emily had left in the kitchen.

The next morning, on the nation's 102nd birthday, Grip rode Brick into Ogden to talk to Bob, who was the 'R' in R. Smith & Sons Surveyors. He'd check with John Browning about his new rifle while he was there. Maybe, if he was having a really good day, he'd find a letter from Julia in his mailbox telling him that she'd discovered her mother's secret. Some businesses shut down for the national holiday, but most remained open, at least for the morning. It was going to be a noisy night of fireworks, but he'd sit on his porch and watch the show.

Bob Smith had shown him the nearly completed map and told him the job would be done tomorrow. Grip asked the surveyor to have them map a good road from the back of the Sandersons to Ogden and noticed that each of the families had added less than a hundred acres to each of their properties.

After leaving R. Smith & Sons Surveyors, he stopped at the post office, found an empty box, then headed for J.M. Browning & Bros., Guns, Pistols, Ammunition & Fishing Tackle. Every time he'd stopped by the shop, John or one of his many brothers had tried to convince him to buy some fishing tackle. Their sales pitch was that the trout were more than happy to take the flies that they were offered at the end of the fishing line. Grip kept turning down the idea and used the excuse that he wanted to wait until the houses were ready. He thought that the men and boys who would soon join him would enjoy the pastime, but he was a gun man.

This time when he walked through the door into the crowded shop, he didn't see John anywhere.

But his brother Ed waved him over and said, "He's up in the workshop. I think your rifle is ready."

"That's great news!" Grip exclaimed before walking quickly around the counter then hustling up the narrow stairs to the workshop.

John Browning heard his loud approach and was already grinning when Grip popped into his workshop.

"You have it done already?" Grip asked in ill-concealed excitement.

"No, I just wanted to get you up here to convince you to buy some fishing tackle."

Grip laughed then replied, "If it will get you to hand over the rifle faster, I'll buy everything you have that'll hook a fish down to the last inch of fishing line."

John grinned, then said, "It's ready and you don't have to buy a single hook. I had Arthur pick up a scabbard for it that wouldn't throw the scope out of alignment."

John didn't have to wait for Grip to ask before he turned and picked up the rifle.

Grip asked, "I'm afraid to sound like a novice shooter, but can you show me how to use your new system?"

John laughed and replied, "I would have been disappointed if you'd grabbed it like a boy finding his first shooter under the Christmas tree, Grip. It's not that much different than the Sharps, but I'll show you those differences."

Grip watched while John gave him the short lesson on loading and unloading the rifle. He'd watched him use the procedure before when he'd first shown him the new design but wanted to be sure he hadn't missed any of the features. He was glad that he did when John demonstrated a switch that would allow the cartridge to be either ejected or manually extracted. There were times when either method was preferable.

John finally handed him his new toy and said, "The ebony stock and forearm do add a good look to the rifle, and the balance with the scope is perfect. Do you have enough Sharps .45 caliber ammunition?"

"I have two boxes, so I'll be okay for a while."

"I heard about how you took down those four men and I'll admit that I was impressed. How bad was it?"

Grip stopped admiring his rifle and replied, "I thought that I'd feel bad sooner or later, but I never did. For a week, I kept expecting to wake up from horrible nightmares, but that never happened. At first, I wondered if there was something wrong with me, but when I recalled what Marshal Guest told me in St.

Louis, I understood the difference between what I had to do and what those evil men wanted to do."

"That's the right of it. There are four families out there now who would be out of their homes or even worse if you hadn't gone out there when you did."

"Did you know that their primary mission given to them by Hatcher was to kill the entire Smith family because they were Mormon? The English lord who bought the land just to win a bet left Hatcher to handle the sale, and that poor excuse for a man decided to use his authority to eradicate the Smiths. That made no sense to me at all at the time. But I've read more about the ongoing feud in Utah, and while it may not be very sensible, I have a better understanding of the situation."

"It's a mess, I'll grant you that. You do know that I'm a Mormon; don't you?"

Grip grinned and replied, "It's not hard to figure out when you have so many brothers. The Mormons are putting the Catholics to shame."

John smiled as he nodded then said, "My father has five wives and I have twenty-one siblings. It must seem very strange to a man who grew up without any brothers or sisters."

"I do have one young lady that I thought was my half-sister, and I pray each night that she isn't. I just don't know how it's possible to ever know for sure. I love her as a woman and not a sister."

"That's an odd situation. And you believe that you will never find out?"

"It's very unlikely, so all I can do is hope."

"Prayer is good too, Grip."

"I'm using that as well. Anyway, I may buy another couple of boxes of the Sharps .45s before I leave, because I think I'll do a lot of target practice when I get home."

"Let's get your rifle into its new scabbard then go downstairs. You can pick up your two boxes of ammunition, pay my outrageous bill, and maybe you should buy that fishing tackle now."

Grip handed him the rifle and as he slipped it carefully into the heavy leather scabbard, he replied, "After everyone joins me next month, John."

"I'll tell you what, Grip. If your lady arrives with the good news you're hoping and praying to hear, then you promise to buy the fishing gear."

Grip took the heavy scabbard from John and as they turned to navigate down the tight stairs, he said, "It would be much more than good news, John. It would be extraordinarily great news. And if that happens, I'll be more than willing to part with some of my non-hard-earned cash to buy a lot of fishing gear. I won't use it, but the other men will probably love to do some fishing."

John's laughter echoed from behind him as they entered the main floor. He paid the bill then exited the gun shop and after carefully securing the new scabbard to Pitch, he mounted and waved to John before riding away at a fast trot. His target range was calling.

Before Grip passed through his two white-washes stumps, Cajun Al was doing the reconnaissance in Coalville. He walked into the county land office and found a large map hanging on the wall nearby. There were no towns far enough to the north to meet their needs, but the map provided a solution. He smiled because it was marked with each of the registered properties in the county.

It was an important discovery because it meant that John Schuler could be a new cowhand from the Double NN ranch. which was on the northern edge of the county. He'd race into town and loudly shout his warning that the evil gang that had robbed the Green River Bank was on a killing rampage on the ranch. It was only twelve miles away, but it was in the opposite direction that they'd use to enter the town after the lawmen left. Mickey was sure that they'd both be riding out of town just minutes after John delivered his warning.

They had divested themselves of the extra horses they'd stolen earlier because they didn't believe they'd have any problems with getting supplies and didn't want to be hindered when they made their escape.

Al mounted and rode out of town confident that things were going according to plan. Their recent narrow escape from the bank robbery in Green River didn't play any part in their plans to take down the Coalville Bank. After all, they were all Mormons and wouldn't pose the same threat as the boys in Wyoming had.

Al hadn't even noticed the number of men wearing sidearms because he'd become so accustomed to seeing armed men ever since they had arrived in Colorado. He should have noticed.

When he told Mickey of the Double NN ranch well north of town, his boss was very pleased with the news, so they began to add the final details to their plan. John would ride into town late in the afternoon an hour before the bank closed.

They expected to be riding west and disappear after sunset, even with the long summer day. No one would chase them and there was plenty of cover to make good their escape even if somebody did show some sand and try to trail them.

———

Grip had fixed himself a very fast lunch before walking out to his new target range with both the Sharps and his new Browning rifle. He had one of his smaller set of saddlebags over his shoulder carrying the ammunition. He wanted to see how much better the new rifle was but knew it had the advantage of having the Malcolm scope. He wished he had the Sharps-Borshadt for a better comparison, but he wouldn't be able to do it until everyone arrived, hopefully before the first week of August.

He didn't have a quite as fancy a target range like the one in St. Louis, but it still had paper targets mounted on proper holders that he'd bought at John's gun shop. He had meticulously marked off ranges of fifty and a hundred feet for his pistols, then one hundred, two hundred, four hundred, six hundred, eight hundred and finally a thousand yards.

Grip had used a stump for his table the first time he'd used his range but had added a few thick leftover boards from the construction to make a heavy table using the stump as a base.

He carefully lowered the new rifle onto the table, dropped his saddlebags to the ground nearby then removed the two boxes of ammunition and set them on the table. He loaded the Sharps and set the vernier sight on the six-hundred-yard target. After taking a stable firing position, he mentally prepared himself and settled the vernier sight on the target. A few seconds later, he sent his first round downrange.

He fired three rounds through the rifle before setting it down and picking up his new weapon with a smile on his face.

After removing the lens caps, he used the scope to mark his first three shots. He was pleased with the results and felt as if he was cheating again because he used the three holes left by the Sharps to make his scope's adjustments for the slight breeze.

He followed the same disciplined preparation and when he was ready, he fired. He was surprised how much of a difference the floating forearm made. The sight hadn't moved at all.

After firing two more shots into the six-hundred-yard target, he skipped the one at eight hundred yards and moved the telescopic sight to the thousand-yard target. The eight power Malcolm scope made a huge difference and he wished he had the Sharps-Borshadt so he could make the more valid comparison.

He took two more shots before walking downrange with both rifles to measure his hits more accurately.

The Sharps and Browning hits on the six-hundred-yard target would all have been killing shots. Two of the Sharps were close to the bullseye and the rest had punched holes in the black center circle.

When he reached the thousand-yard target he was in awe of his new rifle. Each of the three holes were in the six-inch bullseye. Even though he was reasonably sure that he'd hit the center circle, seeing the proof close up was astonishing.

He returned to the house and spent almost an hour cleaning both long guns and almost massaging the Browning. He'd have to sing its praises to the man who'd created it when he visited John again. Maybe he'd buy that fishing tackle after all even if Julia didn't arrive with the hoped-for wonderful news.

After putting his rifles away, he changed into his running outfit, strapped on his new heavy knife in its own sheath and holster-less belt and headed out to the property for his run. The construction crews had gone back to town before noon to celebrate the holiday, so he was alone on his enormous ranch. He hadn't run afoul of the wolf pack again, so he thought he was due but wondered if the knife would make that much of a difference.

As he ran, he was curious if he should even call it a ranch now. He didn't have a brand and he hadn't given it a name, so he'd have to think about it.

When he returned to the house after his ten-mile run, he figured he may as well call it a ranch simply because it was one syllable, and it was closer to being a ranch than it was a farm. He'd have a lot of horses roaming the pastures pretty soon when everyone arrived.

But as much as he looked forward to the arrival of the blacks, he was much more anxious to see Julia again, even if she hadn't discovered her father's identity. His longing to see her again was eroding his decision to assume his father's name was the one that should have been on that blank line on her birth certificate. When she did arrive, he'd find out just how much it had faded. He just hoped that Emily had her baby soon, so she didn't have to remain in St. Louis after everyone else left.

He'd already decided to make good use of his father's money to have the railroads provide one of their executive rolling apartment cars for her and her family to use on the entire trip. She'd be able to rest with her newborn and even enjoy hot meals cooked in the small kitchen in the car. He might have to buy one, but having Julia here sooner was that important to him.

He knew that Julia had been worried about her aunt, but Grip had seen strength in Emily. She'd endured all those years with her lazy husband and still was able to smile. She deserved a good life now and he'd provide it. He wished that she could find a good man to balance her unsatisfactory marriage, but she couldn't divorce Steve. Maybe he'd hire the Pinkertons to find him and offer him some money to divorce Emily.

After a late supper, he spent the first part of the night watching the different firework displays. He sat on his porch with one of the chairs that he'd brought out from the kitchen. Each of the houses that was nearing the end of construction would have wide swings hung from the rafters of their front porches.

The carriage house was already done, but he didn't want to move Pitch and Brick into their new home until the blacks arrived. He was even going to keep the wagon team in the stables when the other horses moved in.

The stables were very impressive with twenty-four stalls and a stone floor, like the one in his father's carriage house. There were two heat stoves, and the four dormers allowed the interior to be well-lit during the day even with the doors closed. There was a half-loft on the west end above the row of stalls for hay and bags of oats, but above the east row was a large room that he'd use for his guns. He'd had them build gun racks and lines of pegs above the built-in workbench that was much like the one that John Browning had in his shop. There was plenty of shelving and storage for pistols and ammunition. He hadn't moved the guns into the room for the same reason that Pitch and Brick were still housed in the barn. It would keep his house free of the smells associated with the upkeep of guns. It wouldn't have bothered him, but he hoped against hope that he'd be sharing his house with Julia.

That night, as Grip locked his doors again, the Mooney gang, just fifty miles southeast of his home, was getting ready for tomorrow's action. They couldn't see any flaws in their plan.

Julia and Tom had reached Denver and after a three-hour layover for the train to Cheyenne, they boarded the Union Pacific train that would take them out of Colorado then across

Wyoming Territory. Then they'd enter Utah and Julia would be able to surprise Grip with her amazing news in two more days.

The construction crews arrived early the next morning and were hard at work when Grip left the ranch to make a supply run to Ogden. He was driving the wagon which was being pulled by his two unnamed work horses. He should really give them names, but he had other things on his mind and would soon have much more.

He hoped to find letters in his post office box, but after so many days without any making an appearance, he was wondering if he should write again and not wait for a reply to his last letters.

The box was empty and after adding all of his supplies from A&M Greengrocer, Falkner's Seed and Grain and Peterson & Son Dry Goods and Sundries, he stopped by to visit John Browning for a few minutes. He didn't want to keep him from his work, which Grip was sure that the gunsmith didn't consider to be anything remotely like work.

Before he returned to his house with his loaded wagon, he rolled to a stop before the sheriff's office and hopped down.

He walked through the open doorway and found the sheriff talking to Deputy John Walker and Deputy Henry Manning.

The lawmen turned to look at him and Sheriff Johnson said, “I was hoping you’d stop by today, Grip.”

“Why?”

“I just got a telegram from the town marshal in Evanston, just across the border in Wyoming Territory. It seems that a family was butchered including four children just outside of town. Their house had been ransacked, but it’s kinda hard to pin down when it happened. He figured it was most likely done by the killers who robbed the Green River Bank a while ago. The posse lost them when they were riding west, and nobody’s seen them since.”

“It sounds like they’re heading this way.”

“That’s what I figured, too. I just wanted to pass along the word. I was just telling John to keep an eye out for four strangers, but that big feller will stick out like a damned elephant. Do you want to let the folks out your way know about it?”

“I’ll do that. After I get back and put my supplies away, I’ll saddle Brick and head that way. I’ll ride over to Huntsville, too.”

“I appreciate it, Grip. I’m sending John and Henry out to tell the folks out in the other towns in the county, too. I wish we’d get a word of where those bastards are now.”

“I’d be happier if we found that they’d been caught and hanged.”

“I don’t reckon a bunch like that is going to surrender, Grip.”

“I don’t either. Well, I’ve got to get going.”

He gave them a short wave then turned and walked quickly to his wagon.

As he drove back to the ranch, he made a decisive leap in his mind. The murders of an innocent family had elevated the four men from thugs to beasts. He would have no qualms with stopping them any way that he could. If he spotted them, he’d use every advantage available, and that included shooting them from a thousand yards without warning.

They couldn’t be allowed to continue their murderous ways. Having his father killed and murdering James Ellis was almost a case of criminal against criminal. But they had murdered innocent people in the bank in Green River and now, they had done even worse. They had killed children and deserved no mercy.

———

Two hours later, Grip approached the Sanderson ranch house because it was the closest.

He didn’t dismount as he passed along the warning to Harry Sanderson, who thanked him and said that he’d tell his family and keep watch. They had two shotguns and two Winchesters, so they could at least keep them at bay if they arrived.

After stops at the Smiths and the Millers, he finally arrived at the Leibnitz ranch house. Not surprisingly, it was Rhonda who walked onto the porch then stepped onto the ground before he reached the house.

She smiled as she looked up at him and asked, “Change your mind about visiting me, Grip?”

“No, ma’am. I need to talk to your father. Is he around?”

“No, he’s out with the herd. What do you need to tell him?”

“There’s a chance that the killers who robbed the bank in Green River are heading this way. They murdered a family just across the Wyoming border a while ago and nobody’s heard a whisper about them since. I’m just letting everyone know, so they can keep an eye out for strangers. There are four of them and one is supposed to be a giant of a man. I’ll ride out to your pastures and tell your father. You’ll want to keep a gun handy, too.”

“What if they show up? We have guns, but I don’t think we can stop them.”

“I know. I told the other families that over the next few days, I’d ride the along the eastern border of my property and if I hear gunfire, I’ll get here quickly. All you’d have to do is keep them busy for a few minutes.”

“That’s comforting.”

“I hope they never get here, Rhonda. The other four men were hired gunmen, but this group is much worse. They’re on the run and won’t hesitate to kill women or children. I’ll tell you just as I told the others and will explain to your father. If you see four men, don’t wait. Start firing shots into the air to let me know and to send them a warning. They’ll probably just go away and look for an easier target.”

“Okay. But I don’t want to see you get shot, Grip.”

“I wouldn’t be too happy about it either, Rhonda,” he replied as he smiled before setting Brick to a medium trot to find Al Leibnitz.

After telling Al, he left their ranch to visit Huntsville. The odds were against the four men appearing in the area was low, and the odds that they were Mickey Mooney’s gang were even lower. Yet Grip felt as if it was fate that kept bringing those four men into his life. He now wondered if it was destiny for them to end his life as they’d finished his father’s or if it was his to be the hand that finally ended their lives and their trail of terror.

He returned to his ranch in mid-afternoon, and after unsaddling Brick and brushing him down, he paid his dogs a visit in their bunkhouse home. After entering his kitchen, he began arranging his weapons for a possible confrontation with the Mooney gang. He’d bring his new Browning rifle, his

Winchester and his Remington. He'd assume the persona that he'd planned to create when he left St. Louis. He'd ride Pitch with his black saddle and carrying the two scabbards with their ebony stocks showing.

As he set them out, he used boot black to darken the leather of the two scabbards and when he thought he was prepared, he started a fire in the cookstove for his late lunch.

John Schumer was approaching Coalville but had to ride around the eastern edge of the town so he could be seen riding in from the north. Mickey had modified his part in the plan by instructing him to tell the first man he spotted about the disaster at the Double NN rather than going to the jail. He was concerned that the sheriff might be suspicious if he received the warning from a stranger.

After excitedly telling the middleman what had happened, John would wheel his horse back north and after a mile or so, he'd retrace his route around the town and join up with the others. Bill Jones would wait to watch the lawmen leave town, then after John returned, they'd hit the bank. There would still be six more hours of sunlight after they raced out of town, but they didn't expect a bunch of Mormon townies to chase after four killers.

John had his gelding throwing a large dust cloud behind him as he raced into Coalville and soon spotted a man leaving Arbuckle Hardware.

He pulled his horse to a dusty stop near the startled man and shouted, “It’s them! Those four killing bastards who robbed the bank in Green River! They showed up at the Double NN and the boss send me to get help. I’m goin’ back there to slow ‘em down!”

Without waiting for a reply, he wheeled his gelding around and sent him back north at a fast trot.

Joe Knott had no idea who the man was, but he didn’t know all of the cowhands in the area, so he didn’t hesitate before he raced to the sheriff’s office to tell him that the gang they’d all heard about had finally surfaced north of town.

In incredibly good timing for the gang, when Joe burst into the room, Summit County Sheriff Lou Gibson was at the small jail’s only desk explaining to his lone deputy, young Ferris Arbuckle what they would do if the murderers of that family showed up in their county.

So, as Joe excitedly relayed what John Schumer had told him, the sheriff didn’t ask a single question. He grabbed his hat and his trusty Winchester and told his deputy to saddle their horses while he sent a telegram to surrounding lawmen.

Bill Jones had seen the man rush into the sheriff’s office and was pleased when the two lawmen soon raced out of the office. He continued to watch as one went into a livery across the street and the other jogged into another building nearby. He couldn't read the name on the building from his angle, but he didn't think it mattered.

He sat in his saddle for another ten minutes before the two lawmen mounted their horses and charged north out of town.

The dust cloud they left behind hadn't even settled to the ground when he waved to Mickey. John had already returned, so the three outlaws soon reached Bill. There was no reason to delay the robbery as the lawmen's horses would be exhausted by the time that they reached the Double NN and discovered the ruse.

"Let's go, boys," Mickey said with a grin.

They didn't pretend to be innocent new arrivals as they menacingly neared the town.

The bank was closer to the southern edge of town, but they weren't unobserved. Before the sheriff left, he'd told Joe Knott that he was now an acting county deputy and to keep an eye out in case those gang members had finished at the Double NN and circled around.

Joe had always wanted to be a lawman, and after the sheriff had disappeared, he had released his Colt's hammer loop and slipped into his tough protector of the innocent mode. But his desire to be either tough or brave evaporated when he spotted the four riders coming from the south. Mickey

Mooney's size had the same impact on Joe as it had on the men he had pummeled in St. Louis.

Joe quickly turned north and ran to Burns Dry Goods. There were always men there telling stories around the pickle barrel, and he needed help.

The four murdering outlaws pulled their horses to a stop before the Coalville Bank and three quickly dismounted. John would remain in his saddle with his Winchester cocked while the other three entered with their pistols drawn.

Mickey used his frightening deep voice which only added to his terrifying visage as he shouted, "This is a robbery. Everybody hit the floor!"

The three customers didn't drop quietly, but almost collapsed onto the pine floorboards. The lone cashier, Will Lafferty, was more reserved as he slowly knelt and then lay on his belly.

The only other men in the bank, the president, John Rolfe and the chief and only clerk, Victor Bristol, were sitting behind their desks, so each of them stuck his hands into the air but remained in their seats.

Mickey was pleased that no one had presented a problem as Cajun Al walked quickly behind the cashier's window with his saddlebags over his shoulder. He had his right bootheel on the cashier's back as he stripped the cash drawer of its contents, even the silver. He looked around for a safe but didn't see one.

"There ain't a safe, boss!" he shouted.

Mickey looked at the older man with his hands in the air and snarled, "Where's the safe, mister?"

"Behind the curtain under the cashier's window."

Al quickly pushed the curtain aside and loudly asked, "What's the combination?"

John Rolfe was honestly trying to remember the numbers, but his mind was a blank.

"Give me a moment. Please. I'm having difficulty remembering them. It was simple, but I can't seem to recall the first number."

"Liar!" Mickey shouted before he pointed his Colt at Victor Bristol and fired.

The bank president was horrified as he watched his clerk fall to the floor then begin to yowl in pain. He had been hit in the right arm, so he wouldn't die if they could stop the bleeding, but the threat was clear and ominous.

He watched as Mickey then pointed his smoking muzzle at him and closed his eyes to help him remember the elusive numbers. If the outlaw shot him, he'd never know.

His sweat was flooding his forehead and what seemed like hours later, the number finally popped into his mind and he quickly said, “Eleven. It’s eleven, then two turns to twenty-two, then one more turn to thirty-three.”

It had only taken him fifteen seconds after Victor had been shot to give Mickey the combination, but John Rolfe still kept his eyes closed. Mickey’s soulless eyes had convinced him that the giant of a man wouldn’t give a second thought before putting a bullet between his eyes.

Cajun Al had the safe open less than a minute later and emptied every penny into his saddlebags.

He rammed his boot heel into the prostrate cashier before laughing and returning to Mickey.

Before they left, Mickey loudly said, “If anyone in here comes outta that door, you’ll be dead before you reach the street.”

As the robbery had been underway, Joe Knott had convinced three other men to help. When they heard the gunshot, the other two joined them. There were only three new Winchesters in the store, but each of their magazine tubes was soon filled with .44s and were in the hands of the men who didn’t have pistols. When they were ready, they didn’t leave through the front doors, but Jack Burns led them through his storeroom before they exited into the back alley.

The six men trotted south behind the building and just as they turned into the space between the barber and the butcher shop, they spotted John Schuster sitting on his horse. He was watching the north end of the town which was now deserted and after hearing Mickey's final warning, knew they'd soon be riding away with a good haul.

As Cajun Al tossed his heavy saddlebags behind his saddle, John turned to look at his boss to comment on how smoothly everything had gone.

He never had a chance to say a word before a shot rang out from across the street and he felt a sharp stab of pain in his left thigh as a .44 slammed into his upper leg.

"Son of a bitch!" he shouted before more gunfire erupted from the shadows on the other side of the street.

Miraculously, after the first shot hit John, not a single one of the others found a home in any of the other outlaws, but one did hit the flank of Bill Jones' horse.

Within a few seconds, the Mooney gang unleased their own barrage into the dark space even as they mounted their horses.

Jack Burns was hit in the left edge of his gut before they all dropped to the ground.

As Mickey and the others turned their horses south to make their escape, Joe Knott scrambled to his feet and emptied his Colt at the fleeing gang.

"We gotta send a telegram to the other sheriffs," Joe said as he slid his empty revolver into his holster.

"I'll check in the bank," Tom Reasoner said, "But we need to get Jack fixed up, too."

"Let's get goin' and hope somebody finds those bastards."

———

After they found a temporary refuge in a nearby forest, Mickey had everyone dismount to assess the damage.

John was in a bad way. The bullet was buried deeply into his thigh and he was bleeding heavily. He knew that it would have to be dug out of the muscle and was terrified at the prospect. In all their years of being the ones to inflict pain, this was the first time that any of them had been shot or stabbed.

But Mickey was inspecting Bill's wounded horse first and after a brief assessment, he pulled his Colt, walked close to the horse's head and after placing the muzzle four inches from his left ear, pulled the trigger. The horse collapsed straight down and then rolled onto its right side.

"What am I gonna ride now?" Bill asked, "Am I gonna ride double with Al or John?"

"Nope," Mickey quickly replied before he cocked his Colt's hammer again, then swung the pistol's sights onto a shocked John Schumer and pulled the trigger.

John never felt the bullet penetrate his face but simply wobbled and then fell awkwardly to his left as Cajun Al and Bill Jones watched in stunned silence.

"Let's take what we can from your horse, Bill. We need to keep moving."

Bill replied, "Okay, boss," and didn't ask why he'd executed John.

They soon left the forest and headed west until they reached a decent creek and used it to mask their tracks as they headed north. They weren't going to go into any towns for a while but knew that there were plenty of ranches and farms in the flatter ground. The rugged landscape they were passing through now wasn't amenable to either enterprise, so they'd have to spend one night outside. They had enough supplies for two days, but they'd find a place to hide out for a week or so after that.

While the three murdering outlaws were winding their way north, Grip had ridden beyond the eastern border of his property to within just a thousand yards of the Sanderson house. He'd decided to patrol the area during the daylight hours and had added a dark gray shirt to his garb to complete the look.

He'd waved his gray Stetson over his head when he was spotted by family members to let them know he was there. He'd continue his patrol until the gang had been spotted. He had little else to do now that the construction was nearing completion. Even his dogs had grown accustomed to his departures and hadn't followed. Their insistence at trailing him on his first runs on his new home only lasted until they realized just how far and fast that he was going. They gave up the chase after three runs but were still happy to see him when he returned.

He finally turned back to his house as the sun set. He still had the premonition that the Mooney gang would soon find him, and he wasn't about to be surprised when they arrived.

When he entered his kitchen, he set his rifles on the table, lit a lamp then started a fire in the cookstove. He walked to the front room hoping to find a telegram on the floor from Julia saying that she had a new cousin and Emily was happy. He saw a sheet of paper near the door, but it wasn't a telegram.

After snatching it from the pine, he quickly read:

Grip

Got a telegram from Coalville. That gang robbed the bank and shot a couple of men, but nobody died. The man who sent it thought he'd hit one and found blood on the ground outside the bank. They rode south, but nobody trailed. They had lured the sheriff and deputy out of town with a phony report.

Be careful.

Zeke

He returned to the kitchen and as he quietly prepared his supper, he hoped that the man who'd sent the telegram was right. He suspected that if his bullet had found its way into Mickey Mooney, it probably would have only made him mad. But if he did hit one of the others, then there might only be three of them now.

In the morning, when he made his patrol, he'd give the families the updated information. He also believed that if he was to see them at all, it would be tomorrow.

After eating his supper, he washed his dishes, blew out the lamp then headed for his bedroom.

As he prepared for sleep, he could almost feel the Mooney gang's presence. He'd only ever met one of them, but he felt as if he knew them. If it wasn't for Mickey Mooney's enormous stature, he might not be able to identify them at all. He wondered if the gang leader's massive physique could survive a hit from his new Browning rifle.

He was only sure of one thing. He wasn't going to be caught by surprise if they did make an appearance in the area.

The surprise that he couldn't have predicted was already snoozing in her first-class passenger car that was crossing western Wyoming Territory. The Union Pacific train was scheduled to arrive in Ogden tomorrow morning at 10:40.

Julia had been so excited after seeing the destination posted on the chalkboard at their last stop that she'd almost forgotten to visit the privy.

But that excitement had worn off and allowed her to sleep. She hoped that soon, she'd be sleeping with Grip beside her. She had already created many different ways of breaking the wonderful news to him and wasn't sure which one she'd use. But it was almost as much fun dreaming them up as it would be to give one of them to him. Almost.

The three remaining members of the Mooney gang were sitting around a campfire just fourteen miles southeast of Grip's large ranch.

Cajun Al finally worked up the nerve to ask, "Why'd you shoot John, Mickey?"

"I reckon that he woulda asked me to do it in a little while anyway. He couldn't see a doctor without facing the noose and sooner or later, that leg woulda been thick with gangrene. I did him a kindness."

"Oh. I was just wonderin'."

Al glanced at Bill Jones but didn't say anything. While neither of them wanted to be shot before, now even a graze might be a death sentence.

CHAPTER 15

The chill of the night, even in the summer, had Mickey and his two partners on their horses just an hour after daybreak. They didn't have much of a choice about their direction as the terrain dictated that they head north.

Grip was up just before they started to ride and after a quick bath and a cold breakfast, he buckled on his black gunbelt and pulled on his hat before leaving the house carrying his two rifles.

He mounted Pitch ten minutes later, and when he walked him out of the barn to make the eight-mile ride across his property, the three outlaws were just seven miles south of the Sanderson ranch.

Grip was riding into the sun as Pitch trotted across his ranch, so his vision was limited. It didn't matter yet as he was still a good dozen miles away from Mooney's bunch as they converged.

He kept the brim of his Stetson just below the fiery ball of the sun to block the glare as he continued to ride east. He was making better time than the three outlaws because he had better ground. That would change in a few more minutes when they exited the difficult terrain south of the Sanderson place.

As Grip rode, he noticed the whitewashed stakes that the surveyors had pounded into the ground every hundred yards to mark where the new road would be built. It would cross the southern side of his property passing near the forest, but even the almost-completed house that was closest to the proposed path would still be four miles away.

He was following the stakes as he continued to ride east into the sun but hadn't seen anyone out in the Sanderson pastures yet, nor had he spotted the roof of their barn.

But riding with the sun on their right, Mickey soon spotted the Sanderson ranch house and barn in the distance and exclaimed, "It looks like we found our new home, boys!"

"My belly would appreciate something hot," Al replied loudly.

"Let's get ready to thank our hosts," Mickey shouted as he pulled his Winchester from his scabbard and cocked the hammer.

Al and Bill followed suit as they continued riding their horses at a slow trot.

———

Harry Sanderson and his two boys, Nate and George, had exited through the back door to go to the barn and saddle their horses. Harry and Nate each had a Winchester while George carried a single-barrel twenty-gauge shotgun as they left the house.

His two daughters, seventeen-year-old Hilda and fifteen-year-old Marie were in the kitchen cleaning up after breakfast.

Harry hadn't ignored Grip's warning, but thought it was unlikely that the gang would come in this direction, so after he'd made a quick scan of his ranch and found it devoid of bad men, he and his sons entered the barn to prepare for the day's work.

Grip had just brought his Stetson's brim as high as he dared when he thought he saw the slightest movement to the south of the ranch. He was still more than two miles from the house and barn but hadn't seen Harry Sanderson and his sons leave the house.

He set Pitch to a faster trot as he continued to try to get a better view of what he might or might not have seen. The sun wasn't the only obstacle to his vision, but the pines that sprouted anywhere they could take root added to the problem.

He finally had a brief clear glimpse and saw the specks of three riders to the southeast.

He hadn't had a long look and at this distance, even if he had more time to study the riders, he wouldn't even have been able to differentiate sizes. Not even Mickey Mooney's bulk could be identified.

But three riders coming from the south convinced him that his belief that their fates were interwoven hadn't been wrong. He was about to confront Mickey Mooney and his men at last.

He still didn't realize that Harry Sanderson and his sons were in the barn and mistakenly assumed that they'd soon be firing their Winchesters at the three men which should at least make them hunker down.

He still pulled his new Browning from its scabbard and popped off the lens caps on the Malcolm scope.

He had six of the .45-100 Sharps cartridges in his vest pockets, so he slid one out and after using the lever to open the breech, he slid it home and pulled the lever to its original position. He appreciated the falling block design even more as everything seemed so clean and he knew he could reload the new rifle faster than the Sharps.

When they had gotten within a mile of the Sanderson house without being spotted, Mickey had them all pick up the pace.

None of them had spotted Grip who was still more than two miles to their left. Their focus was on the house and they were ready to claim it as their own.

Grip knew that they would reach the house before he did and wondered why Harry hadn't started firing yet.

They weren't close to being in range, even with the Browning, but he started to believe that he might need to at least let them know that they'd been spotted and that he was a threat. He couldn't let them reach the ranch house.

After another thirty seconds without any gunfire from the Sandersons, he brought his new rifle to his shoulder and didn't even bother using the telescopic sight. He simply pointed the muzzle in the direction of the riders who were now just four hundred yards from the house and squeezed his trigger.

The ebony stock rammed against his shoulder and the .45 caliber missile screamed from the rifle at more than fifteen hundred feet per second.

He knew that the bullet would hit the ground somewhere close to the riders, but the loud sound would reach them at almost the same moment. The bullet was traveling faster than the speed of sound when it left the muzzle, but even the thinner air at this altitude would start slowing it down until the sound caught up with it and passed it just before it ran out of energy. But in this case, it was the sound that was the weapon.

Mickey, Al and Bill still had their eyes on their target when the Browning's loud report reached their ears. In unison, each of them turned their attention to the direction of the sound and soon spotted Grip riding toward them.

He was still more than a mile away when Cajun Al shouted, "*Who the hell is that?*"

Grip kept his eyes on the three men as he was reloading his rifle, and Pitch continued to close the gap at his fast trot.

"I don't know, but he's gonna be trouble!" Mickey yelled back.

They already had their Winchesters ready, so Mickey had them shift direction toward the southwest where the forest would provide them protection. Even though they hadn't seen where the bullet had struck, the loud report and the willingness of the stranger to fire at that range let them know he had the ability to shoot them without any risk to himself.

As the echo of Grip's shot rolled across the ranch, Harry and his sons suddenly realized that there was danger and left their horses half-saddled as they ran from the barn to protect Hilda and Marie.

They spotted Grip as he quickly rode east less than a mile away. Harry waved, but Grip hadn't seen him as he tried to get within range of the three men who no longer posed an immediate threat to the family.

Grip's direction change was closing the gap rapidly, but he knew he had to take a shot soon before they reached the trees. Once among the pines, any advantage he had would be gone.

Grip pulled Pitch to a sudden stop when he was still six hundred yards from the riders who were racing for the trees. They'd get a little closer before they reached their refuge, and he had to decide who to eliminate. He wanted to put a .45 into Mickey Mooney simply because he was the most dangerous and he was the leader but wasn't sure it would be enough to be fatal at this range. So, he slowed his breathing and set the crosshairs of his scope on the second rider. He was moving quickly across his front and it would be a difficult shot, but not impossible. He could have hit the horse easily, but the horse was innocent.

He set the crosshairs six feet in front of the horse's head and let the scope move with the man for another three seconds to get the proper lead. He squeezed the trigger and the aerodynamic cylinder of lead ripped through the thinner Utah air and just about one second after leaving the Browning's muzzle, the .45 caliber messenger slammed into the right side of Bill Jones' chest. The bullet was following a downward arc as gravity overcame its forward momentum, so when it struck, it shattered one rib then after shredding his right lung's lower lobe, it tumbled through his stomach and then came to rest against the left wall of his abdominal cavity.

Bill screamed loudly when he felt the impact and after dropping his Winchester, he grabbed his side and lurched forward onto his horse's neck. He was still screeching in pain as he dropped to the ground off the left side of his horse and crashed into the hard, rocky ground. He wasn't dead yet but was in immense pain as he writhed and screeched on the Utah dirt.

Mickey and Cajun Al were both shocked when Bill had been hit, but neither bothered to even look back as they ducked onto their horses' necks and raced for the protection of the trees just another hundred yards away.

After seeing the man fall, Grip tapped Pitch's flanks and he soon resumed his fast trot as the gap closed between him and the last two outlaws.

He had reloaded his Browning but wasn't sure he'd get another shot, especially now that they knew they were vulnerable. So, he slid the rifle back into its scabbard, mentally apologizing for not replacing the lens caps then pulled his Winchester free and cocked the hammer.

They were at the extreme range of his '76 when he fired his first round. He knew he'd missed in his haste and the difficulty of making the shot from a moving horse. It had been a low expectation anyway, but now they were in among the trees and he was the one who was vulnerable.

As soon as Mickey and Al were hidden behind the trunks and needle-rich branches of the tall pines, they slowed and then quickly dismounted.

"What'll we do now, boss?" Al quickly asked.

"We have that bastard now. He doesn't know where we are and there are two of us."

"He was dressed all in black and his black horse had all black tack, too. Do you reckon he's a gunfighter?"

"I don't know, but no damned cowhand woulda made that shot, so we're gonna have to be careful with this one. I don't reckon he's a lawman either 'cause he shot without even waitin' for us to fire."

"That makes him a bigger problem; don't it?"

"Yeah, but we're a bigger problem for him now. He's north of here and if he's stupid enough to come lookin' for us, then we'll get him. Let's tie off the horses and leave them like bait. We'll separate by fifty yards or so and stay quiet so he can't sneak up on us."

"Okay, boss," Al replied before taking his horse's reins and tying them to the closest branch while Mickey did the same. They slid their repeaters into their horses' scabbards and drew their Colts. This was going to be a short-range gunfight.

They then walked in opposite directions with their cocked pistols to wait for the gunfighter.

———

Once they'd disappeared into the trees, Grip pulled Pitch to a stop to figure out his next move. They could continue to ride through the forest and soon reach Ogden, but he suspected that they were just a couple of hundred yards away hiding in the trees and waiting for him to hunt them down.

He was still studying the trees when he heard a noise to his left and found Harry Sanderson riding towards him. He shifted his eyes back to the trees in case they appeared but waited for Harry to get close.

Harry pulled his horse to a stop next to Grip and said, “I didn’t see ‘em comin’, Grip. How many are in those trees?”

“Two. One is dead just east of the trees but just let his body stay there for now. I want you to go back to your house and keep your youngsters safe.”

“I can help, Grip.”

“If you want to do anything, send one of your boys to the other families to warn them and then send one of your girls to town to tell the sheriff that two of the gang are in those trees.”

“Are you sure?”

“I’m sure. I’ll figure out what to do with them, but I don’t want them to be able to sneak into town, so the sheriff has to know they’re here. You and your other son stay in the house but keep an eye out.”

“Okay, I’ll do what you asked,” Harry replied, “And thank you again.”

"You're welcome."

Harry wheeled his horse around and quickly rode away leaving Grip to face down his problem.

He pulled his pocket watch and was surprised to see that it was already after ten o'clock and glanced at the sun to verify that it hadn't stopped.

For another ten minutes, he sat in his saddle before he decided how he'd approach the dangerous dilemma.

He heard hoofbeats in the distance, which meant that Harry's son and daughter had ridden away to pass the news. Now he had to act.

Grip walked Pitch closer to the tree line watching for a hint of motion. If they fired, he wouldn't be able to avoid the bullet, but he hoped to spot them setting up for the shot.

He had to remove his hat to wipe the sweat from his brow before he passed the one-hundred-yard mark, but he hadn't seen a shadow move or a flash of color.

When he pulled Pitch to a stop and dismounted, he was just eighty yards from the closest tree. He slid his Winchester home and left Pitch unfettered in case he needed to run. He finally removed his hat and hung it on his saddle horn before he began walking. He pulled his Remington and then his Colt from his shoulder holster. He cocked both pistols as he continued his steady pace.

He had his Remington fully loaded with six cartridges and his Colt Shopkeeper had each of its cylinders filled. He left his black leather vest unbuttoned simply because his hands were full. He didn't expect to reload but it might come down to the dagger he'd used to dispatch Archie Wilcox in Huntsville.

As he drew ever closer to the trees, the Union Pacific train carrying an extremely excited Julia and a very grateful Tom was pulling into the station. If Grip had known of her arrival, there would be little chance that he would be taking this enormous risk.

After passing the first thick pine trunks, Grip stopped and let his eyes adjust to the sudden drop in light. As he waited, he listened closely for any sounds. He knew that if they were still in the forest, they were probably within a hundred yards. He just didn't know where they might be hiding.

Thirty seconds after stopping, he slowly stepped onto the needle strewn ground and had to avoid snapping any of the dozens of twigs and small branches that littered almost every square foot.

After he'd gone fifty feet, he froze when he heard a horse nicker to his left. His heart was thumping against his ribs as he remained in place hoping to hear other evidence of their location. He doubted if they would have remained with their horses, but the animals' presence at least confirmed his suspicion that they hadn't continued through the forest to reach Ogden.

When he had failed to detect any human sounds after another minute of intense listening, he sidestepped behind a three-foot-diameter pine trunk that stood between him and the horses.

He knew that he'd be giving away his position, but he wanted to get them to reveal themselves.

Grip shouted, "I didn't expect to see you in Utah, Mooney! I thought you would have stayed in Kansas City."

Mickey was startled as much by his proximity as he was by Grip's words but was smart enough not to reply in kind and announce his location.

Cajun Al was much more than startled when he realized that Grip was close to his right, probably less than twenty yards away. He then committed a blunder when he believed that he could get the drop on Grip.

He left the safety of his pine protector and began to walk slowly in the direction of Grip's shout with his Colt's muzzle swinging slowly left and right. He had his eyes focused before him as he expected to spot Grip at any moment. He should have been watching where he placed his feet.

Grip wasn't surprised that no one had responded to his revealing shout and was about to insult Mickey Mooney for being a coward when he heard the snap of a small branch being cracked in half just a few yards to his left. He slowly shifted his eyes and his Remington in that direction and soon saw Cajun Al who was looking down at the offending twig.

Just as Grip was preparing to fire, Al looked up, saw Grip and snap fired his Colt. Grip felt his .44 clip his left bicep before firing his Remington. His was a killing shot as the bullet punched into Al's throat and severed his left carotid artery. Al screamed as he spun counterclockwise, dropping his pistol and clutching at his neck.

Grip didn't have time to waste. He knew that Mickey Mooney would either head for his horses to make his escape or try to shoot him. He couldn't run or it would make him an easy target, but he did need to leave.

Cajun Al was sobbing as his life's blood flowed onto the pine needles through the gaps in his fingers that weren't slowing the blood's escape.

Mickey had been stunned by what he'd heard and for a crucial thirty seconds, he remained locked in position as he decided what he needed to do. Now it was one on one and he didn't like the odds anymore. He knew that Grip was good with his weapons, but his own enormous mass now worked against him.

He finally decided that he'd have to get to his horse quickly before Grip found him and expected that the kid would be cautious. He finally left his protection and walked quickly to his horse tied to that branch fifty yards away.

He made no attempt to avoid making noise and Grip soon heard his hurried escape. His left arm was bleeding badly, but he had to stop the big man. He just hoped that he'd be able to do it with .44 caliber pistol rounds.

As he trotted toward the noise, he knew that he couldn't wait to see the results of his first shot. He'd unload both pistols into the giant and hoped that it would be enough. He had been a decent shot with his left hand, but that was before he'd been shot. The arm was still functional, but it would take every last drop of his discipline to ignore the pain.

Mickey Mooney experienced panic for the first time in his life as he jogged toward his horse but kept glancing behind him. If he spotted Taylor, he'd start firing.

Grip knew he was getting close and soon caught a glimpse of Mooney just twenty yards ahead of him. He could have opened fire, but the trees meant he'd have a short window to make a hit and he knew that he'd need every bullet to count.

Mickey thought he was safe when he was just twenty feet from his horse but when he took one last look behind him, he spotted Grip as he passed between two trees just forty feet away.

He turned and fired where he expected him to be, but he wasn't there.

Grip had shifted his direction to the other side of the tree because it would give him a wider field of view. He didn't realize that he'd just saved his own life.

But despite having heard all of the descriptions of Mooney and seeing him briefly in the Malcolm scope, seeing him up close in person was a different matter. He felt as if he was facing a grizzly bear with just pistols.

When Grip did expose himself when he stepped out from the other side of the thick pine trunk, Mickey was surprised and as he quickly shifted his Colt's sights to the left side of the tree, Grip began firing both pistols. He fired the Remington and the Colt simultaneously and then began cocking and firing as quickly as he could to put the bear of a man down.

Mickey fired a second time just as the first .44 from Grip's Remington slammed into his upper left chest. He grunted but never had the opportunity to take another shot as the first bullet fired by Grip's Shopkeeper punched into his big gut and then it was one hit after another until both of Grip's pistols were empty.

Grip was shocked to see Mooney still standing with so many bullet holes in his torso. The blood was dripping from his shirt and his pistol had fallen to the ground, yet he still remained on his feet. He holstered his useless pistols but didn't pull his dagger because he didn't believe it would do any good.

The two men stood twenty feet apart just staring at each other for another thirty seconds without saying a word.

Mickey Mooney found himself fading and felt a warm feeling of peace flow through him that he never had experienced before. He believed that he was now on his way to heaven and that every one of those Bible-thumpers had it wrong. There was no hell.

Grip watched as a smile crossed the big man's face before he finally dropped to his knees and after another ten seconds with an almost rapturous look on his face, he leaned forward and planted his rapturous face into the forest floor.

Grip stared at the body for a few more seconds before the warm rivulet of his own blood reminded him of his own wound. He walked to Mickey's tall white horse, rummaged through his saddlebag and pulled out one of Mickey's tent-like dirty shirts. He wrapped it around his damaged left bicep before untying both horses then slowly mounting Mickey's handsome gelding and walking him out of the trees. Al's horse followed, but he didn't care. He was getting woozy from the loss of blood and needed to find Pitch. He knew he'd never be able to reach town but he'd head for the Sandersons to get help.

When he entered the brilliant sunshine, he closed his eyes and turned the horse toward Pitch who was grazing another hundred yards away.

He wanted to change mounts but didn't know if he'd be able to dismount and climb into his own saddle. He still grabbed his hat and pulled it on to before he started Mooney's horse toward the Sandersons. He glanced back and smiled when he saw Pitch following.

He had his eyes closed, but heard excited voices nearby and when he was lowered from the horse, he thought that he was flying before he passed out.

———

While Grip was engaged in the gunfight in the forest, Julia and Tom were waiting for the four blacks to be unloaded from the stock car.

"Isn't it beautiful here, Tom?" Julia gushed.

Tom grinned and said, "You're just happy because you'll be seeing Grip soon and telling him your good news."

"I'll admit that you're right. He said that he bought a ranch east of town, and I suppose we could ride that way, but let's go ask the sheriff. Grip said that he was a friend."

"The office is right over there. I'll bring the horses with me in a couple of minutes."

Julia smiled then quickly turned and hurried across the platform. Just before she reached the office, a girl pulled up on her lathered horse and ran past her through the open doorway.

Julia followed her inside and was chilled to her bones when she heard the girl hurriedly say. “They showed up at our place, Sheriff. Grip shot one but was going to go into the forest after the other two, including the big man.”

“Son of a bitch!” Zeke exclaimed as he grabbed his hat before he said, “Henry, get our horses saddled. If you can find John, tell him to watch the office and be sure those bastards don’t reach town.”

He then glanced at Julia before looking at the girl and asking. “Is everyone else okay, Hilda?”

“Yes, sir. We didn’t see them coming and if Grip hadn’t been there, we would probably all be dead. I can’t leave because my horse is all worn out.”

“You stay here and take care of the horse.”

He finally looked at Julia and said, “I’d like to help you, ma’am, but we have urgent business.”

Julia quickly replied, “My name is Julia Marley, and I came from St. Louis to see Grip. I’m coming with you.”

Zeke hesitated for a few heartbeats before saying, “I’m sorry, ma’am, but this won’t be any place for a woman.”

"I don't care, Sheriff. My place is with Grip, no matter what the danger."

"I can't stop you, ma'am, but I've got to go."

He quickly walked past her and after Julia glanced at Hilda, she hurriedly followed him out the door. She was wearing her riding skirt because she'd planned to ride to Grip's ranch when she and Tom arrived, so she was ready to go.

She reached Tom who noticed the very different expression on her face, but before he could ask her what was going on, she quickly said, "I'll explain as we ride, but we need to help Grip."

"We'll leave the two mares here. They all have rifles, but I hope we won't need them."

Julia nodded and quickly mounted Ebony. She had to wait for Tom and watched the street to see the sheriff and his deputy. She didn't want to let them sneak off without her.

Sheriff Johnson and Deputy Sheriff Henry Manning weren't trying to sneak off as they raced past the train station and turned east on Second Street. It was closer to the Sanderson ranch and they wanted to make a fast ride. They hoped that they'd be there in time to help Grip.

After they thundered past Julia and Tom, they quickly trailed the two lawmen, but kept a reasonable gap that soon grew bigger. Julia may have wanted desperately to find Grip but wasn't about to make the situation worse by getting in the line of fire.

Grip's temporary bandage had been replaced by a tight, clean towel but everyone who was with him in the Sandersons' main room knew that they had to get him into town and have his wound closed soon.

Hanley Miller had driven his wagon to the forest with his two oldest boys to retrieve the bodies and would take them into town. He'd been warned about Mickey Mooney's bulk, but said they'd manage.

Harry had harnessed his wagon and was bringing it to the front of the house when Al Leibnitz and Rhonda arrived. They were the last of the four families to reach the house because they were the farthest away.

When they stepped down, Harry said, "We're just getting ready to move him into town."

"How bad is it, Harry?" Al asked.

"Not too bad, but he musta been shot early and lost a lot of blood. He should be okay."

Rhonda then said, "I'll ride in the back of the wagon with him."

Al glanced at his daughter before Harry said, “Alright. Climb on board and we’ll bring him out.”

Al and Harry entered the house as Rhonda stepped onto the wagon’s bed and sat with her back against the driver’s seat. She was already planning to stay with Grip in his house to nurse him back to health even if her parents objected. She was a grown woman now and could do as she wished, and she wished to be with him.

Al and Harry soon appeared carrying an unconscious Grip on a blanket. He was an awkward load for the two men, but they soon were able to slide him onto the back of the wagon. Marie Sanderson followed them with a pillow and after seeing Rhonda already near Grip’s head, she handed it to Rhonda who carefully lifted his head and laid it onto the pillow.

As Harry climbed into the driver’s seat, Jason Smith rode up trailing Pitch and the three outlaws’ horses.

“I’ll follow you into town and tell the sheriff what happened while you take Grip to Doc Ripley.”

Harry replied, “I’m surprised he or one of his deputies hasn’t shown up yet, Hilda left here a good hour ago.”

“He’s probably on his way, Harry. Let’s get Grip to the doc.”

Harry nodded and snapped the reins. The horses soon had the wagon moving and followed the stakes for the new road as it was the most level path to Ogden. Al Leibnitz rode alongside Jason Smith to keep an eye on his daughter.

As the wagon rocked and shook across the ground, Rhonda ran her fingers through Grip's thick black hair. He may have professed his love for the woman who might be his sister, but she was in St. Louis and that was far away. While Grip healed, she'd convince him that there was no reason to wait. If her father wasn't riding behind them, she would have kissed him as he lay close to her.

———

They'd been rolling west for ten minutes when Harry shouted, "I think that's Zeke comin' this way with one of his deputies."

Jason Smith yelled back, "I think you're right, Harry. Who's that comin' up behind them?"

"I don't know, but they're ridin' horses that look a lot like Grip's black."

"I noticed that, and I think one of them is a blonde woman," Jason replied loudly.

Rhonda was suddenly ripped from her dreamworld and turned to look west. She had a difficult time seeing past Harry Sanderson, but after leaning to the right side, she spotted the sheriff and two riders trailing about two hundred yards behind them. She couldn't make out the blonde hair that Mister Miller had noted because of the dust but didn't doubt that he was right. If it hadn't been for the black horses, she would have had no idea who the woman might be. But she suddenly realized that somehow that half-sister of his had come to Ogden and would ruin her hastily created plan.

She slid closer to Grip's shoulder and took his hand as the sheriff and deputy raced toward them. She wasn't going to say a word but would wait until the blonde woman arrived.

Zeke had seen the wagon and the trailing rider and empty horses before they spotted him, and loudly said, "Henry, it looks like whatever happened is all over, one way or the other. Let's move a bit faster. We might hafta hunt down those boys."

Before they set their horses to a gallop, Henry yelled back, "My money is on Grip, Zeke!"

As the lawmen pulled away, Tom turned to Julia and said, "Let them go, Julia. We can't do anything but find out what happened. We'd just get in the way."

Julia just nodded as she stared east at the oncoming wagon and riders. She knew that Ebony could outrace most horses and desperately wanted to let him run, but she wasn't a very experienced rider and acknowledged the truth of what Tom had said.

Just a few minutes later, Sheriff Johnson slowed and turned his horse to ride next to Harry Sanderson. He'd glanced into the wagon and seen Grip and his bloody bandage but didn't think he was in danger. He counted three horses with Jason Smith, so he also quickly realized that the gang was no longer a problem.

"What happened, Harry?"

Harry quickly told the sheriff the parts of the gunfight that he had witnessed but said that Grip had entered the forest south of his property to go after the last two, including the giant.

"How bad is he hurt?" Zeke asked.

"I reckon he'll be fine after the doc sews him up. The bullet cut through his arm but didn't hit anything bad. He just lost a lotta blood before he was able to try and stop it and we had to catch him before he fell off his horse. He's been out ever since. Oh, and Hanley and two of his boys will be bringin' the bodies in."

"Okay," the sheriff replied, then turned to his deputy and said, "Henry, head back into town and tell Doc Ripley that we'll be there in about twenty minutes."

"Yes, sir," Deputy Manning replied before starting back toward Ogden.

As he approached Julia and Tom, she waved him down and when he was close, she asked, "Where is Grip? Is he all right?"

"He's in the back of the wagon but he's sleeping. He took a bullet to the upper arm and lost some blood, but he'll be okay. He's just unconscious and almost fell off his horse but Harry Sanderson, the feller driving the wagon, caught him. He said that Grip stopped those three bastards before they got to his house."

"Thank you," Julia said before Henry set off west at a medium trot.

As they started their blacks moving again, Tom said, "He'll be all right, Julia. I imagine that you'll be his nurse now."

Despite her concerns, Julia managed a smile as she replied, "I believe that I have just the medicine for him, too."

When they were about two hundred yards from the wagon, Julia spotted Rhonda's long black hair in the wagon bed. Initially, she thought that she must be Mister Sanderson's wife. But as the gap decreased, she realized how young the woman was. She could be his daughter, or if he was a Mormon, she could still be his wife, or maybe his fourth. But just before they reached the wagon, she noticed that the young woman wasn't even looking at them. She was holding Grip's hand to her breast.

Julia felt a surge of jealousy and anger that she never believed she could experience, but after that instant storm of emotion crashed in her mind, she smiled and let it dissipate into nothing. It wasn't because of the Latin addressed letter she'd received, but from the talk she'd had with Wilma about why he had never married.

She whispered, "Thank you, Mary Duffy," just before she pulled up beside the wagon and turned Ebony to match its speed while Tom rode along on the opposite side.

Rhonda had laid Grip's hand to her bosom when she was sure that Julia could see her and didn't care what her father thought of her. It was only what Grip's blonde half-sister believed that was important.

When she heard Ebony turn and knew that the blonde was close, she waited for Julia's tirade to begin. But she didn't hear a single angry word or even the slightest challenge.

Julia simply asked, "How is he?"

Rhonda finally made eye contact with Julia and was stunned to see her smiling down from her black horse.

"He was shot in the arm, but he asked me to stay with him in his house until he's better."

Harry Sanderson heard her lie and was about to tell Julia that he'd been unconscious since Rhonda had arrived, but Julia was a step ahead of him.

"I doubt that, Miss. The deputy told us that he's been out since the gunfight, but I'll be staying with him now."

"But…but you're his sister!" she exclaimed as she set his hand by his side.

"We were concerned that it might be possible, but it's not true. I was never related to Grip, but that will change soon."

Rhonda opened her mouth to reply but immediately closed it again. The fight for Grip Taylor was over before the first skirmish.

Julia didn't celebrate her victory, but asked, "Where is his ranch?"

"We're on it right now. His houses are over that way," Rhonda replied as she pointed to the east.

"I'm Julia Marley, by the way."

Rhonda smiled as she replied, "I'm Rhonda Leibnitz. I live with my family on our ranch northeast of Grip's."

"It's nice to meet you, Rhonda."

"I'm sorry for my display, Julia. It's just that, well, Grip is a special man."

"He's more incredible than you can imagine."

Julia then said, "I'm going to go talk to the sheriff now."

Rhonda nodded and watched her ride away and despite her earlier intentions, she found that she liked Julia.

Julia pulled up beside the sheriff and asked, "Can you tell me what has happened since Grip arrived? I know the basic information from his letters, but not much of the details, and nothing about what precipitated the gunfight."

Zek replied, "We only have about twenty more minutes, but I can tell you some of it. He told me that you would know about those men he just sent to hell. He said that he knew them in St. Louis, and they'd had his father killed and murdered his father's lawyer."

Julia's face showed her stunned disbelief as she exclaimed, "*That was Mickey Mooney and his men?*"

"Yes, ma'am. I'll start with them and start working backwards until we get into town."

Julia nodded as the sheriff began talking. Tom had pulled up on the other side to listen.

Grip hadn't been totally unconscious for ten minutes but drifting in a dreamlike world where sounds mixed, and motion seemed to be happening to someone else. He thought he'd heard Julia's name mentioned by some ethereal voice and smiled.

Rhonda didn't notice as she was watching Julia while she listened to the sheriff.

The next thing that reached Grip's somnolent mind was when he was being lifted by strong hands and then there were more voices before he felt a prick like a mosquito bite on his left arm. Then he slipped into his land of darkness again.

When the darkness lifted, Grip felt a burning pain in his left arm. He slowly opened his eyes and was thoroughly confused. as he tried to identify his surroundings. It only took a few seconds before he realized that he was in his own bedroom and had no idea how he'd gotten there. *How long had he been unconscious?*

He had barely established his location when he realized that his good right arm was difficult to move and he wondered if he'd been shot in that arm and had somehow forgotten about it.

He was still in a state of confusion when he turned his head to see why his right arm was in rebellion and immediately thought he'd lost his mind.

Just four inches from the tip of his nose, he saw Julia's angelic face. Her eyes were closed, so she was sleeping. He wanted to kiss her, but aside from the potential incest prohibition, there was the much more imperative questions of why and how she had come to Utah. *Was he sleeping with his sister, or did she discover her father's name?*

He delayed waking her as he tried to light the lamp of his mind to its full capacity, so he could evaluate her presence in his bed. It wasn't the big bed that he'd ordered for his new house, so he'd have to find his answer soon. Even in her sleep, Julia was an inspiration and if she hadn't found the answer to their mutual problem, then she'd have to vacate the bed, or he would need to leave before she awakened.

He glanced at the window and estimated that it was mid-afternoon, so he'd been in a different world for at least six hours. It didn't make much sense to him because he had only been shot in the arm.

But before he resolved the Julia question, he spent a few minutes reliving that gunfight with Mickey Mooney. He remembered cocking his hammers and firing his two pistols as quickly as he could and yet, as each bullet left either the Remington or the Shopkeeper, he remembered is dismay that Mooney was still standing. He recalled the first click of the Remington's hammer as it fell on an expended cartridge then soon emptied Colt.

Even though Mooney had dropped his pistol, the fear that Mooney might then strangle him with his enormous paws had ripped through him. It was only when the giant had fallen to his knees that Grip knew his eleven bullets had finally had their effect.

But then his memory's image of Mooney's beatific smile reached his active mind and it bothered him. *Why would a man who was about to suffer eternal damnation seem so content?* He was convinced that he'd never know, but maybe God really did forgive each soul he put on this earth, regardless of the sins they had committed. He wasn't a religious man, so he had no scriptural basis to even try to understand why Mooney had smiled. He was sure that the memory of his face would stay with him until he finally had his answer in the only way possible. He just hoped that it wouldn't be for another five decades.

He pushed the image and the gunfight back into his memory vault then looked at Julia again.

She must be there because she wanted to be with him and if she was still worried about their potential sibling relationship, he couldn't imagine that she'd take the risk of joining him in his bed, even with his wound.

He had no idea how she'd arrived or if she'd come alone, but she was here. He didn't hear any noises in the house, so they were probably alone.

Grip was about to just call her name but decided to take the chance that she had found her father's name. So, with a grimace, he lifted his bandaged left arm and gently placed it across her shoulder.

As her eyelids began to move, he leaned across the short gap and kissed her.

Julia hadn't realized just how tired she'd been after the long days on the train, so when she'd joined Grip in his sickbed, she thought that she'd be awake when he first stirred. Tom had moved the four blacks into the new stables and all of their things into the house before returning to Ogden to meet with the sheriff and the members of the four families.

But she had only managed to keep her eyes open for twenty minutes. She'd kissed him softly shortly after laying beside him and now, she felt his lips on hers and thought that she had somehow initiated the kiss.

When her eyes opened, she discovered that she wasn't the initiator but the recipient.

It had been a short kiss and when she smiled, Grip asked, "I gambled that you discovered the name of your father and it wasn't Lawrence Preston Taylor."

"My father was Farley Edwards."

Grip's eyebrows popped higher as he exclaimed, "*Congressman Edwards?*"

"Yes, sir. I have a note from him if you'd like to read it."

"I trust you, Julia. You'll have to tell me the story later."

"I was going to see him right after I figured it out, but Aunt Emily went into labor. She's doing fine and had a big boy she named Sam. She wanted to name him Agrippa, but I told her that you'd be appalled, so she used your middle name. She left it at Sam rather than Samuel because we both thought it was more appropriate for a boy who'll grow up in Utah Territory. When I first met Sam, she almost ordered me to meet with Mister Edwards and then to leave St. Louis immediately."

"How did you get here? Did you travel alone?"

"Tom escorted me and brought four of the blacks with him, including Ebony. He left them in your new stables and was very pleased with the building. He's in town right now talking to the sheriff and the others who witnessed the shootout. When the sheriff told me that it was Mickey Mooney, I was shocked. Were they really following you all this time?"

"No. I know it was probably just an extraordinary coincidence, but I wonder if our fates were somehow linked."

"Can we talk about what's really important now that I'm in your bed?"

Grip smiled as he replied, "Like how long it will take me to reach the privy?"

Julia laughed but understood that Grip was serious when he slid his feet to the floor. After sitting on the edge of the bed for a few seconds to let the expected dizziness pass, he stood and exited the room as quickly as his stiff muscles would allow.

Julia was still smiling as she watched him leave. Her plans for a romantically charged revelation had evaporated, but she thought that the less passionate first moments of their new relationship were just as memorable.

Grip didn't make it to the privy, but at least was able to avoid embarrassment as no one was there to witness his personal mass evacuation.

The construction crews were gone for the day and he knew that his new house would be ready in three more days because it was the highest priority. If he'd wanted a standard design, they could have had it done in two weeks, but his was far from standard. The other houses weren't standard either, but not as exotic as his because of his special needs.

Julia's unexpected arrival would change everything, but for the better. As he walked back to the house, he wondered if Tom was going to stay or return to St. Louis. If he returned, he would be able to pass along much more information than Grip could include in a letter, even if it was thirty pages long.

When he entered the kitchen, he found Julia on her heels lighting a fire in the cookstove.

She tossed a match onto the kerosene-soaked kindling then after laying three split pieces of firewood atop the flames, she closed the door, stood and smiled at him.

"We have a lot to talk about, so we can start the conversation while I cook supper."

"I'll help, ma'am. Is Tom going to stay here or is he returning to St. Louis?"

"He's leaving tomorrow. He should be returning soon, but I'm not going anywhere."

Grip smiled then stepped in front of her and wrapped both his good and bad arm around her as he replied, "I wouldn't have let you escape, Julia. Do we have to wait for everyone to arrive before we can be married?"

"You haven't asked me yet, Mister Taylor. Earlier today, I saw you with your hand on another woman's breast, so perhaps you've moved on."

Grip exclaimed, "*I did what?* I would never…I didn't…I would only touch…"

Julia laughed, then kissed him and softly said, "Rhonda Leibnitz was taking advantage of your lack of consciousness. I'm sure that she was just trying to irk me, but she dropped the idea."

"*Rhonda did that?*" he asked sharply.

"Don't give it a second thought. Now, I believe that you were starting to say that you would only touch my breasts. Or am I wrong?"

Grip's face slid into a deep shade of red as mumbled, "I just meant…well, I didn't want you to think that I'd ever…"

Julia smiled, kissed him again to end his suffering, then said, “When we don’t have to worry about Tom walking through the door, I’ll grant you that privilege and much more.”

Grip was returning to a dark pink when he asked, “Will you marry me, Miss Marley?”

“Yes, Mister Taylor, I will marry you and we won’t wait for the others to leave St. Louis. I want to share your bed and your life starting tomorrow.”

Grip smiled then kissed her much more passionately as a prelude to their new life.

———

Tom Truax returned to the house just in time to join them at the table. He wasn’t surprised at all to learn that they were going to marry tomorrow and said that he’d appreciate it if they’d have the ceremony in the morning before he boarded his afternoon train.

The rest of the late afternoon and evening was spent sharing stories and Grip was pleased to hear that everyone was still excited about coming to Utah. Grip’s descriptions of the incredible beauty of their new home pushed aside any doubts that they may have had.

The sun had disappeared as they continued to talk in the lamplit kitchen while sharing the last of the coffeepot’s contents.

Tom announced that he was exhausted and left the two young people to find his assigned bed.

After his bedroom door had closed, Julia said, "Tomorrow night will be different."

"I hope so, but I hope my arm feels better. I don't want any distractions."

"I won't let you be distracted, Mister Taylor. I'll have your full attention."

"You always have, Julia. From the moment I first saw you in Claudia's Café, you've been the focus of my thoughts. But now the more lurid thoughts I'd had of you no longer have any restrictions."

Julia smiled as she replied, "I'm ashamed to admit that I never let that blank space on the birth certificate limit my own equally lust-filled thoughts of you, sir."

"But it was much more than just your incredible attractiveness as a woman that made me want to be with you so badly. I've been in awe of many other handsome women in my years, but never even considered sharing my life with them. I never knew if they would be interested in me if I was just a common laborer, but you liked me as me. I was stunned because I imagined that you had drawn the attention of scores of men. Yet you seemed to like me, and I felt is if we had quickly created a bond.

"Just minutes later, when I realized who you were, I was shattered. I knew even then that you were the one woman I had hoped to meet. For a while, I believed that the instant connection was because you were my sister but the more time we spent together, the less valid that argument became. Since that first day, you've always been the one."

Julia smiled as she said, "I thanked Mary Duffy when I saw Rhonda with your hand pressed to her chest. I was right to thank her; wasn't I?"

"As strange as it sounds, you really should thank my father. He sent me to a military school when I was seven and then sent Mary to my room on my sixteenth birthday. She was a very pretty young woman and I'll admit that I was tempted, but it was the discipline I'd already learned and my refusal to give my father a single victory that kept me from using Mary as he had.

"It was only when we talked rather than acted that I fully understood how badly the young women felt who had suffered from my father's abuse. I vowed to her that I'd never hurt a woman and I'd wait until I found the right woman before I, in my father's words, 'became a man'. She probably thought it was just a teenage boy's excuse for not being able to consummate the act, but it meant a lot to me."

"You're wrong, you know. Wilma told me how Mary had confided the events of that night to her and Mary had told her how impressed she was with you. She knew full well that you were not only capable of bedding her but employing all of your willpower to control your urges. She even told Wilma that she hoped that she could be at your wedding to meet the woman you were meant to marry."

"I wish she'd lived long enough, but maybe she'll be watching us tomorrow when we share vows."

"I don't know if she will be, but I've never had a moment's doubt that you were the only man I'd ever love."

"I love you, Julia."

He kissed her softly before they stood and after Grip blew out the lamp, they walked hand-in-hand down the dark hallway. She kissed him before entering her bedroom and closing the door. Grip sighed, then passed Tom's bedroom and soon reached his own.

It was difficult for him to find sleep as he'd spent so many hours in a combination of unconsciousness and sleep. Having Julia laying in her bed just a few feet away didn't help, either.

So, as he lay atop his quilt, he let his mind return to more mundane topics. He wondered if anyone had cleaned his Browning and his pistols, then moved onto the horses.

By the time he finally drifted off, he was designing bridges across the Ogden River to the north side of his property.

CHAPTER 16

The next morning could have been chaotic considering the number of tasks that had to be done before noon, but after Grip, Julia and Tom had bathed and dressed, they were able to share a reasonably pleasant breakfast before they left the house to saddle their horses in the new carriage house.

To the construction crews, it was just another workday, although each of them had heard the incredibly stories about the gunfight and had noticed Julia's presence. None of them had seen her before, but not a single man had heard a whisper of the reason for her arrival.

Grip, Julia and Tom soon rode out of the carriage house on their blacks and Grip waved at the men who were watching, assuming correctly that he wasn't the reason for their attention.

As they rode on the recently improved entrance road, Grip pointed out many of the ranch's features.

He'd told Julia and Tom about the size of the ranch and the amazingly varied features that it encompassed it its sixty-four square miles As she studied the landscape, Julia found herself almost in awe of what her eyes revealed and couldn't wait to explore the ranch with him. She hadn't paid that much attention to her surroundings when she and Tom had ridden out of Ogden behind the sheriff or even on the return to town but knew that it was as beautiful a plot of ground as Grip had described it in his letters.

They rode into Ogden just before ten o'clock and stopped at the sheriff's office to hear of any developments. Tom had updated Grip on the burial of the three outlaws and that the Coalville Bank's stolen money had been returned, but they hadn't decided what to do with the rest of their loot or possessions.

When they entered, Sheriff Johnson and his two deputies hopped to their feet and the sheriff said, "Well, you're lookin' a lot better than the last time I saw you, Grip. How's the arm?"

"Stiff and pretty sore, but it'll be okay. What happened while I was asleep?"

"I just talked to Judge Emerson and he said that if it was alright with you, whatever they had, including the $1640 we found in the big man's saddlebags, should be turned over to the county, and I'd get the horses, tack and weapons. Is that okay?"

"It's fine, but do you mind if I take Mooney's white gelding?"

"I'll hold onto him for you."

"Thanks, Zeke. But speaking of the judge, I need him to perform a marriage if he's available."

Zeke grinned as he replied, “I reckoned that you might be heading that way. He’s in his office. Do you need another witness?”

“Are you volunteering?”

“Only if I get to kiss the bride.”

Grip laughed then said, “Let’s go see Judge Emerson.”

Without being invited, Deputies Manning and Walker followed their boss out of the jail and headed for the county courthouse.

While Judge Gerard L. Emerson was in his courtroom listening to the defense attorney drone on that his client hadn’t stolen the plaintiff’s prize rooster, Grip and Julia filled out the paperwork necessary to satisfy the territorial government.

Each of them was wearing riding clothes and Grip wasn’t even wearing his shoulder harness under his black vest. Tom had told him his guns were cleaned, but Grip still need to take care of them himself and now that he had more weapons stored in the rooms in his carriage house, he’d be spending more time there but not for a few weeks.

As they sat in the outer office and waited for the judge to make his Solomon-like rooster ruling, Grip took Julia’s hand and smiled at her.

"You know, Julia, I was thinking. Now that we're in Utah, I'm thinking of becoming a Mormon."

"Why would you do that?" she asked in surprise.

"Well, I thought that if I did, then you wouldn't mind if I married Rhonda next month."

Julia glared at her smirking groom and whispered, "You can always try to make me your second wife, Mister Taylor. Does it work both ways? Can I have three or four husbands?"

Grip was still smiling when he answered, "I really don't know the answer to that question. It just popped into my head and I thought it was funny."

She smiled back, then kissed him quickly before saying, "It was funny, but let's not follow that line of humor again."

"No, ma'am."

After another five minutes, the pleased plaintiff and the disgruntled defendant left the courtroom with their lawyers and passed through the outer office.

Judge Emerson's clerk waved everyone inside and soon, Grip and Julia stood before the judge who was in a much better humor than he'd been as he'd wasted his time adjudicating the trivial case. He had been close to following Solomon with his ruling when he had ordered that the rooster be cut in half until the defendant had finally admitting to already having done so. He'd ordered the defendant to pay five dollars in damages which was more than he would have had to pay for four full chicken dinners.

He soon stood before the young couple and opened his copy of the marriage ceremony. He barely glanced at the words as he had performed dozens of marriages, but only to those who didn't follow the Mormon doctrine.

Grip hadn't bought wedding bands, so when the judge reached the point in the ceremony when he asked, "Do you wish to exchange rings?", Grip shook his head.

But before he could give a verbal reply, Tom stepped closer and handed him a small box as he whispered, "Julia had me pick these up in St. Louis before we left."

Grip smiled at his bride then selected the smaller ring and when he slid it onto her fingers, he repeated the judge's words and intoned his vow to love, honor and cherish her and to provide and protect her for as long as he should live.

Julia's eyes were threatening to release a steady flow of tears as she slowly slipped the bigger ring onto Grip's finger and said her vows. She may have promised to obey him, but she didn't believe that he would hold her to that promise.

He finally kissed Julia and didn't have one moment of doubt that he would never think of her as his sister again. He would never ask to see that note from Farley Edwards because she was his wife and there would never be another woman in his life.

As the witnesses and even the judge lined up to take their turns kissing the new Mrs. Taylor, Grip smiled and whispered, “Thank you, Mary Duffy.”

EPILOGUE

Tom returned to St. Louis a few days later and spent hours explaining everything that had happened in Utah and his gushing praise of their new home gave each of them a greater incentive to leave the estate. Grip had told him that the new houses would be completed and furnished shortly after he left Ogden which put a timeline on the move.

Emily was growing stronger by the day and little Sam was as robust a baby as imaginable, so they began their preparations to depart the day after Tom had returned.

Grip had wired Warren Stone and told him to sell the estate after they had gone and sent letters to him with added details. He also sent long missives to Joe Trimble and Marshal Guest to fulfill his promise to keep them informed.

He'd also arranged for Union Pacific to provide one of their executive cars to bring everyone to Ogden in the most comfortable fashion. He had to pay the fees that the other railroads would charge for the use of their tracks and facilities, but he wasn't exactly short of funds.

On the sixth of August, the train with the executive car arrived and Julia and Grip were reunited with their extended family. It took a while to move all of the blacks to their new home and Grip had the freighters help to empty and store the contents of the four heavy crates of weapons and four more with the books.

Everyone was stunned by their new homes and the magnificent surroundings, and it took a while to make the adjustments.

Tom had his horses to keep him busy, but now that he wasn't running a household anymore, Rich felt useless.

Emily still rested to build up her strength, and had her children, including Sam to fill her days.

The Albert children were the exception and had adapted quickly and easily.

Grip believed that he'd fulfilled his promise to risk his own safety to help innocents but would still do what he could to help using his vast wealth. He'd never need to fire a gun at another man again and decided to finally put his engineering talents to good use.

By the time that Julia announced her pregnancy in October, Grip had set up his engineering offices in Ogden. He'd built a new building and hired Rich to act as his office manager, which solved his problem.

He set up trust funds for each of the Albert children and became a surrogate father to each of them. Bill became his constant companion when he wasn't with Julia, and Grip introduced him to his world of engineering. So, in addition to acting as Bill's father, he became his tutor and mentor.

Bill proved to be an excellent student, and Grip said that in the fall of '79, he'd send Bill to the University of Michigan. Bill was very uncomfortable when Grip had made the offer because he'd only had six years of schooling, but Grip assured him by the time he left Ogden, he'd be more than well-prepared.

Julia gave birth to their first child on May 29th. She was a pretty, dark-haired girl with deep brown eyes. They named her Charlotte Mary.

Grip had asked Julia if he should move the rest of his father's fortune to the Julia Trust Fund and she'd rejected the idea. She told him that there was an immense amount of good he could do with the money here in Utah.

His idea of having the Pinkertons find Steve Albert to give Emily a chance to remarry proved unnecessary. Julia had mentioned it to her, and Emily had replied that she was very happy just being a mother to her children and didn't want to risk becoming pregnant again.

But just to satisfy his curiosity, he sent a telegram to Joe Trimble and requested that he track down the whereabouts of Emily's husband. He doubted that the man would suddenly appear and demand some form of payment, but simply wanted to know.

Three weeks later, he received a letter from Joe with his answer. Steve Albert had died in February as a result of the mercury he was taking for his syphilis and his excessive drinking. His body had been found in his house when his neighbor had complained about the smell.

The other mystery that Grip never bothered to solve was the disappearance of John Schuler, the only member of Mickey Mooney's men he'd met before that fateful day. His body had never been found and nobody mourned his passing.

After a busy summer, on August 27th, a large group waved goodbye as Bill's train rolled out of the station. He was much more confident as he prepared for his formal education as an engineer. When he returned each summer, he'd put what he'd learned to practice with A.S. Taylor Engineering. When he finished his education, he'd join Grip on a full-time engineer. The town of Ogden was on its way to becoming a city and the train traffic that passed through the station increased each year.

Those trains were the reason that Grip had chosen the city when he'd left the University of Michigan and he never regretted his choice for a moment.

When the last of his father's holdings and the estate were sold, Grip had achieved his purpose of removing almost all vestiges of Lawrence Preston Taylor from St. Louis. There were records of course, but he was convinced that the only place anyone could see his name in public was on his father's gravestone that he'd never seen.

One beautiful autumn day in 1881, he and Julia stood on the bank of the Ogden River near his new bridge. Millie was back at their house watching Charlotte and three-month-old Connor, so they could have some private time.

There was a blanket spread out on the grass behind them with a picnic basket of food and lemonade waiting to be consumed. But it would have to wait. They were here to enjoy themselves.

Julia smiled at Grip as she asked, "Are you sure that I'm doing this right?"

Grip kissed his wife and replied, "Just use your wrist. Let the line flow onto the water."

Julia smiled and after the hook snagged on their blanket, she laughed and dropped her new fishing rod to the ground.

Grip was about to begin the sweeping process to launch his fly onto the flowing water full of cutthroat trout when Julia wrapped her fingers around his pole and pulled it from his hands.

She set it down beside hers and pulled him onto the blanket. It hadn't taken much persuasion to make him forget about fishing.

As he began to unbutton her blouse, she whispered, "Watch out for the hook."

Grip kissed her then said, "You hooked me a long time ago, Mrs. Taylor. I didn't put up a fight and you didn't need to reel me in."

She had his shirt open before she replied, "Then reel me in now, Mr. Taylor."

GRIP TAYLOR

1.	Rock Creek	12/26/2016
2.	North of Denton	01/02/2017
3.	Fort Selden	01/07/2017
4.	Scotts Bluff	01/14/2017
5.	South of Denver	01/22/2017
6.	Miles City	01/28/2017
7.	Hopewell	02/04/2017
8.	Nueva Luz	02/12/2017
9.	The Witch of Dakota	02/19/2017
10.	Baker City	03/13/2017
11.	The Gun Smith	03/21/2017
12.	Gus	03/24/2017
13.	Wilmore	04/06/2017
14.	Mister Thor	04/20/2017
15.	Nora	04/26/2017
16.	Max	05/09/2017
17.	Hunting Pearl	05/14/2017
18.	Bessie	05/25/2017
19.	The Last Four	05/29/2017
20.	Zack	06/12/2017
21.	Finding Bucky	06/21/2017
22.	The Debt	06/30/2017
23.	The Scalawags	07/11/2017
24.	The Stampede	07/20/2017
25.	The Wake of the Bertrand	07/31/2017
26.	Cole	08/09/2017
27.	Luke	09/05/2017
28.	The Eclipse	09/21/2017
29.	A.J. Smith	10/03/2017
30.	Slow John	11/05/2017
31.	The Second Star	11/15/2017
32.	Tate	12/03/2017
33.	Virgil's Herd	12/14/2017

34. Marsh's Valley	01/01/2018
35. Alex Paine	01/18/2018
36. Ben Gray	02/05/2018
37. War Adams	03/05/2018
38. Mac's Cabin	03/21/2018
39. Will Scott	04/13/2018
40. Sheriff Joe	04/22/2018
41. Chance	05/17/2018
42. Doc Holt	06/17/2018
43. Ted Shepard	07/13/2018
44. Haven	07/30/2018
45. Sam's County	08/15/2018
46. Matt Dunne	09/10/2018
47. Conn Jackson	10/05/2018
48. Gabe Owens	10/27/2018
49. Abandoned	11/19/2018
50. Retribution	12/21/2018
51. Inevitable	02/04/2019
52. Scandal in Topeka	03/18/2019
53. Return to Hardeman County	04/10/2019
54. Deception	06/02/2019
55. The Silver Widows	06/27/2019
56. Hitch	08/21/2019
57. Dylan's Journey	09/10/2019
58. Bryn's War	11/06/2019
59. Huw's Legacy	11/30/2019
60. Lynn's Search	12/22/2019
61. Bethan's Choice	02/10/2020
62. Rhody Jones	03/11/2020
63. Alwen's Dream	06/16/2020
64. The Nothing Man	06/30/2020
65. Cy Page: Western Union Man	07/19/2020
66. Tabby Hayes	08/02/2020

67. Letter for Gene	09/08/2020
68. Dylan's Memories	09/20/2020
69. Grip Taylor	10/07/2020
70. Garrett's Duty	11/09/2020
71. East of the Cascades	12/02/2020
72. The Iron Wolfe	12/23/2020
73. Wade Rivers	01/09/2021
74. Ghost Train	01/26/2021
75. The Inheritance	02/26/2021